Judge Walden

Call the Next Case

PETER MURPHY

NO EXIT PRESS

First published in 2019 by No Exit Press,
an imprint of Oldcastle Books Ltd,
Harpenden, UK

noexit.co.uk

A CIP catalogue record for this book is available from the British Library.

ISBN
978-0-85730-297-7 (print)
978-0-85730-298-4 (epub)

2 4 6 8 10 9 7 5 3 1

Typeset in 11.5pt Minion Pro
by Avocet Typeset, Somerton, Somerset, TA11 6RT
Printed and bound in Great Britain by Clays Ltd., Elcograf S.p.A.

For more information about Crime Fiction go to @crimetimeuk

CONTENTS

FOREWORD
by Baroness Hale of Richmond, President of the UK Supreme Court 7

PROLOGUE
by Judge Rinder 11

FEELING ONE'S AGE 13

TOO MANY COOKS 97

A RIDGE OF HIGH PRESSURE 175

AN ISLE FULL OF NOISES 253

SOMETHING BORROWED, SOMETHING BLUE 327

To all our Circuit Judges everywhere, especially our Resident Judges, who, without recognition or tangible reward, labour every day, against overwhelming odds, to save what is left of our court system from the wrecking ball.

FOREWORD

By Baroness Hale of Richmond,
President of the Supreme Court of the United Kingdom

When Peter Murphy and I were Law students together at Cambridge University, from 1963 to 1966, did it occur to either of us what our later careers would be? Perhaps Peter always knew that he would qualify as a barrister and practise as an advocate, but surely not at the International Tribunal for the Former Yugoslavia in The Hague, or that he would crown his career as Resident Judge in the Peterborough Crown Court. It certainly never occurred to me, as I went off to teach Law at the University of Manchester, with a bit of practice on the side, that I would end up as any sort of judge, let alone President of the Supreme Court of the United Kingdom.

Life in an appeal court, especially the top appeal court for the whole United Kingdom, is very different from life "at the coal face", as those who work in trial courts up and down the land tend to call it. We deal in erudite points of law of the sort that Judge Walden, Resident Judge in the Bermondsey Crown Court, tries to avoid if he possibly can. So who would you rather be? Lady Hale, in the Supreme Court, deciding whether outlawing bigamy is incompatible with the rights of (for example) Mormons to manifest their belief that bigamy, indeed, polygamy, is justified in scripture? Or Judge Walden, benignly advising the jury whether duress (of the shotgun sort) is a defence to bigamy? He has a lot more fun than we do.

Bermondsey is an imaginary Crown Court with four

permanent judges who fit each of the stereotypes – the wise, benign and seriously cunning Resident Judge, Judge Walden; the elderly, rather old-fashioned but still fundamentally sound member of the Garrick club; the buccaneering barrister turned Judge, still for some unknown reason nicknamed "Legless"; and the seriously clever who-should-go-further-but-with-family-responsibilities woman Judge. All are supported by some wonderful court staff – the hugely savvy listing officer, Stella, who knows everything that is going on, and Judge Walden's usher, Dawn, always brightly dressed beneath her gown. We all owe these heroines a great debt of gratitude.

What comes over loud and clear is that, despite their differences, each of these judges is equally committed to what the legal process – especially in criminal cases – is all about: the fair trial of those accused of offending against the law. And what also comes over loud and clear is that so are the advocates who appear in front of them. They play by the rules and neither side does dirty tricks – or if they do, they will be found out soon enough and no good will come of it. These stories are a fine description of some sensible and honourable advocacy.

But you mustn't believe that everything that goes on in these pages would really go on – trial judges in disputes between neighbours do not conduct mediations in nearby pubs while the case is going on, for example – but that does not detract from the essential truth of all these stories, that the law and the courts should always be looking for the right solution, wherever and however it may be found.

Nor must you believe that the "Grey Smoothies" from the Ministry of Justice are always out to undermine the independence of the judiciary. They have their role and Judge Walden has his. But somehow he seems to outsmart them every time, which is just as it should be. That his wife is the local vicar, the Reverend Clara Walden, and he buys his daily coffee, sandwich and newspaper from the local market traders, shows how grounded he is in the life of his local community.

But above all, these stories are really funny! His Honour Judge Walden is surely the next Rumpole, a modern, sensible, fair and compassionate judge, not stuck in the past, even when it comes to mastering the new technology and the "paperless court", but staying faithful to the values we both learned all those years ago.

Prologue

by Judge Rinder

This book is the closest one can get to the authentic first hand action of a judge's chambers without having to qualify (perhaps the main reason I love it). The dry wit of Walden and the richly drawn characters, especially his – often frustrating – colleagues, set against the interference of the civil service, make it feel incredibly contemporary.

I don't especially like comparisons, but working in TV, I am often asked to describe a book or a programme. Walden defies description. It's like Rumpole meets Agatha Christie, with a bit of Judge John Deed thrown in – only with none of the absurdity. It could only have been written by someone with years of first hand experience, an acute sense of irony, and an ability to listen and absorb facts and convey them to a jury (or reader) with the type of effortless mastery of detail that only the great advocates possess.

Peter Murphy gives the reader an insight into the hidden – often mundane – world of the court with its eccentricities and often amusing banalities, and never forgets that at the heart of any case (and good book) is the story. The mystery is so utterly absorbing: I found myself walking into a train door. I don't want to give too much away, but Walden is impossible to put down. As soon as you've finished, I challenge you not to order the rest in the series immediately.

FEELING ONE'S AGE

FEELING ONE'S AGE

Monday morning

In sooth, I know not why I am so sad:
It wearies me; you say it wearies you;
But how I caught it, found it, or came by it,
What stuff 'tis made of, whereof it is born,
I am to learn…

Like Antonio in Venice, I arrive at court in Bermondsey this morning in a rather subdued mood. It's a beautiful spring day, and I have all my usual comforts – my latte from Jeanie and Elsie's coffee and sandwich bar in the archway near London Bridge and my copy of *The Times* from George's newspaper stand nearby. But neither the aroma of the latte nor the fresh, cool breeze blowing up off the river dispels the mist entirely. While I do hold the world as a stage where every man must play a part, I don't often see my part as a sad one; and unlike Antonio, I'm pretty sure how I caught it, found it, or came by it. Every year at about this time, my good wife, the Reverend Mrs Walden, priest-in-charge of the church of St Aethelburgh and All Angels in the diocese of Southwark, declares a week to be 'Remember the Elderly Week'. During Remember the Elderly Week everyone has to be nice to anyone older than they are: so we have all manner of events going on in and around the church for our senior citizens – Take your Nan to Church Day, coffee afternoons in the vicarage, bingo evenings in the church hall, slide shows with reminiscences of Bermondsey in the old days – all of them featuring parishioners full of years, escorted by relatives who would never ordinarily darken the door of a church, and who look bored and out of place. The Reverend Mrs Walden is wonderful with them: she can chat away for hours about the old days, and about their families, and about how things aren't what they used to be, and about how the country's going to the dogs, without sounding in any way patronising.

It's a gift I haven't been blessed with, I'm afraid. I'm not sure why. Obviously, I have nothing against the elderly: it's a condition we all face in life barring a worse alternative, and I flatter myself that I can have a decent one-on-one conversation with any elderly person. But I just can't relax when they descend on the vicarage in their hordes. Perhaps it's the inevitable stark confrontation with impending decline – mine as well as theirs. Perhaps it's because I'm only too well aware that some counsel who appear in my court consider me to have reached that stage of life already, my modest age in the mid-sixties notwithstanding, simply because I wear the judicial robe. But whatever the reason, sitting through two services for which the elderly turn out *en masse* with their minders isn't my favourite way to spend my Sunday.

Yesterday too, I was aware of the trial I'm starting this morning, and it's enough to depress even the most cheerful of souls. The Reverend Mrs Walden, rounding off the Week in her climactic Sunday evening sermon, was exhorting the parish to take better care of the elderly: to make sure they are kept safe, are enabled to attend church, and have enough human contact to prevent loneliness and isolation. But my mind was drifting to a different kind of human contact the elderly may encounter in church – and it's one they need to be protected from rather than exposed to. In my case, the human contact is a woman called Laura Catesby, and her victim is a ninety-two-year-old widow by the name of Muriel Jones. Reflecting on Remember the Elderly Week, I can't help thinking that my reaction to it has a lot to do with my fear that somewhere down the road, when the Reverend and I are in our dotage and have been put out to pasture, we may fall victim to something similar ourselves. Age and frailty, I reflect, can make a Muriel Jones of any of us. I suppose I've reached the point where I'm beginning to feel my age.

There's another, even more immediate reason for this dampening of my spirits. This morning is one I hoped would never dawn; one I hoped I might be spared. This morning I truly expect to feel, not just older, but like a man becoming a dinosaur, a relic of the past: because today, after years of false starts and unfulfilled promises – or perhaps threats would be a better word – the Grey Smoothies are poised to introduce the 'Paperless Court'. The Grey Smoothies are the civil servants responsible for the running of our courts. Their twin governing principles, and mantras, are 'business case' and 'value for money for the taxpayer'. Intoning these mantras, they govern the courts using a form of magical thinking, according to which the courts would run just as efficiently, regardless of how much of our infrastructure and resources they degrade or take away, if only we would all just work harder and get on with it. In the universe of the Grey Smoothies, the quality of the courts and of the work we do lacks any quantifiable value. Like Wilde's cynics, the Grey Smoothies know the price of everything and the value of nothing; and sadly, I fear, by the time they have finished with us, there may be little left of a court system that was once the envy of the world.

The Paperless Court is the Grey Smoothies' current value-for-money project, and obsession. It is a system in which all court documents are filed, disseminated, and accessed electronically, so that no longer do we need the traditional court file with its huge piles of dog-eared papers stuffed into overworked cardboard folders. The Paperless Court is touted by the Grey Smoothies as a breakthrough akin to penicillin or the theory of relativity; and I must admit, its potential advantages are obvious even to me. You save on the cost of paper, you make documents available with far less delay, you reduce the risk of losing the documents, and best of all, no one has to carry all those heavy files around. All you need is your computer. But that's where the other side of the equation comes into play.

The Grey Smoothies fondly imagine themselves as inhabiting the same plane as the bankers and commercial wizards of the world, and accordingly, think that the courts should be working with the same technology they use in Canary Wharf or on Wall Street. And unfortunately, someone has convinced them that this is the path to the Grey Smoothie Holy Grail – reducing the cost of running the courts to almost nothing in the interests of value for money for the taxpayer. Unfortunately, whoever told the Grey Smoothies that computerisation was the Holy Grail of cheap and efficient court administration omitted to add an important proviso: that it only works if you spend the money to buy computers and programmes adequate to the complex task of running a court. We've been threatened several times before with the advent of the Paperless Court – it's been an ongoing saga ever since I took over as RJ – but the prototypes the Grey Smoothies have introduced in the past have had the unmistakeable whiff of underfunding about them. They haven't worked very well, and have been abandoned shortly after being trumpeted as the salvation of the court system. None of these failures has been cheap, and after a while you have to question how much value for money the taxpayer is actually getting out of it all.

In addition to those technical concerns, the Grey Smoothies tend to overestimate the human aspects of making the system work – in other words, the talents of those of us on the bench when it comes to computers. Of the four judges at Bermondsey, only Marjorie Jenkins can claim any real expertise with computers. As a busy commercial silk before she became a judge, she mastered modern forms of communication in a way that most of us who spent our lives at the criminal bar did not. It's expected in the world of banking and commerce, which has always seemed to me to revolve around three basic assumptions: that the continuance of human existence depends on the availability of twenty-four-hour phone and internet access; that the sum of all human knowledge can be expressed as a multi-coloured pie chart; and that all information must be capable of being transmitted instantaneously to any place on earth – how mankind survived until these conditions could be fulfilled being something of a mystery.

In the world of crime, that's not exactly the tradition. We work at a slower pace, using such outdated, but time-honoured technology as pens and paper; and most of us think that we are not losing anything because of it. As barristers, many of us were members of chambers that didn't even have a typist until we were getting quite senior in the profession; and even a few years ago, while most barristers had acquired personal computers, you were still looked on as a bit pretentious if you knew much more than how to turn it on. My colleague Hubert Drake, who is not too far from retirement – and, as far as computers are concerned, a confirmed Luddite – may not even know how to do that. Rory 'Legless' Dunblane and I are a little more advanced. We've mastered the art of emails and (at least in Legless's case) texting, and we understand the basics of cutting and pasting and so on. But that's about it. There is some mitigation, at least for those of us, like Hubert, old enough to have been on the bench for a good few years now. If you started your primary school education writing in chalk on a slate tablet, and were already of mature years when the original steam-powered personal computers were making their debut, I think you can be forgiven for not keeping up with every nuance of the computer revolution. Marjorie, by way of contrast, is up with most of them and so by comparison with most judges she is something of an expert. Typically, when my computer is doing something I don't understand or can't control, she's the person I go to for advice, and usually whatever she tells me to do works.

I had hoped that the old paper system might last just long enough for me to retire and allow a new, more computer-savvy generation of judges to get to grips with the new technology. There are some such judges in place already, like Marjorie; and you can see judges-in-waiting, as counsel, with their laptops on the bench in front of them, their PowerPoint presentations in court, and so on. That's what I mean when I say that I'm beginning to feel like a relic of the past, a dinosaur in a post-meteor world. But there's to be no reprieve. We judges, products of another time as we may be, will have to cope with change as best we can. In fairness to the Grey Smoothies, they have done their best to educate us. We've received screed after screed of information – electronically, of course – and several seminars from visiting computer nerds; and we have learned something. But it's a bit like learning a foreign language. If you grow up speaking a language, it's effortless; if you try to learn as an adult, you may achieve a certain fluency, but it will never become second nature. Or perhaps, at the end of the day, it's a cultural question: something to do with teaching an old dog new tricks – it's not that the dog doesn't understand them; it's more that sometimes he just doesn't feel inclined to play ball. I suspect that most of us, when faced with the relentless march of progress, have something of Mr Fezziwig about us.

But you can't tell the Grey Smoothies any of that. As far as they're concerned, they're on the road to the Holy Grail, and now they think they've ironed out the teething troubles that held back Sir Lancelot, Sir Gawain and the rest of them. So the Paperless Court is about to be rolled out, as the phrase is in Grey Smoothie-speak; and Stella, who's done a whole day of training in Cardiff to prepare her for this new era of technological wonders, has been deputed to show all of us how it works this morning, so that we can take our computers into court for the first time. Her presentation ends just before ten thirty – the appointed hour at which the Paperless Court is to be switched on for us simultaneously, rather like the Blackpool Illuminations.

All four judges will be doing a test hearing with our computers in place on the bench. Mine is a plea and case management hearing in the case of a thirty-something defendant called Gerry Farmer. Gerry Farmer is charged with three counts of handling stolen goods, to which Emily Phipson, who's prosecuting, tells me he is about to plead guilty. I've got Stella sitting up on the bench with me, just to make sure that I get off to a good start. Stella is our brilliant list officer, who almost single-handedly keeps the work of the court flowing: scheduling trials and pleas of guilty, and applications of every kind; making sure that each of the four judges has the right amount of work; arguing with solicitors, the CPS, and anyone else who tries to stand in her way. She's also my confidante in sensitive matters, such as those affecting the other judges and the court staff. She is the one person in the building without whom the place would actually fall apart.

Stella has summoned up the file in Mr Farmer's case for me on the screen. I'm feeling less than comfortable about having my computer with me on the bench. It's invading my personal space, taking up room in front of me and to my left, room I'm used to having available for *Archbold* and my notebook. Once the file has come up, Stella whispers to me that if I want to take notes, there's another file I can go to. Together we press a letter on my keyboard, and sure enough up it comes – a blank screen inviting the taking of a judicial note. But I'm not sure I could find my way back to the case file without Stella, and I'm aware of Emily and Piers Drayford, who's defending, grinning up at me. They've been told what's going on, and asked to be patient: but to them, switching between files is second nature and their patience isn't going to last indefinitely. Besides which, I can't spend all day on Gerry Farmer. I need to get on with the case of Muriel Jones before lunch if I'm to finish her evidence today and not have to drag her back to court tomorrow. So the habit of a lifetime prevails: I grab a pen and make my notes in my notebook. Now I need to go back to the Farmer file to look at the indictment, but when I try to return, the screen goes a bright blue colour and there's a message saying, 'Please sign in'. I glance at Stella, panicking slightly.

'I *have* signed in,' I protest quietly.

'Enter your password again,' she whispers.

Recently, I've taken a simple approach to passwords. Until someone told me that the Grey Smoothies insist on frequent changes of password, I opted for rather complicated ones designed to thwart even the most ingenious hacker – like Marjorie, who is working her way through the pantheon of Greek and Roman deities. But when I had to change them regularly, it all started to seem unduly complicated and since then I've resorted to CharlieWOne, CharlieWTwo, and so on. That seems to work well enough. But not today. When I type in 'CharlieWFour', the current version, I get the message, 'Incorrect password: try again'.

'No, it's asking for your new "Paperless" password,' Stella

whispers; and belatedly, I remember that Paperless requires a second password, beginning with a capital letter and containing at least eight digits and including at least one numeral and one other symbol. I duly selected such a password this morning, and I confess that in frustration I went with 'Sodthis!1'. I duly type this in the space provided, and the Farmer file pops back up. Stella smiles benevolently, and points to where it says 'Indictment'. I tap again, and hey presto, there it is.

Perusing the indictment, I see that we have a problem we never seemed to have before draft indictments were sent electronically: namely, that no one ever seems to proofread them before sending them to the court. In the present case, Emily is in the embarrassing position of having to ask for leave to amend the statement of offence in count one, so that it reads: 'Handling stolen goods, contrary to section 22(1) of the Theft Act 1968' in place of the current text, 'Ask counsel to insert appropriate details'. I allow the amendment with a deliberate show of ill grace; only to move to count two and find something that doesn't feel quite right in the particulars of the offence. The particulars of offence in count two allege that Mr Farmer: 'Dishonestly received a solar gorilla, knowing or believing the same to be stolen goods'. My court clerk, Carol, duly puts count two to Mr Farmer, who looks a bit bemused, but as Piers has advised, duly proffers a plea of guilty.

'Are we sure that's correct, Miss Phipson?' I ask.

'Your Honour?'

'Has anyone been in touch with the London Zoo?' Both counsel are staring at me. 'To ask whether they have a record of such a creature going missing,' I explain. 'It sounds like the kind of thing they would notice, don't you think?'

They both look at count two again, and Emily mutters something under her breath. Piers is also looking a bit embarrassed – as he should. Emily turns behind her to consult the CPS representative and the officer in the case, DC Martindale, and after some whispered discussion – and, ironically, some shuffling of old-fashioned paper – it emerges that the item dishonestly received by Mr Farmer was in fact a solar-powered grill. I allow the amendment, and ask Carol to arraign the defendant on count two again. He pleads guilty again, this time more confidently.

And so it goes on. By the time I've released Gerry Farmer on bail pending preparation of a pre-sentence report, I've just about mastered the art of accessing case files and individual documents, and to my delight, I find and open the Laura Catesby file without any assistance whatsoever from Stella. She leaves, assuring me that she is only a phone call away if I need her. For the first time, I find myself alone in the Paperless Court.

'May it please your Honour, members of the jury, my name is Susan Worthington and I appear to prosecute in this case. The defendant Laura Catesby, the lady sitting in the dock at the back of the court, is represented by my learned friend Mr Roderick Lofthouse.'

Susan appears regularly at Bermondsey, both for the prosecution and the defence, but I've always felt that prosecution is her *forte*. She is naturally quite tall and imposing, and when on the prosecution side, has the habit of drawing herself up to her full height and giving the court, defence counsel and defendant alike a particularly menacing stare through her dark brown tortoiseshell glasses. Sometimes she gives the jury the same treatment if she thinks their attention may be wandering a bit; but thus far this morning she has reserved the stare for Roderick.

That's not going to put Roderick off his game – during his long career he has been faced with many menacing stares, including a fair number from me. He will react as he always does, smiling blandly and giving every appearance of ignoring it: nothing new there. What's more interesting about Roderick in this case is that he isn't prosecuting. For some years now he has spent most of his time trying to get convictions rather than prevent them, and I'm curious. Glancing through the file, I see that my first instinct is correct: Mrs Catesby is not in receipt of legal aid. Roderick will have been retained privately, and I'm sure his clerk will have negotiated a very decent fee for her defence. Mrs Catesby comes from monied respectability – it's one of the more puzzling aspects of the case – and I'm sure the prospect of a prison sentence had her solicitors scrambling to retain the most senior member of the Bermondsey Bar before the CPS could snatch him from them. No wonder Roderick is looking so pleased with himself. That's the kind of attention to warm the cockles of any barrister's heart.

'Members of the jury, I'm going to ask the usher to hand out copies of the indictment, which you heard the clerk read to you a few minutes ago.'

Dawn, our usher, also the court's first aid person and expert on home remedies and today wearing a bright orange dress under her gown, flits around the courtroom with truly astonishing speed. Despite her lack of height, she moves like a human dynamo; in a matter of a few seconds, she has furnished the jury with copies of the indictment, one between two, casually retrieving and restoring a pen one of them had dropped over the front of the jury box along the way.

'If you look at the indictment with me, you will see that Laura Catesby is charged with five counts of theft and a sixth count alleging attempted theft. These counts represent what the prosecution say is a pattern of dishonest conduct over a long period of time. You will hear that over a period of about four years, Mrs Catesby stole money from a woman called Muriel Jones. Mrs Jones, members of the jury, is an elderly lady, a widow now almost ninety-three years of age. You will hear that Mrs Catesby met Mrs Jones at the church they both attend, the church of St Mortimer-in-the-Fields, here in Bermondsey.

'Although Mrs Jones is in remarkably good health for her age, like anyone aged eighty-eight, as she was when they first met, she was glad to accept offers of help from friends, doing things like shopping and cleaning, which had become harder for her over the years. Mrs Jones's own family live far from London; she has one son in Yorkshire, and the other living abroad, in South Africa. She didn't see much of them, and her friends replaced them in her life to a large extent. She numbered Mrs Catesby among her friends. But the prosecution say that, far from being a true friend, Mrs Catesby made a pretence of befriending Mrs Jones, so that she could win her trust and pave the way for a campaign of theft which, over a four-year period, enabled her to steal a total of over ten thousand pounds. Mrs Jones was not a rich woman, members of the jury, but her husband, Henry, had left her reasonably well provided for after his death. Sadly, a large chunk of that provision is now gone, stolen by Mrs Catesby.

'How, you may ask, was Mrs Catesby able to steal so much before what she had done came to light? Members of the jury, it was, as I said, a question of building trust. She started by insinuating herself into Mrs Jones's life, volunteering to run errands for her, doing some shopping, picking up cleaning, washing up, making her a sandwich and a cup of soup at lunchtime, and so on. At first, you will hear, Mrs Catesby paid for any shopping out of her own money, presented Mrs Jones with the receipts, and was then reimbursed in cash. But as time went by she persuaded Mrs Jones that it would be easier if Mrs Jones trusted her with her debit card when she went out shopping. Seeing no reason to doubt this woman she knew from her church, Mrs Jones did as Mrs Catesby suggested.'

I see some members of the jury looking in the direction of the dock, and I follow their eyes. Laura Catesby is sitting next to the dock officer with a faraway expression that suggests that the proceedings are boring her. She is dressed in a frilly purple blouse with a black skirt, and she's flaunting a string of pearls around her neck, not to mention a gold watch and two or three impressively sized rings. Now in my experience, regardless of what you're charged with, it's probably not a great idea to appear in front of a Bermondsey jury looking like that; but in a case where you're charged with stealing more than ten thousand pounds from an elderly widow it seems almost reckless. I'm surprised that Roderick or her solicitor didn't send her straight back home to change. Perhaps they tried. She doesn't look like a woman who likes being told what to do. A middle-aged man in a grey suit and a red tie is trying not to look too conspicuous in the public gallery – the husband, I deduce, from the occasional furtive exchange of glances between public gallery and dock. Appearances can be deceptive, of course, but he strikes me as a man who spends more time following orders than giving them.

'Count one,' Susan continues, 'is a count covering the whole four-year period. It deals with all the known occasions on which Mrs Catesby used Mrs Jones's debit card improperly when she went shopping. There are many examples of Mrs Catesby taking more than the cost of the items she bought and gave to Mrs Jones. Her main method of stealing money was to ask for cash back in the amount of twenty-five or fifty pounds, which she then kept for herself. On other occasions she purchased items for herself and used Mrs Jones's money to pay for them. The total amount she obtained in this way over that long period of time, the prosecution say, is in the region of eight thousand pounds.

'Counts two to five relate to specific occasions on which Mrs Catesby stole money from Mrs Jones by inventing stories involving her two daughters. Members of the jury, in many ways this is the most distressing and puzzling aspect of the case. Mrs Catesby didn't need the money she stole. She had a good job as a business manager in a large accountancy firm. Her husband is a fund manager in the City. She has two daughters, Sophie, now aged sixteen, and Emma, now aged thirteen. You will hear, members of the jury, that Mrs Catesby told Mrs Jones a number of blatant lies involving her two daughters. Count two deals with an occasion on which she told Mrs Jones that Emma was seriously ill and needed money for private surgery. She told Mrs Jones that it was just a loan, that it was necessary only because of a temporary financial difficulty, and that she would repay the money as soon as she could. Mrs Jones told Mrs Catesby to take what she needed out of her savings account, and gave her the authorisation to do so. On that occasion, Mrs Catesby took one thousand pounds. That sum was never repaid. Members of the jury, Emma has never needed surgery, and, as far as the prosecution is aware, has never been seriously ill.

'Counts three, four and five deal with similar requests for money, also dressed up as loans, and also involving thefts from Mrs Jones's savings account. In each of these cases, Mrs Catesby told Mrs Jones that because of temporary financial difficulties she was unable to pay school fees for Emma or Sophie at a well-known Christian school for girls in Surrey. She told Mrs Jones that she might have to take the girls out of that school and send them to an ordinary London comprehensive where, Mrs Catesby insisted, they were likely to encounter drugs and immorality. On hearing this, Mrs Jones gave Mrs Catesby the money she asked for: five hundred pounds on each of the occasions dealt with in these three counts. Members of the jury, neither Emma nor Sophie has ever been educated privately. Both girls attend a state comprehensive school in South London.

'The thefts came to light because, when the so-called loans were not repaid, Mrs Jones started to worry, and became suspicious. She contacted Ronald, her son who lives in Yorkshire. Ronald will give evidence, members of the jury, and he will tell you that when his mother voiced these concerns, he came to see her, took charge of her bank statements, and immediately saw the scale of the money that was missing. Rather ingeniously, you may think, having a certain technical expertise as an engineer, he also installed a hidden camera and voice-operated recorder in Mrs Jones's kitchen, where Mrs Jones and Mrs Catesby talked when Mrs Catesby visited. He then arranged for Mrs Catesby to visit Mrs Jones in the kitchen while he concealed himself in one of the bedrooms. As luck would have it, the camera caught Mrs Catesby rifling though Mrs Jones's purse while she was at the stove making coffee, and on his monitor in the bedroom Ronald was able to watch her do it in real time. Ronald left the cover of the bedroom, confronted Mrs Catesby, and saw that she was holding fifty pounds in cash. Members of the jury, that is count six, the charge of attempted theft. Ronald immediately called the police, and detained Mrs Catesby until they arrived.'

Susan scans her notes for a few moments.

'Members of the jury, I needn't take up your time going through the police investigation now. You will hear all about it from the officers. To put it shortly, they carried out a thorough examination of Mrs Jones's bank accounts. They would have liked to go through the receipts Mrs Catesby gave her when she returned from shopping, but the receipts were not in Mrs Jones's flat. The police did find two or three receipts in Mrs Catesby's house when they searched it, but that was all. The prosecution say that she made sure to remove them from Mrs Jones's flat when she left, so as to cover her tracks. It was to be a paperless crime. But fortunately, DC Benson, the police forensic accountant, was able to reconstruct the amounts from the records of two stores where most of the shopping was done.

The police also applied to a judge to order the disclosure of the Catesby family's bank accounts. An examination of those accounts revealed no payments either for private surgery or for private school fees.

'Mrs Catesby was arrested and interviewed under caution at the police station in the presence of her solicitor. She told the police that Mrs Jones had given her permission to take "a little something for herself" whenever she did the shopping. She also claimed that the payments in counts two to five were outright gifts from Mrs Jones to Emma and Sophie, gifts made for no better reason than that she liked the girls and wanted to help them. She denied any mention of loans for surgery or school fees. Members of the jury, the prosecution say that her explanation is patently false and dishonest.

'With your Honour's leave,' Susan concludes, 'I will call the evidence.' She turns to me. 'Your Honour, Mrs Jones is here at court. She's been waiting with one of our volunteers from the victims and witnesses unit. She's in good health, but she has told us that she can't sit in one place for too long. I've promised her that we will give her frequent breaks. Would your Honour rise for a few moments, so that we can bring her into court and make her comfortable?'

With any elderly or vulnerable witness, trials move rather more slowly than in other cases and of course, I've had Gerry Farmer and the Solar Gorilla to deal with this morning before I became free to start the trial. But it's something you can't avoid – you have to work on the witness's schedule until her evidence is concluded.

'Certainly, Miss Worthington,' I reply. 'Coffee break, members of the jury. Fifteen minutes.'

The jurors give me a cheerful nod, but one or two cast rather dark glances in the direction of the dock on the way out of court. I'm finding it hard to resist the temptation to do the same.

Muriel Jones looks small and frail, not quite invisible but hard to see clearly in the witness box. But she has no difficulty in making herself heard. She takes the oath in a strong, clear voice.

'Mrs Jones,' Susan begins, having elicited her name and age, 'do you know the defendant, Laura Catesby?'

Mrs Jones directs a sad look towards the dock. 'Yes, I do.'

'Would you tell the jury how you first met Ms Catesby?'

'It was at church.'

'Is that St Mortimer's church in Bermondsey?'

'Yes, that's right.'

'How long have you been a member of the congregation at St Mortimer's?'

Mrs Jones smiles thinly. 'Oh, goodness, now you're asking, aren't you?'

Susan returns the smile. 'I don't mean exactly. Roughly how long?'

'Well, I've been going to St Mortimer's all my life. My parents started taking me there when I was just a little girl; I went to Sunday school, I had my first communion, and I was confirmed there, and I've been going ever since.'

'Thank you, Mrs Jones. Do you remember when you first met Mrs Catesby?'

At which point, for the first time, Mrs Jones seems hesitant. Susan knows that some patience will probably be required this morning. She gives her a moment, and doesn't press her immediately.

She shakes her head. 'I couldn't tell you exactly.'

'All right, just tell us as far as you remember. We don't need an exact date.' Still, the witness hesitates. Susan glances up at me. 'Would it help you to see your witness statement?'

'Yes. I think it would.'

Witnesses are always allowed to read their witness statements before giving evidence – after all, evidence is supposed to be a test of accuracy, not memory. But if a witness is having trouble remembering the court may permit her to refresh her memory even while giving evidence, and today judges almost always allow it if asked. Roderick could make a bit of a song and dance about it, but we're dealing with a witness in her nineties, and he knows that I'm not about to keep her statement from her if she needs it. Wisely, he decides to keep his powder dry. In any case, an early hint of memory problems does his case no harm.

'No objection, your Honour,' he replies. Dawn quickly takes the statement from Susan and gives it to the witness. Mrs Jones takes her time reading through it.

'She and her husband and her two girls used to come to church most Sundays,' she replies eventually, 'so I can't give you an exact date, but it must have been at least four or five years ago. Her husband was one of the churchwardens for a while.'

'And how did you come to talk to Mrs Catesby?

Another look down at the statement. 'It was when the vicar gave a sermon one Sunday about helping one another.' She pauses, and glances up at me. 'That was the former vicar,' she adds cautiously, 'Mr Canning. He had to leave because of a… well… a scandal, so he's not with us any more. We've got a lady vicar now, who's very nice.'

The jury snigger, and I'm sure they're curious about the details, as we all are when a minister is involved in a scandal. The Reverend Mr Canning had developed the habit of visiting a dominatrix called Madam Rosita and paying her fees from church funds, in respect of which he was convicted of theft in my court, resulting in a premature end to his clerical career. But that's not on the agenda today.

'It was Mr Canning who gave the sermon. And I remember I was standing outside church after the service, and Mrs Catesby was standing there with her husband and the girls, and she asked if she could give me a lift home. So I said yes, that would be very kind, and so they gave me a lift home; and from then on they started taking me to and from church almost every Sunday.'

'Yes. Did Mrs Catesby offer to help you in any other ways?'

Mrs Jones nods. 'Yes, after they'd been giving me a lift for some time, she asked if she could do some shopping for me. She told me she worked for a company that had an office not far from my block of flats, so she could run some errands for me during her lunch hour or after work. She said it was no problem.'

'Did you accept that offer?'

'Yes, I did. Well, I'm not as strong as I was, you know. I've got my shopping cart on wheels and Tesco is only a few minutes' walk. I've been going there for years, but as you get older, you know…' her voice trails away.

'Yes, of course,' Susan says. 'Sadly, Mrs Jones, you're a widow, aren't you?'

'Yes. My Henry's been dead ten years and more now. I've got the two boys, of course, but they're too far away.'

'Your sons?'

'Yes. Ronnie lives up in Yorkshire, near Scarborough, so he does come down to see me now and then. But Jamie's in Durban – he works for a big international engineering company – so I'm lucky if I see him once a year. He's got his own family out there in South Africa.'

'So they can't help on a regular basis?'

'No.'

Susan pauses. 'Mrs Jones, tell the jury how it worked, Mrs Catesby doing the shopping for you. How did you arrange the money and so on?'

She consults her witness statement again.

'Well, I would make a list of what I wanted. I would give her the list, whenever she came, at lunchtime or after work, or whenever, and she would go and get it for me. She would bring me the receipt, and I would give her the money in cash. I still had to go out myself sometimes, of course. She wasn't getting everything for me. I would still go to Tesco and the bank, and so on, at least once a week. But she was a big help. I must admit that. She was very helpful.'

'Yes, I'm sure. Did there come a time when Mrs Catesby suggested a simpler method of dealing with the money?'

'Yes.'

'What was that? Explain to the jury what she suggested, please.'

Back to the witness statement for some seconds.

'She said it would be easier if I just gave her my debit card when she went out shopping for me. I must admit, there were times when I didn't have enough cash to pay her for the shopping, if I hadn't got out to the bank, and then I would have to ask her to wait until the next time. It was only a couple of times, but of course I felt bad about it because she was doing me a favour, so at the time, what she suggested seemed like a good idea.'

'And did you agree to that arrangement?'

'Yes. I would give her the debit card. I'd told her the code, you know, the four numbers, so she could use it.'

'Did she still bring the receipts back for you?'

'Yes, always.'

'Did you look at them at the time?'

Mrs Jones shakes her head sadly. 'At first, I did, you know, when I was giving her the cash. But as time went by, when we'd been doing it all regularly for a while, I suppose I didn't think I needed to. It all seemed to be going well, and I'd met her at church, you know, and I never thought…' again, her voice trails away.

'No, of course. Do you know what happened to the receipts she gave you?'

'Not really. When the police asked about them I didn't have them, so I expect she walked off with them.'

Roderick is rising to his feet. Susan holds up a hand.

'But you don't know? You didn't actually see her taking receipts from your flat?'

'I didn't see her doing it.'

'All right. Were you checking your bank accounts regularly?'

'No,' the witness replies quietly, embarrassed. 'Not like I should. I have, what d'you call it, that electronic banking. They don't send me the bank statements any more, do they? I have to go on the computer, or use that little plastic thing. I don't... I mean, the manager explained to me how to do it, but I'm not really comfortable with it, and when I try to do it, I seem to make mistakes and it doesn't seem to work properly.'

Paperless, I think to myself, without Stella to help her.

'I understand,' Susan says, but I doubt she does. Susan is one of the new generation of computer-savvy judges-in-waiting, who's been using such technology all her life and probably can't imagine the world without it. 'Did Mrs Catesby ever help you in other ways, in addition to doing some shopping for you?'

'She would collect my cleaning once in a while, and to be fair to her, she was always ready to tidy up a bit for me when she came round, and she would sometimes make me a sandwich and some soup for lunch. As I say, she was very helpful.'

'Let me turn to something different,' Susan says. 'As well as getting to know Mrs Catesby herself, did you come to know her family at all?'

'I never really got to know her husband, Larry,' Mrs Jones replies after some thought. 'He never came round to the flat. But Laura sometimes brought the girls if they weren't at school, so I did talk to them from time to time. Very nice girls they are, too. They were always very polite and they seemed very well brought up.'

'Did Mrs Catesby ever mention money in connection specifically with the girls?'

'Several times,' Mrs Jones replies.

'When was the first time, do you remember?'

She thinks for some time, turning over one or two pages of her statement. 'It must be about three years ago now, at least. She came to do some shopping one lunchtime, and she seemed very upset, teary and so forth.'

'Did she tell you why?'

'Yes. She told me that the younger girl, Emma, had some serious medical condition.'

'Did she tell you what that condition was?'

'Not as far as I remember. I assumed it was probably cancer.'

'Why did you assume that? Did she say anything like that?'

'No, but that's always the way, isn't it? No one wants to say the word "cancer", do they? I mean, if someone has a heart attack or a stroke, they will tell you. But it's like bad luck if you actually say "cancer". So they just say that someone's seriously ill. I suppose I just assumed it.'

'And how did the subject of money come up?'

She thinks for some time. 'As far as I remember, Laura said they couldn't get Emma in for surgery on the NHS because of the waiting times. They thought it was dangerous to delay it, so they wanted to go private, but they didn't have the money to hand.'

'But, as I understand it,' Susan interjects, 'both Mr and Mrs Catesby had well-paying jobs, didn't they?'

'As far as I knew, yes.'

'So, why was Mrs Catesby talking to you about money?'

'It was something to do with their investments. If she told me, I can't remember the details. But it was something to do with, they'd made some expensive investments and they had to rebuild their savings. She said it would only be a couple of months because they were due to get dividends from their investments, but they were a bit strapped for cash until then, and could I loan them some money to tide them over and make sure that Emma could have her operation?'

'And did you?'

'Yes, I loaned her a thousand pounds, which is what she said she needed.'

'How did you arrange to make that money available to her?'

'I arranged with the bank to take it out of my savings account, and I gave Laura an authorisation to collect it from the bank.'

'Has Mrs Catesby ever repaid that loan?'

A look towards the dock. 'No. She has not.' Following her eyes, I note that Laura Catesby is still looking faintly bored.

'Is there any question in your mind that it was a loan? Might it have been that you were making a gift of that thousand pounds to Mrs Catesby?'

'What, a thousand pounds? No. It was a loan. I'm not made of money.'

'Did Mrs Catesby ever follow up with you, tell you whether Emma had the surgery, how it went, and so on?'

'She did thank me, and she told me it had been a success, and Emma was fine. But the odd thing was, I didn't see Emma at church for a long time, and she never thanked me personally, which I thought was very strange, because she was always such a nice, polite girl.'

'Before you made that loan to Mrs Catesby, how much money did you have in your savings account?'

'It was something like twenty thousand pounds that my Henry had left me. That was what I had – in addition to my pension, of course. And I do own my flat that I still live in, where I used to live with Henry before he died. But I didn't have any other money.'

'Was that the only occasion when Mrs Catesby raised the

subject of money in connection with her daughters?'

'No.' She's turning over pages in her statement again.

'What other occasions were there?'

'There were times when she told me she couldn't afford to pay their school fees.'

'Did she tell you where they were at school?'

'She said it was a Christian school for girls, St Somebody's in Surrey...'

'St Cecilia's?' Susan asks.

'Something like that.' She looks down at her statement. 'Yes: St Cecilia's, in Surrey. She said it was quite an expensive school, but she and Larry were keen on it because they didn't want the girls going to the comprehensive, because there was a drug problem and the discipline wasn't what it should be. She was afraid they would be exposed to bad influences: that's what she said.'

'Over what period of time was she complaining about not being able to afford the fees?'

'Over the last two, two and a half years or thereabouts.'

'And again, did Mrs Catesby explain why she and her husband couldn't afford the fees?'

'It was due to their investments, and the dividends hadn't been as much as they'd hoped. And then Laura's mother had been very ill, she said, and she'd had to take care of her. So they still didn't have the money. But she was still insisting that it was just a temporary loan, and she would be able to repay me before long.' She looks very sad. 'But she didn't.'

'How much did you loan to Mrs Catesby for school fees?'

'Five hundred each time. She asked me three times.'

'So, fifteen hundred pounds in total?'

'Yes.'

'Plus one thousand for the surgery?'

'Yes.'

'That makes two thousand five hundred pounds, doesn't it? And after looking at your bank accounts and discussing them with your son and with DC Benson, are you now aware that another eight thousand or so…'

'I'm sorry, your Honour,' Roderick intervenes, rising ponderously to his feet, as is his way. His rather-too-light single-breasted jacket has been too tight for him for some time now, but as the acknowledged doyen of the Bermondsey Bar, he is allowed some leeway. 'I must object to that. This witness has no personal knowledge of that amount, or indeed of what happened to it.'

Roderick is right, technically. I'm not sure there's much point in his objection in the long run. Susan shouldn't have any trouble proving it through her police witness and the son, Ronald; but if Roderick really insists, that's what she'll have to do. But I don't think that's Roderick's real agenda. I'm pretty sure he's more interested in taking another early pot shot at Mrs Jones's memory and her credibility as a witness about what happened to her money. Either way, he's made a good point. I glance at Susan and she nods.

'I'll deal with that later in another way,' she replies. 'So far, then, Mrs Jones, we have a total of two thousand five hundred pounds, is that right?'

'Yes.'

'Any of it repaid?'

'Not a penny.'

Susan pauses for some time. 'Mrs Jones, the jury may want to know why you parted with so much money to someone you didn't know all that well, why you trusted Mrs Catesby enough to loan her so much money? What do you say about that?'

I know how Muriel Jones is going to answer that before she opens her mouth, and it's what's made me into such an Antonio today.

'I feel so stupid,' she replies quietly. 'I feel like a complete fool. I can imagine what Henry would have to say about it all.' She bows her head for some seconds before continuing. 'All I can say is that I met the family in my church, they seemed very respectable, they both had good jobs, they had two well brought up children. They were very nice to me, or so I thought, and I fell for it, hook, line and sinker. I'm sure they've been laughing at me, thinking I'm a real mug. It just breaks my heart.'

'I think there came a time,' Susan continues after a suitable pause, 'when you contacted your son Ronald and told him that you were worried about Mrs Catesby. How did that come about?'

'It was after I'd loaned her so much money, and she hadn't repaid a penny,' Mrs Jones replies. 'I just started to get this feeling that something was wrong. It was always, she needed more time, not long, just a few weeks, and everything would be all right. But it never was. So I went to my vicar and I told her in confidence what was going on, and she advised me to ask someone I knew I could trust to look into it. So I asked Ronnie to come down and tell me what he thought. He has a good head on his shoulders. I just needed to know what was going on.'

'And did Ronnie come down to London to see you?'

'Yes.'

'What did he do?'

'He made an appointment to see my bank manager, and got copies of my bank statements going back a few years, my savings account and my ordinary account, and we sat down together and went through them, and he told me…'

Roderick is halfway to his feet to object to the looming hearsay, but Susan raises a hand and deals with it herself.

'I'm not allowed to ask you what Ronnie told you, Mrs Jones,' she explains. 'It's to do with the rules of evidence. But as a result of what Ronnie found when he looked at your bank accounts, what did he do?'

'He went out and bought one of those, what d'you call them, miniature cameras, and a recorder, and he installed them in my kitchen.'

'Why in the kitchen?'

'That's where I always talked with Laura when she came to the flat.'

'Did he do anything else?'

'Yes. He told me to invite Laura to come round to the flat the next day, which I did. I told her I needed some help putting up some curtains.'

'Did Mrs Catesby come the next day?'

'Yes, she did.'

'And what happened?'

'Well, Ronnie told me to behave normally, and I did have some curtains I wanted put up, so I was talking with Laura in the kitchen and I made her a cup of coffee, and Ronnie was in my bedroom, watching and listening to us.'

'He'd set it up so that he could watch and listen from a distance?'

'Yes. He's always been clever with his hands. He's an engineer, you know. Both my sons are engineers, like their father before them.'

'Yes. And what happened next?'

'All of a sudden I see Ronnie running into the kitchen. I was a bit taken aback because it all happened very suddenly and I was turned with my back to Laura. But I see Ronnie run straight over to Laura and grab her arm. She tells him to let go of her, and she's asking him who he is. But then I see that she's got hold of my handbag, which I'd left on the kitchen table, and she has some money in her hand. She'd got it out of my purse. She'd taken fifty pounds, two twenties and a tenner: right under our noses. The cheek of it…'

Glancing towards the dock, I see Mrs Catesby smile briefly before resuming her look of boredom.

'Mrs Jones, did you give Mrs Catesby permission to take any money from your purse on that day?'

'No. I did not.'

'What happened next?'

'Ronnie called the police. Laura tried to leave, but Ronnie wouldn't let her. He told her she had to wait for the police to come.'

'And did the police come, and did they arrest Mrs Catesby?'

'Yes, they did.'

'Mrs Jones, did you ever give Mrs Catesby permission to take money over and above what she needed to pay for the shopping she did for you?'

'No. I did not.'

'Did you ever invite her to take "a bit for herself", or "a little something for herself", or anything like that?'

'No. I did not.'

'Or to take cash back using your debit card?'

'No. I did not.'

'Or to buy things for herself or her family at your expense without telling you?'

'No. I did not.'

'Did you ever make a gift of money, as opposed to a loan, to Mrs Catesby or to either of her daughters?'

'No. I did not.' She pauses for a few moments. 'I didn't mind helping her out because I believed her when she told me why she needed the money. Having met her at church, and with her husband being a churchwarden, and with her girls being so nice and polite, and…'

'Yes,' Susan replies. 'Thank you, Mrs Jones, that's all I have.

Your Honour, I see the time. It's a bit early to break for lunch, but ...'

'I'm sure Mrs Jones would welcome a break,' Roderick agrees immediately. 'May I cross-examine at two o'clock?'

And so to lunch, an oasis of calm in a desert of chaos.

I've brought my own lunch today, as three out of the four Bermondsey judges, myself included, do a good deal of the time, to lessen the risk from exposure to the canteen food. When I take my place at the huge table in the judicial mess, Marjorie is playing unenthusiastically with a mackerel salad. Rory Dunblane, known to us all as 'Legless' because of a now dimly remembered episode after a chambers dinner in his days at the Bar, has brought in some kind of posh-looking soup in a heavy-duty plastic container, and a couple of bread rolls. Only Hubert Drake consistently risks the dreaded dish of the day, which today seems to be some kind of Chinese concoction with noodles and vegetables. Hubert, whose age is somewhat in dispute, is the oldest of us and (according to my calculations, though not his) within sight of retirement; but his constitution seems to cope with the food in the mess remarkably well, and he often claims that he needs his 'proper' lunch to tide him over until his nightly ritual of dinner at the Garrick Club.

'That's a nasty little case you've got, Charlie, that Catesby woman,' Legless observes. 'I did her plea and case management hearing. She turned up dressed to the nines and gave the impression that she couldn't care less about being in court.'

I nod. 'She's giving the same impression now.'

'Is Roderick still defending her?'

'Yes. He's due to cross-examine the widow Jones after lunch.'

'Well, at least you can trust Roderick to be nice to the widow Jones,' Legless says. 'He's not going to beat her up the way some younger members of our bar would.'

'What are you going to give her if she goes down?' Hubert asks. 'I'd give her five years straight inside, and that would be for starters. Taking advantage of the elderly like that: far too much of it going on; absolutely disgraceful.'

'I'm not sure you can get to five years under the sentencing guidelines, Hubert,' Legless replies, with a grin towards me. Over the years, we've had many lunchtime debates over Hubert's views on sentencing, which in general date from the Raj era, but we've long since given up trying to convert him to contemporary practice. The Court of Appeal has also made several attempts without success, and if they can't persuade him, what chance do we have?

'That's what's wrong with the bloody courts these days,' Hubert protests. 'You can't pass a decent sentence without someone telling you it's not allowed under the guidelines. Stuff and nonsense. When you have a case like yours you have to be firm. Otherwise, all the older people are going to go the same way as Harry Buller.'

Hubert returns to his dish of the day without elaborating.

'Who is Harry Buller?' Legless asks after a few seconds.

'What? Oh, Harry's a member of the Garrick. Known him for years. He was telling me about it the other night at dinner. He got one of those, whatsits, emails, apparently from a friend of his, saying the poor blighter was in Tanzania or somewhere on a safari trip, and he'd been kidnapped by these bandits, who were demanding fifty thousand pounds in ransom, and so on; and he'd got two other friends to help him, but he still needed fifteen thousand, and would Harry please transfer it to a numbered account in some bank in the Cayman Islands.'

'You're kidding,' Marjorie says, looking up from her salad.

'But it turned out the email wasn't from his friend at all; it was from some fellow in Nigeria. Complete bloody fraud from start to finish.'

'Imagine that,' Legless murmurs.

'Don't tell me he fell for a story like that, Hubert,' I add.

Hubert shrugs. 'Harry's getting on a bit, Charlie,' he explains. 'He's not as quick as he used to be. It wasn't about the money. Harry's made of money, so he wasn't too bothered about losing the fifteen thousand, but he was asking me what we judges were going to do about it. He was saying that when you catch people like that, you should send them inside for a good long stretch, so they can't defraud people who are less well off; and I agree with him, guidelines or no guidelines. And that's exactly what you should do with the Catesby woman.'

He returns briefly to the dish of the day, but then suddenly looks up. 'It's easy enough to laugh at Harry, but it comes to us all eventually, you know, Charlie,' he adds.

I nod. I'm only too well aware of that today. It's time to change the subject. 'How did you all get on with the Paperless Court?'

'Fine,' Marjorie replies immediately.

'I think I've just about got the idea,' Legless replies. 'But it's taking me forever to find a particular document when I need it; and sometimes it shuts down if it's a big file, and I have to put my password in again. Bloody nuisance.'

Marjorie looks up. 'Oh, not that again', she says. 'That's what happened with the last version. How did you get on, Charlie?'

'Oh, fine,' I reply quickly, and obviously, not entirely truthfully. 'Hubert, were you all right?'

'Right as rain,' Hubert replies with a smile.

'Really?' Marjorie asks. 'Are you sure, Hubert, because if you like, I can always show you…'

'No, thank you,' Hubert replies at once. 'Absolutely fine. No problem.'

The three of us exchange glances.

'How did you manage?' I begin tentatively. 'I only ask because…'

Hubert looks up from the dish of the day. 'Perfectly simple, Charlie,' he replies. 'I got my clerk to print the files out for me.'

* * *

Monday afternoon

'Would it be fair, Mrs Jones,' Roderick begins quietly, almost diffidently, 'to say that your memory isn't quite what it used to be?'

'There's nothing wrong with my memory,' Mrs Jones protests.

'It's just that I couldn't help noticing that you were reading your witness statement quite a lot when you were answering questions from my learned friend. Is that because some of the detail escapes you when it comes to events a long time ago?'

'Everybody has trouble remembering things from a long time ago,' she insists.

'Of course,' Roderick agrees reassuringly. 'I wasn't being critical, Mrs Jones. But as you know, I'm representing Mrs Catesby and I have to try to make sure that the jury know how well you remember what happened between you and Mrs Catesby. I'm sure you understand.'

'If you say so', she replies grudgingly.

'Would it be fair to say that when you first met the Catesby family, you were rather lonely?'

She thinks for some time. 'I suppose so, in a way,' she replies eventually. 'I think most people feel they're on their own by the time they get to my age.'

'Of course,' Roderick concedes. 'Sadly, you'd lost your husband, and your two sons were rather far away, weren't they?'

'Yes. That's true.'

'So when you met people in church who spoke to you and took an interest in you, it must have made a big difference to you, mustn't it, brightened your day a bit?'

'I talk to a lot of people in church, including the vicar. St Mortimer's is a very friendly church, always has been.'

'But the Catesbys went out of their way to take an interest in you, didn't they? They offered you a lift to and from church, offered to do shopping for you, and so on?'

'Yes.'

'And you responded to them; you welcomed the attention?'

'I was grateful to them for offering to help me, yes.'

'Do you have any grandchildren, Mrs Jones?'

'Jamie, my son who lives in South Africa, has two children, a boy and a girl. They're almost grown up now, seventeen and fourteen. I don't see them very often.' Once again, she looks sad.

'But you saw quite a lot of Mrs Catesby's two daughters, Sophie and Emma, didn't you?'

'Yes, I suppose so. I saw them at church, and once in a while Laura would have them with her when she came to see me.'

'And you told the jury earlier that you found them to be very polite, well brought up?'

'Yes, they were: always.'

'Did you come to see them, in a way, as the granddaughters you didn't have – at least, you didn't have close to you, here in London?'

Mrs Jones has to think about that one. 'I suppose I did get quite fond of them,' she admits. 'Yes. But I didn't see them often enough to think of them as my grandchildren.'

'But if Mrs Catesby had told you that Sophie or Emma needed something, something that cost money, you would have helped, wouldn't you – to the extent you could?'

She looks down for just a moment. 'I *did* help them,' she points out.

'That's my point, Mrs Jones…' Roderick begins.

'The only trouble was, she wasn't telling me the truth.'

'Well, Mrs Catesby told you, didn't she, that she and her husband were having some problems because of investments they'd made – they were strapped for cash, I think you told the jury?'

'Yes. That's what she told me.'

'Do you have any reason to doubt that?'

'I wouldn't have any way to know, would I?' she replies after some time.

'So you believed her?'

'At first I did, yes.'

'Yes, and you agreed to help out, didn't you?'

'Not just because they were short of cash. I helped out because she told me they had to pay for an operation or school fees.'

'Are you sure about that, Mrs Jones?' No reply at first. 'If you need to refer to your statement again, please do.'

'I said about that in my statement. It's right here, on page three.'

'You did indeed, Mrs Jones, that's quite right. But if you would turn over to page four with me for a moment…'

'What was that? Page four?'

'Yes, please.'

She's turning over the page slowly.

'Got it? Five lines down from the top, do you say, "I liked Sophie and Emma, and I wanted to make sure they didn't suffer just because their parents had made a bad investment." Is that what you told the police?'

'Yes.'

'Weren't you saying there that you would have helped them anyway? It wasn't tied to operations or school fees, was it? You were just helping to make sure they were all right for money?'

'Yes, but it was because of the operation and the school fees. That's why they needed the money.'

'You told the jury earlier that at some point Mrs Catesby had said something about her mother being ill?'

'Yes.'

'Is it possible that you got a bit confused – that it was her mother who was ill, not Emma?'

'No... I don't think so... no, I'm sure it was Emma...' but there's some hesitation.

'When the girls came to see you, was it after they'd left school for the day?'

'They sometimes came in the afternoon: yes.'

'When they came in the afternoons, would they be wearing school uniform?'

She searches her witness statement: in vain; it's not there. I know this because I'm following it on my screen, and feeling rather pleased with myself.

'They may have done. I can't remember.'

'Do you know Wood Lane Comprehensive School?'

'I know where it is, yes.'

'It's quite close to your flat, isn't it?'

'Yes.'

'Do you see children walking or cycling to and from Wood Lane sometimes? Would you recognise their school uniform?'

She thinks. 'I'm not sure. I think it's a black blazer with a shield on the pocket, a red shield, I think.'

'Something like this?' Roderick asks, holding up a blazer matching that description.

'It could be,' Mrs Jones replies. 'I can't be sure. I see them at a distance, mostly, from my window.'

'Fair enough,' Roderick replies.

'Is my learned friend offering it as an exhibit?' Susan asks, probably for the sole purpose of interrupting Roderick's flow a bit.

'I'd prefer not to,' Roderick says with a smile. 'I don't want Sophie to catch a chill going home.'

The jury chuckle. Susan shoots Roderick one of her looks.

'Mrs Jones, you also told the jury that Emma never said thank you for the money for her operation, is that right? And that surprised you because she's a polite, well brought-up girl?'

'Yes, it did surprise me.'

'But if she never needed an operation in the first place, that would explain the fact that she never thanked you for paying for an operation, wouldn't it?'

No reply.

'Mrs Jones,' Roderick continues, 'what I'm suggesting to you is this: you were understandably lonely; the Catesbys befriended you after you met at St Mortimer's; Laura was very helpful to you, shopping, tidying up, making lunch, and so on; naturally, you were grateful; you came to like Sophie and Emma; and you gave them money – as a gift, out of friendship and gratitude. It's all perfectly natural, perfectly understandable. There was no mention of operations or school fees, was there?'

She stares at him for some time.

'Did you understand my question, Mrs Jones?'

'Yes… no… it was a loan… it wasn't a gift… she kept saying she needed more time to pay me back…'

'And didn't you say to Mrs Catesby, when she went shopping for you, that she should take "a little something" for herself, just for helping you. That, again, would be quite natural, wouldn't it? After all, she was giving up her lunchtime or her early evening to help you, wasn't she? She was giving you her time, her family's time?'

'I suppose she was, yes… but that doesn't mean I gave her permission to take money out of my bank account, or go shopping for herself using my card.'

'She always brought you the receipts when she came back with the shopping, didn't she?'

'Yes, she did.'

'Did you ever, in that four-year period, challenge her about the receipts?'

'Challenge her? What do you mean?'

'Well, for instance, did you ever say to her, "What do you think you're doing? You can't just help yourself to cash from my bank account." Did you ever say anything like that to her?'

Mrs Jones shakes her head.

Roderick looks up at me. 'Your Honour, technically, I'm supposed to put my case to the witness. One interpretation of that is that I should take Mrs Jones through all the various transactions we will be hearing about from DC Benson.' He shifts his glance to Susan. 'If I do that, it will take me the rest of the afternoon, and perhaps into tomorrow morning, because it would only be fair to Mrs Jones to give her at least one break. I would much prefer not to have to keep her for so long. I'm satisfied that I've done enough to indicate the nature of my case to your Honour and the jury, and if my learned friend agrees, I would propose to stop now.'

I nod, and so does Susan. It's a huge advantage of having experienced advocates, that they are not afraid to bend the technical rules in the interests of compassion when the chance offers itself. Roderick has been scrupulously fair in ensuring that Muriel Jones understands his case and has her chance to respond to it, and no purpose would be served by dragging her through each and every receipt and bank account entry. But there are many counsel, on both sides, who would have insisted on it. I tell both counsel that I appreciate what they've just agreed to, which I do, and I tell Mrs Jones that she is free either to remain in court, or make her way home, as she wishes. She says she would like to go home, and thanks everybody for listening to her.

The afternoon concludes with Ronald Jones, the son from Yorkshire. He doesn't have much to say, really. The prosecution is going to get the financial evidence from the forensic accountant, DC Benson, tomorrow: so Susan contents herself with letting Ronald describe finding his mother distressed and worried; going to the bank to get copies of her accounts; going through the accounts and realising that something was wrong, and, in effect luring Laura Catesby into a trap. He also boasts to the jury, with a triumphant flourish, about catching her bang to rights in the act of having fifty pounds away from his mother's purse; though when challenged about it by Roderick, he concedes that she had not made any move towards transferring the money to her own purse. Nonetheless, when Susan plays the video and recording generated by Ronald's covert equipment in the kitchen, the whole episode does look rather squalid and underhand, and it's fairly clear that Mrs Catesby hasn't asked Mrs Jones's permission to be rummaging through her handbag, much less take money from it. All in all, it's a good end to the day for Susan.

I have a few administrative matters to deal with before going home, and Carol has brought me a nice cup of tea to celebrate a successful end to what started as a challenging day. Carol has been in a good mood today: Millwall ended something of a losing streak by winning on Saturday, and as fervent supporters, she and husband Ray had a good weekend on the back of the victory. Carol's other claim to fame is that she trained as a hairdresser before joining the court service, and she has made use of her skills at court once or twice in urgent situations. But no sooner have I settled down to enjoy the tea than there is a knock on the door. Marjorie opens it and pokes her head inside.

'Got a minute, Charlie?' she asks. She sounds rather breathless.

'Yes, of course, Marjorie. Come in. Do you want some tea?'

She waves the offer away and strides briskly over to take a seat in front of my desk. I'm bracing for bad news about the twins again. Simon and Samantha are away at boarding school, and the school tends to summon Marjorie whenever there's a suspicion of illness. Husband Nigel does something frightfully important for an international bank, and spends a good chunk of his time abroad, currently in Geneva, I gather. So whenever the school calls, someone has to cover for Marjorie for a day or two, and it sometimes calls for all my diplomatic skills – and Marjorie's – to pour oil on the troubled waters around whoever has to cover for her. But today, as it turns out, the twins are not the problem.

'I can't get into my computer,' she complains.

'What do you mean, you can't get into it? Has it packed up?'

'Possibly. I've tried all the usual things, including restarting it several times, but it keeps coming back to the same message.'

I'm assuming that Marjorie has run into yet another underfunded technology glitch beyond even her experience, and I'm a bit puzzled as to why she's consulting me about it. The chances of my being equipped to help are remote, to say the least. But since she's come to me…

'What are the symptoms?' I ask.

'It's locked me out, Charlie. The damn thing's frozen solid. There's a message on the screen that says: "Error 32B. Consult system administrator".'

'Who's the system administrator?'

'Stella. But I've already spoken to her, and she has no idea what it means. It's not in the manual, apparently.'

'I thought there was a helpline for this kind of thing,' I suggest tentatively.

'There is. Stella and I called them from her office. They sounded very evasive, and all they would say was that someone would call us back.'

I nod. 'Well, I'm sure they will sort it,' I reply reassuringly. 'Perhaps "Error 32B" is one of the new features of the system and not everyone knows how to deal with it yet.'

'That's what's worrying me, Charlie,' she says. 'Those people know everything there is to know. Usually when you call the helpline, they take over your computer for a minute or two, fiddle around with the settings or whatever, and Bob's your uncle.'

'Well, let's see what they say when they call back. I'm not sure what else we can do.'

She shakes her head. 'It wouldn't matter so much except that I have a judgment to write from when I was sitting in the Family Division as a deputy High Court judge a couple of weeks ago, you remember? I promised the parties I would have it ready by tomorrow. I've done most of it, but I need to finish it and I can't without my computer.'

'Well, if you don't hear from them by tomorrow morning, let me know, and I'll contact them myself and tell them to pull their fingers out.'

Carol has knocked and put her head around the door to tell me she's leaving for the day.

'All right, Charlie, thanks,' Marjorie says. She leaves quickly, and I have the impression that there's something wrong that I can't quite put my finger on.

* * *

Monday evening

'Clara, do you have paperless banking at the church?' I ask the Reverend Mrs Walden over a glass of Chianti as she is chopping up some green onions for tonight's pasta sauce. The vicarage feels cold tonight, even though she's got the heater working in the kitchen. It's a huge old building with high ceilings and leaky windows, and can stay cool even in the middle of an August heat wave – just before it suddenly traps the heat and turns the place into an oven for days after the sun has disappeared.

'Yes, of course. We have for years. There's nowhere to store vast quantities of bank statements at church, and I don't want them cluttering up my study here. Why do you ask?'

'I was feeling sorry for Muriel Jones – you know, the elderly lady in this case I'm trying – having to work out how to do all that at her age. She was giving evidence today and she sounded completely bewildered by it all; and I must say, I have every sympathy with her.'

She nods. 'It must be difficult for her. Of course, Charlie, you know, I'm hearing all about her from Amy Lock.'

'The new vicar at St Mortimer's?'

'Relatively new. It's been eighteen months since we lost Joshua Canning, hasn't it?' She pauses, as if reflecting on how sad it was to lose the Reverend Mr Canning, even in such embarrassing circumstances. Of course, he was her colleague, and inevitably it was a blow to discover the truth about him. It always is, I suppose, when a colleague has a serious problem. 'We had coffee this morning, and she was telling me how shocked she was when Mrs Catesby was arrested.'

'She'd be even more shocked if she heard the evidence,' I reply. I refill both our glasses as the Reverend lights up the stove and starts to fry the onions and garlic.

'Is it that bad?'

'Well, of course, we haven't heard Laura Catesby's side of it yet, so it's early days; but if Mrs Jones is right, it's pretty bad.'

'I'll have a word with Amy,' she suggests. 'Perhaps she can find someone to help Muriel with her banking. I'm sure she's got someone in her congregation who wouldn't mind making a house call.' She is stirring the sizzling spices gently, getting ready to add the tomatoes. She suddenly smiles. 'You do realise, Charlie, that we do paperless banking ourselves, too?'

'Do we?' I ask. She has done our banking for most of our life together. This dates back to my time at the Bar, when I was self-employed and frantically busy, both conditions that can make dealing with a bank something of a nightmare. I've always been grateful that she shielded me from it: I'm doubly grateful now. 'Did it take you a long time to get the hang of it?' I ask.

'Not really,' she replies. 'Once you've done it once or twice it's easy enough. I'm sure it's the same for you at court, with your new paperless system.'

'Oh, of course,' I reply as nonchalantly as I can.

* * *

Tuesday morning

Apparently, yesterday was a quiet news day. In the evening, Laura Catesby made the front page of the *Standard*, and when I stop to pick up my latte and ham and cheese bap – my favourite way of avoiding the hazards of the court cuisine – Elsie and Jeanie, avid readers, are incensed.

'Just imagine, sir,' Elsie says, 'taking advantage of an old lady like that, and her with all that money and a husband with a good job. I don't know what the world's coming to. Of course, you're used to it in your line of work, I'm sure, but I think it's dreadful.'

'I'd like to have seen her try that on with my auntie Nell,' Jeanie adds. 'She'd have given her what for, and no mistake. She would have shown her the door in no time, believe you me. My auntie Nell could get rid of anyone that came to the door, whether it was the Gypsies or the Jehovah's Witnesses, or anyone else. If she'd caught anyone going through her purse, she'd have taken the frying pan to them.'

'A formidable lady, by the sound of it,' I say, handing over my money and making doubly sure it's enough.

'My Nan would have done the same,' Elsie adds. 'Of course, my Nan wouldn't have let anyone shop for her anyway. She always did everything herself. She didn't trust anybody. She would walk all over town looking for the lowest prices – well, you could, in those days, couldn't you?'

'She wouldn't have let anyone rob her blind, would she?' Jeanie asks.

'I should say not. She'd have taken the frying pan to the butcher or the baker, my Nan, never mind anyone going through her purse. She almost gave the greengrocer a black eye once, just for overcharging her by a halfpenny…'

Another customer is hovering, trying to push his way through to the counter in the very tight space of the archway coffee bar. I use him as cover to mouth my thanks and make a diplomatic exit.

'Can you give the son a commendation, guv?' George asks, handing me my copy of *The Times*.

'A commendation?'

'Yeah. I mean, for putting in all that recording equipment and what have you, and getting her bang to rights with her hand in the old lady's purse. We need more people like that, don't we, guv, people who'll have a go? I mean, with all the cuts and that, the police won't even come out for something like that, will they? Unless someone gets shot or a bank gets robbed, they don't want to know, do they? If you ask me, that's the first thing the Labour Party should do once they get back in, but they're not even talking about it, are they…?'

Muttering my thanks, I slip quietly away into the bustle of the morning commute.

DC Benson is a very serious-looking young man wearing a dark suit and red tie, and at Susan's invitation, he has taken his laptop with him into the witness box.

'Officer,' Susan begins, once he's taken the oath, 'in addition to being a police officer, and indeed a detective, have you received training as a forensic accountant, and are you made available as needed to assist with investigations into fraud cases, and other cases involving financial transactions?'

'Yes, Miss, that's correct.'

'And were you asked to assist DS Gordon, the officer in charge of this case, with the investigation into Mrs Catesby's activities?'

'Yes.'

'Please tell His Honour and the jury what steps you took to find out what had been going on.'

The officer nods and taps a key or two on his computer. 'At an early stage, once I'd been advised of the nature of the allegations against Mrs Catesby, I advised DS Gordon to apply to the court for access to Mrs Catesby's bank accounts for the relevant period, and indeed, her husband's accounts also. I'd already been provided with Mrs Jones's accounts by her son, Ronald.'

'What other paperwork did you feel you needed?'

'I was told that there should have been a large number of receipts for items from some shops where Mrs Catesby had gone shopping for Mrs Jones – two shops mainly, Garner's and the Cooperative store, both in Bermondsey. But DS Gordon hadn't been able to find them, except for three receipts dating from about two years ago, which officers found while searching Mrs Catesby's home pursuant to a search warrant.'

'What did you do about that?'

DC Benson smiles. 'To be honest, I thought we were out of luck. I assumed that either Mrs Jones or Mrs Catesby must have thrown them away. But I made inquiries with Garner's and the Coop, and they both told me they could recreate them from their computerised till roll archives, as long as it wasn't a cash transaction, as long as a card was used.'

'A paperless record,' I observe.

'Indeed, your Honour, yes.'

'The point being,' Susan adds, 'that with a card there was something to identify the person paying for whatever had been purchased.'

'Exactly, Miss.'

Susan smiles. 'It sounds like a laborious process, reconstructing records like that.'

'It was extremely laborious, Miss,' DC Benson agrees with a rueful smile, 'to go back over such a long period, and I couldn't have done it without the cooperation of the two shops, both of which placed a member of their staff at my disposal. Fortunately, it turned out that they had a computer search engine, and when we fed in details of Mrs Jones's bank account, we found the relevant entries – the receipts – more than two hundred of them. We then made them up into a schedule.'

'Your Honour, may this schedule be Exhibit one, please?' Roderick nods to indicate that he has no objection. I assent. 'I'm much obliged. Your Honour, there are going to be four schedules in all. My learned friend and I have them on our computers, as does your Honour, but I'm afraid we haven't been able to install screens for the jury or the defendant, so they will have them in hard copy, if the usher will assist.'

The diminutive Dawn is almost hidden by the thick files she has to lug over to the jury box, and although they are given only one between two, once in place they take away almost all the available writing space, so that the jurors have to juggle pens and notebooks with the exhibit. I experience a rare moment of moral superiority.

'Paper, Miss Worthington?' I say. 'How very *passé*.' Roderick, who is of my generation, gives me a grin.

'I'm sorry, your Honour. We do have it electronically, of course, but the CPS budget wouldn't stretch to the screens.'

'Perhaps you should take that up with someone on high,' I suggest.

'Yes, your Honour, thank you. Officer, do you also produce a schedule of the relevant Jones bank accounts, and a schedule of the Catesby accounts?'

'Yes, that's correct, Miss.'

'And those are also in the files the jury have. Exhibits two and three, please, your Honour. Officer, did you examine and analyse the information contained in all three schedules?'

'Yes, I did.'

'And do you also produce a master schedule – Exhibit four, please, your Honour, also in the files – which provides a summary of your findings?'

'Yes.'

'Using that schedule as a guide for the jury, can you explain your findings for the jury?'

DC Benson taps some more keys. I do the same, but in response my screen suddenly goes blank. My first instinct is to panic and call for Stella. But with an effort, I control my feelings and remember how to leave and re-enter the Paperless programme. To my relief, and surprise, I succeed in calling up the page inviting me to enter my password. I type in 'Sodthis!1' and a few seconds later I'm opening Exhibit four. I'm so proud of myself that I have to suppress an urge to interrupt DC Benson to draw attention to my technical prowess.

'Yes,' the officer is saying. 'If the jury would open schedule four – page eighty-two in the file – they will see that in column one we have a list of the receipts, in chronological order.'

'Does that list include the receipts found in Mrs Catesby's house?' Susan asks.

'Yes, Miss, it does.'

'Thank you, Officer. Please continue.'

'In column two we have the total for the value of the goods purchased on each occasion. In column three we have the amount actually paid; and in column four we have the difference between the amounts in columns two and three.'

'On each occasion where there is a difference, which amount is greater?'

'Wherever there is a discrepancy, the amount paid is greater than the value of the goods purchased.'

'Do we know why?'

'Yes. In most cases the difference is attributable to the user of the card asking for cash back, in the amount either of twenty-five or fifty pounds.'

'Are there some other discrepancies also? What is shown in column five?'

'Yes. In column five I have drawn attention to the purchase of items for which Mrs Jones would have no obvious need, and the value of those items.'

'Could you give the jury some examples of these?'

'Yes. On page eighty-five, two pairs of white trainers; on page ninety-one, an item described as a gym bag; on page one hundred and two, a geometry set and a French dictionary. There are a number of others, as the jury will see if they flick through the pages – items of clothing and school supplies and the like, which seem to be inappropriate to Mrs Jones's condition in life.'

'What conclusion, if any, did you draw from column five?'

I see Roderick twitching. If he objects, I might have to stop DC Benson from saying it quite so directly. But Roderick knows that if he makes Susan drag Muriel Jones back to court, just to confirm that she had no reason to buy white trainers or geometry sets, the jury aren't going to like it. Wisely, he contents himself with twitching.

'I drew the conclusion that these were items that Mrs Catesby had purchased for her children, or in some cases, herself.'

'Officer, did you then add up the figures to produce a total of the cash backs, and a total value of the inappropriate items, and do those totals appear on the final page of the schedule?'

'Yes, that's correct, Miss.'

'And is there a grand total of both cash backs and inappropriate items, for the entire period of about four years, slightly in excess of eight thousand pounds?'

'Yes, that's correct.'

'Thank you, Officer. Turning now to Exhibits two and three, I want to ask you about one or two specific matters. First, have you marked certain withdrawals from Mrs Jones's savings account, one in the amount of one thousand pounds, and three in the amount of five hundred pounds each?'

'Yes.'

'In Mrs Catesby's account, have you marked entries that appear to correspond to withdrawals from Mrs Jones's account?'

'Yes. In the case of each withdrawal from Mrs Jones's account there is a corresponding payment into Mrs Catesby's account, for exactly the same amount, on the same day or the day after the withdrawal.'

'Officer, did you find anywhere in Mrs Catesby's account, or her husband's account, any evidence of a payment for a privately funded medical treatment or surgical operation?'

'No. I did not.'

'Did you find any evidence of a payment of school fees to a school called St Cecilia's, in Surrey?'

'No.'

'Or, for that matter, any private school?'

'No, Miss.'

Susan nods. 'Thank you, Officer. Please wait there. I'm sure there will be some further questions.'

'Very few, I'm sure you will be glad to hear, Officer,' Roderick says, rising slowly to his feet. 'You were never in Mrs Jones's kitchen when she gave Mrs Catesby instructions for the shopping, were you?'

'No, sir, I was not.'

'So you don't know what instructions Mrs Jones may have given?'

'No, I don't.'

'If Mrs Jones, out of appreciation for Mrs Catesby's kindness to her, ever invited Mrs Catesby to take a "little something" for herself when she went shopping, you wouldn't know about that, would you?'

'Again, sir, I would not.'

'If she authorised Mrs Catesby to buy something for her daughters, Emma and Sophie, you wouldn't know?'

'That's correct.'

'If she decided to make a gift of money to Mrs Catesby or her daughters, you would have no idea of that, would you?'

'No, sir. I would not.'

'And finally, Officer, you got Mrs Jones's bank accounts from her son, Ronald, didn't you? Not from Mrs Jones herself?'

'That's correct, sir.'

'Did Mr Jones tell you that his mother kept no bank records at home, and that he had to go to the bank himself to get them?'

'As I recall, sir, yes.'

'Mrs Jones had electronic banking set up, didn't she?'

'Yes, sir.'

'But like many elderly people, she was having some trouble coping with it?'

'That's what her son indicated to me, yes, sir.'

'Thank you, Officer,' Roderick concludes, resuming his seat.

The remainder of the prosecution case takes us up to lunchtime, and is remarkably concise. Susan and Roderick have helpfully agreed a number of facts, which are placed before the jury in writing. These include the facts that Emma Catesby has never had a surgical operation, if you discount a slightly difficult birth; and the fact that both she and her sister Sophie have always been educated in the state system, latterly at the Wood Lane Comprehensive School in Bermondsey, and have never attended St Cecilia's, or any other private school.

DS Gordon, the officer in the case, gives evidence about the investigation in general, including Laura Catesby's interview under caution at the police station following her arrest. As foreshadowed in Susan's opening speech, Mrs Catesby told the police exactly what one would expect, namely: that Mrs Jones had given her permission to take 'a little something for herself' whenever she did the shopping; that the payments in counts two to five were outright gifts from Mrs Jones to Emma and Sophie, gifts made for no better reason than she liked the girls and wanted to help them; and that there was never any mention of loans for surgery or school fees.

And so to lunch, but not today to an oasis of calm. As I'm entering my chambers to take off my wig and robe, I encounter Stella almost running along the judicial corridor. She's obviously in a hurry, her short straw-coloured hair bobbing up and down, and for Stella, who's usually a model of stoic calm, she seems almost frantic.

'Oh, Judge,' she says breathlessly, 'I'm so glad I've found you. Can you come with me, please?'

'Yes, of course, Stella. What on earth is the matter?'

'There's some kind of disturbance going on in Judge Jenkins's chambers?'

'Disturbance? What do you mean?' We set out together to walk the short distance to Marjorie's chambers. 'Judge Drake called, and said he heard raised voices. He didn't want to intrude, so I went myself, and I heard some shouting, and then

I put my head around the door and thought I should come and find you.'

'Why didn't you call security?' I ask. 'Judge Jenkins may be in trouble.'

Stella looks at me and shakes her head. 'It's the Grey Smoothies,' she says.

'The Grey Smoothies?'

We are now outside Marjorie's chambers, and I can hear the raised voices for myself. I look at Stella and she looks at me, and we barge in together. Marjorie is standing behind her desk in a defensive posture. Standing in front of her desk is Meredith, our cluster manager – so-called in Grey Smoothie-speak because she manages more than one Crown Court – sporting the usual armful of coloured bracelets over her right grey suit jacket sleeve, and a streak or two of green in her hair. With Meredith is a young man I haven't seen before, wearing thick black glasses, and contrastingly dressed in worn blue jeans and a white T-shirt bearing the legend 'Don't Mess with Mr Megabyte'. Our entry produces a temporary lull in hostilities.

'Can I help at all?' I ask, with what I hope is a calming smile.

'These fascists won't give me my computer back,' Marjorie growls. 'They want to keep me locked out.'

Meredith shakes her head. 'I have instructions from Sir Jeremy, Judge,' she says. 'It's required in this kind of case.'

Sir Jeremy Bagnall is a senior member of the Grey Smoothie High Command, on intimate terms with both the Minister and the Lord Chief Justice. He was knighted in a recent New Year's honours list for services to the court system: and no, that's not an attempt at humour on my part – it's one of those things you couldn't write for television and which make satire redundant. To any Grey Smoothie, any instructions given by Sir Jeremy are to be taken seriously and followed. But they're obviously not going down well with Marjorie. I need to find out what's going on.

'What do you mean, "this kind of case"?' I ask.

'You should ask Shaun, Judge,' Meredith replies, indicating Mr Megabyte. 'He's one of our computer security gurus. It's his case. I haven't seen the evidence.'

'The evidence...?' I ask.

'It's a 32B,' Shaun replies, as if to suggest that the mere mention of 32B makes everything obvious, and requires no further elaboration.

'Well, yes,' I say. 'Judge Jenkins told me she'd got an error message. But we were expecting you to come and sort it, if you couldn't do it over the phone. Haven't you been able to find the problem?'

'It's a 32B,' Shaun insists again, in that irritating tone computer nerds use to express their contempt for anyone to whom their technical ramblings don't immediately make perfect sense.

'Well, for the benefit of those of us unfamiliar with the technical terminology,' I ask, probably with a bit of an edge, 'would you mind explaining in layman's terms what a 32B is?'

There is a silence.

Shaun looks at Meredith. 'Do you want to tell him, or shall I?'

Meredith looks down and exhales heavily. 'An Error 32B message indicates the presence of pornography on a computer,' she explains. 'It's a code our security staff use to avoid being specific about it, for obvious reasons.'

I see Stella's eyes open wide, as I'm sure do mine.

'What...?' I manage to stammer, eventually.

'As I say,' Meredith continues, 'I haven't seen the evidence. I'm not cleared for it. Only Shaun and his supervisor, Paul, have actually seen it. What has to happen next is for them to show the evidence to Sir Jeremy, so that he can assess it and decide what to do. But Sir Jeremy is in urgent meetings with the

Minister today and most of tomorrow, so after court Thursday would be the earliest he could look at it. It has to stay locked down until then.'

Marjorie has sunk into the chair behind her desk.

'What do you mean, decide what to do?' I protest.

'The procedure we follow in these cases,' Meredith continues with some show of reluctance, 'is that if Sir Jeremy concludes that there is pornographic material on the computer, there will have to be an investigation. The judge in question is asked not to sit pending the investigation, and the police are informed.'

'I don't believe it,' I say, almost to myself, after some time.

'Sir Jeremy has no intention of calling the police until he sees the evidence for himself, but he has asked Judge Jenkins not to sit until it's been resolved.'

'That's ridiculous,' I exclaim. Now I'm just as worked up as everybody else. 'I've known Judge Jenkins for years, and this is complete nonsense. Besides which, she's in the middle of a trial.'

'I'm sorry, Judge,' Meredith replies, and I sense that she means it.

Marjorie looks up for a moment. 'It's all total bollocks, Charlie,' she says. 'But you won't budge them. They won't show me what they're talking about, and I'm not saying a word until they do. I want to see the so-called evidence, and I want to make quite sure that no one can fiddle with my computer – including Mr Megabyte here.'

'That is bang out of order…' Mr Megabyte protests, but to her great credit, Meredith immediately puts him in his place, pointing a stern finger.

'That's enough, Shaun,' she insists. 'You will not talk to a judge like that, ever, whatever the situation. Understood? Now, answer me this: is there any way for anyone other than you and Paul to get into the computer?'

Shaun shakes his head sullenly. 'It's locked down tight,' he replies, equally sullenly.

'In that case, it can stay where it is for now. We will come back with Sir Jeremy on Thursday after court.' She turns, not unkindly, towards Marjorie. 'I'm really sorry, Judge Jenkins. Let's hope we can sort this out quickly, and that it's just a misunderstanding.'

'Thank you, Meredith,' I say.

After they have departed, I turn to Marjorie, but she briefly holds up both hands, then springs to her feet, quickly seizing her handbag from the bottom drawer of her desk. She's still angry, and there are tears in her eyes.

'I can't do this any more now, Charlie. I have to go home and call Nigel. He will want to rush back from Geneva, I imagine. I suppose I should call a solicitor as well.'

'Try not to worry about it too much, Judge,' Stella says. 'I'm sure it's just some kind of mistake – isn't it, Judge Walden?'

'Yes, of course,' I agree. 'It's all nonsense. I'm sure we will get it sorted tomorrow.'

After Marjorie has left, Stella and I linger for some time, gazing at the locked computer.

'I suppose I'll have to contact the parties in Judge Jenkins's case and tell them she can't sit for a day or two,' Stella says.

'Yes, but for God's sake, no hint about what's going on. Tell them she's not feeling well, or something.'

'I'm not worried about that,' she replies. 'But if Sir Jeremy thinks there may be pornography on her computer, then what are we going to do?'

'Let's cross that bridge when we come to it,' I suggest. 'I'm not prepared for that yet. I just don't believe it. It's not possible.'

'I agree, Judge,' Stella says at once. She hesitates. 'On the other hand, Judge Jenkins did make a good point. I wouldn't trust Mr Megabyte further than I can throw him.'

I nod silently for some time. 'I wouldn't mind a quick preview of whatever is in there,' I muse aloud.

Stella gives me a look. 'Well, you do have that sentence in Greene tomorrow afternoon, Judge,' she replies. 'Just a thought.'

'So I do,' I reply.

I make my way to the judicial mess to snatch a quick, belated lunch. I tell Legless and Hubert that Marjorie isn't feeling well and has gone home for the rest of the day.

* * *

Tuesday afternoon

Roderick has asked me to sit without the jury so that he can address me about something. Usually, when counsel asks to address the judge in the absence of the jury at the close of the prosecution's case, it can only mean one thing: he's about to make a submission of no case to answer. In other words, he's about to argue: either that the prosecution hasn't adduced enough evidence to sustain the charge; or that the case is so weak that it would be dangerous to leave it to the jury. Either way, he would then invite me to withdraw the case from the jury and direct them to return a verdict of not guilty. But we're not even close to that scenario here. Susan has produced more than enough evidence to sustain a conviction, and Laura Catesby undoubtedly has a case to answer. I'm intrigued. But Roderick isn't terribly enlightening.

'Your Honour,' he begins, 'it's not my practice to waste time, as I hope your Honour knows. But Mrs Catesby has asked if she might have this afternoon to reflect on the evidence, and decide whether or not she wishes to give evidence and call witnesses. We have made good progress with the prosecution case, and if we resume tomorrow morning, we will finish the case without undue delay. I would be most grateful.'

I glance at Susan. She doesn't seem inclined to intervene. It seems odd. Roderick certainly isn't a time waster. There's obviously something going on behind the scenes. The husband isn't here today, I note. It may be that Mrs Catesby is giving Roderick a hard time and proving impervious to advice. If her appearance is anything to go by, that is quite plausible: she's turned out in much the same way she was yesterday, and I'm sure the jury are taking note of it. If she's not listening to Roderick about her appearance, she's probably not listening at all and knowing Roderick as I do, that's likely to lead to an uncomfortable relationship. He's worried, and he needs some time. I wish he'd told me earlier, but trials don't always work like that. Roderick has good judgment, and I am happy to trust him. I agree to his request, and ask Dawn to tell the jury they're free for the rest of the day.

* * *

Wednesday morning

Roderick calls Laura Catesby to give evidence. She's still wearing the smart, well-to-do suburban professional woman's suit, with the pristine blouse, the pearls, the rings and the watch, and as she makes her way to the witness box, I note for the first time the expensive-looking shiny black shoes with just a hint of a heel, their colour and tone exactly matching her handbag. I notice something else, too. The husband is back, now sitting in plain view in the front row of the public gallery. Sitting next to him for the first time are two girls, who must be the daughters and whose school uniform identifies them as pupils of Wood Lane Comprehensive. Sitting next to the daughters, in black clerical garb, sits a woman minister – presumably the Reverend Mrs Amy Lock, successor in unfortunate circumstances to the Reverend Mr Joshua Canning as vicar of the church of St

Mortimer-in-the-Fields in the Diocese of Southwark. They all seem to be staring intently at the defendant as she puts her handbag down and raises the New Testament in her right hand to take the oath.

'Are you Laura Catesby?' Roderick begins. 'Are you the defendant in this case? And are your husband, Larry, and your two daughters, Sophie and Emma, with you in court today?'

'Yes.'

'Mrs Catesby, what do you do for a living?'

'I'm the business manager for a firm of accountants. Our offices are in Tower Bridge Road.'

'Not far from this court, and indeed, not far from where Mrs Jones has her flat?'

'That's right.'

'I think your husband, Larry, is a fund manager in the City of London?'

'Yes, he is.'

'And would it be fair to say that, while you may not be rich, you are a fairly well-off family?'

'Yes, that would be fair.'

'Do your two daughters attend Wood Lane Comprehensive School here in Bermondsey?'

'Yes, they do.'

'How old are they now?'

'Sophie is sixteen, and Emma is thirteen, almost fourteen.'

'Has either of your daughters ever attended a private fee-paying school?'

'No. They've both always been to state schools.'

'Mrs Catesby, how and when did you meet Mrs Muriel Jones?'

For the first time, the air of boredom recedes a little, and there is a slight air of concern. She thinks about her answer.

'It was at St Mortimer's church, at least four years ago, closer to five, I would think.'

'Did you and your family get to know Mrs Jones?'

'Yes. We felt a bit sorry for her. She was on her own, you know, and we noticed that she wasn't as solid on her feet as she had been. So we approached her and got talking to her. We started giving her lifts to and from church; and from there one thing led to another and I offered to do some shopping for her if she didn't want to go out. It wasn't a problem for me. She lives not far from my office, so I could go round to see her during my lunch hour, or more often, after work before I went home. I often went shopping myself on the way home at Garner's or the Coop, so it was no trouble to pick up a few things for her at the same time.'

'Mrs Jones told the jury that at first you would show her the receipts for what you bought for her, and she would give you the amount in cash: is that right?'

'Yes.'

'But after some time, she entrusted you with her debit card?'

'Yes.'

'How did that come about?'

'It was Muriel's idea. There were a couple of times when she hadn't got out to the bank and she didn't have enough cash to pay me back. I wasn't going to take her last pound, obviously, so I would tell her I would wait until I next saw her. It didn't bother me at all, but I think she was a bit embarrassed about it, so she just gave me her debit card and told me the passcode.'

Roderick pauses. 'Mrs Catesby, you've been in court to hear the evidence of DC Benson, and you've seen the schedules he's produced, have you not?'

'Yes. I have.'

'We know that there are instances where you took cash back when paying for the items you bought, usually twenty-five or fifty pounds. Is that also correct?'

'Yes.'

'What was the purpose of the cash backs?'

She hesitates. She looks as though she's finding it a difficult question.

'What I mean,' Roderick continues, 'is: would you keep the cash back, or would you give it to Mrs Jones?'

'I usually gave it to her,' the witness replies. 'She would ask me to get cash for her if she didn't think she would be going out to the bank for a few days. But there were times when I got some cash back for myself.'

I look up. Susan is tight-lipped and is shaking her head. She stands.

'Your Honour, I'm sorry to interrupt, but this was never put to Mrs Jones. I am grateful to my learned friend for not putting all the detailed instances to her during his cross-examination, but she should have been given the opportunity to deal with this. It's not a trivial point. It goes to the heart of the case.'

I have to agree. If Roderick was expecting his client's last answer, it was naughty of him not to cross-examine Muriel about it while he had the chance, so that she had the chance to respond to it. It could be the key to the jury's verdict on count one: if Muriel was the recipient of the cash back, how can she complain that it was stolen? But both Susan and I suspect that he wasn't expecting the answer he got: the implication of which, of course, is that the smartly turned-out Laura is going off-piste, making it up as she goes along. So now, Roderick has to deal with the possibility that his client is spinning the jury a yarn; and although she knows there's nothing I can do about it at the moment, Susan quite rightly wants to make sure the jury get the message that there's something amiss.

'My learned friend will be free to make that point during her cross-examination of the defendant,' Roderick replies stiffly, his manner confirming our suspicions.

'Very well,' I say. 'Let's continue.'

'I'll take you through the instances in the schedule a little later,' Roderick promises. 'But if I understood you correctly, you said a moment ago that there were times when you took the cash back yourself. Why would you do that?'

The witness hesitates again.

'Muriel always told me to take a little something for myself,' she replies eventually.

'Why would she tell you that?' Roderick asks cautiously.

Laura shrugs. 'She was grateful to me for helping her,' she suggests. 'She wanted me to have a little something, to say thank you. It was for the girls, really. I never took anything for myself. It was always for the girls. Muriel was very fond of the girls. She was always telling me how nice and polite they are. I think she saw them as her grandchildren, because the only grandchildren she has live abroad.'

I get the sense that something is going on. The two girls are exchanging glances, and look rather disturbed. Also, I think I'm seeing the prosecutor in Roderick imagining the cross-examination he would be planning if he were on that side of the case – the cross-examination Susan is undoubtedly planning as she sits listening, and taking copious notes. And he is anticipating, as am I, that her first question will have something to do with why an elderly pensioner would give this fairly well-off business manager twenty-five or fifty pounds a time for her daughters in recognition of her charitable services as a shopper. Abruptly, Roderick changes the subject.

'Mrs Catesby, was there a time when Mrs Jones provided you with a thousand pounds out of her savings account?'

'Yes,' she replies, almost inaudibly.

'I'm sorry, Mrs Catesby, please keep your voice up.'

'Yes.'

'Under what circumstances...?'

But before Roderick can even complete the question, the

witness has collapsed in tears in the witness box, and is sobbing uncontrollably. Two or three times, she says she's sorry. Her family and her vicar are again staring at her. The jury are exchanging glances. Roderick puts down his notebook, and turns to me.

'May Mrs Catesby have a few moments, your Honour?'

'Of course,' I reply immediately. 'Let me know when you're ready to resume.'

I take advantage of the break to call Marjorie at home and check on her. Needless to say, she's not in the mood for much conversation. Nigel is quietly returning from Geneva today and she has a solicitor on call, ready to come to court tomorrow in case of need. I encourage her as far as I can with assurances that it's all going to be all right, but I know it doesn't offer her much comfort.

When I'm invited to return to court after about half an hour, I see that Laura Catesby has left the witness box and is sitting in the dock. Her family and vicar are still occupying the front row of the public gallery, and sitting beside them is none other than Mrs Muriel Jones, widow of this parish. Roderick remains standing when Carol invites those in court to sit.

'Your Honour,' he begins, 'we are grateful for the time. It has been put to good use. I would ask your Honour to have the jury brought back into court. Mrs Catesby does not propose to continue her evidence. Once the jury are back, I will ask your Honour if the indictment may be put to her again.'

I must admit that I'm fairly taken aback at first, but thinking back to Laura Catesby's evidence it occurs to me that perhaps I shouldn't be too surprised; at least I was right in thinking that something was going on. I call for the jury to be brought into court. Once they are in place, Carol puts all six counts of the indictment to Laura Catesby in turn, and asks how she pleads.

She pleads guilty to each count. I explain to the jury that, as they have been put in charge of the case they must return a verdict on each count; but as they have heard the defendant freely change her pleas and admit her guilt, after receiving legal advice, the only proper verdict would be one of guilty, and they are to answer the clerk accordingly when she asks for their verdicts. This seems to come as no surprise to the jury. They have already, it turns out, elected a foreman, a woman in her thirties, who without hesitation returns verdicts of guilty on each count as prompted by Carol. It seems pretty clear that the case was travelling in that direction at a speed of knots, regardless of the defendant's change of heart.

'Your Honour,' Roderick says, once the verdicts have been returned and Susan has confirmed that Laura Catesby is a woman of previous exemplary character, 'this is a serious case, and I don't mean to suggest otherwise. But it's also, as your Honour will appreciate shortly, a rather unusual one. I'm sure that in the normal course of events, your Honour would adjourn the case now for a pre-sentence report. But I'm going to ask your Honour not to make that decision yet. What I would like to do is to call a small number of witnesses, very briefly, and when your Honour has heard from them, I may well invite your Honour to pass sentence today. If your Honour still feels that he needs a pre-sentence report, then, of course, that option is still open.'

A pre-sentence report is a prerequisite in almost all cases today, certainly in any case of this kind, and I wouldn't accede to the suggestion Roderick has just made if it were made by just any counsel. But I've known Roderick for years, and I know that he can be trusted not to take up the court's time with frivolous suggestions. Besides, I am really curious to hear what's coming.

'Yes, very well, Mr Lofthouse,' I reply.

The first witness is the husband, Larry, fund manager in

the City, who tells me that his wife has been going through an extended 'bad patch' for the last five or six years. She's been ignored and generally treated with a lack of respect at work; she's had a difficult menopause and has been treated for depression (I'm told that some medical reports have been sent to me – electronically, naturally – via Carol); the whole family has been worried about her. It's the depression that makes her appear bored with whatever is going on around her. She had been behaving strangely for a long time, Larry adds, but the family had no idea what was really going on until she was arrested. They knew, of course, that she was shopping for Muriel Jones and generally assisting her, but they were pleased about that, thinking that it was taking Laura out of herself to some extent. The couple have separate bank accounts, so he wasn't aware of any unexpected monetary credits. He had never seen any receipts from the shops: it was, as Susan observed, a paperless crime.

Last, but of course not least, Larry has come to court bearing a cheque in the amount of fifteen thousand pounds in favour of Muriel Jones, which he is prepared to hand over to the court for onward transmission to Mrs Jones, and which is intended to cover her losses, plus interest, plus some slight compensation for what she has suffered. If Laura is sent to prison, he pleads, it will drastically affect the two girls, who are both at very sensitive stages of their development, as well as Larry himself. She will, of course, lose her job in any case, but if she serves a prison term she may become permanently unemployable, not to mention suffer even more terrible bouts of depression.

Both daughters then give evidence, also pleading with me not to send their mother to prison. Both deeply regret that Muriel Jones was given the impression that they needed money for private school fees; they can't believe that their mother would do such a thing; and Emma, in particular, is mortified that Muriel

Jones was led to believe that she needed an operation when she has enjoyed excellent health throughout her life. She actually apologises to Muriel from the witness box, even though what her mother did is in no conceivable way her fault.

The daughters are followed into the witness box by the Reverend Mrs Amy Lock, whom I suspect, without any hard evidence, of playing the 'I know your wife; we work together' card. It's not what she says; it's more the way she says it. I can almost see the two of them together talking about the case over a cup of tea at one vicarage or the other. But I don't dwell on it – I can't blame her even if she is invoking the spirit of the Reverend Mrs Walden – because what she is saying would be interesting enough even if it came from a wandering Russian Orthodox priest who'd never met either of us. The pleas of guilty that have just been tendered, she reveals, are not a bolt from the blue; on the contrary, they have been under discussion within the family, and with her as the family's religious advisor, for some time now. Everyone was urging Laura Catesby to admit what she'd done, and it was only fear, the vicar confides, that stood in her way – fear and the difficulty of admitting to herself that she had taken advantage of Muriel Jones so shamelessly. Once she reached a place where she could admit to herself what she had done, admitting it to others finally became possible.

For some time, she tried to persuade herself that what she had done, she had done not for herself but for her daughters; but when Sophie and Emma told her in no uncertain terms that they were horrified by it and wanted no part in it, she began to see the light. The family, in particular her daughters, had urged her to plead guilty on Monday morning, and they have continued to urge her ever since. This morning, as the prospect of giving evidence grew ever closer, she began to respond. She tried to give evidence, but the task proved too much for her, and as I saw for myself, she collapsed under the weight. She has been punished – she has punished herself – enough, the Reverend Mrs Lock suggests; and now is the time for forgiveness, in the spirit of the church of which they are all members.

In that same spirit, Muriel Jones has also agreed to give evidence on her behalf.

'She's not a bad person, sir,' Mrs Jones tells me. 'She's made mistakes; but then, we all do, don't we, sir? I know I have, and so did my Henry during his time. But she's obviously had problems I didn't know about, and she's admitted what she's done, so, as the vicar says, perhaps it's time to forgive and forget. She did try to be helpful to me, and as you get older, that's something you really appreciate, sir, isn't it? So I think she ought to be given a second chance, sir, if you're willing.'

So now what do I do? She's admitted to a long-running and serious breach of trust; and surely she could have reached the place where she could admit what she'd done before she put Muriel Jones through the additional anguish of having to give evidence and submit to cross-examination about her memory. But, judging from Muriel's demeanour this afternoon, the experience doesn't seem to have done her any harm, and she's going to get her money back, with a generous bonus for her trouble. After a minute or so of reflection, I tell Roderick he needn't say any more, and that I don't think I would learn anything from a pre-sentence report that I haven't learned this afternoon.

I ask the court probation officer to join us, and with her input I give Laura Catesby a sentence of twelve months imprisonment suspended for two years, concurrently on all six counts. I attach conditions: she is to continue under the supervision of a probation officer throughout the two years; seek treatment for her depression under the guidance of her vicar; perform one hundred and fifty hours of unpaid work for the benefit of the community – not to include shopping for the elderly; and pay compensation to Mrs Jones in the sum of fifteen thousand pounds. The details of the sentence will be transmitted paperlessly to whoever needs them.

* * *

Wednesday afternoon

Stella has found me a couple of applications to lend a pretence of industry to my afternoon, but the main business after lunch is to read and digest the voluminous file in the case I have coming up later. At the unusual time of five o'clock this afternoon, I am due to sentence a young man calling himself Brian Greene, and it's going to take some time. Not that you would know this from reading the list, because you will find no mention of the case of Brian Greene there, and the timing of five o'clock is designed to ensure that the building will be as quiet as possible. Moreover, I will have no court staff with me except for Stella, who will be doubling as both clerk and usher, and one or two security persons from an outside agency.

Brian Greene has pleaded guilty to six offences – the tip, I'm told, of a rather large iceberg – of what is politely termed computer misuse. But in the context of this case, the term 'computer misuse' is a massive understatement, which doesn't even begin to address the scope of young Mr Greene's offending. The Grey Smoothies –not Sir Jeremy Bagnall and his crowd this time, but some people from the same agency as the security personnel – have left Stella and myself in no doubt about the sensitivity of the case. The only reason we've got the case at Bermondsey, they confided to Stella last week, is the hope of avoiding the publicity it would get at the Old Bailey or Southwark. So this afternoon, yours truly, rather than a High Court or Old Bailey judge, will be dealing, in closed court, with a case whose existence isn't officially acknowledged.

The reason for this subterfuge is that it's the government's only chance of avoiding loud demands for Greene's extradition to any one of the several politically important countries his offences have damaged. The government doesn't want that because Brian Greene is generally judged to be, if not *the* most gifted, certainly one of the most gifted computer hackers in the world; and regardless of the sentence I pass on him today, he will be starting a new job within the week with the government agency I mentioned a moment or two ago, for which he has agreed to deploy his talents in a better cause. And I'm sure it won't surprise you to know that Brian Greene isn't his real name. It's all a bit nerve-racking, but I am gratified that we have our uses at Bermondsey and are occasionally attracting a better class of work.

Brian Greene is an unprepossessing young man aged nineteen, but is described by prosecuting counsel, Derek Mapleleaf QC, as a genius – off the charts in terms of the autistic spectrum, but able to function fairly normally in society and possessed of once-in-a-century talents when it comes to computers, and specifically, to hacking. He is, technically speaking, of previous good character, but is known to have been the architect of some of the most damaging hacking attacks on record, in the course of which he has shut down a number of well-protected government and commercial operations both in this country and abroad. When eventually run to ground by the security services as the result of an anonymous tip, Greene could give no coherent account of why he behaved as he did, except that he didn't know what else he would do all day if he wasn't at his computer.

After obtaining extensive psychological reports, the security services concluded that he could be trusted to work in the government service, which – after they had explained to him the likely consequences of being extradited to certain of the countries he'd offended – Greene began to see as an acceptable idea. Abigail Sinclair QC, like Derek Mapleleaf a member of the small cadre of counsel having a high-level security clearance, is representing Greene; and, no doubt aware of its irrelevance, confines herself to a short, boilerplate speech in mitigation, which does little to shed any further light on the defendant. Since it doesn't matter, I give him a concurrent suspended prison term on all six counts – a hopelessly inadequate sentence, but one that at least offers some recourse if his new employment isn't working out a year from now.

To my mind, the hearing's most interesting revelations come from a man introduced to the court as 'Agent A', a member of the security services, whom Derek calls to give evidence about Brian Greene's talents and activities. By way of assuring us of his credentials to give evidence about these matters, Agent A tells us that he was recruited in much the same way about seven years ago, having himself been something of a prodigy in the computer field. But when he speaks about Brian Greene, there is a definite touch of John the Baptist about him: good as he was in his day, Agent A tells us, he is with us today only to proclaim the coming of a man whose computer he is not worthy to switch on. He stands in awe of Brian's achievements, which have involved playing havoc with military, diplomatic and commercial activities seemingly at will, while leaving no real clue about his identity. If, as expected, Brian achieves the same kind of results on behalf of his new masters, Agent A concludes almost reverentially, Great Britain can look forward to a quantum leap forward in its ability to protect its cyber security, and to interfere with that of hostile powers. The Americans, he ventures to add, may even start to take us seriously again.

Remembering Stella's enigmatic hint yesterday, after I've passed sentence I invite Derek and Abigail into chambers for coffee.

I have a good excuse: they were both at Bermondsey in the famous Foggin Island case, whose implications for international law saved the court from closure, and is the subject of a plaque installed by the government of France in the court foyer. I invite Agent A to join us also. After some stilted conversation during which we are all doing our best to avoid any mention of the case we have just dealt with, I ask Derek as delicately as I can whether there might be any chance of borrowing Agent A for a few minutes – with his agreement, of course – to see if he can shed some light on a disturbing circumstance involving the suspected hacking of a judicial computer. Derek has no objection and Agent A, clearly intrigued, agrees at once. It's well after seven o'clock by now. Derek and Abigail are understandably anxious to get away, and once they have gone, I give Agent A a confidential briefing, which he absorbs effortlessly. Like a couple of characters from a John le Carré novel we make our way furtively and, thankfully, unobserved along the now dark and deserted corridor to Marjorie's chambers.

Seating himself in Marjorie's chair, Agent A begins to tap the keys. I've warned him that the computer is securely locked down, to which he reacts with an impish grin. It takes him a little under two minutes, not only to unlock the computer, but also to bypass Marjorie's password.

'We don't want to be too long,' he says, once he's in. 'We don't want to leave fingerprints, do we?'

He stares at the screen for some seconds and smiles. 'I do like your colleague, Judge,' he adds.

'Why do you say that?'

'She's incredibly organised, isn't she? Look at this: everything in files, clearly marked, nothing loose at all. A place for everything and everything in its place. I bet the trains run on time in her house.'

'That would be Marjorie,' I confirm.

'This shouldn't take long at all,' he predicts cheerfully. He taps on some more keys, the screen flashes and flickers for a few moments; and suddenly he sits back contentedly. 'Bingo. Got it. There we are, Judge. There's your pornography.' He laughs. 'That doesn't count as pornography in my book, but each to his own, or her own, I suppose. See for yourself.'

I stand behind Agent A and see for myself. I daresay we all have our own opinions about what constitutes pornography, but I must say that I'm inclined to agree with him. If this is pornography, Error 32B must have a rather sensitive trigger threshold. But I'm also noticing something else, something Agent A would probably have no reason to notice, and what I notice cheers me up even more than the unconvincing state of the 'evidence'.

'Are we sure this is all?' I ask. 'Could there be anything else?'

He shakes his head. 'I did a very thorough search, using the language they're using in their programmes, and she doesn't have any hard-to-find files. No, I've got it all; so now, if you're happy, let's lock it back up before anyone knows we've been here.' He pauses. 'Unless, of course, you'd like me to… I could do it without leaving my fingerprints…'

'No,' I reply at once. 'I have other plans for it. But thank you for offering.'

'No problem,' Agent A says cheerfully. Tap, tap, and the Error 32B message returns to an otherwise blank screen.

'You'd better show me out the back way, Judge,' he suggests, 'just in case your security people are tempted to ask me any awkward questions.'

'Thank you again,' I say.

He grins cheerfully. 'My pleasure. All part of the service.'

We shake hands. I walk him to the door at the end of the judicial corridor, from where he can disappear clandestinely into the Bermondsey night.

I shouldn't have done it, of course, but like the newly converted Brian Greene, I've long been persuaded that sometimes you have to cross a line in a good cause; and I feel sure now that it is in a good cause. I would love to call Marjorie and tell her, but it wouldn't be wise. Sadly, she will have another unquiet night, but things should improve considerably tomorrow.

* * *

Thursday lunchtime

The case of Laura Catesby having collapsed, as the court management terminology for yesterday's events has it, Stella has started me on a short trial, a two-day non-residential burglary. While decidedly the worse for wear, Chummy broke into a store dealing in computer games and helped himself to a good selection from their stock. He's claiming to have been so drunk at the time as not to know what he was doing. But the evidence suggests that, although he'd certainly imbibed enough to reduce his inhibitions when it came to breaking in, he wasn't even close to being inebriated enough to plead temporary insanity. The defence isn't going to fly, as his counsel, Emily Phipson, knows perfectly well. We're going through the motions very efficiently, and we're making good progress. We will get the jury out tomorrow before lunch, with any luck.

And so to lunch, an oasis of calm in a desert of chaos. On my way to the mess I look into Marjorie's chambers, just to make sure that Mr Megabyte hasn't been trying to interfere with her computer. To my surprise, I see her seated at her desk, apparently engrossed in some papers.

'Marjorie, what on earth are you doing here?' I ask. 'I thought you weren't coming in until it's time to meet the Grey Smoothies.'

'This is my bloody court, Charlie, and these are my bloody

chambers, and if the bloody Grey Smoothies don't like that, they know where they can bloody well stuff it.' She smiles thinly. 'I'm sorry,' she adds. 'I didn't mean to get carried away.'

'No,' I reply. 'Actually, that sums it up perfectly.'

'I'm not coming into lunch, if you don't mind.'

'I wasn't expecting you to.'

She pauses. 'Charlie, do you think I need my solicitor with me this afternoon?'

'No,' I reply firmly. 'It's not going to come to that.'

She looks at me curiously. 'Really?' she asks, a trifle sceptically, I think. But then she examines me closely for some time.

'What?' I ask. She gets to her feet and walks across the room to stand in front of me.

'I know that look, Charlie – you're up to something. What is it?'

'Up to something – *moi*?'

'Charlie…'

'I can't tell you any more, Marjorie. Let's just say, I don't think you'll need your solicitor.'

'Oh, come on, Charlie…"

'I can't, Marjorie,' I say with all the finality I can muster. 'Really. Look, I have to go. I'll see you later, after court.'

'I hope I did the right thing, Charlie,' Hubert says, tucking into his escalope Milanese and garlic mashed potatoes, the dish of the day, 'calling Stella on Tuesday afternoon. I was a bit worried about all the shouting and what have you in Marjorie's chambers.' He's obviously dying to ask what was going on. I'm not sure I've completely sold the story about Marjorie not feeling well.

'It was nothing,' I reply quickly, 'storm in a teacup. Stella found me and we dealt with it. Bloody Grey Smoothies again.'

'So, nothing to worry about then?' Hubert asks.

'Nothing at all,' I reply, with as much emphasis as I can

muster. 'Marjorie wasn't feeling too well, so I suggested she take the day off, but I'm sure she'll be back with us soon.' Hubert and Legless look at me questioningly. I give them what I hope looks like a reassuring nod.

'What did you have going on yesterday afternoon then, Charlie?' Hubert asks.

I am alarmed for a moment. 'What?'

'There seemed to be something going on in your court when I was leaving for the Garrick around five. Bit of an odd time for a hearing, or was it something to do with the Grey Smoothies?'

'There was something I had to do,' I reply evasively. Time to change the subject. 'What's this I'm hearing about the Garrick, Hubert,' I retort, 'reconsidering the question of women members? Wasn't there something in *The Times* about it a day or so ago? What's that all about?' Mercifully he takes the bait.

'That's been blown up out of all proportion,' he protests. 'All that's happened is that…'

And mercifully, the rest of the lunch hour passes harmlessly as we catch up on the latest gripping instalment of political goings-on at the Garrick Club.

* * *

Thursday afternoon

By the time we break for the day, we have dealt with the evidence and are ready for closing speeches tomorrow morning. Having claimed to be so comprehensively intoxicated, Chummy didn't have much to say when he reluctantly went into the witness box, and Piers Drayford pretty much nailed him in cross-examination by exploring his admirable lucidity at the police station after his arrest, when he asked, perfectly rationally, to see his solicitor and for a message to be sent to his girlfriend. And now it's time to go and meet the Grey Smoothies, and hopefully solve another paperless crime.

As promised, Sir Jeremy Bagnall is leading the Grey Smoothie delegation. With him are Meredith and Shaun, who, no doubt in deference to Sir Jeremy's presence, has abandoned his Mr Megabyte persona in favour of a rumpled suit and tie. It's all a bit fraught. Both Jeremy and Meredith know all four Bermondsey judges well.

'Would anyone like to say anything before we begin?' Jeremy asks. 'Marjorie? Charles?'

Marjorie is sitting behind her desk, her arms wrapped tightly around her. I'm standing close to her on her left. She shakes her head.

'I think we should just get on with it, Jeremy,' I reply.

'Yes, of course.' He gives a majestic sweep of his arm, ushering Shaun forward. 'Right then, Shaun, if you're ready, please.'

The computer has been turned away from Marjorie and myself, and is perched near the front edge of her desk. Shaun strides forward and seats himself in front of it. He hasn't said a word, but there is the suspicion of a self-satisfied grin on his face. He taps a few keys, and turns towards Jeremy and Meredith.

'There you go, Sir Jeremy,' he says proudly. 'It's all there. All you have to do is scroll down.'

Jeremy approaches the computer, but does not sit down. 'Would you like to come and watch this?' he asks us. I nod to Marjorie, and we walk slowly over to stand slightly behind him, one on each side. Meredith is keeping her distance – she has never liked any of this, I reflect – and she's taken refuge in an armchair across the room. She's holding a notebook, and I'm guessing that, in accordance with standard Grey Smoothie practice, she's the designated note-taker for the meeting.

As soon as Marjorie sees the screen, she positively gasps. I smile. It's a moment I've been looking forward to, seeing her face as she suddenly realises what she's looking at. She has seen what I saw when Agent A gave me my preview. She turns to me excitedly. 'Charlie, it's...' But I shake my head and hold a finger up to my lips. I want Sir Jeremy to discover this for himself – with a little help from me, naturally. She understands immediately, and nods.

'So...' Jeremy begins slowly, 'what we have here are some documents with some extremely bad language in them, which you've kindly highlighted for us, Shaun, thank you. Everyone see?'

'Yes, we can see, Jeremy,' I answer.

'The language would have triggered the 32B, even without the more graphic stuff we've got, that's coming up next,' Shaun observes with satisfaction.

'Yes, I see.'

I'm sure you can imagine what the language consists of. It's the usual Anglo-Saxon terminology for the act of sexual intercourse and related parts of the male and female anatomy. It's nothing you don't hear in the pub on any given Saturday night, but in the Grey Smoothie universe, apparently, it's enough to trigger a 32B. Jeremy has his finger over the mouse, about to scroll down in search of the more graphic stuff. But I intervene.

'Just before you scroll down, Jeremy, may I draw your attention to the header at top right of the pages you've been looking at?'

Shaun frowns and steps forward, as if puzzled, to see for himself. Surely, Mr Megabyte hasn't missed this, I muse to myself? If he has, this could be even better than I'd anticipated.

'It says, "Schedule one", Jeremy reports.

'Indeed, it does,' I reply. 'Now, Marjorie knows much more about all this kind of stuff than I do, Jeremy, but in my limited understanding of such matters, the usual context of a schedule is that it's attached to a parent document, providing additional information that the author didn't want to include in the main document. Let's see what happens when you scroll down.'

By now Marjorie has fully recovered. The colour is back in her cheeks, her arms have disentangled themselves from her waist, and she has an ominous smile on her face. Shaun, on the other hand, is wearing an expression that conveys, for the first time, just a smidgeon of doubt.

'Well, this is different,' Jeremy observes with some distaste, as the results of his scroll present themselves on the screen. He's right. This is very different, and one might well agree with Shaun that it's pretty graphic. What we have is several pages of pictures of a man and a woman, both naked, engaging in various sexual acts. They don't look as though they're aware of the camera: they don't look self-conscious at all, and there's absolutely no effort to draw attention to themselves. Nonetheless, Shaun thinks of it as pornography, and he doesn't need to tell us that it would have triggered a 32B even if the language hadn't.

'Mm...' Jeremy muses, almost to himself, 'so do we think of this as pornography?'

Shaun shrugs. 'Definitely,' he replies, though oddly he doesn't sound absolutely definite.

Agent A and I, of course, have a different view. 'I don't think you can classify something as pornography just because there are images of naked people,' I venture.

'Even when they're... doing what these people are doing?' Jeremy asks. He reflects for some time. 'Didn't somebody once say that it's all in the mind of the beholder, that it depends on one's own reaction to what one sees?'

'It was Justice Potter Stewart of the United States Supreme Court,' Marjorie replies quietly, breaking her silence for the first time, 'and what he said was that he would probably never succeed in defining hard-core pornography intelligibly: but he knew it when he saw it.'

'Ah, yes,' Jeremy says. 'Well, there we are. I suppose that's what I have to decide.'

'Well, just before you do,' I say, 'may I once again direct your attention to the header at top right of the page?'

Jeremy looks closely at the screen. 'It says, "Schedule two",' he observes.

'Yes,' I agree. 'I'm no expert, so perhaps it would be best to ask Shaun to help us. But wouldn't it be sensible to see if we can find the parent document of these two schedules?'

Jeremy nods. 'By all means, yes.' He gives another imperious wave of the hand, and Shaun returns to the computer, rather more slowly this time. He taps twice, as did Agent A before him, and up it comes. Even Meredith is curious now, and she joins us as we huddle in a group in front of Marjorie's computer.

CONFIDENTIAL
IN THE HIGH COURT OF JUSTICE
FAMILY DIVISION *Case number ___*
BETWEEN WILLIAM JAMES JOLLY AND ANGELA JANE JOLLY
Hearing on issues relating to the children of the family following dissolution of marriage
Before Her Honour Judge Jenkins QC, sitting as a Deputy High Court Judge
JUDGMENT

After which the document begins, in Marjorie's crisp, precise prose, to analyse the issues between William James Jolly and Angela Jane Jolly relating to the children of their family.

'This is my draft judgment,' she explains to the silent room, 'in the case I tried in the High Court two or three weeks ago. It's almost finished. I just had one or two things to add.'

No one else seems capable of speech, so I ask her myself.

'Marjorie, I'm sure everyone would be interested to know how these two schedules came to be attached to your judgment.'

'They're evidence in the case,' she explains. She sounds just a tad frustrated, and I can't say I blame her. 'The wife was saying that the husband was an unfit father to his two young daughters, because he wrote those explicit letters to his secretary, and because the wife had those pictures of him in bed with said secretary.' She pauses. 'They're obviously pretty graphic, but just for the record, I don't think of them as pornographic, and I don't think Potter Stewart would have thought of them as pornographic. If you read my judgment, you'll see the view I've formed about it all – though I would prefer you didn't: judgments are supposed to be confidential in the Family Division.'

'As your judgment clearly states at the very beginning,' I observe. 'And that prompts me to ask how you received this evidence on your computer?'

The wife's solicitors sent it to me, in preparation for the hearing,' she replies, 'obviously.'

'Electronically?' I ask. 'A paperless case, is it, using the approved electronic filing system?'

'Yes, of course.'

'So,' I say, doing my best to look suitably judicial, 'are you saying that these two schedules were sent to you electronically, using the system put in place by the ministry to create the Paperless Court, and to ensure that the taxpayer is getting value for money?'

'Exactly.'

'And that while using this system as a judge, in the course of trying to prepare a judgment – a confidential judgment, I may add –' I say with a pointed glance in Shaun's direction, 'you find that not only is your judgment not treated confidentially, but in addition, you have been suspended because of an Error 32B?'

'Yes.'

'I'm sure you must find that rather disturbing.'

'"Disturbing" doesn't begin to describe it. I don't feel safe. I don't think I *am* safe. In fact, I think one might even say that it's become unsafe for judges to deal with sexual cases at all.'

I shake my head. I'm not in a charitable mood, and I decide to approach the nuclear option without any preamble.

'I don't know about you, Jeremy,' I say after a suitable pause, 'but this strikes me as quite a serious matter. It's not very creditable to whoever designed the system, is it? Confidential judgments being read by junior civil servants? Judges being smeared and suspended for doing their job? I shudder to think what the taxpayer might have to say if this finds its way into the newspapers. Actually, I wouldn't be surprised if Marjorie's MP were to ask the Minister one or two questions about it in the House.'

'It's still pornographic,' Shaun whines almost inaudibly, without conviction.

Jeremy gives him a withering look. 'You may leave us,' he replies, turning his head away. Eventually, with Shaun safely out of the room, he turns to Marjorie.

'I can't tell you how sorry I am, Marjorie,' he says. 'I promise you that I will personally look into this, and take urgent steps to remedy the system, and to warn all judges about this… glitch. We will set up a helpline with immediate effect for any judge who encounters an Error 32B message before we have time to fix it.' He looks across at Meredith, who nods and makes a note.

'I hope we can also take it,' I reply, 'that Marjorie is now free to resume her trial. We've lost two days of work already – in a case funded by the taxpayer.'

'That goes without saying,' Jeremy adds, at once.

'I'd prefer that it should go into Meredith's note,' I say, 'just to avoid any doubt about the matter.' Glancing at Meredith, I see that she is already making a thorough record.

Jeremy stands. 'Well, it's been a trying afternoon. I'm sure you have a lot to do. Unless there's anything else, we'll leave you in peace.'

'Well, there is one more thing, Jeremy,' I venture. 'In the light of the distress caused to Judge Jenkins by this whole affair, I would have thought that you might make a suitable gesture of apology – and indeed, of recognition for the sterling work she's doing on the bench.'

'What kind of gesture?' he asks cautiously.

'Oh, I don't know,' I reply. 'Perhaps an undertaking that she might spend a bit more time in the High Court, or perhaps a week or two at the Old Bailey, or even the Court of Appeal once in a while.'

'Well...' he begins, but Meredith cuts him off.

'I'm on it,' she replies.

After they've gone, I ask Marjorie if she has plans for the evening.

'Yes,' she replies. 'Nigel and I are taking you and Clara to Gino's for dinner. And we're not taking no for an answer.'

* * *

Thursday evening

Gino's is one of the hot new restaurants that keep springing up in Bermondsey these days. It's the kind of place the Reverend Mrs Walden and I might go to once a year for some special celebration; and the kind of place Marjorie and Nigel frequent regularly. The food is Tuscan, and wonderful, and the wines are a far cry from the Lidl's Founder's Reserve the Reverend and I would typically be imbibing with dinner on a Thursday evening. It's flowing quite freely, too. Both Marjorie and Nigel are a bit light-headed with relief, and are committed to celebrating without restraint – which I understand completely. The Reverend and I keep off the pace a bit, so that we can make sure they find a safe taxi home when the celebration winds down.

'You have to tell me, Charlie,' Marjorie says as we are

savouring a wonderful Chardonnay grappa to round off our feast. 'You knew exactly what they were going to find before Mr Megabyte opened my computer up, didn't you?'

'Did I?' I ask innocently.

'Yes, you did. How on earth did you do it?'

I hold my hands up modestly. 'Oh, all right' I reply, 'I suppose I may as well tell you. GCHQ have been consulting me about cyber security for years. It's one of my many areas of expertise. To a man with my talents in the field, cracking a Grey Smoothie security code was nothing – child's play.'

She makes a face at me. 'No, Charlie. Seriously.'

'Seriously?' I reply. 'Marjorie, if I were to answer your question seriously, being suspended would be the least of my problems. I'm sorry, and I'm glad it's over, but there are certain things that have to remain locked down, shall we say. Let's invent a name for it. Let's call it a 32C, shall we?'

As we stroll home, having poured Marjorie and Nigel into a black cab, the Reverend and I hold hands. It's a pleasantly cool evening, and there are even a few stars on display.

'Amy Lock called me while I was getting ready for dinner,' she says. 'She wanted to say how grateful she was to you for giving Laura Catesby a suspended sentence.'

'I'm not at all sure I should have done,' I reply. 'It was a dreadful breach of trust. I'm surprised you would have any sympathy for her so soon after Remember the Elderly Week. There's far too much of it going on, you know, bilking the elderly just because they can't pay attention as well as they used to. Today it may be Muriel Jones and Harry Buller; but tomorrow it may be you and me, or even Marjorie and Nigel. We're all feeling our age, you know.'

She turns to look at me. 'Who's Harry Buller?'

'Oh… no one,' I reply. 'Not important.'

'I don't have any sympathy with what she did, Charlie,' she

says. 'But I have a limited sympathy for the condition that allowed her to do it. And as Marjorie's case proves, none of us knows the perils that lie in store for us. All we can do is keep going and hope for the best.'

I look up to the stars, reflecting on Bermondsey Crown Court in general. 'Very true,' I concede.

TOO MANY COOKS

TOO MANY COOKS

Monday morning

As I hand over my change to Jeanie this morning in payment for my ham and cheese bap, I find my mind more than usually focused on food. Like most people, I find thoughts of eating something nice flitting through my mind during the day, even when I'm supposed to be concentrating on other things, and even when I'm not particularly hungry. But having occupied myself during a few idle moments on Friday afternoon by reading the file in the case I'm due to try today, I've prepared myself for the fact that it may be difficult to avoid stirring up the gastric juices a bit. It's likely to be a warm day, apparently, and the false promise of delicious, cooling dishes seems unusually seductive.

It's strange how often cases take you into establishments devoted to food and drink. Usually, the restaurant or bar is just part of the scenery, the backdrop to a case that has nothing to do with eating or drinking as such. Logically, the type or location of the venue shouldn't matter very much. But despite the number of restaurants, pubs and clubs to be found in London, it's interesting how often the same names crop up time and time again in proceedings in front of any of our Crown Courts. Bermondsey is no exception. In any given prosecution for offences involving the supply of drugs, drunken Saturday night fisticuffs, drunken Saturday night sexual escapades, the dishonest handling of high-end stolen goods, or even the odd instance of counterfeit currency, two names spring instantly to mind – and very often on to the pages of police reports and witness statements: the George and Dragon, and the Blue Lagoon. Both seem to play host to a statistically improbable number of transactions that eventually end up in court. As a result two things tend to happen: the police keep a close eye on them, which serves to increase the number of arrests and turn the whole thing into a self-fulfilling prophecy; and the judges and staff at the Crown Court avoid both places like a forensic plague.

But you also have the occasional case in which the establishment is not just part of the scenery, but is more intimately involved with the events in question. In cases like that, the judges and staff, having no reason to fear any adverse consequences, may well have some personal knowledge of the premises acquired during an agreeable night out. The most notorious example at Bermondsey was the case of Jordan's, an up-and-coming restaurant rapidly turning into one of London's leading gastronomic destinations, but which also turned out to be the site of a brothel frequented by a number of men in public life who didn't want that fact to become public knowledge. There were, of course, other men – such as Legless – who just happened to have been there for dinner, but were nervous that their presence at Jordan's might be misconstrued. I tried the resulting case against the proprietor, Robert Jordan, his girlfriend Lucy Trask, and his Russian bar manager, Dimitri Valkov, who ran the brothel. When Valkov, in a futile attempt to save himself, produced a 'black book' containing a number of names, panic broke out in certain quarters that took some time to dispel.

Mercifully, the case of Luigi Ricci, featuring Bermondsey's equally up-and-coming Primavera Toscana, has nothing to do with brothel keeping, as Roderick Lofthouse is about to explain. In fact, it hasn't attracted any suspicion at all in the two years during which it has graced Queen Elizabeth Street, SE1. On the contrary, while it doesn't pretend to be a Jordan's, it has quietly established its reputation for 'excellent affordable Italian food in a family-style setting'. All four judges of the Bermondsey Crown Court have been seen there on several occasions, once or twice together on a Friday evening; and, I suppose, on one or more of those occasions we probably encountered Luigi Ricci and his brother Alessandro, though if so, I don't remember. To err on the safe side, when we had our plea and case management hearing I did suggest to Roderick and to Julian Blanquette, who's defending Luigi, that it might be prudent to move the case to a Crown Court north of the River, or at least import a judge from some such distant clime to try the case. But apparently the Brothers Ricci have no more memory of us than we have of them; counsel saw no need to worry about it, and so on we go.

'May it please the court, members of the jury, my name is Roderick Lofthouse and I appear to prosecute in this case. My learned friend Mr Julian Blanquette represents the defendant, Mr Luigi Ricci, the gentleman in the dock. Members of the jury, with the usher's assistance I'm going to provide you with copies of the indictment, which the clerk of court read to you just a few moments ago. One between two, please.'

Dawn scurries over to Roderick and the jury box in turn, handing out copies while repeating that there is only one between two, just in case they missed it when Roderick told them. Although Roderick and Julian weren't concerned about the judicial familiarity with Primavera Toscana, we all agreed that it wouldn't be a good idea to have a jury of *frequentatores*. So this morning, while I was dealing with my usual hour and a quarter's worth of bail applications and other assorted reasons to delay the start of a trial, we could at least offer the new jury panel something to occupy them during their tedious waiting around time. They were given a short questionnaire asking whether any of them were patrons of Primavera Toscana, or intimates of the Brothers Ricci or any of their employees. It was just as well we did. We received five positive replies from satisfied customers, who had apparently interpreted the questionnaire as the court asking for suggestions of decent places the staff might enjoy going to for lunch. Three supplied particularly effusive recommendations, and one expressed the view that the Riccis should be awarded a Michelin star in recognition of the grilled sea bass. Happily, the jurors concerned were shipped off to panels in the other courts before any damage could be done.

'You will see that the indictment contains a single count of unlawful wounding with intent to cause grievous bodily harm,' Roderick continues, 'contrary to section 18 of the Offences against the Person Act 1861. The particulars of the offence are that Mr Ricci wounded a woman by the name of Linda Galloway by stabbing her with a meat cleaver. Members of the jury, later in the trial the learned judge will direct you about the law, and you must take the law from him, not from me. But I think I can safely tell you this much. A wounding is simply any breaking of the skin, and grievous bodily harm – in the rather archaic language of this old Act of Parliament dating back to 1861 – simply means really serious physical injury. The Crown say, members of the jury, that when you have heard the evidence in this case, you will be driven to conclude that Mr Ricci clearly wounded Miss Galloway, and clearly did so with the intention of causing her really serious physical injury.'

Roderick glances at his notes, and takes a deep breath. The doyen of the Bermondsey Bar is at his deadliest in apparently clear-cut cases of violence. He uses his undoubted gravitas to wonderful effect, and as he increases in seniority the relative lack of detail typical of such cases suits his style more and more. On the other side, Julian Blanquette has a gravitas of his own, but it owes nothing to seniority. Julian owes such gravitas as he has to an infectious energy and a keen wit, which he often employs to good effect against opposing counsel, to the amusement of the jury. I'm wondering with interest what his approach will be to this case. On the face of it, there's not much to raise a chuckle in the papers I've read.

'Members of the jury, it all started at about eight o'clock on a Thursday evening about four months ago. You will hear that the defendant Luigi Ricci and his brother Alessandro, who are both in their fifties, own and operate an Italian restaurant called Primavera Toscana, in Queen Elizabeth Street, SE1, not very far from this court. You will hear that Linda Galloway went to Primavera Toscana for dinner on that evening with a male companion. She arrived at about seven fifteen. It was a quiet evening. Only one other table was occupied, by a Mr and Mrs Snape, and they were several tables away from where Miss Galloway and her companion were seated.

'After two pre-dinner drinks Miss Galloway and her companion placed their orders for dinner. The orders were taken by a young woman called Valentina Ricci, who is the daughter of Alessandro Ricci, and who works part-time at Primavera Toscana while studying for her degree. Members of the jury, you may be surprised by what I'm about to tell you, because generally what the victim of an offence had to eat just before the offence was committed is not of great importance. But in this case you may hear it referred to by the witnesses, and so I will tell you. As it was a warm night, both Miss Galloway and her companion ordered a chilled garlic soup and a Caesar salad with chicken. They also asked for a bottle of sparkling water and a bottle of Vermentino di Gallura – a light, crisp white from Sardegna, which I must say I've rather taken to myself...'

Seeing me looking at him curiously, Roderick holds up a hand.

'I'm sorry, your Honour,' he says quickly, 'I seem to have got rather carried away. I'll move on.'

'The mid-1990 vintages aren't bad,' Julian muses drily, with a sly glance in the direction of the jury box, 'but I must say I've always found the Vernaccia di San Gimignano more reliable myself, certainly in more recent years.'

The jury are having a good snigger.

'I'm sure your Honour would like us to get on with it,' Roderick says.

'I would,' I confirm.

'Yes, of course, your Honour.'

Even given Roderick's seniority, it did sound a bit odd to have him diverge from his theme like that, almost as if he'd momentarily lost the plot. But I have to admit that my own attention wasn't focused one hundred per cent on subject matter either. I must admit, I was somewhat diverted by the image of a nice fresh chilled garlic soup and Caesar salad. I usually look forward to Elsie and Jeanie's ham and cheese bap, but today it's feeling rather pedestrian. I force myself to concentrate.

'The chilled garlic soup,' Roderick continues, 'was served uncontroversially at about eight o'clock. At about eight fifteen Valentina Ricci arrived with the Caesar salad and retreated in the direction of the kitchen, apparently with the intention of leaving Miss Galloway and her companion to enjoy it. On the face of it, all was well. But Miss Galloway will tell you that as Miss Ricci opened the kitchen door, she heard raised voices. The voices were male. The kitchen door closed again, but the voices were still audible. For one or two minutes she did her best to ignore them. But the voices became louder and angrier. Mrs Jennifer Snape will tell you that she also heard the voices, even though she was seated farther away from the kitchen.

Eventually, Valentina Ricci emerged from the kitchen again – this time in tears. And it was just after that, members of the jury, that Miss Galloway's evening went terribly wrong.

'Valentina was followed in a matter of moments by her uncle, the defendant Luigi Ricci. Linda Galloway immediately noticed three things about the defendant: he appeared to be very angry; he was speaking rapidly and loudly in Italian; and he was carrying a large meat cleaver. Miss Galloway initially thought that there must have been some argument between the defendant and Valentina, but she soon realised that she herself was somehow involved. She will tell you that the defendant approached her table, meat cleaver in hand and, still speaking loudly in Italian, stood over her, pointing the meat cleaver at her Caesar salad. It seemed to Miss Galloway that he was remonstrating with her; but as she speaks no Italian she couldn't tell what he was saying. Members of the jury, Alessandro Ricci then emerged from the kitchen, also speaking loudly in Italian, though thankfully, not carrying a weapon. Alessandro also approached Miss Galloway's table, so that she now had both brothers towering over her, one on each side of her and slightly behind her. Miss Galloway then realised that the argument was between the two brothers. Although she doesn't speak the language, Miss Galloway will tell you that she thought she heard several references to the phrase "Insalata Caesar", which she recognised.

'Members of the jury, the next thing that happened was that the defendant Luigi Ricci swung the meat cleaver violently in Miss Galloway's direction. It connected with the right side of her chest, causing serious wounds. There is no dispute about the medical evidence in this case, and it will be read to you. That evidence will leave you in no doubt that the injury Miss Galloway suffered was very serious. She sustained damage to her collarbone, and to two very important muscles in her neck and chest. But, members of the jury, serious as the injury was, it could have been far worse. She lost a considerable amount of blood, but mercifully the meat cleaver, swung with considerable force by the defendant, narrowly missed Miss Galloway's subclavian artery and her anterior jugular vein. Had either the artery or the vein been severed, she might well have bled to death before the ambulance arrived. Fortunately, the meat cleaver stayed away from those areas; Valentina Ricci had the presence of mind to call 999; and medical help arrived promptly. Miss Galloway was taken to Guy's Hospital, where she underwent surgery to repair the damage to her bone and muscles, and where she stayed for almost two weeks. Fortunately, members of the jury, she has made a more or less full recovery.

'The police were called, and took statements from everyone present. Mr Snape saw nothing of the incident because he was sitting with his back to it. Mrs Snape had a partial view, and she will tell you that she saw Luigi Ricci swing the meat cleaver in Miss Galloway's direction. Alessandro and Valentina Ricci saw the incident in its entirety, and they will both give evidence to you: though it's probably best if I warn you now that both of them showed considerable reluctance to cooperate with the police, and they will be at court because they've been served with a court order to attend, called a subpoena. If they failed to attend, the learned judge could hold them in contempt of court. The police also took a statement from Linda Galloway in hospital as soon as her doctors allowed them to do so, and of course, she will give evidence to you today.

'Members of the jury, the defendant was arrested and interviewed under caution at the police station. You will hear that interview read to you. In essence, the defendant told the police that the wounding of Miss Galloway was an accident. Because of an argument with his brother Alessandro about the dish that had been served to Miss Galloway, he intended, he said, to cause a scene and to knock her plate off the table and on to the floor with the meat cleaver; but he lost his grip on the cleaver and it hit Miss Galloway's chest accidentally. In the defence statement provided by Mr Ricci's solicitors, he repeats this account of the events, and suggests that because it was all an accident, he has not committed any offence. He adds that even if he is guilty of an offence, he had no intent to cause her any harm, and so if he is convicted of anything at all he should be convicted only of the lesser offence of unlawful wounding, without any intent, under section 20 of the Act. Members of the jury, the learned judge will explain to you that, as a matter of law, both of those alternatives are open to you. But we anticipate that, once you have heard the evidence, you will have no doubt that what occurred at Primavera Toscana that night was a very serious wounding, carried out deliberately by the defendant with intent to cause Linda Galloway really serious physical injury.'

After a few closing remarks about the burden and standard of proof Roderick concludes his opening, and we're ready for Linda Galloway. The lure of a nice chilled soup or fresh Caesar salad has receded somewhat in my mind, because one or two things are bothering me. For one, it seems strange that Roderick and Julian haven't had a chat about this case and talked about whether a plea to the lesser offence under section 20 might not be a realistic solution. The idea that this was all pure accident, with no element of recklessness – which would be enough for a conviction in this kind of case – seems far-fetched. But equally, in the absence of evidence that Luigi Ricci had a sudden brush with madness, so does the idea that he would take a meat cleaver to a customer in his restaurant just because she ordered the Insalata Caesar. The difference in the maximum sentence as between section 18 and section 20 is life imprisonment versus five years; and given the severity of the injuries, my first reaction as a sentencer is that

I'm going to be reaching for the higher end of the scale in either case. Julian is far too experienced not to have made all this clear to his client, but I haven't heard even a whisper of a possible compromise. Perhaps they did explore it, but for some reason Julian couldn't talk his client into offering a plea.

The second thing bothering me is the absence from Roderick's opening of any information about Miss Galloway's 'male companion'. Whatever became of him, one wonders?

Linda Galloway is thin and slightly built. She's wearing a light blue long-sleeved dress with a white scarf around her neck – to hide the scars she's still carrying, I suspect. Understandably, she doesn't look comfortable. I recall from the file that she's twenty-six, but she looks younger. Roderick will treat her gently, I'm sure, and she looks as though she needs some gentle treatment. After taking the oath she gives him her name and describes herself as currently unemployed.

'Miss Galloway, on the occasion the jury are concerned with, did you go for dinner at the Primavera Toscana restaurant in Queen Elizabeth Street?'

'Yes.'

'As a matter of interest, had you been to Primavera Toscana before?'

'No. It was my first time. And my last.'

'Yes, quite. At about what time did you arrive at the restaurant?'

'We arrived just after seven o'clock, some time between seven and ten past.'

'Were you seated immediately?'

'Yes. The place was empty, apart from one other couple who arrived almost the same time as us.'

'Do you now know that the other couple were a Mr and Mrs Snape?'

'Yes. They sat nearer to the door. We were right at the other end of the restaurant, closer to the toilets and the door to the kitchen.'

'Yes. Thank you. Now, Miss Galloway, you've been using the word "we". Were you with someone else on that evening?'

'Yes.'

'Who were you with?'

'I don't know.'

I glance in Julian's direction just in time to see him give the jury the knowing smile and the raised eyebrows. He shouldn't, really, but I can't say I blame him. It would be hard to resist. From the defence point of view, this is about to get interesting.

'Your Honour, I wonder whether the jury might retire for a few moments?' Roderick asks.

It's a sensible suggestion. We're obviously about to enter uncharted waters. Julian doesn't seem in the least surprised, and it seems that both counsel know something I don't. Clearly, I need to find out what it is. I suggest to the jury that a cup of coffee might be welcome, adding – in the hope of deflecting the disappointment they must feel about being excluded from court at such an intriguing moment – a silly quip about a cappuccino or espresso being in order. It's silly because Bermondsey Crown Court isn't Primavera Toscana, and the jury won't find a cappuccino or espresso they would consider drinking anywhere in the building.

'Your Honour,' Roderick resumes once they've reluctantly left court, 'Miss Galloway genuinely doesn't know the identity of the man she was with. She knew him by the name of Arthur... I don't know whether your Honour sees where I'm going with this?'

'I'm afraid I haven't got the faintest idea, Mr Lofthouse,' I admit.

'At that time, your Honour, Miss Galloway was employed by an escort agency.'

'Ah, I see.' I think about it for a moment or two. 'But even escort agencies must keep some records,' I protest. 'Surely the police have checked. And why didn't they speak to him on the night?'

'In reply to your Honour's second question, the police weren't able to question the man Arthur on the night, because he left the restaurant as soon as Miss Galloway was wounded.'

'What? He just walked out?'

'Yes, your Honour: he walked out and never returned. And in response to your Honour's first question, he paid the agency, such as it is – it's no more than one woman and a dog, really – in cash. They probably don't hold much in the way of records about any of their clients, but they had absolutely nothing on this man.'

I shake my head. 'I didn't see a word about this in the file.'

'It's in the unused material, your Honour. My learned friend has it, but there would have been no need for your Honour to trouble himself with it before trial. The officer in the case, DS McGeorge, who sits behind me, noted the matter in the record of the investigation, of course, and the CPS disclosed the record to the defence.'

By 'unused material' Roderick means material the prosecution doesn't intend to rely on as part of its own case, but is obliged to alert the defence to in case it may help them. Sadly, it's not unknown for the prosecution to bury information it doesn't much care for somewhere in the unused material, in the hope that the defence won't dig too deep. Julian, however, is one of those who is not adverse to a spot of digging.

'That's quite correct, your Honour,' he acknowledges at once. 'They did disclose it. Nonetheless, it is a matter of some concern that it's not mentioned in any of the witness statements.'

'It is,' I agree. 'What are you asking me to do, Mr Lofthouse?'

'Your Honour, as there is no immediate prospect of finding

this man Arthur, I submit that it is unnecessary to bring up Miss Galloway's previous sexual history in front of the jury. She no longer works for the agency. If my learned friend has no objection, Miss Galloway should be allowed to tell the jury simply that her companion left the restaurant, without any reference to her work or his identity.'

'I can't agree to that,' Julian replies, surely to no one's surprise. 'Whoever this man is, he may have valuable evidence to give, and in his absence I would submit that the defendant can't have a fair trial. Depending on what Miss Galloway has to say, I may even have to submit that your Honour should withdraw this case from the jury.'

'Your Honour...'

'And in any case, your Honour,' Julian adds, 'there's no point, is there? The jury are bound to work it out for themselves. There aren't all that many reasons why a young woman would go out to dinner with a man she doesn't know from Adam – or from Arthur, in this case.'

'That makes no difference,' Roderick objects. But I've already heard enough.

'This has nothing to do with Miss Galloway's sexual history,' I rule. 'But the jury must be given a truthful explanation for this man Arthur not being called to give evidence. They must be told why Miss Galloway was with Arthur, and that the police have been unable to trace Arthur, whoever he may be. No one is going to go into her sexual history. I'm sure the jury won't be bothered about it one way or the other, but of course I will direct them about it, just to make sure.'

No one seems unduly distressed by this, and I call for the jury to be brought back to court.

'Miss Galloway,' Roderick resumes, 'you told the jury that you didn't know the identity of the man you were with. Would you please explain to them why?'

'I was working for an escort agency,' she explains in a matter-of-fact way. 'The clients never use their real names, and in his case he paid cash, so we would have no idea. He told me his name was Arthur, so that's the name I used. If he'd told me his name was Merlin, I would have called him Merlin. That's all I know about him.' She looks up at me. 'I don't work for the agency any more, your Honour.'

I turn to the jury. 'Members of the jury, Miss Galloway's previous occupation has nothing to do with the case you're trying. You've only heard about it to explain something that otherwise might seem strange to you, that she was having dinner with a man whose name she didn't know. You mustn't be prejudiced against Miss Galloway in any way because she worked for an escort agency in the past. I'm sure you understand.'

Of course they do. They're all nodding. They're a young London jury, and they aren't turning a hair over Linda Galloway's work history.

'Once you were seated, I take it that you and Arthur looked at the menu and placed your orders?'

'Yes. Well, we had a couple of Proseccos first while we were reading the menu, and then we ordered.'

'All right. What did you order?'

'We both ordered the same thing. Arthur suggested it. He obviously knew his way around an Italian menu better than I did, and he spoke some Italian.'

I see Julian look up and make a note to himself.

'What makes you think that?' Roderick enquires.

'He spoke Italian to the waitress, and she gave him an Italian menu. She gave me the English one.'

'What did Arthur suggest you should have?'

'The chilled garlic soup and a chicken Caesar salad. It was a warm evening, and it sounded very nice. He also ordered some white wine and water.'

'It may be that my learned friend will ask you about the vintage,' Roderick says, with a grin towards the jury, 'but I'm not going to.' Julian is smiling sportingly. 'Did the first course arrive as ordered?'

'Yes, and it was very nice. They gave us some good bread to go with it, too.'

'I'm glad to hear that,' Roderick says. 'What about the second course?'

'The salad was very nice too,' she replies, 'but I never got the chance to taste more than a few mouthfuls.'

'That's a shame,' Roderick says. 'What happened?'

'Well, just as we were getting started, the waitress had opened the kitchen door, and I could hear two men arguing in Italian. They were getting very loud.'

'You don't speak Italian, I gather, so did you have any idea what they were talking about?'

'I didn't' she replies, 'but Arthur did, and he was having a right old laugh about it. He told me...'

'Just pause there, Miss Galloway,' Roderick interrupts, 'in case there's an objection.'

There certainly could be – any answer she gives would be blatant hearsay, and Julian isn't going to miss that – but apparently it doesn't concern him; he shakes his head quickly.

'I'm obliged to my learned friend. What did Arthur tell you?'

'He told me they were arguing about the recipe for the Caesar salad dressing.'

The jury have another good snigger. Julian joins in discreetly.

'The recipe?' Roderick asks, trying to join in the humour himself, but he's a couple of beats off the pace.

'That's what he said. He didn't get the details of it, but one of the men thought the other one had done it all wrong.'

'I see. What happened next?'

'We tried to ignore it and continue with our own conversation, but it was getting louder and louder, even after the kitchen door was closed. And then, a minute or two later, the waitress ran back out of the kitchen. She was crying. She seemed very upset.'

'The waitress being the young woman you now know to be Valentina Ricci?'

'Yes. She was lovely. She came to see me in hospital after my operation. God only knows what they'd said to her, but she was crying her eyes out.'

'Then what happened?'

'Then I heard the kitchen door open again. I turned round in my chair and I saw this man coming out of the kitchen.'

'Yes. So you were sitting with your back towards the kitchen, and Arthur was sitting facing the kitchen, is that right?'

'Yes.'

'You turned and saw a man leaving the kitchen: is that right?'

'Yes.'

'Miss Galloway, I don't think there's any dispute…?'

'None at all, your Honour,' Julian says quickly.

'I'm obliged. Miss Galloway, do you see the man who came out of the kitchen in court today?'

She looks across to the dock. 'Yes. He's the man over there with the officer.'

'The defendant Luigi Ricci?'

'Yes.'

'Thank you. What, if anything, did you notice about Mr Ricci as he came out of the kitchen?'

'He was shouting in Italian. I didn't know who he was shouting at, but he was very loud. He was obviously very angry. And he was holding what looked to me like a meat cleaver, or a very large knife, at least.'

'Yes. With the usher's assistance…'

Dawn picks up an exhibit wrapped in seriously thick plastic, and after showing it to Roderick and Julian in turn, takes it to the witness box. Miss Galloway takes it from her briefly, nods, and quickly returns it.

'Yes,' she replies briefly.

'Thank you,' Roderick replies. 'Exhibit one, please, your Honour. If you would, please, usher…'

Dawn makes her way to the jury box. She stands in front of the box holding Exhibit one in front of her for long enough to allow them all to take a good look. I see some tight lips in the jury box by the time she leaves them to make her way over to the clerk's table, where Carol takes the exhibit from her and hands it up to me. It's difficult to see anything very clearly through the plastic covering, but it's obvious that the blade has several large patches of reddish-brown staining. Linda Galloway is not an expert, so she's not allowed to tell us what the stains are, even though she has a close association with them; but there's no one in court who doesn't know that it's her blood on the blade.

'What happened next?'

'Mr Ricci walked over to where I was sitting and stood behind my right shoulder. He just stood there.'

'Was he doing anything else apart from standing there?'

'He was continuing to shout in Italian, and he was still holding the meat cleaver.'

'Do you happen to remember which hand he used to hold the cleaver?'

'His right hand.'

'What, if anything, did you do?'

'I didn't do anything. I froze, with my fork in my hand. I was absolutely petrified.'

'What, if anything, was Arthur doing?'

'Nothing. He was obviously just as much in shock as I was. His mouth was wide open and he was holding his fork halfway to his mouth. At least, he was the last time I saw him.'

'Did anyone else appear?'

'Yes. A few seconds after Mr Ricci started standing behind me, I heard another man's voice, also shouting in Italian, coming from behind me. I didn't dare turn around, but this man came and stood behind my left shoulder, still shouting.'

'Were you able to see this man?'

'Very briefly. I was so scared, I didn't want to move. But...'

'There's no dispute, your Honour,' Julian says again.

'I'm obliged to my learned friend. Miss Galloway, do you now know that this second man was the defendant's brother, Alessandro Ricci?'

'Yes.'

'What were the two men doing when they were both standing behind you?'

'Well, they were arguing with each other. I realised then that they weren't shouting at the waitress, or me. They were shouting at each other.'

'Again, do you have any sense of what the argument was about?'

'I think it was something to do with the Caesar salad.'

'What makes you think that?'

'Well, it was partly what Arthur had said. But also, Mr Luigi Ricci kept pointing at my salad with the meat cleaver, and I heard both of them say "Insalata Caesar" several times.'

'What happened then?'

'I was about to ask Arthur if we could leave, but just as I was opening my mouth to speak, out of the corner of my eye I saw Mr Luigi Ricci pull his arm back – his right arm – and swing it my direction. I remember screaming, and then...'

'Take your time,' Roderick says.

Dawn walks over to the witness box with a glass of water and a box of tissues. Linda has been composed up to now, but understandably, the experience of her close brush with death is not an easy one to re-live. Gratefully she takes a long draught of water, and blows her nose.

'And then it all went black,' she adds quietly. 'All I remember after that is lying on the floor, bleeding, feeling the warmth of the blood, going in and out of consciousness, people screaming all around me, and then the ambulance coming.'

'When the ambulance came to take you to hospital, where was Arthur?'

'I don't know. He must have left some time after I was stabbed, but I didn't see him leave, and I haven't seen him since.'

Roderick consults his notes. 'Miss Galloway, the jury will hear the medical evidence, so I don't need to take you through it all. Taking it shortly, were you taken to Guy's Hospital, did you undergo surgery to repair serious damage to your collarbone and to the muscles in your chest, and were you in hospital for almost two weeks?'

'Yes.'

'With the usher's assistance, would you kindly look at this bundle of photographs, seven in all...?'

'Yes.'

'Tell the jury what they are, please?'

'These are photographs of the scarring on my shoulder and chest. The first three were taken when I was first admitted to hospital, the second three after my surgery, and then there's one taken by my sister yesterday.'

'Thank you. Exhibit two, please, your Honour. There are copies for your Honour and the jury...'

Roderick waits patiently for us all to look at the photographs.

'Miss Galloway, what have you been told by your doctors about your scars?'

'I've been told that they will fade to some extent over time, but not entirely. I will have some reminder there for the rest of my life. I could try plastic surgery when I've recovered more, but there's no guarantee of how much difference it would make.'

Roderick pauses for effect. 'Were you also told of what

consequences you might have suffered if the meat cleaver had landed, or penetrated, a millimetre or two in any direction from where it did?'

She needs the water and another tissue before answering that one.

'I was told that it could easily have destroyed my breast; or it could have severed a major artery or vein in my neck or chest, in which case I would probably have bled to death before the ambulance got to me.'

'I have nothing further, Miss Galloway,' Roderick concludes. 'Thank you.'

I glance up at the clock: almost one o'clock. I announce that we are adjourned. And so to lunch, an oasis of calm in a desert of chaos.

Despite my earlier concerns, the evidence about the stabbing has taken the edge off my craving for a Caesar salad, and Jeanie and Elsie's ham and cheese bap has regained its attraction.

'Are you doing the wounding at that nice Italian place?' Marjorie asks.

'I am indeed.'

'How is it going? It's such a shame. I really liked that place, what's it called, Primavera something?'

'Primavera Toscana. Yes, we've made a start. We've done the complainant in chief. Julian Blanquette is defending, so I'm sure we've got something interesting to look forward to this afternoon. But, to be honest, I wouldn't give much for Signor Ricci's chances.'

'So we're looking for another Italian place for our nights out, are we?' Legless suggests regretfully.

'It would probably be wise,' I agree.

'Couldn't you get Ricci up from the cells to rustle up a spot of lunch for us?' Hubert asks. 'At least we could have something edible for a couple of days.' His dish of the day is billed as a chicken and mushroom risotto, and judging by its appearance I'm sure anything from the Ricci kitchen would be a distinct improvement.

'Sorry, Hubert, I'd love to, but Julian might have something to say about it.'

'Offer him three months off his sentence for every day he cooks for us,' Hubert suggests. 'Julian wouldn't have anything to say then, would he?'

'Roderick Lofthouse might,' I reply. 'By the way, Hubert, I haven't had the chance to say this, but well done on that case you threw out on Friday.'

'Yes,' Legless joins in, 'absolutely right.'

'It's something we all need to start doing more,' Marjorie adds.

Hubert holds up his hands as if to protest, but he's not fooling anyone – he's obviously pleased with the accolade. 'They didn't leave me much choice, Charlie,' he replies modestly. 'Two thousand pages of technical data, and not a word of it disclosed to the defence, not a single word. It was all to do with the movement of mobile phones, signals bouncing off towers, that kind of thing. All Greek to me, needless to say, but counsel seemed to agree that it was important. What else could I do?'

'And the prosecution told you that they decided not to disclose it because defence counsel would have been paid too much for reading so many pages?' Marjorie asks. 'Is that really true?'

'It is, Marjorie. I couldn't believe my ears. What's it got to do with the CPS how much defence counsel get paid for reading the evidence?'

'Unbelievable,' Legless says. 'I hope you gave them a bloody good bollocking.'

'I certainly did. I gave a proper judgment, the kind of judgment you give in those civil cases of yours, Marjorie – even cited a couple of cases I found in *Archbold* – and I ordered a copy to be sent to the Director of Public Prosecutions personally.'

'Absolutely right, Hubert,' Legless says. 'Very well done. This non-disclosure business is turning into an epidemic.'

'You just can't trust them any more, can you?' Hubert replies. 'Absolute bloody disgrace. Whole bloody system's going down the drain, if you ask me. We have a former Director who's a member of the Garrick. You should hear what he has to say about it after a couple of stiff gins.'

Suddenly, for no reason I can account for, I'm getting this nagging feeling that there's something amiss; and after some reflection I realise it's got something to do with the mysterious Arthur, and Julian's suggestion that I may have to follow Hubert's example by withdrawing the case from the jury. I awake from the reverie to find my three colleagues looking at me curiously. Apparently, my reflection has taken me away from lunch for a few seconds.

'Everything all right, Charlie?' Marjorie asks.

'Oh yes, I'm fine,' I reply quickly. 'Hubert, do you think you could find those cases in *Archbold* again for me, the ones you used in your judgment?'

'Of course, Charlie, be glad to. I'll write you a note and get my usher to drop it off in your chambers. What have you got?'

'A man called Arthur who disappears a bit too easily for my liking,' I reply.

* * *

Monday afternoon

'Miss Galloway,' Julian begins, 'you'd never been to Primavera Toscana before that evening: is that correct?'

'Yes.'

'You'd never met my client, Luigi Ricci, before?'

'No.'

'You hadn't met his brother, Alessandro Ricci, before either, had you?'

'No.'

'Had you met Alessandro's daughter Valentina?'

'No, not before that night.'

'For that matter, had you met any member of the Ricci family?'

'Not as far as I know, no.'

'You came into the restaurant on that evening, you had a couple of drinks, and you ordered dinner, is that right?'

'Yes.'

'You didn't misbehave in any way, cause a disturbance, anything like that, did you?'

'No, certainly not.'

'No. Miss Galloway, can you think of any reason why Luigi Ricci would want to attack you with a meat cleaver?'

'No. I couldn't think of any reason then, and I can't now.'

'It doesn't make any sense, does it?'

'No.'

'You were sitting with your back to the kitchen, weren't you?'

'That's right, yes.'

'Thank you. Let me move on to the time when both brothers had emerged from the kitchen. You told the jury that Luigi was standing to your right, and slightly behind you, and Alessandro was to your left and slightly behind you: is that correct?'

'Yes.'

'So you weren't able to see Luigi directly, full on?'

'No.'

'You had more of a peripheral view of him, would that be fair?'

'Yes, it would.'

'Is it also fair to say that this all happened very quickly?

'Very quickly.'

'You had these two men shouting at each other in Italian; you couldn't understand what they were saying, except for "Insalata Caesar": is that right?'

'Yes,'

'And then, all of a sudden, using your peripheral vision, you see the meat cleaver moving towards you: yes?'

'Yes.'

'And the next thing you know, you're on the ground, bleeding heavily: is that a fair summary of what happened?'

'That's exactly what happened.'

'Is it fair to say, Miss Galloway, that you can't say what may have been going through Luigi's mind at the moment when the meat cleaver moved towards you and struck you?'

'Well…'

'You're not a mind reader, are you, Miss Galloway? I don't mean to be disrespectful. I'm just suggesting that you have no way of knowing what he was thinking at the time.'

She nods, a little reluctantly. 'No. That's true.'

'You can't help the jury to decide whether what Luigi did was intentional, or whether it may have been an accident: can you?'

'I suppose not, if you put it like that.'

Julian pauses for a moment to consult his notes, and resumes unhurriedly.

'Arthur, on the other hand, was facing you, just a few feet away, wasn't he?'

'Yes.'

'So he had a perfect view of what happened, didn't he?'

'Yes.'

'But unfortunately, as you've told us, he left the restaurant when you suffered your injury, or just afterwards?'

'As I said before, I didn't see him leave, but he wasn't there when the ambulance arrived.'

'And you haven't seen him since?'

'That's correct.'

'Miss Galloway, as His Honour has said, we're not concerned with what you did for a living at that time: it's no one's business but yours, and it's got nothing to do with the case.'

'Thank you.'

'But I do want to explore with you whether you have any information about Arthur. First of all, what was the procedure when the office had a client for you?'

'They would text me the details, the name he was using, where and when we were supposed to meet, and so on.'

'Well, you say "and so on". Would "and so on" include a phone number for the client, in case you needed to contact him – to cancel, to suggest a different time or place, to say you were running late: things like that?'

'No. If I had any problem, I was to call into the office. If there was a change of plan on his end they would call or text me. But no, I wouldn't have the client's number.'

'But the office would?'

'As far as I know they would, yes.'

'That would make sense, wouldn't it? You have to be careful, don't you? You never know who you might be dealing with.'

'You can say that again.'

'Yes. And one reason for having a phone number for the client is to make sure you have some idea of who you're dealing with, for safety reasons, if nothing else?'

'That's what I always assumed, yes.'

'You don't need to say the name of the lady at the office, Miss Galloway. But I'm going to ask the usher to provide you with a pen and a piece of paper, and I'm going to ask you to write down her name and the office phone number.'

Dawn takes these items from the clerk's desk and makes her way to the jury box.

'I don't mind saying their names,' Miss Galloway replies as she takes them from Dawn. 'It was Maisie from Monday to Thursday, and Daphne over the weekend. But I would prefer to write the number down, in the circumstances.'

'Thank you,' Julian says, examining the number the witness has given him. 'Miss Galloway, after the incident, after you'd recovered and been released from hospital, did you ever talk to Maisie or Daphne, to ask her whether she had any information about Arthur?'

'I didn't ask her myself, no. I left the agency after what happened with Arthur, and I never went back. It got too dangerous for me. This wasn't the first time I'd had a dodgy one, if you know what I mean. Enough was enough. I was finished with them. But I gave the number to the police when they interviewed me in the hospital and took my statement.'

'Do you remember the name of the officer you gave it to?'

She points across the courtroom. 'It was the officer sitting behind the prosecution barrister.'

'I see,' Julian says, 'the officer in the case, DS McGeorge?'

'Yes.'

'Thank you,' Julian says. He pauses for some seconds. 'Miss Galloway, could you describe Arthur for us?'

'Describe him?'

'Yes. What did he look like? How was he dressed? Let's start with his physical appearance, shall we?'

She thinks for a moment and shrugs. 'His build was tall and thin. He was over six feet tall – I'm sure of that, because my brother's over six feet and Arthur looked taller than my brother.'

'What sort of age?'

'Late forties, early fifties, I would say.'

'Colour of hair?'

'Black, but turning to grey, cut short, what in the old days they called a short back and sides, with a parting on the left side.'

Julian smiles. 'You're very observant, Miss Galloway.'

She returns the smile. 'I trained as a hairdresser,' she replies. 'Hair is something I can't help noticing.' She pauses. 'I'd really like to go back to it. I'm looking for a job as a stylist now.'

'I hope you get one very soon,' Julian says.

'Thank you.'

'Any facial hair?'

'No. He was clean shaven.'

'Colour of eyes?'

She closes hers for a moment, visualising. 'Blue.'

'Any scars, tattoos, other distinguishing marks?'

Miss Galloway suddenly blushes. She looks up at me.

'Do I have to answer that, sir?' she asks confidentially.

'Is there a reason you don't want to?' I ask.

She clasps her hands together. 'It's just that it's a bit embarrassing,' she replies.

'There's no need to be embarrassed,' I encourage her. 'We hear all kinds of things in court every day of the week.'

She nods. ''He has a dark red birthmark on the inside of his right thigh,' she replies.

'Ah, I see,' Julian says. 'So, your assignment with Arthur was…'

'During the afternoon, yes. But then he kindly asked me out to dinner, and that's how we ended up at the restaurant.'

'Yes. How was Arthur dressed – while you were at Primavera Toscana, I mean, of course?'

'He had a very smart suit, a white shirt, red tie, black shoes. He dressed very nicely, like someone who had a very good job.'

'Did you give any details to DS McGeorge about Arthur's appearance? I ask because there's nothing in your witness statement about it. Was that something he asked you about when he came to see you at Guy's Hospital, or at any time, for that matter?'

'Yes. I told him everything – well, everything except the birthmark. I was worried that…'

'Of course. I understand. Did Arthur say anything, at any time while you were with him, to give you any clue about who he was: where he lived; what he did for a living; what his hobbies or interests were? Anything at all?'

She shook her head. 'He's married,' she replies.

'How do you know that?'

'He had a mark on the ring finger of his left hand, where his wedding ring would go. He'd taken it off for me, obviously. They all do.'

'Let me ask you this, Miss Galloway: did the police ever ask you to work with a sketch artist?'

'Like they do on TV?'

'Yes: like they do on TV.'

She shakes her head. 'No. Never.' She sounds a bit disappointed.

'Is there anything else you can tell us about Arthur?'

She thinks for some time. 'Well, the only other thing was: he was a chatty soul. Not like some of them, who just get dressed as soon as we've… you know… and disappear without so much as a thank you. Arthur wanted to talk.'

'What sort of things did he talk about?' Julian asks gently.

'All sorts. He was asking me what I thought about this, that and the other – the trains, the NHS, all the things people complain about – and he was explaining to me who was responsible for it all, government ministers, and civil servants and what have you. And it was the way he talked about them – John this and Jane that – he knew everybody's first name, didn't he? He was talking about them all as if he'd just had lunch with them. Do you know what I mean?'

'I do, Miss Galloway. Thank you.'

Julian turns to me.

'Your Honour, I have no more questions for Miss Galloway, but I would be grateful if she would remain at court for the time being, in case further questions arise. And I would ask that the jury retire for a few moments, so that I can mention a matter of law.'

The jury duly troop off for a tea break. There's no mystery about the matter of law Julian wants to raise. I've been expecting it, and judging by the several whispered conversations between Roderick and DS McGeorge during the latter part of Julian's cross-examination, they've been expecting it too.

'Your Honour, I'm very concerned about the effort – or perhaps I should say, lack of effort – that seems to have gone into trying to track down this man Arthur,' Julian begins. 'He had the best seat in the house; he must have seen exactly what happened. Potentially, he's the best witness we could have. But he's not here, and I can't cross-examine him.'

'The police haven't been able to find him,' Roderick replies urbanely, but I detect the suggestion of unease in his voice.

'As far as I can see, they haven't really tried to find him,' Julian says. 'DS McGeorge's entry in the investigative record says only that he couldn't be traced. It gives no details of what efforts, if any, were made. Miss Galloway says she gave the police quite a lot to go on. Did they talk to Maisie or Daphne, or whoever was in charge of the office? Did the agency have a phone number for Arthur? How did he pay them? In cash or by card? These were all obvious lines of inquiry, and we don't know whether the police pursued any of them.'

'Your Honour...' Roderick begins. But I cut him off. For some reason, whether it's the recent conversation about Hubert's case or just the growing feeling that something's not quite right, I think Julian deserves at least some further inquiry into what went on.

'No, Mr Lofthouse. I agree with Mr Blanquette. The court needs to know more. I'm going to direct that a more senior officer take a witness statement from DS McGeorge, and that both officers give evidence tomorrow morning, and bring with them any materials the police have that might throw some light on who this man Arthur is. We will see what further steps we need to take when we're more fully informed. But there's no need to waste the rest of the afternoon. I'm sure you have other witnesses available.'

'As your Honour pleases,' Roderick replies, rather dispiritedly.

I bring the jury back, and Roderick calls Ethel Snape. She doesn't take very long. As it turns out, she has only one fact of significance to contribute. Although she was facing in the right direction to see the action, she was sitting some distance away and her view was partially blocked by Arthur. She saw the meat cleaver in the air, but can't help about whether Luigi Ricci's handling of it appeared to be deliberate or accidental. Once she realised what had happened she was mainly concerned with trying to help Linda Galloway, by holding towels from the kitchen against her wounds to try to slow down the bleeding until the ambulance arrived. But she did see Arthur leave the restaurant. She told us that Arthur stood up as soon as Linda Galloway collapsed to the floor. He didn't exactly run, she said, but he was walking very quickly and almost bumped into her as she was leaving her seat to make her way to help Linda. She didn't remember Arthur saying anything, and couldn't remember much about his appearance, though such description as she could give was consistent with Linda Galloway's.

Next, Roderick calls Alessandro Ricci. I'm sure he's not exactly overjoyed at the prospect. Alessandro isn't here voluntarily, a fact amply confirmed by his show of reluctance and sullen manner when Dawn invites him to enter the witness box and take the oath. But Roderick really has no choice. He could leave Julian to call him as part of the defence case, of course, but then Julian would be at a disadvantage: he wouldn't be allowed to cross-examine him using leading questions, which, one feels, may be necessary if he's going to get anything worthwhile out of him. It's an issue of fairness, and Roderick is an old-school prosecutor who keeps up the tradition of being scrupulously fair to the defence even at some risk to his own case. Based on what I hear from other RJs, this tradition is on the endangered list in many courts today, and it's always reassuring to find it alive and well at Bermondsey.

'Mr Ricci, are you the brother of the defendant, Luigi Ricci?'

The witness nods.

'You have to answer audibly, Mr Ricci, so that your evidence is recorded.'

'*Sì, è mio fratello.*'

A glance at his expression tells me that Roderick has already had enough of Alessandro Ricci. It would have been made abundantly clear to Alessandro that he could have an interpreter if he wanted one, so there is no excuse for not understanding what is said to him – or for pretending not to. Roderick's patience, you can tell, is already wearing thin.

'Mr Ricci, I'm aware that you speak excellent English, so please reply in English rather than Italian.'

Alessandro answers this without recourse to language at all, with a casual shrug. I decide on a gentle intervention before things get out of hand.

'Mr Ricci, please remember that you are in a court of law, and you have taken an oath to tell the truth,' I remind him. 'If you fail to do so, I have power to hold you in contempt of court, which may mean that you end up in prison.'

'*Non capsico.* Is not so good, my English.'

'You haven't asked for an interpreter, Mr Ricci, and I see that you managed to make a witness statement in English. Do your best, please.'

He looks up at me with a suggestion of defiance. 'What I can say?'

'You can answer the questions Mr Lofthouse puts to you,' I reply. He maintains his stare for a few moments, but the defiance gradually begins to ebb away.

'He is my brother. What else you want to know?' he asks. I gesture to Roderick to continue.

'I'm much obliged, your Honour. Mr Ricci, do you and your brother Luigi jointly own and operate the Primavera Toscana restaurant in Queen Elizabeth Street?'

'Yes.'

'For how long has your restaurant been open?'

The shrug again. 'Two, two and a half years.'

'Before that, did you have a restaurant together in Siena, in Italy?'

'Yes, it's true.'

'Thank you. Now, on the evening the jury are concerned with, were you and your brother Luigi both working at Primavera Toscana?'

'Yes, we were working.'

'How do you work together? Do you both cook?'

'We are both the chefs. Luigi has his – *come se dice*? – his dishes of signature and I have mine; but we are both the chefs, and we can both prepare any dish on our menu.'

'Yes. And was your daughter Valentina working that evening as a waitress?'

'Yes. She is student, but she helps us in restaurant. She is good girl.'

'Yes, I'm sure she is. We've heard that at about seven o'clock that evening, the restaurant was quiet, but that in the next few minutes two couples arrived: is that right?'

'Yes.'

'The two couples were Mr and Mrs Snape, who were seated near the door; and Linda Galloway and the man we're calling Arthur, who were seated nearer to the kitchen: is that correct?'

'Yes, it's true.'

'After Miss Galloway and Arthur had had one or two pre-dinner drinks, did they place an order for food?'

'Yes. Valentina take their order.'

'What dishes did they order?'

'They both order the chilled garlic soup and the chicken Insalata Caesar. It is from our special summer menu – is very good for the warm weather, and, for London, very reasonable. Is very expensive city.' The jury have a quick chuckle.

'Yes, I'm sure. Mr Ricci, who prepared these dishes for Miss Galloway and Arthur? You or your brother?'

'I prepare these dishes. Luigi, he prepare Ossobuco for the other table…'

'I see.'

'For which he need meat cleaver. Is not possible prepare Ossobuco without meat cleaver.'

'Yes, well we'll come to the meat cleaver in a moment, Mr Ricci. But in the course of your preparing the dishes for Miss Galloway and Arthur, did you have any discussion with your brother?'

Silence for some time.

'Mr Ricci…?'

'We have difference of opinion, professional difference of opinion,' he replies eventually, with obvious reluctance. 'Is nothing new. We have this difference many times before.'

'Would you explain to the jury, please, what this difference of opinion was about?'

'*Mio fratello*… my brother, he does not like the way I prepare the Insalata Caesar.'

'For what reason?' I'm sure there's a part of Roderick – his always reliable professional judgment – that is regretting asking this question as soon as the words have left his mouth: with this witness, it's an open invitation to give the jury a lecture on the Italian culinary arts. But it's a lecture we're apparently destined to hear at some point in this trial, and we might as well get it over with. The witness throws both arms high in the air in apparent exasperation.

'Luigi, he think there is only one way to prepare the Insalata Caesar. It must be prepared at the tableside. The oil and garlic you must mix before: this must be ready. Also the croutons. But everything else must be made on trolley at tableside. To the oil and garlic you must add the anchovies, the yokes of two eggs. You must stir to make it – *come se dice*? – more creamy. Then you must stir in the Parmesan cheese, the lemon juice. You must add the salt and Worcester sauce to season. The customer must see all this at tableside. And never, never, the mayonnaise. Never: *capisce*?'

'*Sì, capisco*,' retorts a loud voice from the dock. 'At last you learn. In my restaurant, never the mayonnaise. Never.'

'That will do, Mr Ricci,' I say. 'Don't interrupt, please. You will have your chance later.'

'We may well hear from your brother about this later in the trial,' Roderick continues, no doubt presciently, 'but tell the jury, please: in what way do you use the mayonnaise? How does it differ from your brother's method?'

'I use instead of the eggs,' Alessandro explains.

'*Sacrilegio*!' I hear from the dock.

'Mr Ricci, why do you think your brother is so opposed to that?' Roderick asks quickly before I can warn the defendant again.

Another shrug. 'Because he make Insalata Caesar with eggs, and our father before us make Insalata Caesar with eggs, and his father before him, and his father before him make Insalata Caesar with eggs, and so on until you come to Romulus and Remus who are making Insalata Caesar with eggs for lunch while they are building Rome. With Luigi, there is no change, no – how to say? – *innovazione*. Even, he does not allow me to make my insalata at tableside. I must make in kitchen. Never must the customer see the mayonnaise in Primavera Toscana.'

'Yes. In a few words if you can, Mr Ricci, why do you think your recipe is better? Why do you use mayonnaise instead of eggs?'

'Please to understand,' the witness replies quietly, 'that I am not the first to do this. Many chefs follow this recipe. Why? Is simple: it is more creamy, better to taste for the customers in this country, because they like the sweet things. Perhaps in Italia, the eggs are better. But in this country, not so much. It is for the customers: that is all. So, tell me: why I cannot use my own recipe?'

'*Non*! *Mai!*' the defendant thunders again.

'I won't warn you again, Mr Ricci,' I say, trying to sound more threatening this time. 'If you interrupt again, I will have you removed from court.' Julian turns towards the dock, and adds his own warning with a vigorous shake of the head.

'It might help if we could move on to the events of the evening, Mr Lofthouse,' I suggest.

'Certainly, your Honour. Mr Ricci, do I take it that, despite your brother's views, you used mayonnaise, and not eggs, in the salad you prepared for Miss Galloway and Arthur?'

'Yes, of course. Why I should not?'

'We've moved past that, Mr Ricci,' Roderick replies hurriedly. 'Please concentrate on my questions. Is that what you did?'

'Yes, of course.'

'And was it served to them?'

'Yes, Valentina serve them.'

'What happened next?'

'Luigi see that I am using the mayonnaise, and he is angry. But you understand, is not first time this happen – we have this argument many times. He start to shout at me, and I shout back to him.'

'Were you both shouting in Italian?'

'Yes, of course. It is our language. In what language we should shout?'

'Was Valentina present when this argument took place?'

He nods. 'She comes back to kitchen while we are shouting. But this upsets her – she is sensitive girl, nice girl, not like us. She doesn't like when her father and her uncle are shouting. She starts to cry and she goes out of kitchen, back into restaurant.'

'What happened then?'

He hesitates. 'Luigi, he make the Ossobuco. He has the meat cleaver in his hand. But then, he runs suddenly from kitchen out into restaurant, and still, all the time, he is shouting.'

'Did you follow him?'

'Yes, I follow.'

'What did you see when you got out into the restaurant?'

'I see my brother standing by Miss Galloway, still with the meat cleaver, and still shouting. Everyone in restaurant is looking at him. He is like crazy man. I don't know what he is doing. He is out of control.'

'What, if anything, did you do?'

'I went also to stand by her, because I hope then she would be not so much afraid. But she is very afraid. I can see this.'

'Was your brother standing to Miss Galloway's right, and were you to her left, and were you both slightly behind her?'

'Yes, that is true.'

'What was he shouting about?'

'Still, he is shouting about the Insalata Caesar. I am telling him: for God's sake, Luigi, shut up about the Insalata Caesar, who cares, and can't you see you're upsetting the customers? But he isn't listening to me.'

'Then what happened?'

He hesitates. 'His hand slips, and the meat cleaver hits Miss Galloway. It is accident. We call ambulance, she go to hospital. That's all I see.'

Roderick ponders for some time whether to try to fix this. I'm sure he's been expecting it. You can't hope for much help with your case from a hostile witness, especially when the witness is the defendant's brother. Blood, one supposes, is thicker than mayonnaise. But having already come this far, Roderick decides to give it a spin.

'Well, Mr Ricci, what you saw was the meat cleaver strike Miss Galloway in the shoulder and chest. You don't know what was in your brother's mind at the time, do you?'

'It is accident,' Alessandro insists stubbornly.

'What did Luigi do immediately after striking Miss Galloway with the meat cleaver?'

'The witness didn't say he *struck* her with anything, your Honour,' Julian objects, not unreasonably.

Roderick grits his teeth. 'What did Luigi do after Miss Galloway had fallen to the floor, bleeding extensively from her wounds?' he asks.

The witness shakes his head. 'He sit down in chair. He is in shock. We are all in shock. Valentina call ambulance. She bring towels from kitchen and holds them to stop the blood. Mrs Snape also help her.'

'Thank you, Mr Ricci,' Roderick concludes insincerely. 'I have nothing further, your Honour.'

'Just one matter,' Julian says, leaping to his feet. 'Mr Ricci, did you see what happened to the man we're calling Arthur after the accident?'

'He leave restaurant,' Alessandro replies. 'He does not return. Where he go, who knows?'

'Had you ever seen Arthur before that evening?'

'No.'

'Or since?'

'No.

'Nothing further, your Honour. Thank you, Mr Ricci.'

Roderick seems to have little enthusiasm for taking matters any further this afternoon. By common consent we adjourn until tomorrow, to see whether any further information will come to light about the elusive Arthur.

* * *

Monday evening

Finding myself in something of an Italian frame of mind this evening, I suggest to the Reverend Mrs Walden that we take ourselves off to La Bella Napoli for dinner, a suggestion to which she offers no resistance. I dutifully peruse the menu, but I'm aware that I'm simply going through the motions. I think I could recite the Bella Napoli menu from memory if called upon to do so, but this evening my mind was made up before I ever left home. The temptation to sample the Insalata Caesar is overwhelming, and as I've been regaling the Reverend with the saga of the Ricci family salad wars on the way to the restaurant, she is also keen to know whether or not we can tell eggs from mayonnaise. There's no chilled garlic soup on the menu, so we start with a tasty *antipastiera*, a basket of bread, and a bottle of the house Chianti, a vintage I doubt Julian Blanquette would approve of, but more than adequate to the occasion.

We are slightly disappointed when the salads arrive from the kitchen. I'd hoped that Tony, La Bella Napoli's owner and head chef, might fancy giving us a demonstration of the classic tableside procedure, which would not only add a piece of culinary theatre but would also tell us on which side of the egg–mayonnaise divide the Bella Napoli kitchen stands. Instead, the salad is presented to us fully formed on the plate. Nonetheless it is delicious, and although I'd been fairly sure that I would know one way or the other more or less instantly, by the time I've eaten the final mouthful I've changed my mind three times, finally opting without any real conviction for the mayonnaise. The Reverend Mrs Walden, after similar vacillations, comes down on the side of the eggs. There's nothing for it but to ask.

After dessert, as is his wont, Tony approaches with the offer of a Sambuca or Limoncello on the house to go with our coffee. I invite him to stay and have one with us, and as it's getting late and his sous-chefs can manage the remaining sprinkling of diners easily enough, he cheerfully agrees, pulls up a chair, and pours us all a stiff Limoncello.

'The eggs,' Tony informs us without hesitation after I've explained the reason for my inquiry. 'That's the way I was taught. I know there are some chefs who use mayonnaise, but to be honest, if you're going to do that, you may as well serve some commercial Caesar dressing out of a bottle and have done with it.'

'Told you,' the Reverend beams, sticking her tongue out at me. I reciprocate.

'So, there's definitely a right way and a wrong way?' I ask.

'In my opinion, yes. But all chefs have strong opinions about the food they prepare. And yes, it's true that British tastes are different: you know, there are people who want salad cream on everything, and there are people who want ketchup or brown sauce on everything. But I don't think we should change our cuisine just for that reason. If you make it properly with the eggs, an Insalata Caesar should be plenty sweet enough, in addition to the other tastes, the anchovies and the cheese and so on. The only question is whether it's a well-made salad.'

'Do you ever make it tableside?' the Reverend asks.

'In the old days, in Napoli, always,' Tony replies, wistfully. 'But in Italy people have more time. It takes up a lot of time to prepare the salad tableside all evening. Service takes longer throughout the restaurant. The problem is, people are always in such a hurry here. They have some place to be after dinner, or they have to go back to work after dinner – you know what I'm saying. We're losing the art of the leisurely dinner, when everything may take a bit longer but the whole evening is devoted to dinner, so it doesn't matter; when everyone is talking and enjoying the wine, and no one minds if it's all a little slower. Then, we can practise the old skills. But as things are in this country...' he sees her looking disappointed. 'But I tell you what, Mrs Walden, next time you're here, ask for me, and I will make it for you tableside – if I can still remember how to do it.'

She laughs. '*Grazie, Signor Antonio.*'

'*Prego, Signora.*'

'Tony,' I ask, 'do you know these Ricci characters by any chance?'

He smiles. 'Primavera Toscana? Oh, yes. They're what you might call a bit of a local legend.'

'In what way?'

He nods, and refills our glasses. Then he raises the first finger of his right hand, and taps the right side of his nose several times.

'I probably shouldn't say too much, Mr Walden. But I'll guarantee you one thing: whatever the problem was with those guys when this incident happened, it's not about the right way to make Insalata Caesar. I'll guarantee you that.'

* * *

Tuesday morning

The *Standard* having done full justice to the Insalata Caesar controversy overnight, with several of its regular columnists thoughtfully contributing their own recipes, Elsie and Jeanie are left questioning whether it's even safe to go out to dinner any more. It's not a question of whether the Caesar salad is prepared tableside or in the kitchen: it's a question of whether anyone's even safe in restaurants any more, what with mad cooks stomping around everywhere waving meat cleavers.

'I mean, what had that poor girl ever done to him, sir?' Elsie asks. 'All she did was go for an evening out, and the next thing you know, she ends up being stabbed because the chef doesn't like the way his own kitchen made her dinner.'

'It's like a postcode lottery, innit?' Jeanie replies. 'Except, it's not the postcodes, it's what's on the menu. If you choose the wrong thing from the menu, the chef comes after you with a big knife. How are people supposed to know what to choose with all that going on?'

'I blame those chefs on TV,' Elsie says, 'the famous ones, the so-called chefs to the stars. I mean, just look at them. They're always swearing and carrying on, aren't they? Some of them even throw things at the people working with them while they're abusing them. And then they blame them for making a mess of the salad. Their nerves must be in shreds, poor things. I'm surprised they can even find the lettuce, let alone make a salad. And these people are on TV. What are young people supposed to think when they see that kind of thing going on? They're paid enough, aren't they, these chefs? They should set a better example.'

Jeanie smiles. 'Here you are, sir. One latte, and one ham and cheese bap with mayonnaise. Or I can do you one with raw eggs, sir, if you prefer.'

'No, thank you, Jeanie, this one will be fine,' I reply.

I hear them giggling as I make my way over to George's newspaper stand.

'Got a nice salad for lunch, have we, guv?' he chuckles.

'Don't you start, George,' I reply.

'No, but it's shocking, guv, innit? And it's only because it's foreign food, innit? I mean, you don't see people knifing each other over the best way to make fish and chips or bangers and mash, do you?'

'My mother had her own way of making Yorkshire pudding,' I reply. 'She and my aunt argued about it for years.' I'm not quite sure why I've volunteered this information.

'I don't suppose they took a knife to each other though, guv, did they?' George persists.

'Not as far as I know.'

'No, well, that's it, innit? It's just your foreigners, innit? Anyway, guv, I've got a little something you might want to take a look at this morning.'

'Oh, yes?'

George has an uncanny knack of finding news items affecting his customers. It's almost like having your own personal archivist, and over the years he's unearthed any number of stories affecting the court, or yours truly, stories which otherwise would have passed me by until it was too late. How he does it, I have no idea. This morning he's brandishing a copy of the *Daily Telegraph* in addition to *The Times*. I don't usually buy anything other than *The Times*, but I've learned to take George at his word when he says there's something worth reading elsewhere.

'Page eighteen,' he says with a grin, handing me my change.

I take my seat behind my desk, take my first sip of my latte, and turn to page eighteen. Once again, George is right. Page eighteen contains today's letters to the Editor and one letter, in a prominent position at the top of the page, catches my eye immediately.

Failures to Disclose Evidence
From His Honour Judge Hubert Drake

Sir,
I am writing in the hope that you will allow me to bring to the attention of your readers the disgraceful and increasingly common practice of the prosecution in the Crown Court of withholding relevant and sometimes exculpatory evidence from the defence. I need hardly point out the potential of this practice to cause miscarriages of justice.

Recently I had occasion to stay proceedings as an abuse of the process of the Court when the prosecution failed to disclose a large quantity of relevant evidence to the defence, which put the defendant at a hopeless disadvantage and might well have resulted in an incorrect verdict of guilty. When I confronted prosecution counsel with this conduct on the prosecution's part, he was unaware of the reason for it. I asked him to take instructions, which he did. I was then told that if the evidence had been disclosed, defence counsel would have been paid too much of the taxpayer's money in fees for reading it. I was scarcely able to believe my ears. Leaving aside the fact that the amount of fees payable to defence counsel is no business of the prosecution, it is a piece of extraordinary arrogance for the prosecution to think that they are somehow the guardians of the public purse, and as such are entitled to dispense or withhold evidence in accordance with their own view of the country's economic situation. I make clear that counsel was not to blame for this situation. He had not known of the reason for the decision and was visibly appalled by it.

I understand from colleagues that this practice is becoming widespread. Whether it is the result of deliberate malpractice, or of prosecutors being overworked, lack of experience or training, or simply administrative chaos caused by having too many cooks in the kitchen, I have no way of knowing. But it must be stopped before fair trials in this country become a thing of the past. We judges can't do it all. The lead must come from our politicians. But so far, they seem to be burying their heads in the sand, as usual.

Yours sincerely,
Hubert Drake
Bermondsey Crown Court

Stella knocks and enters my chambers, *Daily Telegraph* in hand.

'Good morning, Judge,' she says in the doom-laden tone of impending disaster for which she is renowned at court. She sees the copy already open on my desk. 'I didn't know whether you'd seen it, so I thought I'd better bring my copy, just in case.'

'Good morning, Stella. Have you seen Judge Drake?'

'Yes. But I didn't say anything. I know you'll want to speak to him yourself. He's in chambers, if you want to catch him before he goes into court.'

I shake my head. 'No. I'll talk to him later. I need some time to work out what to say.'

'Well, I'm afraid you won't have as much time as you might like for that, Judge.'

'Oh? Why might that be?'

'Because the Grey Smoothies are coming for lunch, and they want to speak to you and Judge Drake together. They called a few minutes ago.'

Roderick has asked for the jury to be kept out of court so that he can bring me up to date about the hunt for Arthur.

'We haven't found him yet, your Honour,' he explains. 'But we have had what may be a piece of luck. DS McGeorge checked the emergency call records again, and it appears that there were two 999 calls made that evening about the events at Primavera Toscana, not just one. The jury have been told about the call made from the restaurant by Valentina Ricci. But there was also a call made about five minutes later by a man who refused to give his name. That call was made from a telephone box in Tower Bridge Road, a short walk from Queen Elizabeth Street and Primavera Toscana. The piece of luck we've had is that there is CCTV footage showing a man answering Arthur's description entering the phone box at the time the call was made. It's surprising to find footage that hasn't been erased after such a long time, but it seems that the local authority held on to a number of tapes from that period because there had been an upsurge in vandalism in the area, and when DS McGeorge checked they were able to provide it to him.'

'Does that mean we may be able to identify Arthur?' I ask.

'DS McGeorge is working on it with other officers as we speak, your Honour. The question is going to be whether the CCTV image corresponds with any pictures the police may have, or with any in the public domain. The quality of the image is quite good, so DS McGeorge thinks it will be possible to match it. The question is whether there's anything to match it with.'

'I see. All right. What do you want to do while that search is going on?'

'I see no reason not to press on with the evidence, your Honour,' Roderick replies. 'I can read the medical evidence, and then take the next witness.'

'Mr Blanquette?'

'I have no problem with any of that, your Honour,' Julian

replies, 'as long as it's understood that if Arthur is found, and depending on what he has to say, I may ask for certain witnesses to be recalled; and I wouldn't want to be called on to start my case until we know one way or the other.'

'I quite understand that, your Honour,' Roderick says, 'and of course, I'll give my learned friend every assistance.'

'Yes, all right,' I agree. 'Let's have the jury back.'

As foretold in Roderick's opening, the undisputed medical evidence leaves no doubt that Linda Galloway had a near brush with death. The meat cleaver hit her shoulder and the right side of her chest, causing serious wounds. She sustained damage to her collarbone, and to the muscles in her neck and chest. She also lost a lot of blood: but not as much as she might have – the cleaver missed Miss Galloway's subclavian artery and her anterior jugular vein by a matter of millimetres. Had either been severed, she might well have bled to death before the ambulance arrived, in which case Luigi Ricci would now be at the Old Bailey facing a more serious charge. As Roderick reads the evidence to the jury in his usual dry measured tones, you can see their lips tightening. To help that process along, Roderick also produces her heavily bloodstained dress and shoes in plastic exhibit bags, which Dawn happily holds up for the jury to peruse to their heart's content.

Next, Roderick calls Valentina Ricci. She's a strikingly pretty young woman with dark eyes and long black hair, dressed in a sharp red shirt and designer jeans, with moderately high-heeled black shoes. She doesn't want to be here any more than her father, you can tell, but she's not going to be sullen about it. For her, it's more of a sad occasion. She will go through the motions of protest, but at the end of the day she knows that there is nowhere to hide. After giving Roderick her name and age, and the fact that she is Alessandro Ricci's daughter and Luigi's niece, she quietly tells me that she doesn't want to give evidence that might hurt a member of her family.

'What would happen if I don't answer any questions?' she asks me.

'I would give you every chance,' I reply, 'but if you persist I would have to find you in contempt of court and keep you in custody until you change your mind.'

She looks down at her shoes.

'If I may ask, Miss Ricci,' I add. 'What are you studying at college?'

'Political science, your Honour. But then I want to study law and become a solicitor.'

'Well, it's not going to help if you have a conviction for contempt of court on your record, is it?' I say.

'No,' she replies. She turns back towards Roderick. 'All right.'

'Thank you, your Honour. Miss Ricci, there's been no dispute about the sequence of events, so let me come straight to the argument between your father and your uncle. We've heard that it started in the kitchen and then moved out to the restaurant where Miss Galloway was sitting. Is that your memory of it also?'

'Yes.'

'And we've heard that they were arguing over the finer points of making a Caesar salad.'

She is silent almost long enough for Roderick to ask if she has understood the question.

'Yes, that's what you've heard,' she replies, just as he's about to.

Roderick looks at her. 'I'm not sure I understand, Miss Ricci. Are you saying that's not what the argument was about?'

'Were they shouting at each other about the Insalata Caesar? Yes: but they shout at each other about that all the time. My whole life I've listened to them arguing: yes, about Insalata

Caesar, but if not Insalata Caesar, then about Ossobuco; or if it's not about Ossobuco it's about Pasta alle Vongole; or if it's not about Pasta alla Vongole, it's about the right sauce for grilled sea bass. These men can argue their way through the whole menu in a week. Trust me: if there are two ways to prepare any dish in the world my father and my uncle will argue about it.' She has become animated. She pauses for breath, and ends up almost shouting. 'But nobody is waving meat cleavers around, for God's sake.'

There is a silence for some time, and suddenly I'm remembering Tony's enigmatic comment about the Caesar salad last night.

'Are you saying, then,' Roderick resumes cautiously, 'that there was something else going on, that it wasn't just about the salad?'

'It's never just about the salad,' she replies.

'Well, what *was* it about?' Roderick asks.

There is a loud burst of Italian from the dock, to which the witness replies in kind. Before I can call for a translation, Luigi holds his head in his hands, and shouts 'No!' several times.

'I'm sorry, Uncle Luigi,' Valentina replies, and translation becomes unnecessary. 'I must tell the truth. I have no choice.'

After one last protest the defendant subsides.

'My father Alessandro gambles,' she says simply. 'Cards, horses, football: whatever there is to bet on, he will bet on it. The trouble is, he isn't very good at it. He has lost a lot of money over the years. But recently, it's got worse...'

'How much worse?' Roderick inquires gently.

'I can't give you an exact amount. But listening to them arguing, I know it's a large sum. And unfortunately, at some point my father used his interest in Primavera Toscana as collateral to borrow money to fund his gambling. He and my uncle own the restaurant jointly, you see.'

Roderick is nodding. 'And now the bank is calling in his

loans, and the business may have to be sold?' he asks.

'I wish,' she replies.

'You're going to have to explain that, Miss Ricci...'

'There's no bank involved,' she says quietly. 'There's a man who lends money to my father, and every so often he comes calling to collect whatever my father owes him.'

'You mean, your father has been borrowing from a loan shark?' Roderick asks, glancing up at me.

She nods. 'We hoped, maybe he would let them sell the restaurant, but he doesn't want to wait that long for his money. He would rather have the cash, and I have the impression that if he doesn't get it, he would be quite happy to torch the place with us in it. My uncle had just found this out a day or two before.' And then, suddenly, she adds, 'I think, the night Miss Galloway was hurt, the man was going to give my father a final warning.'

I react before Roderick can even ask.

'Members of the jury,' I say, 'there's a matter of law I need to discuss with counsel. Take a break for a few minutes, if you would, please.'

Everyone is so stunned that even the usually nimble Dawn is slow getting to her feet to escort the jury out of court. Their eyes are wide open. They know exactly what Valentina Ricci has just said, and I'm sure they're wondering why they can't remain in court to hear it confirmed. But there are a number of implications involved, and each of them represents a potential Pandora's box. They need to be out of court long enough for us to sort it out.

'Miss Ricci,' I say, after the jury are safely out of earshot and things have calmed down a bit, 'are you saying that this same man was in the restaurant when Miss Galloway was stabbed?'

'Yes. He's the man – Arthur. But that's just the name he was using that night. It's not his real name, obviously.'

'Just answer "yes" or "no", for the moment. Do you know his real name?'

'I only know what I've been told.'

'Told by whom, your uncle?'

'Yes: and by my father.'

I gesture to Dawn. 'Miss Ricci, don't say the name out loud, please. The usher will give you a pen and paper. Please write it down for us.'

She does. Dawn hands the paper to me, and then to both counsel in turn.

'Your Honour,' Roderick says, 'I do have some further questions for Miss Ricci, but I wonder whether your Honour would be good enough to rise for some time. I should get this information to DS McGeorge and his team with as little delay as possible, and there are matters I should discuss with my learned friend about where we go from here.'

'Yes, of course,' I agree at once. 'Let's tell the jury they have time for coffee, and I'm going to order that for the time being, the evidence given by Miss Ricci is not to be reported or disseminated outside this courtroom. Miss Ricci, please don't discuss your evidence with anyone during this adjournment, and if anyone tries to approach you, don't talk to them, and tell the usher straight away. Do you understand?'

'Yes, sir. Thank you.'

'I'm withdrawing the defendant's bail until further notice,' I add. 'He must remain in custody for now.'

I leave court before anyone can protest. He can probably have bail again later in the day, but I can't have him running around talking to people and making phone calls at this particular moment. Fortunately, his brother hasn't attended court this morning, so with any luck we can control the situation until DS McGeorge tracks Arthur down. But it's a situation everyone needs to consider carefully, and I'm not in the least surprised when, shortly after arriving back in chambers, I receive a note from counsel indicating that they will need until after lunch. I release everyone, wishing that lunch today would be an oasis of calm in a desert of chaos, and knowing that it won't.

Carol has brought us some dreadful canteen sandwiches, a few bags of crisps, and some sparkling water which seems to have lost most of its sparkle. The Grey Smoothies are out in force, led by Sir Jeremy Bagnall of the Grey Smoothie High Command, attired in a solemn dark grey suit and a red tie. Our cluster manager and note-taker-in-chief, Meredith, is with him, decked out in a white blouse and grey slacks, with the usual assortment of bracelets dangling from her right wrist and jangling whenever her wrist comes into contact with the table. Meredith has brought her sidekick, Jack, who still looks about fourteen and still wears the same light grey suit, a little too small for him, with a violent pink tie scrunched up against his collar. They are all looking grim, and I don't think it's just because of the sandwiches. I've insisted that Stella sit in with us, with her hand-held recorder, just to make it clear to Meredith that she doesn't have a monopoly of recording today's meeting.

Hubert is looking defiant, though knowing him as I do, I sense that he's also anxious about this meeting. He should be. Hubert is perpetually worried about any inquiry that might focus attention on his age or raise any suggestion that retirement may be on the cards. That's the one thing that puzzles me about this affair. Hubert is certainly outspoken enough at lunch at court and, so I gather, at the Garrick Club; but with anything that might attract the notice of the Grey Smoothies he's usually desperate to keep his head down. So his letter strikes me as markedly out of character. To make matters worse, I've only had a few minutes to talk to him in advance, when we had both risen for lunch, and he wasn't very forthcoming. So I've got absolutely no idea what to expect from him.

Sir Jeremy has placed a copy of the offending letter in the middle of the table between the two sides. He sits back and eyes it with distaste for some time.

'Hubert,' he begins, 'I'm sure, with your experience, you know perfectly well that it's not acceptable for sitting judges to write letters to the newspapers – certainly not about any subject that has to do with the law. What's this all about?'

'There's no need to talk to me like a prefect dressing down a naughty schoolboy, Jeremy,' Hubert replies brusquely.

'I'm not. I'm speaking to you quite reasonably.'

'It didn't sound at all reasonable.'

'I'm asking you, perfectly politely, to account for your writing a letter to a newspaper as a sitting judge. It's something the Minister, perfectly reasonably, needs to know. I don't see why you should be so upset about it. I'm simply asking why you did what you did.'

'I should have thought that was perfectly obvious.'

'Well, I'm sorry, but I don't find it obvious at all,' Jeremy replies with a sniff.

It's already getting a bit tense. I decide to intervene.

'Hubert, I think Jeremy's simply pointing out that it's unusual for judges to write letters to the press for publication. It's generally discouraged, as you know. He's just asking what drove you to write to the *Telegraph* about this particular subject.'

'Once again, I should have thought it was quite obvious.'

'Perhaps so,' I reply before Jeremy can jump in again, 'but so that we're all sure we understand, why don't you explain it to us?'

'The case I wrote to the editor about was an outrage,' Hubert explodes. 'Telling a judge that you won't disclose evidence you're legally obliged to disclose because you don't want defence counsel to be paid properly for reading it. I've never heard of such a thing. Something has to be done about it.'

'I agree with you, Hubert,' Jeremy concedes, spreading his arms out wide. 'But there are proper channels for communicating concerns such as that.'

'Are there?' Hubert asks. 'Perhaps you wouldn't mind enlightening me.'

Meredith looks up from her busy note taking. 'We encourage judges to send a copy of any ruling of that kind to the Director of Public Prosecutions,' she says, 'as you did; and you're always welcome to copy them to Sir Jeremy.'

'And what good would that do?' Hubert asks, not unreasonably. 'It's not an isolated case. This kind of thing is happening all the time, but no one ever does anything.'

'The more information we have, the more we can put pressure on those responsible to make changes,' Meredith replies.

'I'm not seeing any evidence of that,' Hubert grumbles.

'Hubert does have a point, Meredith,' I say. 'This kind of non-disclosure is cropping up far too often. It used to be rare, but recently it seems to have become almost routine, and from what I hear from other RJs it's not just Bermondsey – it's everywhere.'

'The Minister is aware of the problem, Charles,' Jeremy replies. 'But I will talk to him, I will pass on your concerns, and I'm sure he will look into them.'

I like the sound of that, and I have the momentary illusion that perhaps the meeting will end amicably and constructively. But it's not to be.

'If history is anything to go by, Jeremy,' Hubert replies, 'I doubt that will help. Our impression is that the Minister prefers to keep his head below the parapet until he has MPs sniping at him in the House. As far as I can see, that's the only thing that gets his attention,'

'That's quite unjustified,' Jeremy protests. 'The Minister is always busy behind the scenes...' he pauses long enough to replace his conciliatory tone with a rather more insistent one. 'In any case, that's not the point. We can't have judges writing to the newspapers, and that's all there is to it.'

'Somebody has to let the public know what's going on in their courts,' Hubert says.

'That's for the Minister or the Lord Chief Justice to do – when it's necessary to do it at all. We don't make policy in the press, Hubert. We make policy very carefully, behind the scenes, and we calculate our statements to the press very precisely.'

'What statements?' Hubert asks. 'As far as I know, there's been a deafening silence about these non-disclosure cases.'

'You're entitled to your opinion, Hubert,' Jeremy replies. 'But I say again, we are aware of the problem and we're working on it behind the scenes. It doesn't help to have circuit judges shooting from the hip and giving newspapers like the *Telegraph* the wrong impression.'

'What wrong impression?' Hubert demands.

'The impression that there's some great conspiracy going on to deprive defendants of their right to a fair trial.'

'I didn't say that,' Hubert insists.

'He's right, Jeremy,' I add. 'The letter clearly says that Hubert doesn't know whether this kind of thing is deliberate malpractice, or what does he call it...?' I glance over to the paper. 'Or simply a case of administrative chaos, too many cooks in the kitchen, and so on.'

Jeremy shakes his head. 'That's not what the papers are likely to read into it. In any case, that's not the point. It's not proper for a sitting judge to write to a newspaper in this way, and that's the end of it.'

'Excuse me, but where does it say that exactly?' Hubert asks, more quietly, after a silence.

'Where does it say what?' Jeremy asks.

'That a judge can't write to a newspaper to express his views. You see, Jeremy, as a lawyer, my impression is that judges have the same freedom of speech as everybody else. Has there been some change in the law that I've missed?'

Jeremy and Meredith exchange glances. She reaches into her briefcase and produces a copy of the Judicial Code of Conduct and hands it to Jeremy. Of course: Meredith is always prepared. I'm sure she doesn't leave home without a copy of the Code ready to hand. I bet she was a girl scout in her younger days. Jeremy starts flicking through the pages.

'Let me save you the trouble, Jeremy,' Hubert says. 'I have read the Code very carefully, I assure you. There are a lot of platitudes in it about the role of a judge. But you're not going to find a prohibition on writing to the press.'

'It's strongly discouraged,' Meredith points out.

'But not prohibited,' Hubert insists.

'Well,' Jeremy says, 'you may dismiss what the Code says as platitudes if you wish, Hubert, but I'm afraid the Minister takes a different view – as do I. I'm afraid the bottom line, if I may be permitted to use that expression, is this: unless within the next twenty-four hours you assure the Minister in writing that this will not happen again, you will receive an invitation to meet the Minister personally, and if that happens, I would be very surprised if he doesn't suggest that the time may have come for you to retire.'

I see Hubert take a deep breath. 'And if I may be permitted to use an expression of my own, Jeremy – do bugger off, there's a good fellow.'

Alarmed, I place a restraining hand on Hubert's arm. 'I'm sure all Hubert means to say is that he would like some time to think about it, Jeremy. He's a little overwrought, that's all.'

'I am not in the least bloody overwrought,' Hubert replies loudly.

Jeremy nods and starts to get to his feet.

'Well I've said all I have to say.'

'In any case,' Hubert adds, 'the Minister's not going to do anything to me, is he?'

'Why not?' Meredith asks.

'I'm a whistle-blower, aren't I?' Hubert replies. 'I'm a protected species.'

I see both Jeremy and Meredith form up as if to respond to this, but neither does. Jeremy quietly resumes his seat.

'That's preposterous,' he mutters eventually.

I gaze at Hubert, and can't resist a smile. They didn't see that one coming, and I suspect that someone will be making a call to the Government Legal Department during the course of the afternoon.

'It's illegal to retaliate against whistle-blowers,' Hubert continues blandly. 'They tried it in the NHS, didn't they, with all those doctors and nurses? They may have got away with it for a while, but the chickens eventually came home to roost, didn't they?'

'That only applies if the whistle-blower couldn't get anything done through internal channels,' Meredith protests.

'I rest my case,' Hubert replies.

Jeremy shakes his head and gets to his feet once more.

'Twenty-four hours, Hubert,' he says. 'I shall be back tomorrow afternoon after court, and I sincerely hope you have your written assurance ready for me to take to the Minister.'

'Well, that didn't go too badly,' Hubert says, after they've gone.

'Didn't it?' I reply. 'I don't think Jeremy's bluffing, Hubert. If I were you, I would give serious consideration to giving him what he's asked for. Whatever came over you to write to the *Telegraph*, anyway?'

He sighs 'Oh, I don't know, Charlie. I think it was just how bloody casual the prosecution were about it. It was like they were saying to me, "We're going to get this defendant by fair means or foul, and save money at the same time, and there's nothing a superannuated old git like you can do to stop us." Well, I'd finally had enough. I just wasn't going to have it. And you know as well as I do how much the Minister is going to do about it – bugger all, as usual. So I thought I'd fire a warning shot across their bow.'

'Well, you certainly did that,' I say. 'But you are going to promise us all that you won't do it again, aren't you?'

He gets up to leave. 'I'm a whistle-blower, Charlie. They mess around with me at their peril. You'll see.'

Watching Hubert as he departs, I can't honestly say I share his confidence on that score. Looking around, I see that for the most part the sandwiches are lying almost untouched on their plates. I should be hungry, but I seem to have lost my appetite. I'm not even sure an Insalata Caesar would help. Besides, I'm due back in court in five minutes.

* * *

Tuesday afternoon

Roderick has asked for the jury to remain out of court again.

'Good news, your Honour,' he begins brightly. 'Arthur has been found and is currently being interviewed by DS McGeorge. I'm not sure yet exactly what he has to say, but at least we are moving in the right direction.'

'Are we satisfied that we have his real name?' I ask.

Roderick hesitates. 'I'm not ready to go into that in open court yet, your Honour. There may be, shall we say, complications about it. In any case, DS McGeorge is fairly sure that he won't be ready to produce Arthur until tomorrow morning. May I suggest that we continue with Valentina Ricci's evidence? It may be that she is as far as we're able to go today, but once Arthur has given evidence I'll be able to close my case, so we are making good progress overall.'

We bring the jury back and Valentina makes her way to the witness box without so much as a glance towards the dock. Luigi Ricci stares at her impassively.

'Miss Ricci,' Roderick says, 'when we interrupted your evidence you had told us about the argument you heard between your father and your uncle. I now want to ask you about what happened after that. I think we agreed that your uncle Luigi, the defendant, was standing to Miss Galloway's right and slightly behind her, and your father to her left?'

'Yes.'

'Your uncle was still holding the meat cleaver in his right hand?'

'Yes.'

'And what happened?'

'My uncle hit out with the meat cleaver and accidentally struck Miss Galloway on her shoulder. She fell to the floor. She was bleeding heavily. I called the ambulance.'

Roderick looks down for a moment or two, and exhales audibly: two reluctant witnesses, and two suggestions that the whole thing was no more than an accident. Once more, Roderick has to consider whether to try to salvage the situation. But left unattended, so to speak, Valentina seizes the opportunity to ram her point home before he can try.

'He didn't intend to hit her. Why should he? He had no quarrel with her. It was Arthur he was trying to impress.'

It's too late now. The cat is out of the bag. In fairness, this was a determined cat and there was never any way to keep it in. Besides, this is coming as no surprise to the jury, I'm sure. They've had plenty of time to work it out for themselves.

'What do you mean, "impress" him?' Roderick asks.

'Arthur was there to warn my father what would happen if he and his friends didn't get their money. My uncle actually thought that he could put the frighteners on Arthur. He wanted to let him know that there were two big men for them to worry about, not just one, and they were armed with meat cleavers. It was a really stupid idea, obviously. But then, even more stupidly, he thought he'd demonstrate on Miss Galloway. He didn't know she was an escort, did he? He thought she was Arthur's girlfriend.'

'Demonstrate on her?'

'He was going to bury the meat cleaver in the table right in front of her. They were using the argument about the salad as cover, because they knew that Arthur spoke a bit of Italian. My uncle realised she would be scared, but he hoped Arthur would think twice about whatever he had in mind if he thought they were ready to come after his girlfriend. But his hand slipped, and he hit Miss Galloway instead of the table.'

'*È vero*,' I hear, coming quietly from the dock.

'So that the jury will understand,' Roderick adds, 'the money Arthur wanted was money he or others had loaned your father so that he could finance his gambling: is that right?'

'Yes.'

'What did Arthur do after Miss Galloway had been stabbed?' Roderick asks.

'He left, very quickly.'

'Did you see him again that evening?'

'No: and I haven't seen him since.' She smiles thinly. 'And no one has torched the restaurant. Stupid as it all was, maybe my uncle's plan actually worked.'

I turn towards the dock, and see the defendant smile in return. And suddenly, the mood of the trial has changed. Roderick may have to downgrade his expectations to a reckless wounding without intent. True, the story that has emerged isn't the same story the defendant gave the police when he was interviewed under caution; but Julian's not going to have any problem explaining to the jury why Luigi Ricci wasn't entirely forthcoming with the *carabinieri* at that stage, against the backdrop of what looks like a brush with organised crime. Ruefully, Roderick passes Valentina to Julian for cross-examination. But Julian is far too experienced to pick away at something he couldn't really improve on, and he cheerfully declines.

'Miss Ricci,' I say, 'I'm sure everyone would agree with me that it was very nice of you to visit Miss Galloway in hospital.'

'I had to apologise to her,' she replies. 'The poor girl hadn't done anything to deserve that, had she? She was an innocent bystander. Unfortunately, she got mixed up in our family business without knowing it. It was the least I could do,'

We adjourn for the day to allow DS McGeorge to complete whatever inquiries he's making.

* * *

Tuesday evening

Arriving home I find the Reverend Mrs Walden in the kitchen, standing proudly beside two bowls of salad.

'My curiosity was aroused,' she says.

'Oh? Curiosity about what?'

'The big eggs versus mayonnaise controversy, of course,' she replies. 'I thought it was really odd that we weren't sure of the difference last night, and I wondered what would happen if I tried to make it myself. So this afternoon I went online and found a couple of recipes for Insalata Caesar, and then I paid a visit to that Italian Deli on London Bridge Road and got a few supplies in. This is a taste test. I used eggs in one bowl and mayonnaise in the other; otherwise they're identical. I would have done it tableside during dinner, as one should, but that would give the game away, wouldn't it? So we have a surprise starter, and the lucky winner gets a glass of this.'

She reaches across her work surface to where she has a bottle of Amaretto cunningly concealed behind her blender.

'That's not fair,' I protest. 'You already know which is which.'

She shakes her head. 'I've forgotten,' she replies unconvincingly. 'They look exactly alike.'

We take the taste test, and this time, there's no doubt about it: we both identify the eggs and mayonnaise immediately and without hesitation.

'Perhaps there's something about the way they do it in restaurant kitchens,' she suggests, pouring us both a glass of Amaretto, 'some hidden secret.'

'Perhaps there is,' I reply. 'Apparently there are a lot of secrets hidden away in restaurant kitchens – Italian ones, particularly.'

* * *

Wednesday morning

It's becoming a regular ritual. Once again Roderick wants to address me without the jury, and this morning he has sitting behind him, not only DS McGeorge, but an obviously senior uniformed officer I don't remember seeing before, but who somehow looks familiar. Roderick seems troubled, and Julian, who usually has a cheerful smile to bestow on everyone, is also wearing a grave expression.

'Your Honour, I have two applications to make this morning,' Roderick begins slowly, 'both of which my learned friend opposes. By way of introduction, I can tell your Honour that DS McGeorge has completed his interview of the man we're calling Arthur, and he has taken a statement from him. Arthur is at court, and the prosecution intend to call him as a witness. But before we do, I am instructed to make these applications dealing with the manner in which he should give evidence. If I may elaborate, your Honour?'

'Yes, I think you should,' I reply.

'Your Honour, my first application is that Arthur should give evidence as an anonymous witness, without revealing his true name to the court, except privately to your Honour, of course. My second application is for special measures, to enable Arthur to give evidence behind a screen, so that your Honour, counsel and the jury can see him, but he is not visible to the public or the press.'

All manner of speculative thoughts flit through my mind. The first is that Arthur must be an undercover police officer, or even an officer of the security services. That seems just possible, given the threats made against the Ricci family, but it doesn't seem awfully convincing. More likely, perhaps, he's a villain acting as a police informant. Either way, they wouldn't want to compromise Arthur by revealing his identity, and the court would normally do whatever it could to protect him. But if that's the case, why is Julian opposing it? I ask him.

'Your Honour,' Julian replies, 'first, I haven't been given any notice of these applications until just now and I haven't been given any reason why they are necessary. I'm entirely in the dark, as is your Honour. A witness may only give evidence anonymously if it's necessary, if it is consistent with a fair trial, and if it is in the interests of justice for him to give evidence because his evidence is important and he wouldn't give evidence otherwise. I've heard nothing to suggest that any of those conditions is present. As for the screen, I'm not necessarily opposed to that, but your Honour is bound to inquire why the quality of Arthur's evidence might be affected if a screen is not allowed. Again, I've been told nothing about why that is a concern.'

I nod. 'I think you will have to give the court some explanation, Mr Lofthouse,' I say. 'Mr Blanquette is quite right. I can't make the kind of orders you're asking for without some basis for them.'

Roderick sighs. 'In that case, your Honour, I will have to ask your Honour to close the court to the public and press for the time being. In due course, much of what I'm about to say may have to be repeated in open court, but I'm instructed to do my best to keep certain matters confidential.'

'Very well,' I agree. 'I will ask members of the public and the press to leave court for the time being. I will reopen the court as soon as possible.'

Dawn cheerfully ushers out the few members of the public who have been observing the proceedings, though they include one or two representatives of the press, whose presence, needless to say, is now guaranteed as soon as the court is open again.

'I'm all ears, Mr Lofthouse,' I say. 'What on earth is this all about, some matter of national security?'

Roderick closes his eyes and shakes his head. He looks tired.

'Something far less exalted, your Honour, I'm afraid. I regret to say that important information relevant to this case has until now been withheld, from the court and from the defence. It was withheld from me too, until I was provided with Arthur's real name yesterday. I have brought my learned friend Mr Blanquette up to date this morning, and I must now do the same for your Honour.'

Visions of Hubert, Sir Jeremy Bagnall, and the *Daily Telegraph* flash through my mind.

'Are you saying that there has been a failure of disclosure, Mr Lofthouse?'

'That's exactly what I'm saying, your Honour, and for the record, I wish to state that I told those instructing me this morning that I could not allow myself to be associated with it, and unless disclosure was properly made, I would be professionally obliged to withdraw from the case.'

He pauses for effect, but it's a dramatic enough statement in its own right, not to mention exactly what I would expect of Roderick.

'They have persuaded me that I can properly ask the court for anonymity and special measures, but I have made it clear that I must put the court fully in the picture. Frankly, your Honour, I have told them that if they fail to do so, I will not resist my learned friend's application that your Honour should withdraw the case from the jury. They have agreed that we should proceed on that basis. Your Honour, I have with me Assistant Commissioner of Police Leonard Smith, who can deal with the matters in question. May I call him?'

Now I recognise him. He's on television all the time, answering for the Metropolitan Police on a whole range of topics.

'Mr Blanquette,' I say, 'do you have any observations before I decide what to do?'

'Your Honour,' he replies. He seems to have recovered his good humour now. 'I accept what my learned friend says without reservation, of course, and I'm waiting agog to hear all these fascinating secrets, as I'm sure your Honour is.'

I nod. 'Come forward, please, Mr Smith,' I say.

He's a tall, grey-haired man, his pristine uniform sporting several police medals, and he takes the oath in a quiet, precise voice.

'Assistant Commissioner,' Roderick says, 'please tell his Honour what you know about this man Arthur, and about the way in which the evidence has been dealt with.'

'Yes, sir. Your Honour, police were aware of Arthur's true identity on the day following the incident at Primavera Toscana. They became aware as a result of the 999 call he made from the phone box in Tower Bridge Road. Because Arthur had refused to give his name, and given the seriousness of the offence, an officer seized the CCTV footage later the same day. But once Arthur's identity became known, the word came down from on high that no information about the 999 call or his identity was to become public.'

'From on high?' I ask. 'What on earth do you mean by that?'

'I don't know, your Honour,' he replies. 'I myself was only made aware of these events yesterday afternoon. But I can tell your Honour this: that decision was taken at a higher level, a level above the police, and in particular DS McGeorge knew nothing about it. As far as he was concerned, the CCTV footage and the second 999 call were new information, and he certainly wasn't involved in any decision not to disclose them.'

'A level above the police?' I ask.

'Yes, your Honour.'

'Continue, please,' Roderick says.

'Arthur's name,' the Assistant Commissioner continues, 'is Sidney Rockwell.'

I put my pen down, close my eyes and nod silently for some time. The witness has given us the same name as Valentina Ricci. When she gave it, I dismissed it as a coincidence, but now that it's been confirmed I finally understand what is going on, as, I'm sure, does Roderick.

'Mr Rockwell is known to police,' Mr Smith is saying. 'I have copies of his antecedents. He has three previous convictions, one for robbery, and two for assault occasioning actual bodily harm. We have reason to believe, your Honour, that he was involved in making threats to Mr Alessandro Ricci and his family in order to recover monies his associates had loaned to Mr Ricci to enable to him to cover his gambling debts. We further have reason to believe that his presence at the Primavera Toscana restaurant on the evening in question was directly related to those threats.'

'Did DS McGeorge interview Mr Rockwell,' Roderick asks, 'and did he make a witness statement dealing with the matters relevant to this case?'

'He did, sir: although with respect to any possible criminal conduct on his part, on the advice of his solicitor he refused to answer the questions put to him.'

'I take it that, at some point, he will be further interviewed – under caution – about his possible involvement in such offences?'

'Yes, sir. I understand that DS McGeorge intends to do so as soon as this court has finished with him.'

I can't let it rest there.

'Is it your understanding, Assistant Commissioner,' I ask, 'that the reason why someone on a higher level was anxious to keep all this a secret has less to do with Mr Rockwell's rather mundane criminal record than with his family tree?'

'That is my understanding, your Honour, yes.'

'I see,' I say. 'Thank you, Mr Smith. Mr Lofthouse, I am against you on the two applications you have made. Mr Rockwell will give evidence under his own name, and in full view of the public.'

'Yes, your Honour,' Roderick replies quietly. 'May I have a few moments to take instructions?'

'Certainly, Mr Lofthouse.'

I adjourn for half an hour, at the end of which Roderick advises me that he is not obliged to withdraw from the case, and that he proposes to call Sidney Rockwell to give evidence. I'm glad to hear it. If it had been otherwise, I would have withdrawn the case from the jury, which would have been the only way to guarantee no miscarriage of justice for Luigi Ricci, but would also have guaranteed a distressing failure of justice for Linda Galloway.

Sidney Rockwell bears little resemblance to the image of the suave man-about-town described by Linda Galloway. He is wearing a cheap grey jacket and blue jeans, and looks as though he hasn't shaved for several days. Predictably, he refuses to answer any questions about any criminal conduct on his part. There's nothing I can do about that – he has the right not to incriminate himself, and his solicitor has apparently done a very thorough job of explaining that right to him. So Roderick glosses over all that and asks him how Linda Galloway came to be wounded.

'Luigi was trying to put on a show for me,' he explains, 'Mr Big Guy with a meat cleaver. It was rather funny, if you want to know the truth. Of course, I had to keep a straight face. But I've picked up the odd word or two of Italian over the years, and I knew exactly what was going on.'

'And what happened?' Roderick asks.

'Well, he swings the meat cleaver, and he's trying to make it look like he's going for her, but he's probably going for her food, or the table next to her. That's how it looked to me. I mean, he's got no reason to harm Linda, has he? He's never seen her before. But it goes wrong, doesn't it? He's so busy jabbering away that he's not concentrating. He hits her instead of the plate or the table. It was pathetic. It was a real shame, too. She's a nice girl.'

'Yet when this nice girl was severely wounded,' Roderick continues, 'you left the restaurant as quickly as you could, didn't you? Why was that? Why didn't you stay and help?'

The witness looks at me for some time, as if asking for guidance about how to answer the question. Eventually, having realised that he's looking in vain, he replies, 'I think I'd better decline to answer that on the advice of my solicitor. But I did call 999.' He smiles. 'They've got me on CCTV doing it.'

Roderick calls DS McGeorge to take us through the defendant's police interview, in which he offered the explanation about knocking Linda Galloway's salad on to the floor as a dramatic contribution to the great eggs versus mayonnaise debate. As the officer in the case, he must also answer any questions about the investigation generally. I've been expecting Julian to have a go at him and try to unearth further damaging evidence of non-disclosure and cover-up, but wisely he's very low key about it. It's clear that DS McGeorge had nothing to do with the failure to disclose evidence. All that went on at a far higher level, but as far as Julian is concerned it doesn't matter. As soon as Roderick has closed the prosecution case he asks me to withdraw the case from the jury. I send everyone away for the rest of the day, to think about it overnight – and to allow the parties to regroup and come to terms with the evidence that's been given, and the verdict that's now looking more and more likely.

And so to lunch, an oasis of calm in a desert of chaos.

By now, of course, everyone knows that Hubert is in hot water. Copies of the *Telegraph* have been circulating clandestinely throughout the court, and interestingly, as far as I can gather from Stella and Carol, the staff are solidly behind Hubert, seeing him as a whistle-blower who's courageously broken the rules to protect the court from abuse. The opinion in the judicial mess is more nuanced.

'I'm not sure that was the right thing to do, Hubert,' Marjorie says gently. 'You'd made your point in your judgment, and you'd got some press coverage for that. Why stick your neck out with a letter?'

Hubert looks up from his ham and cheese bake, a particularly unappealing variant of the dish of the day.

'I did what I thought was right, Marjorie,' he insists. 'And it doesn't say anywhere that I'm not allowed to write a letter to the *Telegraph*.'

'About trout fishing, perhaps,' Marjorie replies, 'but not about the law.'

'I don't know anything about trout fishing,' Hubert says. 'Why would I write them a letter about that?'

'Well, I for one admire you, Hubert,' Legless chimes in, 'and I've had several emails from judges elsewhere who wish they'd done it themselves. Finally, someone is standing up to be counted. Well done, that's what I say.'

'That's all very well, Legless,' I say 'but the Grey Smoothies want Hubert's head on a silver platter. Unless he gives them a written assurance this afternoon not to do it again, he may have to go before the Minister – and we all know what that means.'

There is a silence.

'You're not ready to retire, Hubert,' I say. 'What would you do with yourself? You can't spend all day at the Garrick. Surely you want to go on as long as you can?'

'Of course I do,' he concedes. 'But I can't back down. I'm a whistle-blower.'

'Actually, Hubert,' Marjorie says, 'that's a bit dodgy legally, unless you can show that you tried to get a result through internal channels and failed. Sorry.'

'Hubert,' I suggest, 'what if you didn't have to give them a written assurance? What if you gave me your word that you wouldn't do it again, and they accepted it, and the whole thing went away?'

'I'm not sure I wouldn't do it again,' Hubert objects, 'if I had to.'

'I think you've fought as much of a battle as anyone could expect you to fight,' I reply. He doesn't disagree: in fact, I think I see a look of relief cross his face. 'Let me see if I can sort it.'

'Charlie's right, Hubert,' Marjorie adds.

'Do you think they would agree to just let it go?' Legless asks.

'I have a hunch that I might be able to arrange it,' I reply. 'And you know, Hubert, you've achieved what you set out to achieve. You've drawn attention to the abuse of disclosure. It's a matter the Minister can hardly ignore now. The *Telegraph* has made an issue of it, and they've even had a few retired judges writing and taking it up. So don't throw what's left of your career away unnecessarily. Let me try to resolve this.'

'What do you want me to do, exactly?' he asks after some time.

'Nothing. Let me deal with the Grey Smoothies on my own. Stay in chambers in case I need you. Don't push off to the Garrick until I tell you the coast is clear.'

He sighs. 'All right, Charlie, whatever you say. You are my RJ after all.'

And there are days when you don't make it easy, I think, but don't say.

* * *

Wednesday afternoon

'Where's Hubert?' Sir Jeremy asks. 'Is he still in court?'

We're in my chambers with cups of tea and biscuits supplied by Carol, and the mood is tense.

'No,' I reply. 'Hubert is in his chambers. He will join us if we need him. But before we come to Hubert, there's another matter I need to talk to you about – something that's just come up today, as a matter of fact.'

Jeremy looks at me. 'But Charles, this meeting is specifically about Hubert. Is it something serious enough to take precedence?'

'It's connected to Hubert's situation, in a sense, and it may possibly have some influence on the view you take of Hubert's situation.'

'All right,' he concedes with a show of reluctance. 'What's all this about?'

Meredith grasps her pen expectantly. I'm letting her make

the record today on her own: I don't want a taped record of what might be said in the next few minutes.

'Well, actually, Jeremy, it may concern the Minister too.'

He and Meredith exchange glances. I can't help wondering whether word has already reached them of this morning's goings on.

'The Minister?'

'Yes: Sir Edward Rockwell MP.'

'I'm well aware of the Minister's name, Charles,' he says, a little too quickly. 'What does that have to do with anything?'

'Well, it's just that a man by the name of Sidney Rockwell gave evidence in my court earlier today.'

'He's the Minister's younger brother,' Jeremy acknowledges, again just a fraction too quickly.

'So I gather. They see quite a lot of each other too, don't they? One hears that the Minister has Sidney to lunch at the House, and so on.'

'Why shouldn't he? Again, Charles, I can't see…'

'Sidney Rockwell has previous convictions for robbery and assault.'

'The Minister knows all about that,' Jeremy insists. 'So does the rest of the world, for that matter. There's nothing new in it. He's been in the papers often enough. Sidney is the black sheep of the Rockwell family, always has been.'

'Yes, but it would seem that he's turning a shade or two blacker than he used to be.'

'What on earth do you mean by that?'

'Well, Jeremy, street muggings and fights as a younger man are one thing: but blackmail, involving threats of violence and arson and links to organised crime – well, that's moving up in the world, isn't it, playing in a different league?'

No reply.

'In fact,' I continue, 'I believe the police are interviewing

Sidney under caution at the police station about matters of that very kind as we speak.'

'What matters, exactly?' Meredith asks. She sounds somewhat alarmed, which is exactly what I intend.

'It's alleged that he was acting as an enforcer for an underworld consortium bent on doing violence to an Italian chef and burning the poor fellow's restaurant to the ground because he hadn't paid his gambling debts. Very nasty. He'll do some serious time if he goes down for that.'

Jeremy recovers. 'I don't know why you're telling us all this, Charles,' he protests. 'If what you say is true it will be all over the papers tomorrow, I'm sure, and the Minister will say what he always says: he's not his brother's keeper, he's not responsible for Sidney's conduct, and he acknowledges that the law must take its course. It's not his fault that his brother has gone off the rails.'

'I agree entirely,' I reply. 'I'm telling you this, not because of what Sidney did, but because what he did very nearly didn't see the light of day. You see, Jeremy, someone took a deliberate decision to withhold disclosure from the court and the defence – not only about what Sidney had been doing in the restaurant on the evening in question, but also about his identity. He was using the name Arthur at the time – a kind of stage name, one supposes.'

This time, there's an even longer silence.

'The failure to disclose threatened to make it impossible for the defendant to receive a fair trial,' I continue. 'In fact, there's still a defence application pending to withdraw the case from the jury. Now that Sidney has given evidence, I'm probably not going to grant it, but I might have had no choice if he hadn't. It's a serious matter, Jeremy. If it hadn't been for prosecuting counsel who is not only very good, but also highly ethical and conscientious, it might never have come to light, and there might have been a miscarriage of justice. I find it all very disturbing. In fact, to be frank, it even occurred to me to write to the *Daily Telegraph* about it.'

'Well, it's unfortunate that the police tried to cover it up, Judge, obviously,' Meredith jumps in. 'But all's well that ends well, surely.'

'Except that it wasn't the police,' I reply. 'An Assistant Commissioner of the Metropolitan Police took the trouble to come to court this morning to explain that to me under oath. He said that the decision was made "at a higher level". He didn't know what level, exactly. But all of us in this room know, don't we?'

Jeremy springs back to life. 'Are you saying the Civil Service had something to do with this?' he asks indignantly. 'Because if you are…'

'What I'm saying, Jeremy,' I interrupt, 'is that I don't know whether there was any deliberate malpractice, or whether it was just a case of administrative chaos, too many cooks in the kitchen, that kind of thing. But when the case comes to an end in a day or two, depending on the outcome, I may have to refer the matter to the police for a criminal investigation.'

'That's ridiculous. Even if what you say is true, it's the sort of thing that can be handled internally, by disciplining those responsible.'

'In normal circumstances, perhaps. But where there's been an attempt to conceal evidence that has the potential to embarrass a Minister of the Crown, I'm not so sure. There might be allegations of a cover-up further down the line, and if I let it go people may even say that the Court was involved in it. No, in a case like this a police investigation is fully warranted, and I expect that the officer in the case, DS McGeorge, will be more than happy to take the lead, given that he almost took the blame for something that wasn't his fault.' I pause for effect. 'As

I say, Jeremy, it all depends on how the case ends, and whether anything else comes to light.'

'Does it also depend on what happens in Judge Drake's case?' Meredith asks. I can't help smiling. Say what you like about Meredith, and I often do, she doesn't miss much and she's quick on the uptake.

'Well, obviously, the two matters are closely related,' I reply.

Her jaw drops. 'But that's... that sounds like... with respect, Judge, almost like... blackmail.'

'Not at all,' I say. 'I leave that kind of thing to Sidney Rockwell. No, all I'm saying is that if I have to order an investigation, it might not be the wisest thing for the Minister to force a judge into retirement for blowing the whistle on the same kind of failure of disclosure. It's the kind of thing certain newspapers would have a field day with, isn't it? I'm not trying to pressure anyone, Meredith. I have the Minister's interests at heart, I assure you.'

Meredith is about to reply, when Jeremy cuts her off.

'What are you suggesting, Charles?'

'Jeremy, I don't condone what Hubert did. We all know that sitting judges shouldn't be writing to the newspapers. But I've had a word with Hubert, and he's got the point. He won't be doing it again. I'd like to suggest that you accept that assurance from me, as his RJ, and that we all move on.'

Jeremy drains his teacup and appears to meditate for some time, with Meredith seething silently alongside him.

'If I were to agree to that proposal,' he asks eventually, 'can the Minister expect that you would take a responsible view of how to deal with the failure of disclosure?'

'I hope the Minister understands that I always try to act responsibly,' I reply. 'It's just that being an RJ isn't always an easy job. One has any number of responsibilities at any given time, and sometimes they can appear to conflict.'

We shake hands. Meredith slams her notebook shut, furiously grinding her teeth against the pen in her mouth.

'Would he have to resign?' Jack suddenly asks, 'the Minister, if there was a scandal about his brother?'

A Meredith, Jack is not. Jeremy and Meredith are on their feet, ready to leave, and looking down at the floor.

'I'm no expert on that kind of thing,' I reply. 'But at the very least he might have to ask himself a question or two in the House.'

I call into Hubert's chambers and tell him he's free to take himself off to the Garrick for a drink. I wend my way homeward. The Reverend Mrs Walden and I are dining at the Delights of the Raj this evening. We're taking a break from Italian cuisine for a night or two.

* * *

Thursday morning

It doesn't take a crystal ball to predict what's likely to happen this morning. I foresee that Roderick will ask to address me in the absence of the jury, and that he will say –

'Your Honour, my learned friend Mr Blanquette and I have spent some considerable time discussing the case, yesterday and this morning, and my learned friend has taken further instructions from his client. I understand that Mr Ricci will ask for the indictment to be put again and will offer a plea of guilty to unlawful wounding without intent, on the basis of recklessness.'

'That is correct, your Honour,' Julian chimes in.

'Your Honour, I have also taken instructions, and in the circumstances that plea is acceptable to the Crown.'

I smile benignly.

'Yes, very well, Mr Lofthouse,' I say. 'Let's have the jury back, and the indictment will be put again.'

I've adjourned the case of Luigi Ricci for a pre-sentence report. His plea was well advised. If he'd gone down for the charge on the indictment, wounding with intent, he would be looking at ten to twelve years, but with the lesser charge and the way the evidence has developed it's going to be closer to three or four. I tell the defendant that it's going to depend partly on the impression he makes on the probation officer, as reflected in the report, which it will. I don't expect to see Luigi Ricci back in court, ever; and there's a part of me that feels sorry for him. One way of looking at this case is that he reacted stupidly to events not of his making, and had some really bad luck. But Linda Galloway was stabbed within an inch – actually, within a few millimetres – of her life, and despite the probably terminal damage it will do to the family and to Primavera Toscana, I have no choice but to send him inside for a good while. We can't have people brandishing dangerous items like meat cleavers in public places when people might get hurt.

Not even if they order Insalata Caesar made with mayonnaise.

A RIDGE OF HIGH PRESSURE

A RIDGE OF HIGH PRESSURE

Sunday morning

'Recently,' the Reverend Mrs Walden begins, 'a young man, a member of our congregation, came to me with a page from a popular magazine and complained to me that the magazine had promised him something that hadn't materialised; and he asked me what he should do about it. I'm afraid I told him to grow up and get a life.'

I bet she did, too. The Reverend Mrs Walden has acquired something of a reputation in the diocese of Southwark for dispensing spiritual advice in down-to-earth language that everyone can understand, rather than in the theological platitudes preferred by many of her colleagues. This trait is generally admired, though there are those critics who sometimes find her approach just a little too direct, and those same critics would no doubt find their view confirmed by her treatment of the young man in question, whoever he may be. But if this young man is present this morning, I'm confident that he wouldn't agree with them. He would have found that the Reverend's pithy admonition to grow up and get a life was merely the prelude to some warm and insightful counselling, from which he emerged encouraged, or at least much better informed. The Reverend's sermons are the same way. They sometimes begin with a deliberately administered shock to the system, but go on to offer a good deal of wisdom, and end with a conclusion that most of the congregation couldn't have imagined when she started.

'The page he showed me,' she continues, 'contained an astrological forecast for the coming month, the main feature of which, as far as this young man was concerned, was the prediction that – and I quote – "As a Capricorn, with Neptune currently retrograde and transiting in Pisces trine to the Sun and Venus in Scorpio, you are in line for a new and exotic romantic relationship." Inexplicably, more than two months later no such relationship is anywhere in sight, and the young man says he feels cheated.

'I suppose there are many levels on which one could approach this episode in his life, and perhaps the most obvious one would be to dismiss astrology as a load of hocus-pocus and to conclude that anyone who puts their trust in such nonsense gets everything they deserve. And perhaps you think that my reply to this young man indicates that I was trying to convey just that. I wasn't.

'I have no particular brief for or against astrology, but I don't think that's where the problem lies. After all, if we had an astrologer with us this morning, I suspect that she might reply that you have to read forecasts in a sensible way. There are twelve signs of the Zodiac – so Capricorns make up about one twelfth of the population. But the article gives only one forecast for Capricorn, as it does for each of the other eleven signs. Was the author claiming that all of those millions of Capricorns were destined to start exotic new relationships last month? It seems unlikely, doesn't it? So perhaps you have to read the forecast less literally, in terms of the energetic patterns themselves rather than any particular expression of those patterns. But then, perhaps the author of the column should have made that rather clearer than he did.

'It's been fashionable for more than a hundred years now

for the Church to decry astrology and other esoteric practices as being at best superstitious rubbish and at worst the work of the Devil. But before writing it off entirely, I think we should bear one or two things in mind. In earlier times, all the major religions had respect for astrology and it formed part of their teachings, certainly in the esoteric canons. The Jewish Kabbalah is an essentially astrological construct. Early Islam made wide use of astrology alongside the astronomical, mathematical and medical aspects of its culture. Today, the Hindu Jyotish remains one of the pillars of the wisdom of that religious system. Even in our Christian religion, until relatively recent times many popes and bishops employed astrologers to advise them: the famous seer Nostradamus was such an astrologer who worked for a bishop. The dating of Easter was originally an astrological calculation, as was the start of the Muslim feast of Ramadan.

'And the next time someone on the more evangelical wing of our Church tells you that astrology is contrary to Scripture, you might ask them what the prophet Daniel did for a living. Does anyone remember? No? It's a great pub quiz question, by the way… no? The answer is that he was an astrologer: and apparently he was rather good at it, because he became the chief astrologer to several Persian emperors, from Nebuchadnezzar to Cyrus.

'But as Shakespeare's Cassius rightly reminds us, "The fault, dear Brutus, is not in our stars, but in ourselves." This young man's problem wasn't that he read an over-general astrological forecast in an uncritical way, but that he used the forecast as a way to avoid taking responsibility for his life. He sat back and waited for something to fall into his lap, without any effort or commitment on his part. Whenever we do that, we condemn ourselves to failure. God doesn't want us to sit around all our lives in a passive way, waiting for something good to happen. He wants us to be proactive, with His help, in seeking out good things for ourselves. That's what I meant when I told this young man to get a life. I wasn't trying to be unkind to him. I was trying to get him to see that blaming others for your failures when you haven't made any effort to succeed isn't a productive way to go. This morning, I want to look at some ways in which we can all work on getting a life, or an even better life, by taking responsibility for our own lives and wellbeing…'

As usual, the Reverend is right on point. But what's remarkable about it, as has happened with many of her sermons over the years, is that, sitting in my pew on Sunday morning I not infrequently detect an echo of what awaits me at court on the following morning. How she does it, I don't know, but she often provides insight into a case I'm about to try – and never more so than this week.

***

Monday morning

'May it please your Honour,' Susan Worthington begins, 'I appear for the prosecution in this case. My learned friend Mr Aubrey Brooks represents the defendant, Gerard Busby. Your Honour, I understand that my learned friend Mr Brooks has an application before we swear in a jury, so may I defer to him before we go any further?'

'Yes, Miss Worthington. Mr Brooks?'

'Your Honour,' Aubrey begins, rising to his feet gradually in his usual urbane manner, 'this is a somewhat unusual case, and I have a somewhat unusual application.'

Aubrey is at his elegant best in his trademark double-breasted jacket, and as one of our regulars who himself sits as a recorder from time to time, he has acquired a certain gravitas to go with his understated but potent skills as an advocate. He's going to need it this week, I suspect.

'As your Honour knows, the defendant Mr Busby is charged with a single count of fraud. The prosecution say that Mr Busby dishonestly made a false representation to a woman called Edith Hunter, the alleged misrepresentation being that he had the ability to predict correctly that Mrs Hunter would be successful in obtaining a high-powered job abroad, in Paris. In fact, Mrs Hunter didn't get the job, and in addition to having to resign from the job she had in London, she incurred the expense of renting a flat in Paris for a year. Your Honour, the skill Mr Busby claimed to possess – and indeed does possess, so he instructs me – is that of using astrological techniques to forecast future events with some degree of accuracy.'

'Not, apparently, in this case,' I observe.

'Well, his prediction wasn't fulfilled in this instance,' Aubrey concedes at once. 'Mr Busby doesn't deny that. But that doesn't necessarily mean that what he told Mrs Hunter was false, or that he was acting in any way dishonestly. That is what the jury will have to decide, and my application concerns the jury.

'Mr Busby, quite naturally, wishes to know more about those involved in his trial. As an astrologer, the most natural way for him to do that is to have everyone's natal charts – their birth charts, that is. He would like to prepare charts for your Honour, my learned friend and myself, and most important of all, for the members of the jury. It's a fairly simple procedure, I'm told. Charts can be prepared in a matter of minutes using a computer programme. The information Mr Busby needs to input is each person's date, time, and place of birth.'

I must admit, I'm rather taken aback. I've known Aubrey to make applications that have little chance of success before – he sometimes does it deliberately to draw attention to aspects of the case that may be important later in the trial, or just to wind his opponent up – and this may be one such. But even by that standard, this one is on the edge. Susan takes advantage of my being taken aback to launch an immediate counter-attack.

'Your Honour, this is the most ridiculous application I've ever heard in my life,' she protests in her most severe tone of voice. 'There is no basis whatsoever for asking jurors to divulge that kind of personal information, and it smacks of trying to undermine or intimidate them in some way. For my own part, your Honour, I flatly refuse to supply the information my learned friend is asking for, and if your Honour were to rule that I must, I would ask for an adjournment to allow me to seek professional advice from the Bar Council.'

'I don't know what my learned friend is so upset about,' Aubrey replies. 'All the dates of birth are public information. Jurors provide their dates of birth to the court. In your Honour's case, as in mine, it's available in the current edition of *Who's Who*; and in my learned friend's case, I got it from her chambers website before coming into court this morning. All Mr Busby is seeking additionally is the time and place of birth, and I don't see why that should ruffle any feathers if the date is freely available.'

Susan doesn't immediately spring to her feet again.

'Why does he want the time and place?' I ask.

'Your Honour, he instructs me that the date alone is not precise enough for a detailed assessment of someone's personal traits. A date is a period of twenty-four hours, anywhere in the world. Without knowing the precise time and place of birth, the chart is not specific to the individual and so isn't of much use.'

I have a flashback to yesterday's service and the Reverend Mrs Walden's observation that a twelfth of the world's population are Capricorns. A date doesn't distinguish between them. As she suggested, one size can't fit all.

'In this day and age, your Honour,' Aubrey goes on, 'people are more curious than they used to be about the people with whom they have to deal, and Mr Busby is no exception. Natal charts are what people used as a source of information before we had the internet and social media. It's an older system, but it's one Mr Busby trusts.'

'He's not entitled to subject judges and jurors to that kind of personal intrusion,' Susan insists, 'and that's before you take into account that, as this case shows, his so-called older system is arrant nonsense.'

'It's done in America every day,' Aubrey says.

'What's done in America every day, Mr Brooks?' I ask. 'Are you suggesting that every American court has an astrologer on standby in case someone wants information about the jury?'

Susan turns to Aubrey with a smirk, but he seems unperturbed. 'Not astrologers, your Honour, no. But counsel are allowed to ask jurors all kinds of questions to try to find out what prejudices they may have. In some cases, they have jury consultants to look into the jurors' backgrounds, or even to investigate the demographics of the jury pool in the area.'

'That's not the practice in this country, thank goodness,' Susan intervenes.

'It's the practice to ensure that jurors have no connection to the defendant, or the offence charged, that might affect their ability to be impartial,' Aubrey replies at once. 'We do that all the time.'

'That's not the same thing. You don't need astrology for that. All you have to do is to ask them a few basic questions.'

'It's exactly the same thing,' Aubrey insists, 'and even if your Honour is against me when it comes to the natal charts, I'm going to ask your Honour to question the jury panel about their attitude to astrologers – whether they approve, disapprove, whether they've ever consulted one, whether they read newspaper horoscope columns, and so on. I don't want a juror who thinks that anyone who dabbles in the dark arts is Lucifer incarnate and should be condemned accordingly.'

There is a pause. Susan nods.

'Well, that's a different thing,' she replies. 'I have no objection to your Honour asking the jury panel whether they have a belief or attitude that might get in the way of their giving Mr Busby a fair trial. I don't mind them being asked whether they have ever consulted an astrologer – but with the understanding that the answer does not necessarily disqualify them from sitting on this jury.'

Aubrey nods. 'I can live with that, your Honour. But I would like your Honour's ruling on whether we can ask for their time and place of birth.'

'No,' I reply. 'I'm not going to allow that, Mr Brooks – whatever they may get up to in America. Moreover, I do not propose to divulge that information about myself, or to require Miss Worthington to divulge such information about herself.'

Susan flashes me a grateful smile.

'As your Honour pleases.' Aubrey says. 'I see that your Honour has a sentence listed before we begin the trial. It might save time if my learned friend and I can agree on the wording of the questions, and then, if your Honour approves them, we will ask the jury bailiff to supply them to the jury panel. Hopefully the answers will be available by the time your Honour is ready to start the trial.'

'I agree, your Honour,' Susan says.

'Yes, all right,' I reply. 'Just as a matter of interest, Mr Brooks,' I add as they are making ready to leave court, 'have you supplied the defendant with your date, time and place of birth?'

'Of course, your Honour,' Aubrey positively beams in reply.

The subject of the sentencing hearing is Tony Morales, a resident of Bermondsey old enough to know better, who was convicted in front of me recently of inflicting grievous bodily harm. While drinking and playing pool in the George and Dragon one evening with his mates, Tony encountered a face he didn't recognise, but that turned out to belong to a young man called Owen Wiles. Since he didn't know Wiles, and since he'd downed an impressive number of pints of lager by then, Tony jumped to the conclusion that Owen probably hailed from Lambeth or Vauxhall, or, even worse, somewhere north of the River. It's well known, of course, that no one from outside Bermondsey is allowed in the George and Dragon if they're of an age to drink too much and get involved in fights for the fun of it – that privilege being reserved for Tony, his mates, and other local residents. So Tony and his mates gathered round and suggested that Owen Wiles might like to find somewhere else to drink. Wiles's reply, admittedly, was lacking in factual information and somewhat undiplomatic, but in fairness he probably didn't anticipate Tony's response – which was to crack his pool cue over Wiles's head six or seven times, and to continue the assault by kicking him after Wiles had collapsed to the floor until his mates thought enough was enough and pulled him off.

Owen Wiles was unconscious for some time after arriving at hospital, and was diagnosed with a hairline fracture of the skull, in addition to two broken ribs and numerous lacerations and bruises. He spent several days in hospital, four weeks recovering at home, and was unable to return to work for more than two months. Ironically, Owen was born in Bermondsey, had lived in Bermondsey his entire life, and had been to the George and Dragon any number of times before.

Tony Morales has form for actual bodily harm – an assault on an opposing supporter after a game at Millwall – and driving with excess alcohol, plus a couple of cautions and juvenile findings of guilt for shoplifting and non-residential burglary. Cathy Writtle is representing him, which is a good choice.

Cathy can be a bit excitable, but she's realistic and is not in the habit of making exaggerated claims on her client's behalf. Not that claims of any kind favourable to Tony Morales are easy to come by: the pre-sentence report makes bleak reading. The only glimmer of light, hidden away amid the observations on Tony's apparent aversion to work, growing fondness for alcohol, and generally wayward lifestyle, is what seems to be a genuine attachment to his elderly mother, who suffers from some form of dementia and has recently entered a care home.

Cathy has been around far too long to think that his attachment to his mother is going to get him off the hook for this. Her best point is that she somehow persuaded the jury to acquit Tony of GBH with intent, which would have carried a vastly greater sentence, and to convict him only of the lesser offence of inflicting grievous bodily harm without intent, for which I now have to sentence him. It was a remarkable result that surprised everyone, including Cathy; and today she has put together a seductive proposal involving a suspended sentence with unpaid work and treatment for alcohol addiction, which would leave him at liberty to visit his mother. She presents it with all her usual skill and flair, and I congratulate her on it just before they take Tony Morales down to the cells: but she knows I'm not buying it. I weigh Tony off for four years, which is at least two years less than he deserves. It's slightly on the high side for the sentencing guideline I have to apply, but I don't think the Court of Appeal is going to show any interest in interfering – and neither, I know, does Cathy.

'Members of the jury,' Susan begins after introducing herself and Aubrey to the jury, supplying them with copies of the indictment and explaining it to them. 'This is a classic case of a fraud committed on a gullible victim by a man dishonestly claiming to have supernatural powers. Unfortunately for his victim, Edith Hunter, that claim was untrue, Mr Busby knew it to be untrue, and as result, you will hear, Mrs Hunter suffered not only considerable distress but also a significant financial loss.'

We have a typically mixed Bermondsey jury, mostly fairly young but with two older men of Bangladeshi extraction. While sitting upstairs waiting for me to finish sentencing Tony Morales, they occupied themselves by answering a makeshift questionnaire devised by Susan and Aubrey and approved by me, which asks them the following questions:

1. *Do you know, or have you heard of the defendant, Gerard Busby?*
2. *Do you know a woman called Edith Hunter?*
3. *Have you ever consulted an astrologer?*
4. *If so, when and for what purpose?*
5. *Do you regularly read horoscope columns in newspapers or magazines?*
6. *Do you have any religious or other belief that would make it difficult for you to judge a case fairly and impartially if the case involves astrology?*

All sixteen members of the panel have answered 'no' to questions one and two, and almost all of them have answered 'no' to questions three, five, and six, ignoring question four in consequence. One man discloses that his Auntie Vye used to read tea leaves, though he does not suggest that he benefitted from her skills personally, and confirms that he has never consulted an astrologer. But one woman reveals that she once consulted an astrologer to see whether he could help her find her missing cat, a valuable Siamese. She adds that she found the cat a day later in the kind of place the astrologer had suggested looking for it, but she is objective enough to add that she's not sure whether that was because of his advice, or sheer good fortune. She is confident that she can judge the case fairly.

That's less obviously true, however, of another woman who describes herself as a 'Bible-believing Christian', and is totally opposed to astrologers and any other 'fortune-tellers', whose prospects for the afterlife, she implies, are not to be envied. I agree with Susan and Aubrey that we should excuse her from service in our case, and it seems to cause no problem – we still have fifteen potential jurors from whom to select a jury of twelve. One of the fifteen is an attractive young woman who ends up sitting as juror number four, and who has commented on question six by writing 'live and let live' by way of an answer.

'Members of the jury,' Susan continues, 'in the early part of last year Edith Hunter was working for Girl's Best Friend, which as you may know, is a leading international jewellery retail company with branches throughout the world. She was a senior manager of the company's London retail operation, she was earning a substantial salary and good benefits, and her career prospects seemed bright. Mrs Hunter is married. She and her husband Jim, who is a partner in a City law firm, live in Hampstead. Their daughter, Amber, was away at university in Durham.

'In May of last year, Mrs Hunter was head-hunted by an agent representing Le Chat Bien Paré, a French competitor of Girl's Best Friend, based in Paris. The agent said that she could expect a substantial increase in salary and benefits, in addition to greater responsibility in Le Chat's corporate structure. Mrs Hunter will tell you, members of the jury, that she was attracted to the possibility, not only because of the financial benefits, but also because she was an admirer of Le Chat Bien Paré and rather liked the idea of living in Paris. But she also had one or two concerns. One was her husband's job. Jim wasn't averse to spending some time in Paris – his law firm has an office there – but making arrangements for his transfer would not be straightforward and it would have to be handled delicately. Another concern, of course, was her own job. If it were to become known at Girl's Best Friend that she was talking to a competitor, it would be bound to cause problems for her: indeed, it might well result in her being asked to resign her position immediately.

'At this critical point in her life, members of the jury, a friend told Mrs Hunter about the defendant, Gerard Busby. In fairness, I should say that this friend, a Mrs Wilson, told Mrs Hunter that she had consulted Mr Busby on a matter concerning a personal relationship, and had found him helpful and insightful; and it may be appropriate now for me to say that the Crown does not deny that Mr Busby has satisfied customers to boast of – and indeed he does boast of them freely on his website – but we say, members of the jury, that this is due to his charm and accomplished bedside manner rather than any actual professional skills. Be that as it may, Mrs Hunter visited Mr Busby's website, and reviewed the claims he made about himself and his work.

'Members of the jury, we have printed off copies of three pages taken from Mr Busby's website on Friday, by way of illustration. They are identical to the pages up on the site when Mrs Hunter visited it last year. Your Honour, I understand my learned friend has no objection...'

'None whatsoever,' Aubrey confirms, smiling.

'Then may these pages become Exhibit one? With the usher's assistance, there are copies for your Honour and the jury.'

Dawn, today sporting a bright lime green blouse under her black gown, scurries back and forth, distributing the copies in a matter of seconds. They do make interesting reading. The first page is as follows:

GERARD BUSBY BA (Oxon)
Holder of the Diploma of the College of Astrological Studies of Wales
More than 20 years' Experience as a Professional Astrologer
Gerard applies the millennia-old wisdom of astrology to help you with your problems in all areas of life. Among the questions he can answer are –
Will the man or woman of my dreams come along – and when?
Why am I having problems in my relationship?
Will I get that job I've applied for?
Where is that valuable item I've misplaced?
Should I change career or go back to college?
Should I invest in this new stock?
I have to go to court: what will happen?
Gerard works with couples, as well as individuals

Pages two and three summarise Gerard's successes in various of these areas, including questions about relationships, investments and new careers, and offer a selection of laudatory comments from clients about the accuracy of his predictions, his helpful manner, and his thorough, professional approach.

'Members of the jury,' Susan continues, 'at this critical point in her life, Mrs Hunter decided to consult the defendant. She will tell you that she had reservations about it: she had never done anything of the kind before, and as a well-educated woman, she felt that she was in danger of trying to solve her problems emotionally rather than logically. She will tell you about her visit to Mr Busby's office, which is in his home in Kennington, here in south London. She doesn't remember everything Mr Busby said in a meeting that lasted for more than an hour, members of the jury, but she is clear that Mr Busby advised her as follows: she should pursue the offer of the new job with Le Chat Bien Paré in Paris; she would undoubtedly be offered the job; her husband would be given a transfer to his law firm's Paris office; and she would be very happy with her choice. She remembers repeated references by Mr Busby to the planet Jupiter and her tenth house.'

I glance across to the dock, where I see the defendant nodding.

'By that time, members of the jury, Mrs Hunter had spoken to the agent for Le Chat a number of times, and shortly afterwards she was invited to Paris for an interview. Unfortunately, relying on what Mr Busby had told her, she had made no secret of what was going on at work, and on her return from Paris she was asked to resign her position with Girl's Best Friend with immediate effect. Mrs Hunter wasn't too concerned about that, members of the jury, as it was what she had planned to do anyway. Not only that, but she and her husband took a lease for a year on a flat in Paris, and he duly applied for a transfer to join her there.

'But sadly, members of the jury, her dreams unravelled when the directors of Le Chat Bien Paré decided not to offer her the position, despite the recommendations of their agent, and despite the fact that, in her eyes, at least, the interview had gone well. Suddenly, in a matter of a day or two, she went from being a woman with a good job to a woman out of work and with no immediate prospect of work. Her husband had also made no friends at his law firm with his suddenly announced departure, and it was difficult for him when he had to apply to withdraw his request for a transfer and ask to remain in London. In addition, the Hunters were stuck with a lease for a year on an expensive flat in Paris.

'Members of the jury, the prosecution doesn't seek to avoid the fact that, leaving Mr Busby out of the picture, Mrs Hunter could have handled the situation far better than she did. It would no doubt have been wiser to make sure of the job in Paris before making it known that she had been head-hunted; and surely acquiring a flat could have been done when she knew that the job was on offer. We don't seek to blame Mr Busby for those decisions on her part. What we seek to blame Mr Busby for is this.

'He accepted money from Mrs Hunter – his fee being two hundred and fifty pounds – representing to her that he could accurately predict whether or not she would be offered the job she wanted. That misrepresentation was untrue and he knew it to be untrue, but he falsely and dishonestly assured her that his predictions were based on logic, or, as he put it, on sound astrological wisdom. He preyed on Mrs Hunter's emotional condition and the difficult decisions she had to make, and lulled her into a false sense of security for which there was no logical basis whatsoever.'

I see both Aubrey and the defendant taking copious notes.

'Members of the jury, in due course Mrs Hunter complained to the police, an eventuality Mr Busby apparently failed to predict. DC Trent, the officer in the case who sits behind me, interviewed Mr Busby at the police station in the presence of his solicitor. You will hear the interview read to you. I can summarise it for you quite simply. Mr Busby agreed that he was a practitioner of astrology, and that his work included answering questions calling for some degree of prediction, though he claimed that prediction was only one part of his work. He admitted having read charts for Edith Hunter, and to having predicted that she would be offered the job with Le Chat Bien Paré. He also admitted that Mrs Hunter did not in fact get the job, but he sought to explain that by saying that predictions reflect probabilities and not an absolute guarantee that the predicted event will occur.

'He also suggested that Mrs Hunter had sabotaged her chances of getting the job, and caused difficulties for herself, by the way in which she pre-emptively moved to Paris without waiting for an offer. As I have already said, members of the jury, the prosecution accepts that Mrs Hunter could have handled the situation better. But we say, nonetheless, that Mr Busby predicted her success, that his prediction was dishonest and fraudulent and that he did this in return for a fee of two hundred and fifty pounds. Mr Busby was later arrested and charged.'

Within the next few minutes Susan concludes her opening with a few standard remarks about the burden and standard of proof, and we are ready to begin the evidence. But we're not going to do it immediately. Tony Morales and one or two other interruptions have taken us within striking distance of one o'clock, and we agree to adjourn a bit early. I extend Mr Busby's bail throughout the trial, and rise. And so to lunch, an oasis of calm in a desert of chaos.

A snigger runs round the judicial mess as I enter. Despite having risen early, when I returned to chambers I found several written applications on my desk needing my urgent attention, so I'm the last to arrive.

'Have you got the famous astrology case started?' Marjorie asks. I've been expecting a few humorous asides – the case of Gerard Busby has achieved a certain notoriety at Bermondsey Crown Court – and I'm bound to get some ribbing about it. 'Has Chummy predicted fame and fortune for you?'

'Never mind fame and fortune,' Hubert says with his most annoying grin, 'has he predicted what's on the menu for lunch? That's the real question. The dish of the day is Breton fish pie, by the way. Not bad, but it would take a bit of predicting, wouldn't it?'

'No, Hubert, the real question is whether he's predicted the outcome of the trial,' Legless counters. 'You know, that could be a useful skill. It would save the court a lot of time if he could predict the results of all our cases, and think how much money it would save for the Grey Smoothies. We'd be in their good books forever.'

'Well, obviously he can't do that,' Marjorie insists. 'If he'd predicted that the jury would convict, he would have pleaded guilty early on and made sure of the one-third reduction in his sentence.'

'Well, in that case he must have predicted that he's going to get off,' Hubert replies.

They all laugh.

'Very funny,' I say. 'He hasn't predicted anything, as far as I know, though he did ask us all to tell him when and where we'd been born, so that he could analyse our characters.'

'Did you tell him?' Marjorie asks.

'No, of course not.'

'Oh, you should have, Charlie,' she says. 'It would be fun to see what he has to say about you. Perhaps he sees the Old Bailey in your future.'

'If he sees anything in my future,' I reply, 'it's probably the Grey Smoothies, and I can do without any more of that, thank you.'

'Who's representing him?' Hubert asks.

'Aubrey Brooks.'

'What,' Marjorie says, 'with Susan Worthington prosecuting? I'd pay good money to see that.'

'Aubrey, needless to say, has given Chummy his birth details. He told us.'

'Well, of course,' Marjorie says, 'he probably had no choice if he wanted the case. Chummy would have insisted on making sure they're compatible.'

'Oh, Aubrey would do it anyway,' Legless points out. 'He's so full of himself, and I'm sure Chummy is telling him he's a sure thing for Lord Chief Justice in a few years' time, if he can just get him a not guilty.'

We all laugh at that thought, and the conversation drifts to other topics. At ten to two Stella knocks on the door and comes in.

'Sorry to disturb, Judge Walden,' she says, 'but just to let you know, the Grey Smoothies are going to be here after court – Sir Jeremy and Meredith.'

'You see, Charlie,' Legless says, 'you don't even need an astrologer. You predicted that all on your own.'

'Not by means of astrology,' I reply, 'just the voice of long experience. Did they say what they want?'

'They've received a complaint of religious discrimination,' Stella replies.

I look around the table. 'All right then, who's been mean to the Salvation Army?'

'Not me, Charlie,' Hubert replies. 'I'm always very nice to them.'

'It's in your court, actually, Judge,' Stella says.

'Mine?'

'Yes. One of the women in your jury panel thinks her freedom to express her religion has been denied her.'

I shake my head. Not for the first time, and without any help from Gerard Busby, I predict that it's going to be a long week.

* * *

Monday afternoon

'Mrs Hunter, what is your full name?'

'Edith Dorothy Hunter.'

'Do you live with your husband, Jim, in Hampstead, and is your husband a solicitor and a partner in a law firm in the City?'

'Yes, that's correct.'

'And do you have one daughter, Amber, who's currently

studying for her degree at Durham University?'

'Yes.'

'Mrs Hunter, what do you do for a living?'

Mrs Hunter pauses for some time, appearing rather distressed. She's smartly dressed in a conservative dark blue suit, her makeup neat and understated, but there's no hiding that life has dealt her a blow from which she hasn't yet recovered. She removes a tissue from her handbag, though she doesn't deploy it immediately.

'I'm currently unemployed.'

'How long have you been unemployed?'

'Since September of last year.'

'What was your occupation at that time?'

'I had a senior managerial role with Girl's Best Friend in London.'

'Girl's Best Friend being a well-known international jewellery retail company?'

'Yes.'

'Mrs Hunter, in May of last year, did anyone approach you regarding possible alternative employment?'

'Yes. I was approached by an agent acting for the French jewellery company Le Chat Bien Paré, who asked if I might be interested in relocating to Paris to work for them.'

'You were head-hunted, in effect?'

'Yes.'

'Did the agent give you any information about the salary and terms of employment you could expect with Le Chat Bien Paré?'

'Yes. Putting it bluntly, the salary and perks were considerably better than I was getting with Girl's Best Friend.'

'How did you react to the agent's suggestion?'

She smiles sadly. 'That's not an easy question to answer. I was very attracted to the idea of moving to Paris – my husband and I adore the city, and we both speak French fairly well – and the terms were very generous. Also, Amber had effectively left home, so she wasn't tying us down.' She pauses for some time. 'But we are a two-career family. Jim is a senior partner in his firm. They do have an office in Paris, but he would have to apply for a transfer; it wasn't certain that there would be a position for him, and even if there was, if might not have been at the same level.'

'So this was something of a difficult crossroads in your life?'

'Yes, you could say that.'

'Around that time, did you have a conversation with a friend, whose name, I believe, is Mrs Wilson?'

'Pat Wilson, yes. I've known her for years.'

'Was it within your knowledge that Mrs Wilson had recently been through some marital difficulties?'

'Her husband was having an affair with his secretary, so you could say that, yes.'

Susan glances across at Aubrey. 'Give me a moment, Mrs Hunter: I just want to check that there's no objection to hearsay.'

'None whatsoever, your Honour,' Aubrey replies with a smile. Well, of course not – his client is about to get a ringing endorsement.

'I'm much obliged. Mrs Hunter, did Mrs Wilson tell you about something she had done in that situation?'

'Yes. She said she'd been to see an astrologer, and that he had given her a good deal of insight into her husband and the situation that had developed, and laid out various options for her. She said that she found him very helpful and professional. She gave me his card.'

'I don't think there's any dispute about it. Was the astrologer in question the defendant Mr Busby?'

'Yes, that's correct.'

'What did you decide to do?'

She pauses again, shaking her head. 'I don't know why,

because I'd never had anything to do with fortune-telling of any kind before, but I decided to go and see him. All I can say is that I felt really conflicted, I didn't have much time to think – the agent was pressing me for a quick answer – and I needed to decide what to do. Jim was willing to go with whatever I decided, but he needed to know. I thought, if this man was able to lay out the options for Pat, he might be able to do the same for me. I don't know – looking back it seems mad now – but I thought he might somehow help me to reach a decision.'

'Did you contact Mr Busby?'

'Yes, I called him and explained the situation.'

'How did he respond?'

'He said he would be able to help, he told me his fee would be two hundred and fifty pounds, and he asked me for some information.'

'What information did he ask for?'

'He wanted to know when and where I was born, including the time I was born, and the date and time of the first approach by Le Chat's agent. It was in an email, so I had it available.'

'Did you provide that information to him?'

'Yes, I did.'

'Did Mr Busby explain why he wanted it?'

'Yes. He said he needed it to prepare the astrological charts he would be using.'

'And did you subsequently go to his office in Kennington?'

'Yes. This would be two days after the phone call.'

'What happened during that meeting?'

She thinks for some time. 'He seemed very professional, as Pat had said. He was dressed in a suit and tie. His office seemed tidy and well organised. He had a lot of different papers on the table, including what I took to be astrological charts. We talked for the best part of an hour.'

'Did he put anything in writing for you, or was this just talk, just a discussion between you?'

'No, there was nothing in writing. He did give me a copy of my natal chart, as he called it, but there was nothing else in writing.'

'What advice, if any, did Mr Busby give you regarding your employment situation?'

'He said that I would definitely receive a formal offer from Le Chat, and there was no need to worry about Jim's situation. If I really wanted to make the change I should go ahead and do it.'

'I want to press you about that, Mrs Hunter. You said that he told you that you would "definitely" get an offer? Is that right?'

She hesitates. 'I can't remember whether he used the word "definitely", but he was telling me that it was going to happen – there was no doubt about it, in his mind.'

'I see. I know this may be difficult for you, Mrs Hunter, but can you reconstruct for us at all anything Mr Busby said to explain his prediction that you would get an offer from Le Chat?'

'I didn't pay much attention, to be honest. It went over my head. It all sounded like a load of mumbo-jumbo. The only thing that's stayed with me is that he kept referring to Jupiter...'

'The planet Jupiter?'

'So I assumed – something about Jupiter being in the tenth house of my chart, the house relating to career, and that pattern being repeated in some other chart for the year...'

'Your solar return for the year,' a voice from the dock interjects to aid her memory, 'the chart for the moment of the Sun's return to its natal position.'

'Don't interrupt, please, Mr Busby,' I say.

'I'm sorry, your Honour, but I told her all this at the time – just trying to help.' Aubrey turns and gives him a severe shake of the head, and he subsides.

'That will do, Mr Busby. Miss Worthington?'

Susan is flicking through her notes.

'Thank you, your Honour. Mrs Hunter, did your meeting with Mr Busby play any part in what you did next?'

'Yes, it did.'

'Explain to the jury, please, in what way it affected you.'

'Well, I'd paid the man two hundred and fifty pounds. He'd said that I was going to be offered the job. But I hadn't received an offer. I had an interview scheduled by then, but no offer had been made.'

'Did you believe that whether or not there was an offer depended on the interview?'

'I assumed so, yes.'

'So what difference did Mr Busby's advice make?'

'He persuaded me that it was safe to go ahead.'

'In what sense, safe?'

'In the sense that I would be getting the job.'

'And what steps did you think would be safe to take in reliance on that advice?'

'It was safe to announce to my colleagues at Girl's Best Friend that I would be leaving; to ask Jim to put in for a transfer to Paris; to find a place to live in Paris.'

'And did you do all of those things?'

'Yes, I did.'

'Before you'd received an offer from Le Chat Bien Paré?'

'Yes.'

'And, just to make sure the jury are clear about this, Mrs Hunter, you did these things why?'

'Because Mr Busby told me that I was definitely going to get the job.'

'Let me ask you briefly about the consequences of those steps you took. First, what happened at Girl's Best Friend?'

'That was the end for me. In that business, you can't continue to work once you've told them you're leaving to join a competitor. It's a small industry in some ways. There are too many trade secrets. You have to leave straight away.'

'So you had to resign your position?'

'Yes.'

'What happened with your husband at his firm?'

'It caused him all kinds of grief. His managing partner had gone out on a limb to find him a place in the Paris office, and when he went in and said he was staying after all, people were very upset. They'd even lined up his replacement, and he was moving from somewhere, and so they'd made certain promises to him. It made things very difficult for him.'

'But he did retain his position?'

'Yes, he did.'

'And finally, what about the flat?'

'We were stuck with it. It's a beautiful flat on the Rue des Écoles, not far from the Boulevard St Germain. We had agents looking for us, and they sent us a virtual tour of the flat online. It's lovely: but we had to take a lease for a full year, which didn't seem like a problem at the time, but of course, now is a huge problem.'

'Tell the jury, please, how much you're out of pocket for the rent.'

'The rent is two thousand euros a month. We're trying desperately to sublet it, but we haven't had any luck yet.'

'Thank you, Mrs Hunter,' Susan says, resuming her seat. 'There will be some further questions. Wait there, please.'

But we are given a welcome reprieve by a note from the jury asking for a comfort break. I think we're all grateful for it. I adjourn for fifteen minutes, and when I return I see that Aubrey has a few documents in front of him which, to my admittedly untutored eye, look as though they could be astrological charts. Aubrey looks at the witness for some time, almost as if he is unsure where to start, which, knowing Aubrey, I find very unlikely.

'Mrs Hunter,' he asks eventually, as I'm on the point of asking him if he wouldn't mind beginning, 'when you told everyone at Girl's Best Friend that you were leaving, you were burning your bridges, weren't you?'

'Burning my bridges?'

'There was no way back after that, was there? Wasn't that what you told my learned friend?'

'Oh, I see. Yes, that's true.'

'Your husband could have asked for his transfer after you received an offer, couldn't he?'

'Yes.'

'Another bridge almost burned, would you agree?'

'Yes.'

'And that lovely flat – well, as you said yourself, you're stuck with it, aren't you?'

'Yes.'

'And again, you could have taken the lease after an offer had been made, rather than before?'

'Yes.'

'Mr Busby never advised you to do any of those things, did he?'

'He told me I would get the job.'

'No. Listen to my question, please, Mrs Hunter. Mr Busby never advised you to do any of those things, did he?'

'If you put it like that, no.'

'No. Now, would you look at Exhibit one with me for a moment, please. If you would be so kind, usher…

Dawn is so kind, and hands the exhibit to the witness.

'The jury have copies. These are the pages from Mr Busby's website that my learned friend asked you to produce earlier, aren't they?'

'Yes, that's correct.'

'From which I take it that you had visited Mr Busby's website before you went to meet him?'

'Yes.'

'You see on the first page that after his name, he puts "BA (Oxon)". That refers to the degree of Bachelor of Arts from the University of Oxford, doesn't it?'

'I believe so, yes.'

'You believe so? You're a university graduate yourself, aren't you?'

'I went to Bristol.'

'Perhaps you did, but you know perfectly well what "BA (Oxon)" means, don't you?'

'Yes.'

'Yes. Mrs Hunter, do you have any reason to doubt that Mr Busby holds that degree?'

'No.'

'The same page also states that he holds a diploma from the College of Astrological Studies of Wales. Do you have any reason to doubt that he holds that diploma?'

'No.'

'It goes on to say that Mr Busby has more than twenty years of experience: any reason to doubt that?'

'No.'

'No. The only other information you had about Mr Busby was what your friend Pat Wilson told you; and she said that she found him to be professional and helpful to her: is that right?'

'Yes, she did.'

'And after you'd had your meeting – your reading, as he would call it – with Mr Busby, you felt confident that you would get the job with Le Chat Bien Paré: yes?'

'Yes, I did.'

'I'd like to show you a document, Mrs Hunter, and I

understand that you won't be able to comment on it in any great detail because it's an astrological chart, and I'm sure that, like me, you find such things something of a mystery. But there are one or two things I would like to ask you about it. Usher, if you would, please, there are copies for His Honour, the witness, and the members of the jury.'

Dawn duly obliges.

'This is your natal chart. It's got your birth details, hasn't it? I won't read them out, but the date, time and place of your birth are given there, top left, aren't they?'

'Yes. This is a copy of the chart Mr Busby gave me.'

'Thank you, Mrs Hunter. Exhibit two please, your Honour.'

I assent.

'Now, the chart is drawn in the shape of a circle, isn't it?'

'Yes.'

'And at the top of the circle, there's a vertical line that goes all the way down the middle of the circle, dividing it into two semi-circles, do you see?'

'Yes.'

'And we see a symbol that looks almost like a bridge, with a curved horizontal line above a straight horizontal line. It's actually a representation of a set of scales, a symbol of balance. But do you see what I'm pointing to?'

'Yes.'

'Do you all see, members of the jury?' They nod. 'Now, I'm going to ask you to accept from me that the vertical line represents the start – or cusp – of the tenth house of the chart: are you with me so far?'

She nods. 'Yes, I do remember him saying that.'

'Do you also remember that the symbol on that cusp is the sign of Libra?'

'Yes, I believe so.'

'If we now look in the tenth house, to the left of the vertical line, we see another symbol – this time like the number four, except that the line on the left is curved instead of straight, yes?'

'That's Jupiter.'

'You recognise that symbol?'

'That's what Mr Busby told me.'

'Thank you. Did he explain that Jupiter was in the tenth house of your chart?'

'Yes.'

'And did he also explain that Jupiter was in the same position in your solar return chart for the year – in other words, that Jupiter was making a return to its natal position?'

'I seem to remember something like that. But please understand, I didn't really have any idea what he was talking about.'

'Of course: but you do remember that much?'

'Yes.'

'Mrs Hunter, Mr Busby instructs me that Jupiter operates on a roughly twelve-year cycle in making a return, so one would expect this to happen when one's age is a multiple of twelve. If I may, Mrs Hunter, how old were you at the beginning of this year?'

'Forty-eight.'

'Thank you. I'm not asking you to comment on this, Mrs Hunter, because I don't think it would be fair: but did Mr Busby tell you that a Jupiter return with Jupiter in Libra in the tenth house was a very positive indication for a career move, particularly a move to another country?'

'He told me that I would get the job.'

Aubrey pauses. 'He told you that the charts strongly supported your making the move. That's what he told you, wasn't it? He told you that the charts provided strong evidence that you would get an offer.'

'He told me I would get the job.'

'Well, Mrs Hunter, on his behalf, I must dispute that. Please understand. I'm putting it to you that he said there was strong evidence in the charts, but he never said it was a certainty.'

'He did say that.'

'Did he say that, or was that what you wanted to hear?'

'What do you mean?'

'Oh, come on, Mrs Hunter: a new life in Paris, more money and better perks, a lovely flat near the Boulevard St Germain. You were desperate to say "*oui*" to Le Chat, weren't you?'

'Desperate? No…' but she has hesitated, just for a moment.

'Really? Isn't that why you told Girl's Best Friend straight away? You couldn't wait to be out of there and in Paris, could you?'

'No. That's not true.'

'That's why you leased the flat before you even had an offer. You'd made your mind up that you were going to Paris long before you ever went anywhere near Kennington, hadn't you?'

'No,' she protests.

'How did you behave during the interview with Le Chat Bien Paré?'

She seems momentarily startled by the abrupt change of direction.

'What do you mean?'

'Were you enthusiastic, hesitant? Did you treat it as a formality?'

She hesitates. 'That's what the agent led me to believe, subsequently.'

Aubrey nods.

'I would imagine that you've interviewed a large number of people for jobs in the course of your career, haven't you, Mrs Hunter?'

'A very large number.'

'And what would you think of a candidate who treats the interview as a formality?'

She looks away. Aubrey sits down without waiting for a reply.

Susan asks her a couple of easy questions in re-examination, mainly to ensure that Aubrey hasn't had the last word. She then calls Jim Hunter. He can't add much of any real interest. He's very upset by the whole episode, naturally, but that's mainly because of the embarrassment he suffered at his firm, and the small matter of two thousand euros a month for a flat he will probably never stay in, with no sign of a sub-tenant on the horizon. As to his wife's foray into astrology, he has almost nothing to contribute, for the perfectly good reason that he knew nothing about it until Le Chat Bien Paré pulled the plug on the whole venture by not making her an offer. Apart from the odd comment about 'charlatans' he is largely silent about the whole subject of astrology, and Aubrey wisely lets him go without provoking an argument about it.

Susan then produces some agreed evidence: the lease for the lovely flat in the Rue des Écoles; Mr Busby's receipt for his fee of two hundred and fifty pounds; a letter to Mrs Hunter from the chairman of the board of Girl's Best Friend requiring her immediate resignation and surrender of any trade documents in her possession; Mrs Hunter's letter of resignation in response to same; and a selection of emails between Mrs Hunter and Le Chat's agent tracing the history of the whole ill-starred project. Next she will call the officer in the case, DC Trent, but nobody has the energy for that this afternoon, especially myself with a meeting with the Grey Smoothie High Command to look forward to.

'There's been a complaint from a juror, Charles,' Sir Jeremy begins, 'a woman by the name of Deidre Streeter. She telephoned our office at lunchtime to say that she had been excluded from a jury panel in your court.'

The High Command is out in force. At Sir Jeremy's right hand, literally and figuratively, we have Meredith, today in her light grey suit worn with an off-white scarf and the usual selection of plastic bracelets dangling from her right wrist; and on Meredith's right hand, Jack, the perennial Peter Pan of Grey Smoothie Central, whose suit is always a bit too small and whose tie looks as though the knot was tied by a two-year-old brother during a temper tantrum. But Stella is with me, and we are prepared. Stella quietly hands me a document. It's Deidre Streeter's response to the questionnaire we gave the jury panel for the case of Gerard Busby, and it reads as follows.

1. *Do you know, or have you heard of the defendant, Gerard Busby?*
   No.
2. *Do you know a woman called Edith Hunter?*
   No.
3. *Have you ever consulted an astrologer?*
   I am shocked to be asked such a question. I am a Christian. See answer to question 6.
4. *If so, when and for what purpose?*
   See answer to question 6.
5. *Do you regularly read horoscope columns in newspapers or magazines?*
   See answer to question 6.
6. *Do you have any religious or other belief that would make it difficult for you to judge a case fairly and impartially if the case involves astrology?*
   Yes, I certainly do. I am a Bible-believing Christian, and I believe the word of my Lord and God, which says that fortune-

tellers, witches and the like shall have no place in the Kingdom of Heaven but shall be cast into eternal darkness.

'She's complaining that she was excluded from the jury panel in the case you've just started on the ground of her religious beliefs,' Meredith adds.

'She's absolutely right,' I confirm. 'She was.'

'But you can't...'

'Meredith, did she happen to tell you what the case is about?' I interrupt.

They look at each other, rather shiftily, it seems to me.

'Jack dealt with her, I believe,' Jeremy replies after a pause. Both he and Meredith look in Jack's direction. He makes a momentary effort to adjust his tie, but it's knotted far too tight for that. It's hanging below his collar, and it's not going to move from that position; I'd take odds that he will have to cut it off when he gets home.

'She said it was something to do with her religion,' he replies nervously, 'but she didn't say what it was about, exactly.'

'Allow me to enlighten you,' I say. 'The defendant, a man called Gerard Busby, is charged with fraud, the allegation being that he is, or at least claims to be, a professional astrologer; and that he predicted, wrongly as it turns out, that a female client would get the job of her dreams in Paris.'

Jeremy and Meredith exchange glances.

'Sounds like a rather strange case to find its way to the Crown Court,' Jeremy observes.

'My current view,' I reply, 'is that, if anything, it's a civil case that belongs in the County Court, but because the alleged victim went to the police instead of her solicitor, we're stuck with it here. Actually, I'm not sure it doesn't belong in the Astrologers' Professional Conduct Panel, if there is such a thing.'

I pause. That is exactly what I think. So far, it seems to me that

Gerard Busby may have a somewhat unusual profession, but quite how Susan proposes to translate the events Edith Hunter has related into fraud and dishonesty on his part is eluding me at the moment. But it's early days, I suppose. So –

'Of course, that view may change as the evidence develops,' I add.

'I see,' Jeremy says.

'This is how she answered a few questions we put to the panel,' I say. 'Perhaps you'd like to look at it?' I hand the response to Meredith, and all three of them have a good look.

'I felt that her ability to judge the case fairly and dispassionately might be in question,' I add. 'I have two very experienced counsel in the case, both of whom agreed with me. Under the fraud sentencing guideline, being cast into eternal darkness is a bit on the stiff side for a first offence.'

There is silence for some time.

'She really wanted to serve on a jury,' Meredith ventures without much conviction. 'I understand that.'

'She *is* serving on a jury, Meredith,' Stella replies. 'She's in Judge Dunblane's court, a GBH committed during a pub brawl. Don't worry about her. I'm sure she'll find lots of things to disapprove of in that case, too.'

Sir Jeremy nods. 'We'll write to her and tell her that we're satisfied with the court's decision,' he says.

'How very kind,' I reply.

'But it would probably be a good idea for you to send me a formal written report, Charles – just in case she decides to take it further, you know.'

'Of course,' I reply.

'There is one other thing,' he adds. He reaches out his hand to Meredith, who digs into her briefcase and hands him a copy of the *Standard*. 'This is hot off the press. We noticed it on the way over here. You probably haven't had a chance to see it, but we felt you should – in case you want to say anything to your jury, you know.'

Stella leans over my shoulder so that we can both read it.

'Is this the Trial written in the Stars?' the headline reads. 'Astrologers compete to Predict Verdict in Fraud Case.' It goes on to record the views of six 'leading astrologers', each of whom has obligingly forecast the result of my trial at the close of the first day, without having heard a single word of the evidence. They are going for a not guilty, by a majority of four to two. I shake my head.

'Thank you, Jeremy,' I say. 'Absolutely right. I will have to say something. What on earth are they doing over there at the *Standard*? I've a good mind to report the editor to the Attorney General for contempt of court.'

'I would advise some reflection about that, Charles,' he replies. 'There could be complications: you know how these things are. Let me speak to the Minister and ask him to have a quiet word with the editor. They're old friends. That should do the trick.'

* * *

Tuesday morning

I discuss yesterday's press coverage with Susan and Aubrey before bringing the jury down to court. With George's help, flicking rapidly through the papers on his stall, I think I've established that the likelihood of any real damage is confined to the *Standard*. Today's dailies mention the case, but in a strictly factual way; and between us the Reverend Mrs Walden and I covered the TV news channels yesterday evening. To my relief, both Susan and Aubrey agree – they haven't found anything else similar to the *Standard*'s prediction of the verdict exercise. I allow them every chance to ask me to discharge the jury and start again with a new one in a couple of weeks' time, by which time the present intake of jurors will have departed and will no longer be able to gossip about the case in the jury room. Neither does. I can't say I'm surprised. Susan undoubtedly knows that her case isn't going to improve at the second time of telling. It may even be that by now she's wishing that the CPS had left it to the Astrologers' Professional Conduct Panel. Aubrey must be feeling that his cross-examination of Edith Hunter went as well as he could expect, and he may be contemplating asking me to withdraw the case from the jury once the prosecution closes its case, so a new trial may be the last thing he wants. We settle for my directing the jury to disregard whatever they may come across in the media.

'Members of the jury, you may have seen a report of this case in yesterday evening's *Standard*,' I begin, 'in which a number of persons claiming to be astrologers presented what they claim to be their predictions about the outcome of this trial – in other words, they are claiming to know what verdict you will return. Now, unlike you, not one of these self-proclaimed astrologers has heard a word of the evidence, so it's hardly surprising that they are not even unanimous about it.'

Several members of the jury are looking at me in such a way as to suggest that, not only did they read the *Standard*, but they also disapprove of anyone, astrologers or otherwise, telling them what their verdict should be. It's what I'd expected from a Bermondsey jury; it's a good sign, and I press on.

'Members of the jury, let me repeat what I said just after you were sworn in to try this case. It is your job, and yours alone, to return a verdict. The fact of the matter is that at this early stage of the trial, no one – not even you – knows what the verdict will be. Do your best to avoid coming into contact with media reports of the trial. Remember that you know far more about this case than anyone in the media, so please disregard anything you may see or hear. Remember the oath you took when we swore you in – to return a true verdict in accordance with the evidence. Don't let any outside influences interfere with your consideration of the evidence. The evidence is all that matters.'

The jury seem to react very positively to this, and I assume that we are now ready to proceed with the evidence. But Aubrey has a surprise up his sleeve.

'Your Honour,' he begins, 'I'm very grateful to your Honour for his very clear direction to the jury. But as an astrologer himself, Mr Busby is extremely concerned that others in his profession may be making use of their skills to try to influence the jury – to influence the outcome of the case.'

For a moment I feel some annoyance. Aubrey's already told me that he's not asking for the jury to be discharged, and I've already told him that I'm not referring the article to the Attorney General, so there's no reason for bringing it up again with the jury present. But Aubrey's capacity to amaze me knows few bounds and I certainly wasn't prepared for what comes next.

'Accordingly, your Honour, Mr Busby has prepared his own prediction of the outcome of the trial.'

Susan is on her feet immediately. 'Oh, really, your Honour…'

Aubrey holds up a hand containing a small brown envelope. 'If my learned friend would allow me to finish… Your Honour, Mr Busby does not propose to reveal his prediction. I have not seen it; and as far as I know, no one has seen it apart from Mr Busby himself; it is contained in this envelope, and Mr Busby has no intention of making it known until the trial has been concluded. He would like to entrust the envelope to the court, so that everyone knows that it is secure until then.'

'What on earth is the point of that?' I ask, to vigorous concurring nods of the head from Susan.

'Your Honour, Mr Busby's reputation as a professional astrologer has been impugned in this case. He has been accused of fraud and chicanery. He wishes to point out that the true charlatans are those who publish predictions in the press and so court publicity for themselves at inappropriate times. He instructs me that, professionally, an astrologer may always announce that he has predicted the outcome of some event of interest to the public; but the only ethical way to do that is to keep the prediction under seal until such time as the outcome is known: to do otherwise risks influencing the outcome by improper means, and Mr Busby wishes the jury to understand that he is a professional astrologer to whom professional ethics are important.'

As court clerk, Carol is looking to me for guidance about whether to accept the envelope on the court's behalf. I think for a few seconds.

'Yes, very well, then,' I reply. 'The court will take custody of the envelope. It will not, of course, become an exhibit. I rule that it is not to be opened, or its contents examined, until the trial has ended and the court has approved that course.'

Carol nods to Dawn, who duly takes possession of Mr Busby's as yet unknown prediction of his own fate. Susan is fuming silently, but I can't see any harm in it. If Aubrey had applied to me to discharge the jury I would probably have done it, and I'm not averse to giving something back to him for his forbearance.

DC Lawrence Trent, a distinguished-looking young officer in a very sharp dark grey suit, takes the oath and tells Susan that he is the officer in the case.

'By which you mean that you are the officer in overall charge of the investigation and handling of the case?'

'Yes, Miss. It's my job to look for evidence, to interview witnesses, then to preserve the evidence, consult with the CPS about the charges and disclosure of the evidence, and to stand ready to assist the court about all aspects of the investigation.'

'Yes, thank you. Officer, did your association with this case begin when Edith Hunter came to the police station to make a complaint against Mr Busby?'

'Yes, Miss.'

'What did you do?'

'I took a statement from Mrs Hunter, after which I consulted with the CPS.'

'Is that usual?'

'No. It's a bit early to get the CPS involved in an investigation, but to be perfectly honest I felt a bit out of my depth with this case. I'd never come across anything like it before.'

'I know exactly how you feel,' Susan says. 'What did the CPS have to say about it?'

'They pointed out a few possible charges, and sketched out the kind of evidence I should be looking for, and they advised me to interview Mr Busby and see what he had to say about it.'

'And did you do that?'

'Yes, Miss. I went to Mr Busby's office in Kennington in company with another officer, DC Morgan. I introduced myself to Mr Busby and told him about the complaint made by Mrs Hunter. I asked Mr Busby if he would accompany me voluntarily to the police station for an interview. He agreed immediately, and telephoned his solicitor, asking her to meet us at the station. He agreed to my taking possession of a number of documents pertaining to his work with Mrs Hunter, and his computer. Later that same day, with DC Morgan, I interviewed Mr Busby in the presence of his solicitor, Miss Glasgow.'

'Yes. Just before we come to the interview, was Mr Busby's computer interrogated, and apart from the charts relating to his meeting with Mrs Hunter, is it right to say that nothing of relevance to the present case was found?'

'Yes, Miss, and the computer was returned to him after the interrogation was complete.'

'Thank you. Let's move on to the interview.'

These things are never all that gripping. Most counsel and officers don't have the gift of storytelling, and try as they may to liven it up, the process of reading to the jury a longish interview, one question and answer at a time, is rarely a compelling spectacle. Usually, the jury's attention starts to flag long before they've reached the end, and breaks are often desirable. To be fair, Susan and DC Trent are distinctly above average in this department, and they are aided by the fact that as interviews go, this one is actually quite interesting. The defendant makes no secret of his work as a professional astrologer, a field in which he has been practising, as his website claims, for more than twenty years. He agrees that he had a consultation with Edith Hunter about her prospects of getting the job with Le Chat Bien Paré, and that he advised her that she had an extremely good chance. He doesn't accept that he said or implied that it was certain, suggesting that he doesn't believe we can be certain of anything in this world – a philosophy with which, as a judge, I must admit, I have a good deal of sympathy. He admits that Mrs Hunter did not get the outcome he had predicted, but suggests that had more to do with her haste in rushing to Paris and out of her job in London than with any error on his part. Indeed, he stands by his findings as completely reasonable, given the information she provided.

Susan thanks DC Trent and passes him to Aubrey.

'Officer,' Aubrey begins, 'I just have a couple of questions. First, is it right that Mr Busby is a man of previous good character: he has no cautions or convictions recorded against him?'

'That is correct, sir.'

'Second, would it be fair to say that Mr Busby was cooperative with you from the first moment you approached him, and gave you every assistance in your investigation?'

'He was extremely cooperative and easy to deal with, sir. In fact, I would say he was remarkably open and candid with me at all times.'

'Thank you, Officer.'

This effectively ends the prosecution case, which Susan closes a few minutes later. Aubrey asks me to send the jury out and makes a short and persuasive argument that I should withdraw the case from them. That application can only succeed if either the prosecution has failed to offer any evidence to prove an element of the offence of fraud, or if their evidence as a whole is so tenuous or discredited that it would not be safe to leave the case to the jury. As I told the Grey Smoothies, I'm not at all sure that this case even belongs in the Crown Court. There's no law against practising astrology, and contrary to what the prosecution has sometimes appeared to suggest, the practice of astrology is not fraudulent in itself – if both astrologer and client believe that there is some legitimate value in it, they are free in law to conduct their business. On the other hand, fraud can be committed in the course of almost any human activity and I can't honestly say that there is no evidence to support the prosecution's claim, or that Aubrey has discredited it so thoroughly that there is next to nothing left of it. I can't substitute my own feelings for the opinion of the jury. With some reluctance, I announce that I'm going to leave the case to them.

Aubrey announces that he will call Gerard Busby. Mr Busby makes his way to the witness box, clutching a file of papers. I don't know what I expected an astrologer to look like, but a part of me is surprised by his appearance, a conservative grey suit and a pink tie over a light blue shirt, his hair neatly trimmed. I'm not sure what profession I would assign him to if I had to guess, but I don't think it would be anything as esoteric as astrology.

'Mr Busby,' Aubrey asks, after the defendant has taken the oath and given the court his name – volunteering, without being asked, the date, time and place of his birth – 'if you would look at Exhibit one with me, please. Your Honour, these are the pages downloaded from Mr Busby's website; the jury have copies. Mr Busby, you state that you hold a BA from Oxford University: is that correct?'

'Yes, it is.'

'Which college did you go to?'

'I was at Christ Church.'

'What did you read?'

'Modern history.'

'You also state that you hold a diploma from the College of Astrological Studies of Wales: is that also correct?'

'Yes, it is.'

'Tell the jury a little more about that, if you would. For how long has the college been established?'

'It was founded in 1921.'

'Where is it based?'

'The college has its headquarters in Aberystwyth, but classes are provided at various locations throughout the country.'

'What do you have to do to earn the diploma?'

'It's a one-year course, which is done on a part-time basis, although it's quite intensive. You do twelve complete weekends and one evening a week of classes, with one break during August. It requires a lot of private study, and there's a two-day examination at the end of the course. If you pass the exam, you then have to spend a minimum of forty hours sitting in on consultations with a practitioner.'

'Where did you study for your diploma?'

'In London. I had a part-time job teaching history, to tide me over during the year.'

'Did you successfully complete the course and receive your diploma?'

'Yes.'

Aubrey pauses for a moment. 'Mr Busby, the jury may be interested to know why a man such as yourself, who's been to Oxford and is obviously very bright, chooses to become an astrologer. What do you say about that?'

He laughs. 'If I had a pound for every time I've been asked that… I can only say that I've always been fascinated by astrology – and by astronomy for that matter, which is just the other side of the coin – and I couldn't see myself teaching history for the rest of my life, which seemed to be the other option. So I thought I would at least give it a try and see what happened.'

'And here you are, more than twenty years later. How has your practice gone?'

'I've been fortunate enough to have built up a good client base over the years. I've been very successful. I also teach for the college myself now in London.'

'You also list on your website a number of questions you can answer by the use of astrology: is that right?'

'Yes, though that's not the bulk of my work.'

'Explain that to the jury, please'

'Most of my clients initially come for a natal chart reading, which is based on the chart for the date, time and place of their birth. Many of them are referred to me by therapists and counsellors.'

'Why would therapists send people to see you?'

'Because the natal chart can provide information about the client that might take months to get through conventional talk therapy. The chart gives both therapist and client access to the real issues far more quickly, which is useful for them.'

'But you also do some predictive work, with clients who come to you solely for the answer to a particular question?'

'Yes. Predictive work of that kind is not so common in the West. In India, where they have a very strong predictive astrological tradition, it's the norm; but that's because it's what people are interested in. Will my father recover from his illness? Will I find my missing cow? These are the kinds of practical questions they address. But in the West, less so.'

'But there are predictive techniques in the West?'

'Yes, indeed. The main text is a book called *Christian Astrology*, by a seventeenth-century astrologer, William Lilly.'

'He's an actual historical character?'

'Yes, indeed. When he was in London he lived in a house on the site of what used to be Strand tube station – there's a plaque on the wall to commemorate him. '

'He gave his book an interesting title,' I observe, recalling the Reverend Mrs Walden's sermon. I see the jury smiling.

'A politically astute title, your Honour,' Busby replies. 'By Lilly's time, the Christian churches were losing their attachment to astrology, and you had the Puritans to deal with. Lilly was aware that not everyone would approve of him or his book, and the title offered a certain degree of protection. Actually, he led something of a charmed life.'

'What makes you say that?' I ask.

'He advised both sides during the Civil War at the same time,' he replies. 'He gives us examples of charts he prepared for both Royalist and Commonwealth commanders – and neither side chopped off his head.'

The jury laugh, and I sense them warming to him.

'Remarkable,' I agree, handing him back to Aubrey.

'Mr Busby, how does astrology work?'

He laughs again. 'I only wish I knew. There are almost as many explanations as there are astrologers. Personally, I don't subscribe to physical explanations such as magnetic or gravitational forces acting on the earth. With the exception of the Moon, the bodies we deal with are too far away to make anything like that realistic. In my personal opinion, the closest analogy is with meteorology.'

'What?' Aubrey asks. 'Weather forecasting?'

'Yes.'

'Explain, please.'

'Meteorology and astrology are both based on the study of cycles,' he begins, entering teaching mode. 'By studying recurring patterns in atmospheric conditions, meteorologists have learned that when patterns repeat they tend to produce the same effects in terms of weather. So, for example, experience shows that when you have a trough of low pressure you're likely to have some rain and cooler temperatures, whereas if you get a ridge of high pressure, you're likely to have clear, sunny conditions and higher temperatures.'

'What patterns and cycles does astrology work with?'

'The apparent movements of the Sun, the Moon and the planets relative to the earth, and the angles they form as they move. Scientists also observe these cycles for many different purposes, of course, but astrology is a symbolic science. It goes back, in various forms and across various civilisations, for over two thousand years; and during that time, astrologers have learned to correlate those cycles to our life on earth. But the astrologer's work is more difficult than the meteorologist's.'

'In what way?'

'They don't have to deal with human nature and conduct, which is based on free will and is notoriously unpredictable. We do.'

'All right,' Aubrey says, 'let's come to your consultation with Edith Hunter. What did Mrs Hunter want you to do?'

'She asked me whether she would get a job she'd been approached about in Paris.'

'The job with Le Chat Bien Paré?'

'Yes.'

'When someone asks you a question of that kind, what do you do?'

'The first thing you do with any question is prepare a chart for the date, time and place of the question itself. If the question concerns an event and its date, time and place have been fixed, you also run a chart for the event. She didn't know when she might get the job, so I used the chart for the time of the question. Of course, I also ran her natal chart, with progressions and her solar return for the year.'

'That sounds like a lot of material.'

'As with weather forecasting, the number of indications is important. We look for pieces of evidence pointing to, or away from a particular conclusion. The more evidence you accumulate, the more confidence you have in your conclusion.'

Aubrey nods. 'It sounds like a lot of work, though. I'm asking because the prosecution have placed some emphasis on the fact you charged Mrs Hunter two hundred and fifty pounds. What amount of work is involved in answering a question like this?'

'First, I have to prepare the charts. Actually, the computer does that for me these days, so it doesn't take long. But I still have to study them, and that does take time. I go to Lilly or one of the more modern authors to remind myself of the rules for questions about getting a job. Then I apply the rules to the charts and see what I've got. We're talking about at least two or three hours of preparation, and then I'm going to spend an hour or so with the client, going through it with her. So I don't think my fee is unreasonable. I reduce it sometimes if the client can't afford it, but I've never had any complaints about it.'

'Mr Busby, when you talk about the "rules" for a certain kind of question, what do you mean?'

'Predictive astrology follows well-established rules. Certain combinations of planets and houses, and the aspects – angles – between the planets lead you to certain conclusions. You can get the rules from Lilly, but his language can be difficult for modern readers, so there are more contemporary authors too.'

'Is the kind of question Mrs Hunter asked a complicated one?'

He smiles. 'Actually, no. "Will the client get the job?" is one of the easier ones; the rules are pretty straightforward. You still need to sit down with the client to find out the exact circumstances – the chart won't help much unless you understand what's going on in her life – but the rules themselves aren't difficult. The tricky questions are: "I've lost my cat, or my diamond broach, or what have you: where is it, and will I get it back?" Those can be horribly complicated.'

'Mr Busby, Mrs Hunter told the jury that you had, in effect, predicted that she would certainly get the job in Paris, that there was no doubt about it. Did you say anything like that?'

'No. I did not. You can never answer a question with certainty, any more than the weather forecaster can guarantee the weather. You give your best forecast based on the evidence, but once in a while it doesn't work out as you predict.'

'You might have a ridge of high pressure, but you can still get the occasional thunderstorm?'

'Exactly.'

'Can astrologers simply get it wrong?'

'Of course. Like anyone else we can make mistakes.'

'How could that happen?'

'You can misread the charts or the rules. But more often, it's a case of trying too hard to satisfy the client. You want to give the client an answer, but sometimes the evidence isn't there, or it isn't all pointing one way. Of course, its best just to say so, but there's a temptation to give the client some answer, even if it's not really supported by the evidence. Then, once in a while, the client may have given you bad information, or you've made a mistake inputting the details into the computer, so you're working with an incorrect chart.'

'What happened in Mrs Hunter's case?'

'I gave Mrs Hunter a totally correct opinion based on what

she told me. The evidence in the charts was very strong. I had four concurring pieces of evidence.'

'Without going into detail, did this have to do with Jupiter and the tenth house?'

'It did. Mrs Hunter remembered that correctly. Jupiter in the tenth house is very favourable to a new job, particularly one abroad, and she was having a Jupiter return at the time. Actually, there were four separate indicators across the various charts I was looking at, which was more than enough for the conclusion I reached.'

'You found your ridge of high pressure and you predicted some sunshine?'

'Yes.'

'So why didn't she get the job?'

He shrugs. 'There could be many reasons. Certain things happened after I'd given my prediction that could have altered the course of events. That happens sometimes. Circumstances change, and unless you look at a chart for the changed circumstances your prediction may be overtaken by events. In this case, there was the interview. I didn't know the details of the interview and I didn't have a chart for it. But the way she behaved, treating it as a formality, as you put it to her, and all the rest of it…'

'That may have changed things?'

'It may have. I can't say. That's not astrology, that's about human behaviour. But I stand by the forecast I gave her.'

'Thank you, Mr Busby,' Aubrey concludes. 'Wait there, please.'

It's feeling like a long morning, and by common consent we leave cross-examination until two o'clock. And so to lunch, an oasis of calm in a desert of chaos.

Legless and I are the first two to arrive.

'I'm glad to get you alone for a moment, Charlie,' he says. 'I thought I'd better let you know. I've had a problem with one of my jurors, a woman. I've had to discharge her. I don't think she's very happy about it.'

I feel a slight chill on the back of my neck.

'Not Deidre Streeter, by any chance?' I ask.

He looks at me in surprise. 'Yes, as a matter of fact. How did you know?'

'You're not the first one,' I reply. 'Does she disapprove of pub brawls?'

'She sent me a note just before lunch. I've brought it with me.' He hands it to me.

'Judge, drunkards and brawlers shall not by any means enter into the Kingdom of Heaven. This is the Word of the Lord, and no human court can stand against the Word of the Lord.'

I assure Legless that he has done the right thing in discharging her. But predictably, a message from Sir Jeremy Bagnall is waiting for me when I return to chambers after lunch. He's received another complaint of religious discrimination, and would I kindly consult Judge Dunblane and include our response to it in my report?

* * *

Tuesday afternoon

'So, Mr Busby,' Susan begins, with an unexpected touch of venom, 'what's your prediction for the jury's verdict? What's in the brown envelope you gave to the court?'

Aubrey is on his feet in a flash.

'Your Honour, that's entirely improper, as my learned friend well knows.'

'I don't see why,' Susan persists. 'Presumably he prepared a chart of some kind, and applied Mr Lilly's rules to arrive at his prediction. He's put his working methods before the jury – actually, he's relying on them as part of his defence. The jury should know what conclusion he's reached.'

'As I explained at the time,' Aubrey replies, 'Mr Busby presented the envelope to the court to make a point, namely: that the professional way to present a forecast is to keep it sealed until after the event, unlike those who seek publicity by publishing their findings in the *Standard* before the jury even retires. His prediction is as irrelevant as theirs, as your Honour explained to the jury this morning.'

I nod. 'I'm against you, Miss Worthington. Let's move on, shall we?'

'Yes, your Honour.'

I'm sure she's not too displeased with the result. She must have known I wasn't going to allow her to peek inside the envelope, but she's woken everyone up after lunch, and perhaps even thrown the defendant – and Aubrey – to some extent.

'As a matter of interest, Mr Busby, does Mr Lilly give any rules for forecasting the outcome of trials?'

'Yes, he does.'

'Really?'

'Yes. The law and the court procedures have changed since Lilly's time, obviously, so you have to be careful, but with a little adaptation you can make the rules work very well.'

'Have you ever been asked to predict the outcome of court cases?'

'Yes, many times.'

'Really? With what degree of success?'

'With a great deal of success.'

'So we could do it all without the court, could we, Mr Busby – without any need for His Honour, without any need for the jury? All we need to decide a case is a couple of charts?'

'Your Honour...' Aubrey is on his feet again.

'That's enough, Miss Worthington,' I say. 'Please move on.'

'Yes, your Honour.'

But the witness turns to me. 'Your Honour, if I may explain: yes, we can forecast results, but without access to the people involved in the case, relying solely on charts would be a very dangerous thing to do; and we would give up all the transparency of a public trial. I could never agree to that.'

I nod. 'Neither could I, Mr Busby,' I agree.

I look at Susan. Something about this case is getting to her. She's always a rather combative cross-examiner, but she's not usually given to this kind of personal animus. It occurs to me that perhaps, despite finding it obvious that astrology is bogus, she can't actually find a knock-out punch. In that case, a couple of well-chosen barbs followed by sitting down contemptuously might be the way to go. But if that's the plan, the barbs weren't well chosen, and may even have backfired. The jury seem less than impressed thus far.

'Do you intend your clients to act on the forecasts you provide for them, Mr Busby?'

'I'm not sure what you mean by "intend" them to act. If a client consults me and pays me two hundred and fifty pounds, I tend to assume that the question she's asked is important to her. So I would expect her to take account of my answer, but I wouldn't expect her to ignore whatever else is going on in her life. She knows her own situation better than I do.'

'Your learned counsel criticised Mrs Hunter for letting Girl's Best Friend know about her interest in moving to Paris, and for taking a flat in Paris, didn't he, Mr Busby? Does that criticism reflect your views?'

I see Aubrey rise halfway to his feet to object, but the witness takes the chance away from him.

'Yes, it does,' he replies.

'So you think she acted stupidly?'

He takes a deep breath. 'I wouldn't want to use that word about Mrs Hunter. I don't think she's a stupid woman. But doing those things before she'd even had an interview? I just don't get it.'

'It's tempting fate, is it, Mr Busby? But of course, you'd know all about fate, wouldn't you?'

This time Aubrey makes it to his feet.

'Your Honour, this isn't cross-examination, it's badgering the witness…'

I'm about to agree with him, when –

'No, I'd like to answer that, your Honour,' Busby intervenes. 'I don't deal in "fate", Miss Worthington. My clients have free will, just as we all do.'

'There's no room for "fate" in astrology, then?' I ask him myself.

'There are things we can't change,' he replies. 'For example, in this life I was born a man and I will never have the experience of being a cat. So you could say I'm fated to live the life I have, and not a cat's life. But within the lives we are given, we take decisions of our own free will. So when I supply a forecast for a client, I'm not saying she has to act in a particular way. I'm just giving her information. What she does with that information is up to her.'

'What about when you forecast that someone is going to die?' Susan asks suddenly. 'Do they have free will about that?'

There is a silence for some time, and it feels as if the oxygen has been sucked out of the courtroom.

Then Aubrey says, 'Your Honour, really, this is too much. He hasn't…'

I agree, and at this point, I admit, I'm more than ready to pounce on Susan – but Busby has been staring at her.

'Has something like that happened to someone you know?' he asks her, kindly and gently.

'It happened to my mother,' Susan replies. 'She was diagnosed with cancer and she went to an astrologer, who said...' she stops abruptly. 'I'm sorry, your Honour, I shouldn't have started this line of questioning. I'll stop.'

So that's what's getting to her, that's where the personal animus is coming from. I'm about to invite everyone to move on, when Busby pre-empts us all once again.

'That should never have happened to your mother,' he replies. 'I'm very sorry that it did.'

'She asked him the question,' Susan concedes quietly.

'Let's move on, shall we, Miss Worthington?' I suggest.

'No astrologer has to answer a question just because a client asks it,' Busby replies.

'Would you have answered that question?' I ask, sensing that Susan needs a few moments.

'No, your Honour.'

'Why not?'

'Because my role is to help my clients to make positive decisions about their lives using their free will, and I can't imagine how answering that question would help. And that's before you take into account that even if I see a ridge of high pressure, the weather doesn't always play by the rules.'

'I have nothing further, your Honour,' Susan says.

I give everyone a twenty-minute break. Susan's not the only one who needs some recovery time.

'Your Honour, I call Lydia Howell,' Aubrey says when we resume.

Lydia Howell is a small, energetic, grey-haired woman wearing bright clothes, with a pair of large, garish spectacles dangling from a silver chain around her neck.

'Mrs Howell, do you live in London?'

'Yes, in Islington.'

'What do you do for a living?'

'I'm a professional astrologer.'

'For how long have you been an astrologer?'

'For many years. I graduated from the College of Astrological Studies of Wales in 1972 and I've been in practice ever since.'

'Do you know the defendant, Gerard Busby?'

'I do indeed. I've known him since before he qualified. The college asked me if Gerard could do his hours sitting in on consultations with me, after he'd passed his exams. You have to do forty hours of sitting in before you can get your diploma. He didn't do all forty hours with me. I don't think it's good to spend the whole time with the same person; it does you good to see different styles and different approaches, so I arranged for him to spend some time with other astrologers I knew. But he did the bulk of his hours with me.'

'During that time, did you have the opportunity to assess Mr Busby's ability as an astrologer?'

'Both then and since. Since then we've kept in touch, we've spoken at conferences together, and we both teach for the college from time to time.'

'And what is your opinion of him as a professional astrologer?'

'Gerard is extremely competent. That was obvious even when he was sitting in with me. I always asked him what he thought of the charts before we saw a client, and he was almost always right on the money. Before long, I was letting him conduct part of the reading – with the client's approval, of course. He is a very safe pair of hands. I would trust his judgment implicitly.'

'What do you say about his honesty, his professional integrity?'

'They are of the highest order. I've never had any cause to question them.'

'Thank you, Mrs Howell. Now, did my instructing solicitors ask you to assist by looking at some charts and then answering a question based on those charts?'

'Yes, they did. I've brought them with me if anyone wants to see them.'

'Thank you. Would you tell the jury what you were asked to do?'

'I was given a chart for the time of a question posed to Gerard by a client, together with the client's natal chart with progressions, and her solar return for the year.'

'Was that client a Mrs Edith Hunter?'

'So I've been told since. I wasn't given her name at the time – privacy concerns, you understand.'

'Yes, of course. Do you know Mrs Hunter at all?'

'No, not at all.'

'What was the question asked?'

'The client had asked whether she would get a new job in Paris, about which she had been approached, although no offer had been made to her, and she wanted to know whether it was going to work out for her.'

'Before we go any further, Mrs Howell, did the solicitors tell you why you were being asked to look at these charts?'

'Yes, they explained that Gerard had been charged with fraud in connection with a judgment he had made for a client, and they wanted an independent opinion about the work he had done.'

'Did they tell you what Mr Busby had concluded about the charts?'

'No. They said they wanted my independent opinion.'

'Did you have any communications with Mr Busby about the question?'

'No, of course not. As I say, they wanted my independent opinion.'

'What, if any, conclusion did you reach?'

'Well, please understand that I didn't have the advantage of meeting the client, which I would always do if she were my client…'

'I understand…'

'So I was working only with the charts…'

'But with that reservation…?'

'With that reservation, my opinion was that there was a very high probability that she would get the job.'

'Was it certain?'

'That's a word I don't use. Certainty doesn't exist. There was a very high probability.'

'I'm not going to ask for your reasoning, Mrs Howell, but are you ready to explain how you reached your conclusion if anyone wants you to?'

'Yes, of course.'

'Thank you very much, Mrs Howell. Wait there please.'

'I have no questions, your Honour,' Susan says after some thought.

We have some time left before we have to adjourn for the day; but we're ready for closing speeches now, Susan has to go first, and I'm not sure she's in the right frame of mind to do it this afternoon. She looks thoroughly miserable. I tell the jury that for administrative reasons we can't go any further today, and release them until tomorrow morning.

* * *

Wednesday morning

'My Nan used to read people's palms,' Elsie says, as she wraps up my ham and cheese bap, following a lengthy discussion of the case while she was assembling it.

'What kind of things did she tell them?' Jeanie asks, handing me my latte and taking my money.

'Well, the usual things – you know, they were going to meet a tall, dark stranger, or they were going to win the pools. They never did, of course, but they all thought it was very interesting.'

'My auntie Nell did the Tarot cards,' Jeanie says.

'Oh yes?' I say, 'and what kind of things did she predict?'

'The same as Elsie's Nan, as far as I remember, sir, though in Auntie Nell's case someone actually did win the pools.'

'You're joking,' Elsie protests.

'No, she did. I mean, it wasn't the whole thing, the million pounds or whatever it was if you got all the results right. But she had five draws on the coupon, so she won a fair bit, didn't she? Enough to keep her in Guinness for a while, let's put it that way. Of course, everybody started coming to see auntie Nell after that; but nobody won anything else, so they left her alone eventually.'

'You got it all sorted, guv, did you?' George asks as I hand over my change to pay for *The Times*. 'It was a bit naughty of the *Standard* to put all that stuff in there with your trial going on, wasn't it?'

'It was indeed,' I agree.

'If you ask me, guv, the *Standard* hasn't been the same since they started giving it away for free. In the old days, when you had to pay for it, it was all right, wasn't it? And in those days you could always buy the *News* if you didn't fancy the *Standard*, couldn't you? But ever since they stopped charging for it – I don't know, but it's just not the same, if you know what I mean. Perhaps it's all the advertising.'

'Perhaps it is,' I say.

'I tell you what, guv,' he adds, 'what you ought to do is have all those astrologers, or whatever they call themselves, hauled up before you for contempt of court. Then, you could ask them to predict what sentence you were going to give them, and you could give them more than they were expecting. You could have a right laugh with them, couldn't you?'

Susan still isn't quite herself, but she makes a brave show of it. She's brief and to the point and, actually, quite effective. She avoids the mistake of launching a full-scale attack on astrology and concentrates on the case at hand. The moment Gerard Busby accepts two hundred and fifty pounds from Edith Hunter to predict the obvious, she argues, he must take responsibility for the certainty of success he plants in her mind. And it was always a good bet that he'd be proved right, wasn't it?

'I mean, come on, members of the jury, she'd been head-hunted for goodness sake. It doesn't take an astrologer to forecast that the job is as good as hers, does it, when an agent has been plying her with offers of more money and better perks and an idyllic new life in Paris? You and I would reach the same conclusion after chatting with her for five minutes, wouldn't we, using nothing more than our common sense? We wouldn't need to consult the stars, would we?'

But once he takes her money and talks to her about the charts, Susan argues, he steps into the shoes of Le Chat Bien Paré's agent, he takes over where the agent left off. Now Gerard Busby is the one making all the promises, the one seducing her with the prospect of this wonderful change in her fortunes. And once he does that, he has to take responsibility for her reaction to the promises he makes, because in promising her that her fortune is written in the stars, he invests common sense with an aura of scientific method that it doesn't have. Left to her own devices, left to her own common sense, Edith Hunter would have been more circumspect, wouldn't she? She wouldn't have counted her chickens before they hatched. But if your fate is written in the stars, you can assume that they're already hatched and running around the yard, and you can start buying the ingredients for your Chicken Kiev.

Except, you can't: because if you do, you risk sabotaging the result in the real world, because if there's one thing that's going to kill an interview it's treating it as a formality and being arrogant enough to assume that the job is already yours.

In all probability, that's what happened to Edith Hunter, just as the defence said. But unlike the defence, we say that the blame falls fairly and squarely on Gerard Busby, not on Edith Hunter. The blame falls on Gerard Busby because he's the one who took an obviously likely event and placed on it the spurious seal of inevitability offered by this pseudo-science of astrology. He knew what he was doing, and what he was doing was dishonest and fraudulent. Turning Aubrey's strong point back on him is clever, and effective, and for the first time for a while, the case seems to swing back somewhat towards the prosecution's side.

'Gerard Busby is not on trial for being an astrologer,' Aubrey reminds the jury.

For the moment, that's as far as he's going to get. I haven't paid much attention to the public gallery, which is quite crowded this morning after all the publicity the case has attracted. If I had, I would have recognised a familiar face. As it is, the first thing I'm aware of is her voice, which isn't familiar, shouting very loudly. Then I see that she's holding a home-made banner, a huge sheet of paper she must have rolled up and secreted into the building inside her coat. Its message, scrawled untidily in a bright red marker is, 'Christians have rights too! End discrimination!'

'Christians have a right to serve on juries!' Deidre Streeter is screaming at the top of her voice. 'But I've been slung off two juries in two days. This is blatant religious discrimination!'

'That will do, Mrs Streeter,' I say. 'Either you will leave court at once, or I will hold you in contempt and have you arrested.'

'You can't do that to me,' she replies. 'I know my rights.'

Dawn is following her training and leading the jury quickly out of court. I see Carol pressing the button under her desk, which will bring security to our aid in a minute or two.

'He should be put away,' Deidre continues to bellow. 'What

do you need a trial for? Those who practise fortune-telling and devilry shall be cast into eternal darkness!'

I give it a few seconds, but she's showing no sign of stopping. It has its funny side, I suppose, if you like that kind of thing – a woman who's perfectly happy to condemn people without trial, ranting on and on endlessly about discrimination because we won't let her serve on a jury; while the other occupants of the public gallery remain frozen in their seats, staring straight ahead of them, unsure whether to ignore her, try to intervene somehow, or make a run for it. But I'm afraid, if I ever had any sense of humour about Deidre Streeter, it has long since evaporated.

'Detective Constable Trent,' I almost shout over the din. 'I'm holding Mrs Streeter in contempt of court. Will you please assist the court by detaining her until the security staff can take her down to the cells?'

'Yes, your Honour.'

'I will rise for a few moments,' I say, as DC Trent provokes fresh outbursts by restraining her. 'I will deal with her after court this afternoon. She will remain in custody until then.'

'I think Emily Phipson is at court, Judge,' Carol says. 'Shall I ask whether she would represent Mrs Streeter *pro bono*?'

'Good idea,' I agree.

'Gerard Busby is not on trial for being an astrologer', Aubrey reminds the jury for the second time, order having now been restored thanks to the joint efforts of DC Trent and security. The jury don't seem fazed by the outburst they were exposed to, but I've directed them to ignore it, just in case. 'He's not on trial for practising as an astrologer, and he's not on trial for accepting a fee of two hundred and fifty pounds for rendering an astrological opinion. He's on trial because the prosecution say he acted dishonestly and fraudulently. But where is the dishonesty? Where is the fraud?

'The practice of astrology is a lawful occupation, in which people have engaged for centuries. We may disagree about whether there is any validity in astrology, but not about the principle that people are free to decide that question for themselves. I'm not asking you to approve of what Mr Busby does, only to remember that there are those who do, and they have the right to consult people like Gerard Busby and Lydia Howell if they wish. Otherwise, how could we allow practitioners of alternative medicine – practitioners of acupuncture, of chiropractic, of homeopathy, to treat patients? For that matter, how could we allow priests, or ministers, or rabbis, or imams to counsel people and offer them spiritual comfort and guidance? Because there are as many people who are sceptical about all of those practices as there are those who are sceptical about astrology. The point is that in a free society, we allow people to believe in things we may not believe in ourselves.'

There's not a shred of evidence, Aubrey continues, that Gerard Busby acted in any way dishonestly. If he were taking money from clients, not caring whether what he told them had any basis or not, not caring whether his answers to the questions they asked were right or wrong, is it conceivable that he could have been carrying on his practice for more than twenty years, that he could have got away with it for so long, that he could have built up and maintained such a loyal clientele? Wouldn't he inevitably have been exposed years ago?

'And what of the prosecution's claim that Mr Busby told Edith Hunter that it was a certainty that she would get the job? Members of the jury, Mr Busby has answered that more than once in the course of this trial, hasn't he? He told you that he never gives his clients answers with absolute certainty, because he can't – and any honest professional, be he a lawyer, a doctor, a priest, or a practitioner in any field will tell you the same: that's just not how life works. Certainty doesn't exist in human affairs, members of the jury: all we have are degrees of probability, and that applies in this trial as much as it does in any other area of life. When he sums the case up to you, His Honour will tell you that the law itself makes that very same assumption. The law requires a high standard of proof to be satisfied before anyone can be convicted of a crime; but it doesn't rise to the level of absolute certainty, because we can't attain that level.

'My learned friend Miss Worthington told you that Mr Busby took a fee from Edith Hunter for "predicting the obvious". Well, members of the jury, many things can seem obvious to those who aren't intimately involved with them, can't they? But if it's your life and you have very serious, and perhaps irrevocable decisions to make, things have a way of looking less obvious to you than they might to those around you. So it's not totally surprising, is it, that Mrs Hunter wasn't as sure of her ground as Miss Worthington seems to be; it's not surprising, is it, that she wanted an opinion from someone uninvolved in the emotion of it all, someone who could stand back and look at the situation more objectively? And at the end of the day, members of the jury, let's not forget that this event that my learned friend says was so "obvious" did not in fact occur.

'During her cross-examination of Mr Busby, my learned friend challenged him to call Mrs Hunter "stupid" for telling her existing employers about her intention to leave, for taking a lease on an expensive flat in Paris before any offer had been made, and for treating her interview as a "formality". Perhaps out of politeness, Mr Busby was reluctant to apply the word "stupid" to what she did. But it doesn't matter what you call it. Call it stupidity, call it ill advised, call it whatever you like: Gerard Busby did not advise Edith Hunter to do any of those things. She made those decisions using her own free will, all on her own.

'If Gerard Busby gave Edith Hunter an answer to her question in good faith, he wasn't dishonest and he wasn't fraudulent; and having heard Gerard Busby and Lydia Howell talk about their work, isn't it clear that, whatever else they may be, they are people of good faith? You've seen Mr Busby and heard him in the witness box. You know that he's a man of good character, and you've heard Lydia Howell, a woman who has known him well for a long time and was partly responsible for his training, say that Mr Busby is not only a highly competent astrologer, but perhaps more importantly, an honest man, a man of integrity. I hope that having seen and heard him yourselves, you have drawn the same conclusion.'

When my turn comes, I keep it as simple as I can. I've decided to steer clear of the formula the Court of Appeal prefers judges to use when explaining the standard of proof. The Court of Appeal likes judges to tell juries that they have to be 'sure' of guilt before they convict – as opposed, that is, to being 'absolutely certain'. In the rarefied atmosphere inhabited by the Court of Appeal there's a difference. But even if there is, it's a lot to expect a jury to absorb at the best of times, and this jury has heard quite enough about certainty, or the lack thereof, already in this trial. So today I'm winding the clock back and using some well-tried older language, and if the Court of Appeal doesn't like it, I'm afraid that's just too bad.

'As Mr Brooks has rightly told you,' I direct them, 'this case isn't about astrology: it's about an allegation of fraud, an allegation of dishonesty; and you can only convict Mr Busby if the prosecution has proved fraud and dishonesty beyond any reasonable doubt. If you have any reasonable doubt about whether Mr Busby has been guilty of fraud and dishonesty, your verdict must be one of not guilty.'

It's nearly lunchtime by the time I conclude the summing-up and send the jury out to start work, but I'm satisfied that they understand the standard of proof.

* * *

Wednesday afternoon

Stella has thoughtfully held back some bail applications and plea and case management hearings for me so that I don't become bored by having nothing to do during the afternoon. But I'm fully expecting to bring the jury back to court at some point this afternoon, to give them a further direction about the law. It's common in fraud cases for juries to have problems with the words 'dishonest', 'misrepresentation' and 'fraud'. It's odd – or perhaps it isn't – that jurors often have the most difficulty, not with the most abstruse legal terms, but with those that are also words in everyday use in the English language. They often send a note asking what exactly those words mean – and it's a strangely difficult question to answer. But in this case, the note never comes. Instead, at four o'clock when I release them for the day, the jury give every impression that they are making good progress, and are looking forward to resuming deliberations tomorrow morning.

I have Deidre Streeter brought up from the cells. She's had a conference with Emily Phipson, but has decided to represent herself rather than accept Emily's kind offer of a *pro bono* defence. It's not altogether surprising. Emily would have left her in no doubt that she doesn't have a leg to stand on, and that she should offer the court an apology. I doubt that such sage advice holds much appeal for Deidre.

'Mrs Streeter,' I begin, 'earlier you disrupted a trial in this court and had to be removed to the cells so that the trial could continue. I held you in contempt of court, and this is your opportunity to tell me why I should not impose some punishment on you, which might include imprisonment. I understand that you were offered a barrister to represent you, but you prefer to represent yourself: is that correct?'

'Yes: that's correct.'

'All right. What do you want to say to me?'

'I don't want to say anything to you, except that I have my principles, and I believe that as a Christian I should be entitled to serve on a jury and express my views.'

'You had the chance to serve on two juries,' I point out, 'and in each case you made it clear to the court that you were not prepared to judge the case fairly, on the basis of the evidence; you made it clear that you couldn't be fair to the defendant.'

'All I made clear to the court was that, as a Christian, certain things, such as fortune-telling and carousing, are not acceptable to the Lord. I was exercising my right to express my religious beliefs. I don't expect you to understand.'

'As it happens,' I reply, 'I do have some understanding of religious expression. I understand that you have your principles. But I also have my principles – one of which is that when defendants come before the courts, they are entitled to a fair trial by an impartial jury, and another of which is that the courts must be free to do their work without disruption. Are you prepared to apologise for your behaviour in disrupting the trial?'

'I have nothing to apologise for. I am doing the will of the Lord my God. Evil-doers will be cast out into eternal darkness.'

From her tone I'm sure she's expecting the martyrdom of a prison sentence, but I'm not going to give her the satisfaction. Neither am I going to give her any more of the court's time as a platform to condemn evil-doers.

'Mrs Streeter, you are a woman of previous good character, and I'm going to assume that what happened today was an isolated case of bad judgment. In those circumstances I'm going to discharge you conditionally for twelve months. That means that if you commit no further offence during the next twelve months, you will hear no more about this: it's over and you can put it behind you. On the other hand, of course, if you should commit a further offence, you may be brought back and sentenced for this offence of contempt in addition to being prosecuted for the new offence. Do you understand?'

She nods silently.

'Very well. I should also make it clear that your term of jury service at this court is now over, with immediate effect.'

As I'm leaving court and the officer is releasing her from the dock, I add, 'Oh, by the way, Mrs Streeter, do you by any chance happen to know what the prophet Daniel did for a living?'

I decide not to wait for a reply.

* * *

Thursday morning

This morning I'm told that we have six or seven protesters outside the main entrance to the court, carrying placards protesting against the court's suppression of religious freedom and its generally godless approach to our public life. Opposite them are three or four secularists demanding an end to religious privilege in the courts. Neither group has made any attempt to enter the building and there's no sign of Deidre Streeter, so security aren't worried about them. After yesterday they're on the lookout for anyone trying to smuggle a placard into court, but no one has attempted it yet. Arriving in chambers and taking a first sip of my latte, I find a message from Sir Jeremy Bagnall. There's been a further complaint, it seems, this time about a woman being dragged down to the cells and held in captivity for several hours for expressing her religious beliefs, and would I kindly address this episode also in my formal written report?

Initially all goes according to my expectations. I send the jury back out at ten o'clock, and start on the day's applications. At ten forty-five, Dawn approaches and indicates that the jury are ready to return a verdict. I rise and return to chambers for a few minutes to give Carol and Dawn time to prepare the courtroom. Carol knocks and comes in, but instead of the cheerful invitation to return to court to take the verdict, she looks rather worried.

'Judge, I'm sorry, but counsel say they have to see you in chambers before we bring the jury back down. It's something very sensitive.'

She's right to look worried. Whenever counsel say that they want to mention something 'very sensitive', what they mean is that something has gone seriously wrong. I suddenly have a very bad feeling about it. I ask Carol to invite them to join us. She does, bringing her hand-held recording device with her. We all sit down, and Carol puts the date and time on tape before handing over to Susan.

'The officer in the case, DC Trent, brought this to me a short time ago,' Susan says. 'I've shown it to Aubrey, of course, and we agreed that we had to bring it to you immediately, before any further steps are taken in the trial.'

She hands me what appears to be a hand-written note, several lines in length, written in blue ink on a piece of white paper torn from a note pad of some kind. It is accompanied by a small white envelope, on the front of which the name 'DC Trent' appears in the same handwriting as the note itself. My assumption is that this is a further assault on the trial by Mrs Streeter and her cohorts. If they've tried to interfere with the jury, of course, it's going to be considerably more serious than causing a scene in court. I'm bracing myself accordingly. But in fact, the note reads as follows:

Dear DC Trent,

I've never done anything like this before, but I feel I have to now. I'm Julie, juror number four, the brunette on the front row. I don't know whether you've noticed, but we've been on the same tube train coming to court two or three times, and I've nodded and said good morning to you. The thing is, I really fancy you, and I want to see you away from court. Would you like to call or text me once the case is over, and we could go out for a coffee or a drink?

It concludes with Julie's signature followed by an xx, and her home and mobile numbers, accompanied by a couple of heart symbols and what I believe is termed a smiley-face.

I close my eyes. 'Live and let live,' I mutter.

'I'm sorry, Judge?' Susan says.

'Nothing.' I pause for some time. 'Am I going to have to discharge the jury?'

'I would say yes, Judge,' Aubrey replies immediately. 'There's obviously a strong attraction on this young woman's part to DC Trent, and that may well have translated into some sympathy for the prosecution.'

'Not necessarily, Aubrey,' Susan insists. 'There's no reason to think she's incapable of trying the case fairly – she's asking to see him after the case is over, and there's no suggestion that any other members of the jury know about it. Worst case scenario, we discharge her and continue with the remaining eleven.'

'Even so…' Aubrey replies.

'Even so,' I say, 'I need to find out what's been going on. Carol, I'm going to sit in chambers and hear evidence in the absence of the jury and the public.'

'Right you are, Judge.'

'I'll start with DC Trent; but before Dawn goes to get him, she is to go upstairs to the jury room and separate Julie from the other jurors and hold her somewhere else until we're ready for her. Make sure Dawn understands that she's not to tell Julie or the other jurors why. We need to cut off any further possibility of discussion about this if we can – although I have a terrible feeling that we're closing the stable door after the horse has bolted.'

'It's probably already galloping down through Kent,' Aubrey observes pessimistically. I can't help feeling a bit sorry for him. He must feel that the trial has been going his way and I'm sure he'd like to continue, but he can't take a risk like this.

'Judge,' Susan says as Carol leaves to make the arrangements, 'they've already reached a verdict. I see no reason not to take it. If you want to deal with Julie for contempt, you can still do that later.'

I shake my head. 'I need to find out what's going on,' I insist.

'Detective Constable Trent,' I begin after he's taken the oath, 'how did you come into possession of this note?'

'I'm based at Bermondsey Police Station, your Honour, and I called into the nick on my way to court this morning. The desk sergeant told me it had been delivered for me a few minutes earlier by a young woman. The sergeant said she didn't leave her name, but his description of her is consistent with juror number four.'

'You do understand the implications of this?'

'Yes, sir.'

'Good. With that in mind, Officer, has there been any contact between juror number four and yourself out of court?'

'I do remember seeing her on the tube yesterday morning, sir. She wished me a good morning. I nodded in return, but then I moved away down the carriage to avoid any further contact. Apparently, she thinks she's seen me on the tube more than once. That's certainly possible, but I honestly don't remember anything except that one occasion.'

'Officer, has there been any romantic contact, or any planning of any romantic contact between you?'

'No, your Honour, none of any kind.'

DC Trent's manner is sincerity itself, and I believe him completely. But there's also a gleam in his eye which suggests that the answer to that question may well be different a week from now.

Julie Burke is brought down to court alone, without her colleagues on the jury. She is distressed and tearful, and by now, fully aware of the trouble she's got herself in. She goes into the witness box and takes the oath, handkerchief in hand.

'There is to be no mention of what verdict the jury may have arrived at,' I begin. 'Is that clearly understood?'

'Yes, sir.'

'Miss Burke, do you remember the directions I gave the jury at the start of the trial?'

'Yes, sir.'

'Do you remember my saying that you were not to approach anyone in the case, and not to allow anyone to approach you?'

'Yes, sir.'

'You will find a note and envelope in front of you. Are they in your handwriting?'

'Yes, sir.'

'Did you deliver them to Bermondsey Police Station for Detective Constable Trent this morning?'

'Yes, sir.'

I shake my head. 'Would you mind explaining why you disobeyed the court's instructions in this way?'

She breaks down and cries for some time. I would like to summon up some sympathy for her in her embarrassment, but at the moment I can't. The consequences of her approach to DC Trent are just too serious.

'I didn't think it could do any harm,' she replies eventually, making liberal use of the handkerchief. 'We'd actually agreed on our verdict yesterday afternoon. If you'd given us another half-hour, we might have returned the verdict then. But it was time to go home. So we waited, and told Dawn we were ready this morning after we'd had a cup of coffee. But I thought the trial was over, so it couldn't do any harm.'

Susan is looking at me. I think for some time.

'Miss Burke, has your attraction for DC Trent affected your view of the case, influenced how you thought about the verdict, in any way?'

She looks genuinely surprised by the question.

'What, you mean, made me take the side of the police or the prosecution? No. Of course not. When we discussed the case, I said what I thought. It had nothing to do with it.'

For just a moment I think I see a chink of light. But one more question is required before I can be sure.

'All right. Please think about this very carefully indeed, Miss Burke. Have you discussed your feelings for DC Trent with any of the other members of the jury?'

'Only the women,' she replies. 'We all thought DC Trent was rather dishy.'

The chink of light is extinguished as quickly as it was born. I ask Dawn to take her back upstairs and reunite her with the four other women and the seven men serving on the jury. I look questioningly at counsel.

'I say this with some regret, your Honour,' Aubrey begins, 'but I'm afraid I see no alternative to discharging the jury.'

'She said her interest in DC Trent didn't affect her view of the evidence,' Susan replies, though there is little conviction left in her voice now.

'She also said that all the women on the jury had something of a collective attraction to DC Trent,' Aubrey points out. 'If your Honour were to leave it up to me, I would have to ask your Honour to discharge them.'

'I'm not going to leave it up to you, Mr Brooks,' I reply. 'I don't think that would be fair. It's my responsibility to ensure that Mr Busby has a fair trial.'

'Your Honour,' Susan asks tentatively, 'if we could at least ask the jury, not to return a verdict, but what the verdict would have been, it might be of assistance to me in advising the CPS whether the prosecution should proceed with a re-trial.'

'Tempting, Miss Worthington,' I reply, 'but I'm afraid not. Sadly, the jury must take the verdict with them to wherever they may go when they leave court.'

I ask Dawn to bring the jury down to court, announce that we are now back in open court, and advise them that for reasons I'm not allowed to go into – although by now, I have no illusion that there's any secret about it – I have decided to discharge them from returning a verdict. I thank them for their service and try to assure them that their work has not been entirely wasted, a form of words we tend to use on these occasions to make juries feel better about their experience – and indeed, it is often true, though I have some difficulty in believing so in this case. I ask Julie Burke to remain behind, and explain to her that she will receive a summons to appear back at court in a week or two to show cause why she should not be dealt with for contempt of court. I add that she would be well advised to bring her solicitor with her. I allow Susan the usual seven days to consult with the CPS and decide whether or not the prosecution wishes to retry the case, and extend Mr Busby's bail until then. I ask Carol to invite Susan and Aubrey into chambers for coffee.

'I must apologise for my meltdown in court yesterday, Judge,' Susan says once we're alone with the coffee.

'Please don't worry about it,' I say. 'These things happen; there are times when a case gets to all of us, and you were dealing with a very difficult cross-examination.'

'Even so, I should have kept my cool. It's just that my mother was never the same once that astrologer told her that the cancer was going to kill her. It was almost as if she gave up.'

We are silent for a few seconds.

'On the other hand, Susan,' Aubrey says kindly, 'doctors say that kind of thing all the time, too, don't they? I suppose someone has to, sometimes.' Susan nods. 'Actually, I talked with Busby about what you'd said, and he was really horrified. He said that whoever said that to your mother crossed a red line. There would have to be a very, very good reason to tell a client she's dying, and he can't think of one.'

The silence is longer this time. I decide to break it. I open the middle drawer of my desk, where I know Carol has left the infamous brown envelope.

'Come on,' I say, 'if we can't have the real verdict, we can at least have Mr Busby's prediction of it. Let's see who's better at predicting verdicts, lawyers or astrologers. What do you think?'

'Not guilty,' Susan replies at once.

'Not guilty, I agree,' Aubrey says.

'Then we're unanimous,' I say, opening the envelope. 'Let's see whether Mr Busby agrees.'

I open the envelope and extract a single sheet of A4, on which the defendant has printed out the following from his computer.

Bermondsey Crown Court
The Queen v. Gerard Busby

I prepared a chart for the first moment of the trial, which I took to be the moment when the jury was sworn in. Following Lilly's rules for forecasting the outcome of trials, I assigned the Moon to represent the jury. The Moon is in the 12th house of the chart, with challenging aspects to both malefics, Mars and Saturn. Mercury, representing clear communication, is also in difficult aspect to the Moon and has just gone retrograde. There are also indications of some external disruption of the trial. Although the chart is relatively favourable to the defence, and a verdict of not guilty is possible, the greater probability is that, for some external reason, the jury will not return a verdict.

Gerard Busby, Defendant and Astrologer.

'Any thoughts?' I ask, smiling, as I watch the two of them read it.

'There are more things in Heaven and Earth, Judge,' Aubrey comments. 'I must admit, getting to know Mr Busby has been something of a revelation.'

'I'm going to advise the CPS that we don't need to do this again,' Susan says.

'That's awfully kind of you, Susan,' Aubrey says. 'It will come as a welcome ridge of high pressure for Mr Busby. He will be very relieved to hear it.'

'He probably knows already, doesn't he?' she replies.

* * *

Thursday evening

I relate the events of the day to the Reverend Mrs Walden, for whom astrology evokes images of India, and from there it's a predictably easy step to take ourselves off to the Delights of the Raj for dinner – a veritable feast of samosas, Chicken Madras and Sag Aloo, washed down by a couple of Cobras.

'What are you going to do with that young woman on your jury?' the Reverend asks. 'Are you going to send her to prison?'

'I should,' I reply.

'Oh come on, Charlie, all she did was tell a man she fancied him.'

'That wasn't all she did, Clara, not by a long way.'

'Well, all right, she went to the police station to drop off a note with her telephone number.'

'A note for the police officer in a case in which she's on the jury.'

'Well yes, and I know you have to disapprove, officially. But I also know that there's a part of you that admires her initiative. You can't deny it, Charlie. I know you too well. You're a romantic at heart. There's a part of you that's cheering her on for having the gumption to do something like that.'

'That's not the point, Clara,' I insist. 'She disrupted a four-day trial, wasted a huge amount of public money, and she's put both the complainant and the defendant at risk of having to go through the stress of a trial all over again.'

'I thought you said that the prosecution weren't going to retry the case?'

'Susan Worthington is going to advise them that the case isn't strong enough to warrant a second trial, but you never know with the CPS – they're quite capable of ignoring counsel's advice when it suits them.'

'All the same…'

'All right. I did want to lock her up this morning,' I admit. 'But when it comes to it, I'll probably fine her and let it go at that, and then she and DC Trent can fancy each other to their hearts' content.'

'Good for you, Charlie,' she says.

Our friend Rajiv, the owner of the Delights, stops by to inquire into how we have enjoyed our meal. We assure him that it's been as good as ever.

'Rajiv, let me ask you something,' I say. 'Is astrology still widely practised in India? Do people still believe in it?'

'Oh, indeed, yes, Mr Walden,' he replies, taking a seat next to our table. 'You see it everywhere. You know, when my wife and I were married in Mumbai, not only did our parents arrange the marriage, as is the custom in India, but each of the two families consulted an astrologer. The astrologers prepared our charts and compared them. If the astrologers had not approved of our union after reading the charts, our parents would have called the wedding off.' He laughs. 'But fortunately, the charts were favourable. We have been married for more than thirty years, and we have four wonderful children.' He stands. 'Though we have not tried to arrange any marriages for them, nor have we consulted an astrologer about them.'

'So, do you think our parents should have consulted astrologers for us before we got married?' the Reverend asks after Rajiv has made his way back to the kitchen.

'I think we've done perfectly well without them, thank you,' I reply.

'Still,' she persists, 'this fellow, what's his name, Busby, seems to have made quite an impression on everybody, doesn't he? And he certainly nailed his prediction of the verdict, or lack of verdict. Perhaps I'll suggest to the Bishop that Southwark should revive the tradition of the diocesan astrologer. What do you think? Should we take a look at Busby?'

'I think the diocese could do a lot worse,' I admit.

AN ISLE FULL OF NOISES

AN ISLE FULL OF NOISES

Last Friday

I've never understood why judges of the Crown Court are called circuit judges. It conjures up romantic images of a bygone age, of the itinerant judge mounting his horse to administer justice in some far-flung corner of the realm, his faithful clerk, a judicial Sancho Panza, bearing his books behind him on his donkey, to be greeted by the cheering crowds of citizens who have flocked to the town square to welcome his portentous arrival. Nothing could be further from the truth. All right: perhaps it worked, just, in the old days, when the itinerant Assize judge arrived at a town, tried a murderer, sentenced him to death, reserved judgment in the one civil case before him, and moved on to the next venue. But today? Not a chance. The system would collapse under its own weight in a matter of weeks. The last thing the Grey Smoothies want today is an itinerant judge.

Just imagine the travel costs, for one thing. How could they be sure that the taxpayer is getting value for money from the privatised feed and stable for the horse – or the judge? Then there would be the nightmare of trying to keep to the itinerary in the face of the volume of work, the problems of case management, the accidents of overrunning trials, the reality of delayed sentencing hearings, and all the rest of it. No, circuit judges don't ride the circuits today.

Quite the contrary: when you're appointed they tell you

exactly where you will be sitting and warn you in no uncertain terms not even to think about applying for a transfer to another court for the first five years. So, if you live in Leeds and they want you to sit in Swansea, you either say 'thank you' politely and move the family to South Wales, or you turn the job down. And even after five years, they may then suggest that Manchester wouldn't be a bad career move for you, even though there's a Mancunian who would love to sit there who they're sending to Basildon. It makes their lives much easier, you see, if they can treat judges as pawns in a game of administrative chess and don't have to worry about them as people who may also be trying to have a life. They don't have to lie awake all night – assuming they would anyway – worrying about some poor sod they're forcing to choose between his family and the job he's always wanted. How to put this? Viewed from the judicial perspective, human resources issues don't seem to loom large in the administration of the courts.

So on the rare occasions I'm called upon to sit away from my base court, Bermondsey, it comes as something of a surprise: and never more so than today. Today I am to be asked, figuratively speaking of course, to saddle up my trusty steed and make ready to ride the circuit, to become a circuit judge in the literal sense of the term. It all starts innocently enough. Every Friday, usually before court sits in the morning, Stella comes to see me in chambers to discuss the schedule for the coming week; and today is no different, except that today she has Marjorie with her.

'I've got a bit of an unusual one for you next week, Judge,' Stella begins. She sounds unusually hesitant, and I'm already suspicious.

'Really?' I reply, taking a hasty draught of Jeanie and Elsie's latte. 'Well, that will make a nice change, I'm sure.'

'It's all because of Judge Jenkins's case overrunning, you see.'

I've been wondering what impact that would have on the list. Marjorie is doing an importation of class A drugs with four defendants that was supposed to last for two to three weeks. It's already run for two weeks, and the prosecution hasn't even closed its case. It's not Marjorie's fault. It's not anybody's fault. First, she had an important witness go down with some kind of virus that's making the rounds, and then, no sooner had the witness recovered sufficiently to drag himself to court when two members of her jury complained of similar symptoms. Marjorie had no real choice: she sent everyone home until they were feeling fully fit. It's one of those things that happen sometimes during a trial, and you just have to deal with it. But of course, in the process she lost several days of trial time.

'It's got another week to run yet, hasn't it, Judge?' Stella asks.

'At least a week,' Marjorie says, 'and the thing is, Charlie, next week I'm supposed to be sitting as a deputy High Court judge out in the country.'

I remember. We were all excited when the Powers That Be added Marjorie's name to the exclusive and – by Bermondsey standards – exotic list of deputy High Court judges: excited, but not surprised. Marjorie is the lawyer on the Bermondsey bench, and we are all hoping that she will be asked to move up to the High Court full-time in due course – she's undoubtedly fully qualified. But she has to pay her dues sitting as a deputy first, and I know she's been looking forward to it.

'But obviously now, I've got to stay here and finish this bloody trial.'

'Oh, don't worry,' I say, doing my best to reassure her. 'They'll understand. They'll ask you again before too long.'

She smiles. 'Oh, *che sarà, sarà*, Charlie. I'm not going to worry about it.' I see her exchange a glance with Stella. 'I just need to make sure they can cover the case I was going to do. The one thing they won't thank me for is leaving them without cover.'

'Cover?' I ask.

'Yes, Judge,' Stella says. 'After Judge Jenkins told me she would be overrunning I talked to our senior Presider, Mr Justice Gulivant, to let him know. I assumed he'd give the case to someone else on the list, but yesterday he called me and said he wants you to do it.'

I am silent for a few seconds, and then I laugh nervously.

'What? You mean a civil case?'

'Yes, Judge.'

'*Moi*? Sit as a deputy High Court judge and try a civil case? He can't be serious.'

'He seemed perfectly serious, Judge.'

'But I can't… I mean, it would disrupt things here too much, wouldn't it? I'm sure you have a trial planned for me this week…'

Stella shakes her head. 'Judge Dunblane and Judge Drake both have trials starting in longish cases, so I'm not listing much other work this week. The only fixture I would have for you is a residential burglary, two to three days. I can get a recorder in to deal with that.'

I stare at her open-mouthed. A slight sense of panic is starting to set in. I appeal to Marjorie's better nature.

'But I don't know anything about civil cases, Marjorie. You know that. I wouldn't have the first idea where to begin.'

'Oh nonsense, Charlie,' she replies with a smile. 'Of course you would. It's not a complicated case. I can walk you through it.'

'What did you tell Mr Justice Gulivant?' I ask Stella.

'I told him I was sure you'd be very pleased to do it,' she replies. 'It would be quite a feather in Bermondsey's cap to have two judges on the list, wouldn't it?'

'It would,' Marjorie agrees.

'I rather like our cap the way it is,' I mutter.

Stella stands to leave. 'I'll leave the two of you together, and make some calls about getting a recorder,' she says cheerfully.

'I won't have to decide the facts of the case myself, will I?' I whine after Stella has gone. 'Please tell me I'll at least have a jury to work out who's telling the truth.'

'I'm afraid not, Charlie: we don't have many civil jury trials these days,' Marjorie replies. 'But don't worry. You'll get used to it. You don't have to find anything proved beyond reasonable doubt – it's a simple balance of probabilities.'

'It doesn't sound simple at all. And I'll have to write a judgment, won't I? I'm not used to that kind of thing.'

She laughs. 'The secret is to take good notes from day one and keep your papers organised,' she promises me. 'Writing the judgment is easy once you've made your mind up which way you're going. Besides, you don't have to do it there and then. You can take a couple of weeks, more if you need it – in fact, that's what the parties will expect.'

I shake my head.

'Don't worry,' she adds. 'As I said, it's not a difficult case. It's a dispute between near neighbours, all to do with who owns a plot of land between their two houses in a village somewhere in rural Cambridgeshire.'

'Cambridgeshire?'

'Oh, didn't I tell you?' she replies innocently. 'The trial's in Huntingdon. Charming town: you'll love it.'

We are silent for some time.

'You'll have to take over as RJ for the week,' I say eventually, by way of reprisal.

'I always do when you're away, don't I?' she reminds me. 'I'm sure I'll manage. There's nothing brewing, is there?'

'Not unless the Grey Smoothies have an unexpected rush of

blood to the head,' I reply, 'which one can never rule out. But barring that, no: it should be calm and peaceful.'

'Just like Huntingdon,' she says.

The Reverend Mrs Walden and I are not agoraphobic as such, but we are hard-core, card-carrying townies. I'm not saying we don't enjoy the odd weekend as guests in a nice hotel or someone's country retreat on the rare occasions when she can get a weekend off – especially when the hotel or country retreat happens to be in Provence or Tuscany – but in normal circumstances we both feel more at home in the smoke. So I'm sure I come across as rather despondent when I tell her over our pre-dinner glass of Lidl's Fine Amontillado that I am duty bound to saddle up my horse and gallop towards darkest Cambridgeshire.

'I'm sure you'll have a very good time,' she ventures consolingly. 'Have they found you somewhere decent to stay?'

'An old coaching inn called the George,' I reply, 'said to have been in Oliver Cromwell's family at some point. Hopefully it's been redecorated since then.'

'I'm sure it will be very nice.'

'And I won't have my daily stroll to court to start the day with.'

'I'm fairly sure that coffee and *The Times* will be available locally,' she says. 'What's really troubling you, Charlie? Is it doing such a different kind of case?'

'Clara, I know nothing about the ownership of land,' I confide in her. 'I remember studying land law at Cambridge. It was an absolute nightmare. There was something called the Rule against Perpetuities that could have been written by James Joyce on speed. It's incomprehensible. God only knows how I ever passed that exam.'

'Yes, He does,' she smiles.

'It's all very well for Marjorie. She understands that kind of thing. But I'm just a criminal hack.'

'You're a criminal *judge*,' she replies. 'Look, Charlie, what do you always tell your recorders when they're about to sit for the first time?'

'Listen to counsel, take your time, and ask for help whenever you need it,' I say.

'Exactly. So, take your own advice. Tell the barristers it's not the kind of case you usually do, and make sure they explain it all to you. Then trust your judicial instinct. You'll know which way to decide.'

I pour us another glass of the Amontillado.

'Why don't you come with me?' I suggest.

'What?'

'Well, we could have a week away, see the sights, sample the local cuisine and what have you – enjoy the country air for a few days.'

She shakes her head. 'I can't, Charlie. This week is really busy. I've got the Parish Council meeting, the engaged couples counselling, the youth club, the…'

'Yes, all right,' I say by way of resignation.

'I'm sorry.'

She takes a break from cutting up the ingredients for our noodles and spicy chicken – an experimental dinner she's been planning for some time – and brings her glass of sherry around the table to be with me.

'Look on the bright side, Charlie. You don't have to worry about being RJ for a week. You can try something different. Who knows, you might even find that you enjoy doing the odd civil case now and then.'

'I doubt it.'

'And it might be fun to be out in the country. Don't you remember what Shakespeare had to say about it?'

'What was that?'

'"The Isle is full of noises, sounds and sweet airs, that give delight and hurt not."'

'We shall see,' I reply dourly.

* * *

Monday morning

'May it please your Lordship, my name is Robert Mason, and I appear for the claimants, Andrew and Gwendolyn Pearce, in this matter. My learned friend Miss Ruth Bannerman appears for the defendant, Archie Barratt.'

It sounds strange to hear myself referred to as 'your Lordship'. I have to resist the temptation to look around the courtroom, in case there's a High Court judge with us I somehow haven't noticed. It's quite flattering in a way, I suppose; but it's not something I've ever aspired to, and it seems rather weird. It's not the only thing that seems weird. Sitting without robes is something I've only done once or twice for a short time and for special reasons; but that's what most civil judges do all the time and I will have to get used to conducting an entire trial wearing a suit and tie. But the weirdest thing of all is not having a jury. The courtroom has a jury box, but it's empty. I'm used to having twelve people in the box, and I keep seeing a jury there in my mind's eye. I only just caught myself in time, about to give them my usual pre-trial directions, before Robert Mason began his opening speech. Thank God I did: the last thing I need is counsel worrying that they've got a judge who talks to imaginary juries.

Actually, it's not just the start of the trial: my whole experience since arriving at the Huntingdon Combined Court Centre at about nine o'clock this morning has been weird. I couldn't help noticing that there was an eerie silence about the place. The only other human being in evidence when I arrived was the security guard, Ernie, who wasn't expecting me and at first refused to believe that I was a judge – partly because he'd never seen me before and partly because no one had told him that any cases were scheduled for hearing in the building today. It was only when I produced my judicial identity card that he reluctantly allowed me to pass through the security apparatus into the court's foyer.

'It's bloody typical, isn't it?' he volunteers once my briefcase and I have both successfully negotiated the scanner. 'They never tell me anything, do they? I'm always the last to know. What kind of case is it?'

'It's a civil case,' I reply, 'High Court.'

He shakes his head. 'They're supposed to do all those kinds of cases at Peterborough, aren't they?' he insists. 'Unless they've changed it all again. They change it every other bloody day. I can't keep track of it all. It's hopeless.'

Mercifully, just when all is beginning to seem lost, help is at hand. My court clerk is here, having come all the way from Peterborough, where they're supposed to do the civil cases, recording equipment in tow. He greets me cheerfully as he lugs the equipment through the revolving main door and deposits it on the desk for Ernie's inspection. Ernie insists that it must pass through the scanner.

'I'm Anand Gupta, Judge,' he says cheerfully. 'I'm your court clerk for Pearce and Barratt. Sorry to keep you waiting.'

'Not at all,' I reply as we shake hands. 'Actually, I'm not sure what we're waiting for, if anything. Ernie here doesn't think there are any cases scheduled for today.'

'They probably haven't sent him the list,' Anand explains. 'They should, of course, but they forget as often as not, don't they, Ernie? Nothing much happens here, you see. But we're booked in for court four, Judge; of that I can assure you.'

When we arrive at my assigned chambers we meet our usher for the day, Molly, a thin, forty-something with hair straight out of the 1960s, who tells me that she's a permanent fixture at this court at which nothing much happens.

'I was trained for the Magistrates' Court,' she confides to me apologetically. 'That's all I've done, really. I did do Crown Court once, but I lost a jury.'

'What do you mean exactly, lost a jury?' I ask.

'I let them go to lunch, didn't I, when they weren't supposed to leave the building,' she replies regretfully. 'Apparently they were meant to stay together. They wouldn't let me do Crown Court again after that. I've never done civil.'

'Well, that makes two of us,' I reassure her. 'We'll have to learn together, won't we? And you won't have to worry about losing the jury because we won't have one.'

When Molly leaves to prepare the courtroom, I ask Anand why nothing much happens at Huntingdon.

'Your guess is as good as mine, Judge,' he replies. 'This is a nice enough building, and it's only ten or so years old. I don't know how much it cost to build, but it couldn't have been cheap, could it? As a combined court centre, it's designed to accommodate all the courts: Crown Court, Magistrates' Court, and County Court. But the Crown Court has given up on it because they don't have the staff; the County Court has always sat at Peterborough and doesn't want to move; and the Huntingdon magistrates may be merging with another bench elsewhere in the county. We had the employment tribunals for a while, but they moved to Watford. The coroner sits here now and then – and that's about it, really. They'll probably sell it to a developer to build more flats eventually, but meanwhile they're spending a lot of public funds keeping it up. There's no knowing what they'll get up to next, is there?'

'No, there isn't,' I agree. 'Just as a point of interest: do you know why we're sitting here for this case instead of at Peterborough?'

'The defendant, Mr Barratt, is over eighty, Judge, and he didn't want to travel as far as Peterborough. So they agreed to let us use Huntingdon. They do that once in a while, you see, so that no one can say that the building isn't being used.'

'So that everyone can see the taxpayer is getting value for money?'

He nods knowingly. 'It's the same down in London then, is it, Judge?'

'Exactly the same.' I change the subject. 'Do you know counsel?'

'Yes. Both very good, Judge, both members of chambers in Cambridge. They'll do a good job for you.'

'My Lord,' Robert Mason continues, 'this is a case about a relatively small plot of land, about three-quarters of an acre in total, in the village of Lower Wattage, about ten miles into the fen country from Huntingdon. My learned friend and I have prepared agreed copies of all the documents your Lordship is likely to need. If I might ask the usher to assist…'

Molly happily collects four large file folders, and helpfully arranges them in front of me on the bench. They feel quite heavy, and it takes her two trips to bring all four, but having done so she retreats with a smile, as if to say, 'There's nothing to this civil stuff really, Judge, is there, once you get the hang of it?' I successfully suppress an urge to inquire about copies for my imaginary jury.

'My Lord, the land in dispute is in a street called The Ramblings, and it lies between two houses in that street: the Post House, which is owned by my clients, Andrew and Gwendolyn Pearce; and the Old Rectory, which is owned by the defendant, Archie Barratt. The Ramblings is a wide street, which runs the length of the village and is in effect its high street.

'If your Lordship would open the yellow folder… you will see that it begins with an agreed plan of the area. We have marked the disputed plot. It's always been known as the Middle Plot – probably because it is more or less the midpoint between the two ends of The Ramblings. Your Lordship will see that there are a number of houses up and down the street on both sides, and several streets leading off The Ramblings to newer residential developments. Lower Wattage isn't a big place – the total population is less than five thousand people. Looking up and down the street, your Lordship will see various buildings of interest, some of which we've marked specifically – Miller's grocery, St Mary's Church and the adjoining vicarage, the Post Office, and the Black Bull public house.'

'And the Freeman's Hall,' Ruth Bannerman adds, 'next to the Post Office. That's also an important local landmark, originally a masonic building but now something of a civic centre.'

'I'm obliged. My learned friend is quite right,' Robert agrees. 'My Lord, the dispute between the parties boils down to this: Mr and Mrs Pearce bought the Post House about three years ago. They bought it from an elderly gentleman called Pitt, who had lived there for a very long time. His family had lived there for over a hundred years. That's not uncommon in fen villages such as Lower Wattage. Indeed, the same is true of Mr Barratt, whose family has owned the Old Rectory for some one hundred and fifty years.'

'Two hundred, more like,' I hear from the row behind Ruth. It comes from the defendant, who is sitting with folded arms and an air of concentration on his wrinkled face. He certainly looks his age, although he doesn't seem at all frail. I would put money on his making it as far as Peterborough without undue difficulty if he had to. In contrast to the claimants, who are neat and tidy in business attire, he's dressed in rough working clothes and looks as though he has every intention of putting in a shift taking care of the livestock as soon as court rises for the day.

Robert smiles. 'A long time, anyway. My Lord, my clients have an unbroken title to the Middle Plot going back through their predecessors to the year 1651, at the end of the Civil War, when their predecessor in title John Hammond purchased it from a Mr Lampeter, who apparently left the area in some haste in consequence of having backed the wrong side during the war. It remained in Mr Hammond's family until 1894 when it was acquired by an ancestor of Mr Pitt. From 1894 there is an unbroken paper chain – or parchment chain, I should probably say – up to the present day. My clients took title when they bought from Mr Pitt. Simply stated, all the deeds clearly show the Middle Plot as part of the Post House. The two plots are treated as a single property.

'Your Lordship will be able to see the original deeds if he wishes, of course, but because some of them are quite fragile at this point in their long history, my learned friend and I have agreed to use certified copies for the purposes of the case. Your Lordship will find them in the blue folder.'

'That seems eminently sensible,' I say, flicking through the blue folder. I don't want to have to look after a collection of historic documents and be blamed if anything happens to them. I'm not the best custodian of original documents: I have form for misplacing such things in chambers, as my colleagues and the court staff at Bermondsey will attest.

'My Lord, there's no dispute about the claimants' paper title,' Ruth adds. 'It's clear that they own the Middle Plot as far as the deeds go.'

'Why don't I defer to my learned friend to explain that?' Robert suggests.

I can't help smiling. If counsel said that in a criminal trial at Bermondsey, it would be said in a sarcastic vein, meaning, 'Please do shut up; I'm trying to make my opening speech and I don't need you interrupting me', and I would have to issue a ruling on the subject. But in Cambridgeshire, in a civil case and with no jury to impress, that's clearly not what's going on. It's not about grandstanding. They are working together to help me to understand the case: the trial is a cooperative effort. They've agreed on the documents I need to see, and they're not going to allow formality to stand in the way of explaining the case to me in the most efficient way. If making a joint opening speech is the best way of explaining the case, that's what they will do. Moreover, they both have calm and thoroughly professional attitudes. So far I'm pleasantly impressed with Cambridgeshire.

'Your Lordship will find the pleadings in the green folder,' Ruth says. 'The issue your Lordship has to try is this: yes, the claimants have a paper title to the disputed land; but their title is unregistered – apparently they have chosen to rely on the deeds alone as proof of title – and so Mr Barratt is legally entitled to assert title by adverse possession.'

'You mean, possessing the land without Mr and Mrs Pearce's permission?' I ask.

'Using the land, my Lord, yes, without their permission and without the permission of Mr Pitt before them, because a continuous period of adverse use of twelve years is required. If Mr Barratt can show that he has continuously used the land without permission, but peacefully and undisturbed, for that period, he will have acquired title to the Middle Plot by adverse possession. Mr Barratt will say that he has regularly used the Middle Plot for various purposes over the years, mainly to grow fruit and vegetables for his family, and that his father did so for many years before him. Your Lordship will find the witness statements in the red folder.'

Marjorie has prepared me for this. In civil cases there is an exchange of witness statements, which then take the place of live evidence-in-chief. The witness is allowed to clarify what he has said in this statement, but otherwise the only live evidence is his cross-examination. Well, it saves time I suppose, and I'm sure it works well enough for cases in which there's no jury, but it's not something I'd want to introduce in the Crown Court. Every minute a witness spends in the box is an opportunity to evaluate his evidence, and I don't like being deprived of seeing how he tells his story – especially as I'm the one who has to decide who to believe. As a compromise, I've asked counsel to read the witness statements aloud, so that I can at least see the faces of the witnesses as the story unfolds.

By agreement, we begin with Mrs Gwendolyn Pearce, who, it appears, was the moving force behind the purchase of the Post House and so has become in a sense the lead claimant – or as the defendant might prefer it, the ringleader. She's wearing a smart light grey suit with a blue neck scarf, and she's sitting rigidly upright, staring somewhere past me into space.

My name is Gwendolyn Pearce. I am 62 years of age, and one of the claimants in this action. I am the wife of the other complainant, Andrew Pearce. We have been married for about 35 years. For most of our married life we lived in London, where my husband was a stockbroker in the City and I served on the boards of a number of charitable organisations. But about five years ago my husband decided to retire, and we agreed that we had had enough of London. We decided to find a place in the country in which to spend our remaining years. We both had happy memories of our undergraduate years at Cambridge, where we met, and we felt that we would like to return to the area.

We instructed one or two firms of estate agents in Cambridge and spent some time looking for property in a number of towns and villages. We have no children and our house in Hampstead, where we had lived for many years, had appreciated in value, so we were prepared to buy a property and restore it if necessary. Eventually one of the agents alerted us to the Post House in The Ramblings, Lower Wattage, and we went to see it. It was everything we had dreamed about. It is a grade two listed building with an amazing history – apparently, the owner during the Civil War used to hide Royalist fugitives there – and although it needed some restoration, we were sure we could afford it. We made a generous offer, which Mr Pitt accepted immediately. We moved in a month or two after completing. From that point onwards, what we intended as our dream has turned into a nightmare. This is because of the defendant, our neighbour, Archie Barratt.

The title to the Post House includes title to a plot of vacant ground known locally as the Middle Plot. This is clearly shown on all the deeds. The Middle Plot is a plot of about three-quarters of an acre midway along The Ramblings, and midway between our house and Mr Barratt's house, the Old Rectory. After we had moved in and settled down a bit, we gradually started our work of restoration. I also decided that the village needed tidying up a bit. There are a number of old buildings in Lower Wattage which could look really amazing with some effort, but the place has been allowed to fall into a state of disrepair. A lot of it is just a matter of a coat of paint, though some of the buildings, such as the Freeman's Hall, are in need of some serious repairs. Also, The Ramblings itself needs brightening up. So I embarked on a campaign to make this happen. I spoke to Dennis, the landlord of the Black Bull, and got the names of the people who owned the various buildings. I approached them and suggested that they take action. I even suggested that once The Ramblings looked brighter, we could enter Lower Wattage in the Cambridgeshire Best Kept Village Competition.

As my contribution, I decide to plant several young trees and a wide variety of plants in the Middle Plot. I started up several flowerbeds. I did some of this work myself, but two local boys, Harry and Matthew, agreed to do some of the digging in return for some pocket money. During this process, I encountered what appeared to be some abandoned vegetable plantings. I assumed that these dated back to Mr Pitt's time, so I simply removed them. But when I woke up one morning a few days later, I saw that someone had devastated the Middle Plot. My trees and plants had been dug up and cast aside, and the flowerbeds had been ploughed under. This must have been done overnight, otherwise I would have noticed.

I immediately suspected Archie Barratt. Mr Barratt is a widower. He is always scruffily dressed, and is surly and uncivil. He has hardly spoken a word to us since we moved in, and when we have reached out to him, for example by taking him a flask of hot soup one cold evening, he has been unwelcoming and, in fact, brusque to the point of rudeness. His two sons, Bernie and Mickey, are just as rude and they present as threatening. When I confided my suspicions in Dennis, he told me that my plans to brighten up the village had not gone down well with some of the older established families, including the Barratt family, and that they particularly resented my suggestion of entering Lower Wattage in the Best Kept Village Competition.

In view of the threatening demeanour of Mr Barratt and his two sons, I decided not to approach him myself. Instead I asked my solicitor to write him a letter, in which I demanded compensation for the trees and plants he had destroyed, as well as the cost of paying Harry and Matthew. I also threatened to sue him if he trespassed on our property again. My solicitor told me that he did not receive any reply to his letter. But about a week later, I found a hand-written note that had been pushed through my letterbox. It read: "Why don't you fuck off back to Londun [sic] and leave us in peace? We're doing very well without the likes of you. And while you're at it, tell your fancy solliciter [sic] he can fuck himself as well.' I produce this note as Exhibit GP 1.

'Your Lordship will find that note in the yellow folder, page twenty-two,' Robert interrupts helpfully.

'Yes, I'm much obliged,' I reply. In her witness statement Mrs Pearce offers no actual proof of authorship, but there is no protest from the defendant or his counsel; and with my admittedly urban prejudices, the handwriting and spelling certainly don't seem inconsistent with a rustic hand, shall we say. I glance sadly at the jury box again. Twelve citizens of Huntingdon and environs would have a much better feel for this, I reflect, and they would really enjoy the story that's unfolding. This case was made for a jury.

Following this incident, Mr Barratt and his sons entered on to the Middle Plot frequently and started to plant vegetables and other plants. At first they did this during the night, but later they were at it quite brazenly during the daytime. They had been poisoning people in the village against us, saying that we were 'foreigners' and 'interlopers' from London. The atmosphere in the Black Bull and Miller's store became unfriendly, and even the vicar said something to the effect that we should be careful not to cause offence to people. We received several anonymous phone threats, saying that they would burn our house down or run us out of town.

We actually considered moving for some time, but eventually we decided that we were not going to be driven from our home by people like the Barratts. I instructed my solicitor to write to Mr Barratt again, pointing out that he and his sons were trespassing on the Middle Plot, and that if we caught them at it again we would sue to enforce our title. Despite this letter, Mr Barratt and his sons have continued to trespass on our land at will, quite blatantly, at all hours of the day and night. We are now seeking a declaration that my husband and I are the exclusive owners of the Middle Plot, and an injunction restraining Mr Barratt from entering on to the Middle Plot or using it in any way.

I believe that the facts stated in this witness statement are true.

Robert asks Gwendolyn Pearce to come into the witness box. She takes the oath, confirms that what we have just heard is true and he passes her to Ruth for cross-examination.

'Mrs Pearce, you and your husband have lived in the Post House in Lower Wattage for a little more than two years: is that right?'

'Yes, it is.'

'And until you travelled to Lower Wattage from London to see the Post House before purchasing it, you had never visited the village, is that also right?'

'Yes.'

'So, would it be fair to say that you have no way of knowing whether Mr Barratt and members of his family may have made use of parts of the Middle Plot, prior to your arrival?'

'That's true.'

'For all you know, they may have made use of it during the many years when Mr Pitt owned the Post House before you?'

'Perhaps Mr Pitt didn't object.'

'But you don't know that, one way or the other, do you?'

'No. I suppose not.'

'No. But your evidence was that, when you first arrived to take up residence at the Post House, there was evidence that someone had been growing vegetables on the Middle Plot?'

'Yes.'

'You assumed that it was Mr Pitt?'

'Yes, I did, since he was the owner of the Middle Plot before us.'

'But, for all you know, it could have been Mr Barratt, couldn't it?'

'Yes, I suppose so.'

'After all, Mr Barratt showed every sign of wanting to grow vegetables on the Middle Plot after you moved in, didn't he?'

'Yes, he did.'

'Which you construed as an act of trespass?'

'Yes, I certainly did.'

'But didn't Mr Barratt explain to you that he and his family had been using the land to grow vegetables, and even fruit and other plants, at different times?'

'He did make that claim, yes.'

'How did you react to that?'

'I told him in no uncertain terms that the fact that he had trespassed on our land in the past did not entitle him to continue to trespass now that we were in possession.'

'When you spoke to local people, in the Black Bull or Miller's for example, did you tell them what Mr Barratt was doing?'

'I did eventually. After a while, everyone found out about it, because he was spreading the word that we were foreigners and interlopers. People took sides. So, yes, I did speak to certain people.'

'Did those people include Dennis, the landlord of the Black Bull, and the vicar, the Reverend Mr Jacobs?'

'Yes.'

'And what did they tell you?'

This is another thing Marjorie, thankfully, prepared me for. In a criminal case at Bermondsey Robert Mason would be on his feet objecting, screaming that the question calls for blatant hearsay, which it clearly does. But in fact, he is sitting in his seat perfectly calmly, awaiting the answer. In civil cases, where they rarely have to worry about juries, the Rule against Hearsay apparently disappeared years ago. It's now up to judges such as myself to decide how much weight to give to it. Actually, in this case, even at Bermondsey I might have allowed it. It is necessary to establish Gwendolyn's state of mind and how much she knew, and I've noticed that Dennis and Mr Jacobs, together with a number of other prominent residents of Lower Wattage, have made witness statements and may give evidence later in the trial. If so, no harm can come from it. Even so, I find myself tempted to ask my imaginary jury to retire for a while so that I can check the position with counsel.

'It all depended on who you asked. Dennis said that Mr Barratt was always taking liberties, and he wouldn't care whether we objected to what he was doing or not. He always treated the Middle Plot as his own, and never worried about what Mr Pitt or anyone else thought.'

Ruth smiles, for a reason that escapes me for the moment, though I have the sense that a significant moment may have come and gone. This is confirmed by Robert, who is suddenly trying very hard to look unconcerned – generally a sign that he thinks something has gone wrong with his case.

'Mr Jacobs said that as far as he knew, Mr Barratt's family had grown food for the village on the Middle Plot during the war, but they hadn't used it since, certainly not regularly,' Gwendolyn continues uninvited. 'Mr Jacobs said he only started it again because he didn't like Andrew and me.'

'Really?' Ruth asks, doing her best to feign surprise. 'Why would that be, do you think?'

Gwendolyn sniffs dismissively. 'Mr Barratt couldn't stand the fact that we wanted to let people see Lower Wattage in all its glory, that we wanted to put a few coats of paint on some of the buildings, tidy the street up, take away the debris and the dead branches, plant a few flowers, brighten the place up a bit. It's such a pretty village, but Mr Barratt and the others had let it go to rack and ruin. The Ramblings looked like a tip. They couldn't stand that we were showing them up, and doing what they should have done years ago.'

'And entering Lower Wattage in the Best Kept Village Competition?' Ruth asks.

'Yes. Why not? It's as pretty as any other village in Cambridgeshire.'

'And you really have no idea how anyone could possibly dislike you and your husband for that, do you?'

'No. I don't. We were doing them all a favour.'

Ruth nods and pauses. 'Mrs Pearce, there's nothing on the deeds to suggest that Mr Pitt, or any of your predecessors in title, ever granted Mr Barratt or anyone in his family an easement or licence to use the Middle Plot, is there?'

'You mean, that anyone gave the Barratts permission to use the land?'

'Exactly.'

'No. The deeds just say that our title to the Post House includes title to the Middle Plot. Our solicitor checked the title before we completed.'

'And there were no easements or licences, were there?'

'No.'

'Mr Pitt – Mr George Pitt, the gentleman you bought from: did you ever ask him whether he had given Mr Barratt permission to use the Middle Plot?'

She shakes her head. 'We only met him once, at the completion, for a few minutes. The solicitors were dealing with it. So, no. We had no idea it had been going on.'

'Quite so,' Ruth says. 'And sadly, I understand that Mr Pitt passed away not long after completion, didn't he?'

'So I'm told. I heard he'd gone to live with a son in Dawlish, but then someone – I think it was Mr Jacobs – told me that he had died.'

'So we can't ask him now, can we?'

'No.'

Ruth turns around briefly to confer with her instructing solicitor and Mr Barratt, both of whom nod.

'Thank you, Mrs Pearce. I have nothing further, my Lord,' she says, resuming her seat.

'Mrs Pearce,' Robert asks, 'you have told his Lordship that your efforts to improve the village of Lower Wattage led to certain of its inhabitants resenting you: would that be a fair way of putting it?'

'That would be something of an understatement.'

'Yes, no doubt. But for whatever reason, your plans to improve the village's appearance proved controversial and turned some people against you?'

'Yes.'

'Is it your opinion that this animosity on Mr Barratt's part had anything to do with the matters his Lordship has to consider in this case?'

'Yes, of course.'

'In what way?'

'Mr Barratt is claiming an interest in our land simply to get back at us for showing him and the others up by trying to take better care of the village. It's sheer vindictiveness, as simple as that. Anyone can make up a story about using land continuously for a number of years when we weren't around to see it. But if he had, I'm sure Mr Pitt, or his solicitor, or the agent would have told us when we bought the Post House. Otherwise, it would have been – what do you call it a…?'

'A misrepresentation?'

'A misrepresentation, yes. It would have been a

misrepresentation otherwise, wouldn't it? He's just made up this story to punish us for trying to make the village look better.'

'Unless your Lordship has any questions?'

I don't, at least for now. I will have to hear what Archie Barratt has to say about all this before I know what questions I need to ask anyone, and it's as if Robert and Ruth have read my mind. They have agreed that we should take Andrew Pearce next, which will take us to lunchtime, but then we will indeed hear from Archie Barratt. I can't help smiling. In a criminal case we would have to hear from all the prosecution witnesses before anyone gave evidence for the defence. But in the flexible world of civil litigation, without a jury to worry about, we can vary the order of witnesses as much as we like, and counsel have suggested that I should hear from Mr Barratt first thing after lunch. I couldn't agree more. After that, there are further witnesses on both sides, order to be determined... and, as I'm about to learn, something else that I hadn't expected.

'Tomorrow morning,' Robert says, 'we propose to go on a view, to let your Lordship see the land in question for himself, and indeed to see the village as a whole. As your Lordship has heard, Lower Wattage is only about ten miles out of town. I've spoken to your Lordship's clerk, and he will make arrangements for travel for your Lordship, my learned friend, myself, the usher and himself. The parties and their solicitors will meet us at the property.'

I glance at Anand. He turns around to me.

'No problem, Judge. The parties will pay for the transportation, but I will make the arrangements. And I'll arrange for some refreshments from the Black Bull, so that we can use their facilities in case of need.'

I nod. 'Yes, very well. Mr Mason, in a criminal case the rule would be that no one should speak during a view unless it's strictly necessary,' I say. It's true, and it makes the whole experience not only very uncomfortable, but a recipe for potential disaster. Try keeping a defendant and twelve jurors quiet for an hour or two at the scene of an alleged crime some time. It confounds human nature, 'But, as we have no jury, I suppose…'

He smiles. 'My Lord, as long as anything said is said in the presence of everyone, we wouldn't see a problem.'

'I agree, my Lord,' Ruth adds.

I really am quite getting to like civil cases.

Andrew Pearce doesn't take long. He has nothing of substance to add to what his wife has already told us. She, it turns out to no one's surprise, was the moving force behind the move from London to the country, the choice of Lower Wattage and the Post House, and the ill-starred campaign to win the Best Kept Village Competition. He played along happily, and naturally supports her entirely in relation to the depredations committed by Archie Barratt, but he wasn't the prime mover. Ruth asks him one or two *pro forma* questions, just so that he doesn't feel ignored, and that takes us neatly to one o'clock. And so to lunch, an oasis of calm in a desert of chaos.

Except that today, of course, the oasis is a far cry from the judicial mess at Bermondsey. Molly has kindly offered to go out and bring me a sandwich if I want to eat in chambers, but I thank her and say I'll fend for myself. I'm surprised at how relaxed I feel. I've asked Marjorie to be on standby in case I need an urgent consultation, and I've had visions of calling her in panic as soon as I could escape the bench for lunch, with God only knows how many questions. But not at all: thanks to my cooperative counsel and the adaptable nature of the civil case, I'm actually feeling in control. I think briefly about calling her just to tell her that, but she's probably got enough to do acting as RJ in my absence, and instead I embark on my half-minute reverse commute across George Street to the George Hotel.

I was pleasantly surprised when I arrived late yesterday afternoon. My room is comfortable enough and the hotel is a delight, featuring an original Jacobean courtyard, where, Darla tells me, a local theatre group puts on an outdoor Shakespeare production every summer. Darla is the manager of the hotel and couldn't be more helpful, although there is one slight qualification to that. I had tried to make it clear that I wanted to keep a low profile – you never know, with local feeling running high about the case – and she seemed to understand. But an hour so later in the bar, after I'd enjoyed a dinner of bangers and mash, she suddenly bellowed, 'Another pint, Judge?' which had the effect of focusing every eye in the place on me. She did look suitably contrite when I grimaced, and I'm sure it won't happen again.

She's more than made up for it today by saving me a corner table, and serving me herself to make sure lunch doesn't take too long. I cast my eye over *The Times* while savouring a delicious smoked salmon and horseradish sandwich. I must admit, the George gives Jeanie and Elsie more than a run for their money, and it knocks spots off the judicial mess. Altogether, a very agreeable interlude: so far, the noises, sounds and sweet airs are indeed giving delight and hurting not. But you know what they say: if it seems too good to be true, it probably is. And sure enough, when I arrive back in my chambers after lunch -

'There was a call for you from Judge Jenkins at Bermondsey,' Molly says. 'It sounded urgent. I wrote the number down for you.'

'Oh, right, thanks,' I reply. 'I'll call her now.'

Molly clearly feels that she hasn't yet quite captured the urgency of the matter. 'She seemed really upset, Judge,' she adds. She is not wrong.

'"Calm and peaceful", Charlie?' Marjorie shrieks down the phone, without any pleasantries at all. '"Calm and peaceful"?

Wasn't that what you said, it would all be "calm and peaceful" this week?'

I hold my phone away from my ear for a few seconds.

'Well, as far as I know it should be. What on earth has happened?'

There is a silence, during which I sense her making an effort to control herself. I'm worried now. Of the four judges at Bermondsey, Marjorie is undoubtedly the most composed, which is exactly why she is my automatic choice for deputy RJ whenever I'm away. I'm not sure I've ever seen her really lose her cool. If Marjorie's in this kind of state something must really be wrong. It occurs to me briefly that the catastrophe I have long dreaded has finally visited itself on us: the dish of the day has caused an outbreak of mass poisoning. Judges, lawyers, jurors, and members of the public are lying, helpless and groaning, in the corridors as their toxic lunch begins its deadly work. I've always thought it was only a matter of time. We came close once with a terrifying paella, the perpetrator of which, a Spanish assistant cook, fled the jurisdiction shortly afterwards. On that occasion the damage was limited; perhaps now our luck has finally run out. But, on the other hand, it's only just after lunch: surely, there hasn't really been time for the effects of a mass poisoning to become apparent? I can hear her breathing heavily on the other end of the phone.

'We've got gangs of violent protesters laying siege to the court, Charlie,' she replies. 'That's what's happened. I've had to close the bloody building and call the police. If that's your idea of "calm and peaceful"...'

'What? Marjorie, what are you talking about? Protesting about what?'

I hear a deep sigh.

'I'm sorry, Charlie. It's not your fault; I know that. It's just been scary, that's all.'

'Of course,' I say. 'Are you all right? Has anyone been hurt?'

'No – well, not so far. It's quietened down a bit now. They did try to force their way into the building, but security managed to hold them off long enough to lock the doors. The police are outside with them now, but you know how narrow the street is outside our front door. They're having trouble dispersing them. They're talking about calling in riot police.'

'For God's sake,' I say. 'What's this about? We don't have any cases listed this week that would cause something like that. We'd have warned the police in advance if we did.'

'The defendant in Legless's case didn't turn up for a pre-trial hearing on Friday afternoon,' she explains eventually, 'so Legless revoked his bail and issued a warrant for his arrest, as any of us would have. The police found him late yesterday afternoon. They did arrest him, but he resisted and there was a bit of a struggle. No one really knows what happened, but they had to use some force to restrain him and somehow Chummy was injured. He stopped breathing in the ambulance and he's in Guy's Hospital in a coma.'

'Oh, God,' I reply. 'And the locals have risen up in revolt?'

'He's a member of some right-wing group that's not without its adherents in South London, and most of them are now outside Bermondsey Crown Court carrying baseball bats and God only knows what else. They've been shouting and carrying on non-stop. I'm surprised you can't hear them. I'm standing in the foyer now, with Stella. It's chaos out there. Bob is liaising with the police, and we're waiting for further instructions.'

'So everyone's trapped inside the building for now?'

'We have smuggled one or two people out of the back door, including a pregnant woman who's on Hubert's jury. They aren't targeting the rear of the building as yet. But the police are advising everyone to stay put until they can clear them away.

I've called a halt to all the trials for now, and we will see what happens. Any advice?'

I think for some time.

'If they're targeting the court rather than the police station, maybe they're blaming Legless for this for some reason. What's Chummy charged with?'

'Racially aggravated GBH. He's a nasty piece of work, and so are his mates, by the look of them.'

'In that case, Marjorie, call in the Judicial Protection Unit. You remember, there was a DI Derbyshire who came when those Free English Men, or whatever they called themselves, made that death threat against me. Bob will have the number. Legless should have some protection for a while – whether he thinks he needs it or not.'

'Good thought,' she replies. 'You know Legless. If he had his way, he'd be out on the street at this very moment helping the police to sort them out – and Hubert would be right behind him: he wants to fire up the cannon and turn it on them.'

'I knew there was a reason I always pick you to be deputy RJ,' I say, and she actually laughs for a moment. 'Look, Marjorie, you'll be all right. You're doing all the right things. Stay in touch, and keep me up to date. I have to go back into court, but I'll tell the staff to get me off the bench immediately if you call again. If I don't hear from you, I'll call once I've finished for the afternoon.'

'How's Huntingdon?' she asks after a short silence. She sounds like Marjorie again now: the composure is back.

'Calm and peaceful.'

'How are you doing with your civil case?'

'Loving it,' I reply. 'I really should do this more often.'

* * *

Monday afternoon

My name is Archie Barratt. I am 82 years of age and a retired farm manager. I am a widower, my wife having predeceased me in 1995, and I live alone at my family home, the Old Rectory, The Ramblings, Lower Wattage. I am the defendant in this action. I have two sons, Bernie and Mickey, who have been referred to. But they do not live with me. They both live with their own families in Dry Drayton, where they work as farm labourers. They visit me occasionally.

My family has lived in the Old Rectory for the best part of two hundred years, or so I've always been told. From what I understand, my ancestors took the Old Rectory over when the village built the new vicarage by the church, and that was in 1830 or thereabouts. I remember my grandparents and parents living here. I've never lived anywhere else, and never intend to. George Pitt's family lived in the Post House next door for over a hundred years, too. George was the last surviving member of the Pitt family. George is dead now. But unfortunately, before he died, he sold out to the interlopers from London.

My understanding of the Middle Plot is as follows. I was always told that for several hundred years, the Middle Plot was treated as common land for all the villagers to use. Of course, in those days, there was almost nothing to Lower Wattage except The Ramblings and a few other houses here and there. It wasn't much more than a hamlet then, nothing like what you've got today with the new housing estates. So it made sense that a small plot like the Middle Plot could have been used as common land. But in the chaos of the Civil War it was somehow included by mistake in the deed for the Post House, and because there is no actual evidence that it was supposed to be common land, it has been passed on from owner to owner of the Post House down the years. My grandfather and father always said that the Pitts recognised that they should not have had the title to the Middle Plot, and although they never officially consented to anyone else using it, in practice they turned a blind eye to it. Certainly they always did during my grandfather's time and my father's time, and I never had any comment or problem about it from George, even though he and I had a pint or two together in the Black Bull a couple of evenings each week, so he had plenty of opportunity to tell me if he objected.

Although people in Lower Wattage were aware that the Middle Plot was supposed to be common land, I don't remember anyone using it except for my family. I think that was because, when you look at it, it does seem that it should belong to either the Post House or the Old Rectory, as it is very close to both houses. But my family has made frequent use of it throughout my lifetime. We've always grown vegetables and fruit on the land. When the war broke out, my dad couldn't enlist for active service. He had one leg that didn't work properly because of a tractor accident in his youth. But he was in the Home Guard and he organised the local 'Dig for Victory' campaign, and throughout the war we used the whole plot to provide food for local people, including ourselves. That wasn't all we used it for, of course. My grandfather, my father and I used to play cricket and football there, often with my cousins from Over and Wisbech, and we had parties and picnics on the land during summer months.

When the interlopers came, I was expecting things to continue as they always had. But it wasn't like that at all. Almost as soon as they moved into the Post House, she was on the warpath, complaining about how 'run down' the village was, and how everything needed to be renovated and painted. She hadn't been in Lower Wattage five minutes, and she was giving orders to people whose families had lived in the village for centuries, and criticising them for not taking better care of the place. I agree, there are some buildings that have seen better days, but that's true of any small town or village in the Fens, and you can't just go barging in and demanding that people change everything overnight. I sometimes think she wanted to make us look like London. Then one morning, I saw her on the land digging, and over a weekend she tore up and destroyed all the patches I used for growing our vegetables and filled the Plot with flowers and such like. When I asked her about it, she told me she wanted to brighten the place up so that she could enter Lower Wattage in the Best Kept Village Competition – without so much as a by-your-leave to me, or any of the local inhabitants.

I admit that I took that as a declaration of war. I asked Bernie and Mickey to help me, and together we cleared all the trees and flowers away, and planted our vegetables again. But I did something else, too. I could smell trouble, so for the first time in my life I went and saw a solicitor in Cambridge and asked him what he thought I should do. I was amazed by what he said. He said because of what he called 'adverse possession' over many years, my family had acquired legal title to the Middle Plot, and so I was entitled to do whatever I wanted with it, and to stop Mrs Pearce from using it, if I wanted to. But I would need a court order to establish my title. I didn't know what to do. I was happy for the land to be common land, as it always had been, as I saw it. On the other hand, it was obvious that Mrs Pearce didn't see it that way, and was determined to keep it for her own exclusive use. When I received a threatening letter from her solicitor, that confirmed it, and from that time on I've used the Plot as much and as often as I can, because my solicitor said I should keep on doing it, regardless of any threats from her. As he requested, I also obtained witness statements from people in the village who know the history, including the vicar, Mr Jacobs, Dennis from the Black Bull, and Tina Miller from the store.

I am now asking the Court to declare that I now have legal title to the Middle Plot, based on adverse possession by myself and my family for many years, many more than the required legal minimum of twelve.

I believe that the facts stated in this witness statement are true.

'Mr Barratt,' Robert begins,' let me start with more recent matters, if I may. After Mr and Mrs Pearce moved into the Post House, did you ever ask them whether they were willing to turn a blind eye to your use of the land, like George Pitt?'

'Did I ask them?

'Yes: did you ask them?'

'No, I didn't ask them anything. Why would I?'

'Well, how did you know that George Pitt had explained the arrangement to Mr and Mrs Pearce – the arrangement that he turned a blind eye when you used the Middle Plot?'

'I didn't know whether he had or not.'

'Well, if he hadn't, how were they expected to find out about it?'

Archie shakes his head. 'I don't know, do I?'

'After all, as you're fond of pointing out, they were newcomers, weren't they?'

'Yes, they were.'

'And if they didn't know, and they saw you on the Middle Plot planting vegetables, they would have every right to assume that you were trespassing on their land, wouldn't they?'

'I don't know what they thought, do I?'

'Well, it's only common sense, isn't it, Mr Barratt? If you saw someone on your land planting something, and you didn't know of any arrangement, you'd assume they were trespassing, wouldn't you?'

'I might.'

'Of course you would. And you couldn't have any complaint if Mrs Pearce ripped out whatever you'd planted, and planted her own flowers, or whatever she wanted to plant. You could hardly object to that, could you, because you'd been trespassing?'

Ruth stands, quietly.

'With all due respect, my Lord, that's the very point your Lordship has to decide.'

I have to smile. I think someone has finally objected to something in this very polite, jointly managed civil trial. But I'm not sure exactly what the objection is. Perhaps Robert will clarify it for me – or perhaps not.

'I'll move on,' he replies, with a smile towards Ruth. 'Mr Barratt, is this right: despite your claim that the Middle Plot is common land for the whole village, you've never known anyone else to use it? It's always been your family and no one else?'

'Yes. Well, as far as I know. I don't know who might have used it in the past, do I?'

'But not during your lifetime? Even during the war, when everyone was "digging for victory"? No one else used it?'

'I explained that. If you look at it…'

'Yes, I understand. But if land is regarded as common land by an entire village, and has been for several centuries, it's a remarkable thing, isn't it, that no one else has ever tried to use it?'

'I couldn't say.'

'It must have been the best-kept secret in the fen country, Mr Barratt.'

'My learned friend is making a comment rather than asking a question, my Lord,' Ruth observes, almost apologetically.

Finally: an objection I understand – and agree with.

'So I am,' Robert agrees, without my prompting. 'Mr Barratt, the truth of the matter is this, isn't it: that the Middle Plot has never been common land? That's a figment of your imagination, isn't it? At least since 1651, title to the Middle Plot has gone with title to the Post House, hasn't it?'

'It was the tradition that it was common land. That's what I was always told.'

'Do you know of anyone outside your family who is aware of that tradition?'

Silence.

'All right, Mr Barratt, I won't press you. Now, you told his Lordship that when you went to see your solicitor, he told you all about adverse possession: yes?'

'Yes.'

'Did he explain to you that, for adverse possession, you have to be in possession of the land *continuously* for a period of at least twelve years?'

No response for some time. 'I can't remember everything he said.'

'Fair enough. But wouldn't you agree with me that you were never in possession of the Middle Plot continuously? You went there from time to time to play football or cricket. Presumably that was when you were a boy?'

'Yes, that's true.'

'Whereas you're now eighty-two?'

'Yes. But I played with Bernie and Mickey when they were lads.'

'And how old are Bernie and Micky now?'

'They're in their fifties.'

'So, is it fair to say that there's been no cricket played on the Middle Plot for some years now?'

'That doesn't mean we didn't play there.'

'No, of course. Let me move on to the growing of vegetables.

I'm sure your father did a lot of that during the war?'

'Yes, he did.'

'Yes: everyone was "digging for victory" then, weren't they? But again, you were a young boy during the war, weren't you?'

'Yes, I was.'

'And once the war ended, if you or your father planted anything there, it would only be for your own family wouldn't it? You wouldn't be digging for the whole village after the war, would you?'

'There were a couple of elderly people in Lower Wattage – Mrs Brown and Mr Ankers. They were on their own, and they were a bit frail, and my father did give them some cabbage and lettuce and tomatoes, and what have you.'

'I'm sure he did. But it was on a much smaller scale, wasn't it?'

'I don't know what you mean.'

'I'm suggesting that you weren't planting anything regularly: certainly not every year; just now and then. Isn't that fair to say?'

Archie is looking a little defensive, but he does his best to hit back.

'We always knew we could. We planted whenever we wanted to.'

'You never lived on the Middle Plot, did you?'

'Lived on it? No, of course not. We had our own house.'

'Indeed you did. The Middle Plot was a place you used occasionally, wasn't it?'

'It was much more than "occasionally".'

'Mr Barratt, do you have a garden at the Old Rectory?'

'Yes.'

'In fact, you have a quite large garden at the rear of your house, don't you?'

'Yes.'

'What do you use your garden for?'

'We have some fruit trees.'

'And some flower beds?'

'Yes.'

'And some areas where you grow vegetables?'

'One or two, yes.'

'And a quite large greenhouse?'

'Yes.'

'Which would be a good reason not to play cricket or football in the garden, wouldn't it? You wouldn't have been very popular with your father if you were breaking panes of glass all the time, would you?'

Archie snorts. 'He would have taken his belt to me, as I would have to Bernie and Mickey if they'd done it.'

'Yes,' Robert says, apparently doing his best to sound disapproving of parents taking belts to children: if so, it doesn't seem to make any immediate impression on Archie Barratt. Robert pauses for some time, under cover of consulting his notes. 'Mr Barratt, this case isn't about adverse possession, is it?'

Archie lifts his head and stares at him. 'Well, if it's not, I'd like to know what it is about.'

'It's about you not liking Mr and Mrs Pearce, isn't it?'

Archie shrugs. 'I don't like them. That's true enough.'

'They're foreigners, aren't they, interlopers?'

'Yes, they are.'

'They hadn't been in Lower Wattage five minutes before they were berating you older inhabitants for your neglect of the village, and trying to brighten the place up, and entering it in the Best Kept Village Competition, and all the rest of it. They disrespected you and made a thorough nuisance of themselves – and it made you furious, didn't it?'

'I didn't like it, it's true.'

'And you thought you'd teach them a lesson, didn't you?'

'No.'

'You decided that you wouldn't allow them to use their own land without interference, and then you invented this story of continuous use to persuade your solicitor that you had a case of adverse possession for more than twelve years.'

'I do have a case.'

'The truth of the matter, Mr Barratt, is this, isn't it: you're nothing more than a trespasser who goes on to other people's land now and then, just to annoy them because he doesn't like them?'

'Certainly not.'

'I have nothing further, my Lord. Thank you, Mr Barratt.'

Next, again with Ruth's agreement, Robert reads five witness statements: from the vicar, Mr Jacobs; Dennis from the Black Bull; Tina from Miller's grocery store; and from the Barratt boys, Bernie and Mickey. Both parties are going to decide whether they want to cross-examine any of these witnesses after we've had the view, and I am politely invited to indicate whether there are any questions I would like to ask any of them. It's a fair question, because none of them takes matters very much further, as far as I can see. Bernie and Mickey, needless to say, support their father's evidence in every detail, including several from periods pre-dating their own births.

Mr Jacobs, Dennis and Tina agree on three things. They agree that Mr and Mrs Pearce were a real pain in the neck – self-important, condescending newcomers who thought nothing of parachuting into a village inhabited by the same families for centuries, ordering people around and disrupting their way of life as if they owned the place. They agree that Archie Barratt, and his father before him, used the Middle Plot from time to time to grow vegetables. But they also agree that they couldn't possibly say when or how often this happened, or for how long it had been going on. Not one of them describes the Middle Plot as common land.

'My Lord,' Anand announces as I'm about to rise for the day, 'arrangements have been made for the view tomorrow. Our car will leave from the George's car park at nine thirty, and the parties will be waiting for us at the property at ten o'clock.'

Everybody agrees that this will be satisfactory.

'No further word from Judge Jenkins?' I ask Molly as we walk together from court to chambers. It's not the easiest walk of its kind involving, as it does, two flights of stairs and two doors you can only open with a fob. How a judge would ever escape if a mob of violent protesters gained access to this court, I really don't know: apparently it's an eventuality that escaped the notice of whoever designed the security system here in calm, peaceful Huntingdon.

'Not a word,' Molly replies. 'Is she all right, Judge? She sounded ever so upset.'

'She would have called if there was a problem, I'm sure,' I reply soothingly.

'But according to the news, there's been a real riot at your court,' Molly continues blandly. 'Do you get a lot of that at Bermondsey?'

'No. It's quite unusual, really,' I reply.

'I wouldn't want to do Crown Court again if I thought that kind of thing was going to happen,' she observes.

'I'm sure you're safe here in Huntingdon,' I assure her.

'Nothing much has changed, Charlie,' Marjorie tells me. 'The police have given them several warnings to disperse, but they haven't tried to make them yet.'

'Oh, for God's sake, why not?' I ask. 'They've had all afternoon. What are they waiting for?'

'They were waiting for the riot police to arrive. But they're in position now, so we're hoping it won't be too long. It's just all so worrying for everyone. Simon and Samantha even got their teacher to call from school to see if I'm all right. Someone had seen it on the news. Legless and Hubert are fuming.'

'Has someone been in touch with the Protection Unit?'

'Yes. DI Derbyshire will come to meet Legless as soon as the street has been cleared and we can open the building again. I'm sure it won't be –'

But before she can complete the sentence, I hear a bang in the background – a loud bang.

'Marjorie? Marjorie? What's going on? Are you all right?'

But the line has gone dead.

* * *

Monday evening

I leave the court building and run across the street to the George, straight into the bar, where Darla greets me cheerfully, mercifully without calling me 'Judge', and pulls me a much-needed pint of Abbot. As I had hoped, the TV in the bar is on. Some kind of quiz show is in progress, but fortunately no one is taking any notice of it and at my request Darla switches to the BBC news channel. As I'd expected, they are covering the scene outside Bermondsey Crown Court, where a regular pitched battle is taking place. There seems to be some damage to the glass in the court's front doors, and there is some smoke around, but I'm not seeing anything worse than that; and as the coverage unfolds, it becomes clear that the riot police are quickly gaining ascendancy over Chummy's mates, many of whom are already legging it while they can, and others are being detained without much resistance.

I call Marjorie's number, and she answers at the third time of asking.

'Marjorie, are you all right? I heard this almighty bang and then I lost you.'

'Yes, I'm fine, Charlie. There was some kind of explosion outside. The police are saying it was probably a home-made device of some kind, but it can't have been anything too serious – we haven't had any reports of casualties.'

'Thank goodness for that. I'm watching the BBC news in my hotel, and from what I can see the police are making good progress.'

'Yes, I'm still in the foyer with Stella and it's looking good from here too. I expect we will be all clear in a few minutes. Why don't you call me back in an hour or so, and I'll update you then?'

'All right, but I'm going to keep watching, and you can call me any time if you need me.'

'Thanks, Charlie, but it's all under control now.' It's said confidently, and my worries are subsiding to some extent. She will have to make sure that Legless cooperates with DI Derbyshire, and she will probably have to close the court for repairs for a day or two. It's going to be a nightmare for Stella too, with trials to re-schedule. But there have been no casualties, and everything else is negotiable.

I call the Reverend Mrs Walden, just to make sure that no stray protesters have appeared in the vicinity of the vicarage. She assures me that all is well.

'I hope you don't have anything like that going on in Huntingdon,' she says.

'No. It's all very quiet,' I reply. 'It's different from the big city.'

'Do you think you're starting to prefer the country to town?' she asks.

'Not as a way of life,' I reply. 'But I must say, I'm coming around to it, at least on an occasional basis.'

* * *

Tuesday morning

I haven't had as much sleep as I wanted. I was on the phone with Marjorie until late as she kept me up to date with what was going on. The BBC lost interest in Bermondsey Crown Court as a developing news story once the riot police had finally routed the protesters at about seven o'clock, and their coverage of events at the court from that time onwards was spasmodic. So Marjorie stayed on the line and supplied the news in real time, while I dined on Abbot and Darla's goujons of plaice with chips and mushy peas. At about seven thirty, the police gave the all clear for those inside the building to make their way home. The court staff, without exception, gallantly remained at court to lend a hand until the jurors, defendants on bail, counsel and solicitors, and members of the public were clear of the building.

DI Derbyshire, with some difficulty, eventually talked Legless into accepting a police driver and a panic alarm at his house for the duration of his case. Hubert called a taxi to take him to the Garrick, where he no doubt regaled his fellow members with any number of interesting stories of the day's excitement.

Once the building was largely empty, with only Marjorie, Stella, Bob and an enhanced night security team left, our cluster manager, Meredith, arrived with a building inspection team from Grey Smoothie Central. Marjorie followed them for more than an hour as they combed every inch of the building before concluding that the court would have to remain closed for repairs until at least Thursday – something Marjorie thought should have been pretty obvious from a quick inspection of the front doors and surrounding areas, which were in fact the only areas ever to have been threatened. The police recovered the remains of a small home-made explosive device, not very efficient or powerful, but sufficiently so to do some damage to the front doors, and render some repairs and a thorough security check essential.

By now it was somewhere between nine thirty and ten o'clock. Stella said that she would have to email the solicitors in each of the cases to tell them they were adjourned at least until Thursday, so that they could stand down defendants and witnesses. She would also have to email the staff, to confirm that it was business as usual and that they should all be back at work bright and early this morning. Marjorie and Meredith insisted on staying as late as necessary to help her, and as they settled themselves in Stella's office, Marjorie confided in me that Stella had just produced a bottle of Jameson's and three glasses. Well, fair enough: if ever three women had earned a drink, it was these three.

At ten forty-five, Guy's Hospital called Stella to say that the defendant's condition was less serious than first believed. He had woken up, and his injuries were not thought to be in any way life-threatening. He would be moved out of intensive care some time this morning. In view of the afternoon's events, the hospital's publicity department was giving this development as much exposure as possible.

At about eleven fifteen Marjorie was alone with the security staff and ready to make her way home. By now, everything outside on the street was quiet. Two uniformed officers were stationed outside the doors of the court in case of further trouble, but there was no sign that they would be called into action. Nonetheless, I insisted that Marjorie call a taxi to take her home. She didn't argue the point. While she waited for the taxi, I told her with absolute sincerity how sorry I was that I hadn't been there, and how beautifully she'd handled everything the day had thrown at her, and how very proud I was of her. Then I realised how patronising that sounded, and apologised. It was then that I realised how much guilt I was feeling about being away and leaving Marjorie to deal with this mess: not that there was any way I could have anticipated it, but as RJ you do tend to think it's all somehow down to you, and it becomes very personal when anything goes wrong at your court. Marjorie told me that she hadn't found anything I'd said patronising; she was grateful for the compliment. She asked me again if I needed any help with my case.

When I finally got to bed after midnight, I lay awake and stared at the ceiling into the small hours.

The drive from Huntingdon to Lower Wattage takes about half an hour. By nine thirty the rush hour traffic has subsided, and we soon find ourselves meandering at a leisurely pace, in the light of a grey, cloudy morning, along flat fen country roads past fields of rough, clumpy grass and black soil, bordered by an occasional line of tall, thin trees – ash, perhaps willow? I don't know: the Reverend Mrs Walden would identify them immediately, but trees have never been my strong point. I am in a comfortable limousine, with Robert and Ruth, Anand and Molly.

The atmosphere is relaxed. Robert and Ruth tell me about their chambers in Cambridge. Both are graduates of the University who have always loved the Cambridge area. Ruth did her pupillage in Cambridge and stayed on to become a member of chambers. Robert started out in practice in London but felt irresistibly drawn to the countryside. Although the range of work may be more limited in Cambridge, they both like the more forgiving pace of provincial practice, and the more trusting, collegiate relationship that exists between members of a small local bar. They express concern about yesterday's events at Bermondsey – Ruth knows Marjorie slightly from events at Lincoln's Inn, of which they are both members, and is not at all surprised by her brilliant handling of the crisis. But there's a definite subtext: that in their eyes the violence only serves to confirm the wisdom of their choice in opting for Cambridge. Anand is well thought of at all the local courts, and has a promising career ahead of him in the court service. But his true passion is cricket. He captains a local town team, and despite two unsuccessful trials still harbours ambitions of playing at the county level. Molly is happy enough in her job, but is waiting for her prince to ride up to her door on his white charger and whisk her off to warmer foreign climes.

We park in front of the Middle Plot. The parties and their respective solicitors are waiting for us, as arranged, standing separately and apparently nervously in their own gardens. No one knows quite what to do, and I have to take charge. Fortunately, without twelve inquisitive jurors wandering everywhere and trying to see and hear things they shouldn't, this is one view that's unlikely to cause problems. But I decide to keep the parties separate, asking Anand and Molly to walk with me, placing the Pearce party to my left, and the Barratt party to my right; and in that formation we begin our tour of the street.

We walk in silence around the grounds of the Post House to its rear garden, then around the Middle Plot, and finally around the periphery to the garden of the Old Rectory, with its vegetable patches and its greenhouse. There is no sign of current horticultural activity on the Middle Plot at all, though a few fruit trees survive towards the back of the plot, and there are numerous indications of past plantings. I find myself surprised to see that the Post House garden is a disaster area, with cracked paving stones overgrown by weeds, and a ruinous wooden shed near collapse, with broken window panes. Ruth is obviously tempted to giggle, while Robert shakes his head sadly. There is no Best Village Competition to be won here, especially if the judges take a peek behind the scenes. Gwendolyn Pearce might have been anxious to turn the Middle Plot into a local attraction, but evidently her ambition doesn't extend to her own garden, which looks as though no one has taken much interest in it since Mr Lampeter left in such a hurry in 1651.

For some reason, we then walk the length of The Ramblings in both directions. I'm leading the view, so I probably ought to know why we're doing this, but I don't. The walk seems to start spontaneously, and I see no advantage in stopping it. Perhaps I'm trying to get a feel for this place, so remote from everything I'm used to. Perhaps I'm expecting the local families to be looking out on me doubtfully, perhaps pulling aside their lace curtains to offer me some subtle, mystic indication of where the truth in this odd little case lies. But the whole place looks deserted, and for a moment it feels as if we've travelled back six hundred years in time to find that there's been an outbreak of the Plague and the surviving inhabitants have fled for their lives. But there are lights burning in the Black Bull, and a customer or two to be seen in Miller's grocery, and once in a while a disinterested pedestrian or cyclist passes us with no overt sign of curiosity. I decide that it's time to return to the scene of the dispute. We walk to the middle of the Middle Plot and gather around in a circle.

'Tell me, Mr Barratt,' I ask, 'how much of the plot did you and your father use when you were growing vegetables and so on? Can you point to the parts you were planting?'

He looks around several times.

'It was mostly up at the top end there, by the fruit trees, sir,' he replies. 'We tried to keep all the plants in the same area, and then we used the rest for playing cricket sometimes, and for parties in the good weather.'

'You would plant closer to the water supply from the house or the back garden?'

'Exactly, sir, yes. But during the war we used almost the

whole plot. We had a lot more people to feed then, you see, and my father being in charge of the Home Guard for the village…'

He stops abruptly and looks around again, almost as if something is puzzling him.

'Yes, Mr Barratt,' I say after we have waited for some time. 'Did you want to add anything?'

'No,' he replies quietly, just before his knees begin to give way. Ruth and his solicitor are there in a flash to support him, and a moment or two later, Robert joins them. They sit Archie down on the ground.

'Quick, fetch him some water,' Andrew Pearce says to his wife.

'Yes, of course,' Gwendolyn replies, rushing without actually running towards her front door. Molly, uninvited, goes with her.

'There's a bench up there by the fruit trees,' Anand points out. 'Let's get him over there.'

Between them, they stand Archie up again, and walk him slowly over to the bench, where he can sit in greater comfort. Anand squats by his side. Gwendolyn appears with a large glass of water, which she insists on presenting to Archie herself.

'Take small sips,' she advises, holding the glass for him. 'Drink as much as you need, but take your time.'

He takes several sips, and nods. Perhaps for the first time ever, their eyes meet. 'Thank you,' he says. She puts the glass in his hands and stands nearby.

'Mr Barratt, is there any medicine you need?' Anand asks. 'If you tell me where it is and give me your key, I'll get it for you.'

Archie shakes his head. 'No. I don't need anything. I'll be all right in a minute.'

'Are you sure? I can call a doctor if you like, or we can run you over to Cambridge, to the A & E at Addenbrookes.'

'No. I don't need a doctor.' He looks at me strangely. 'The

thing is, sir, I've just remembered something. It's just come back to me, and it's come as a bit of a shock. But I think I'd better tell you about it, all the same.'

'Is it something to do with the case?' I ask.

'Yes, sir. It's about the use we made of the Plot here.'

'In that case,' I suggest, 'perhaps you might like to talk to Miss Bannerman and your solicitor first, in case they want to give you any advice. The rest of us will move over to the Post House, out of earshot, while you talk.'

Another shake of the head. 'No. It's something I've just got to say.'

Ruth looks at me doubtfully. But there's nothing I can do. I can't stop the man talking if he's determined to do so. If I had a jury, perhaps, but not in this case.

'I'll allow both sides to ask any further questions once we're back in court,' I assure her. She nods.

'Do you feel up to it?' Gwendolyn asks.

'Yes.' He glances at all of us in turn. 'I was just a little boy during the war,' he begins, 'so my memory of that time isn't perfect. But I do remember my father and my grandfather digging for victory, and there were other men from the village, older men who weren't away fighting, and the women too, of course, who helped them. I remember that very clearly. But there's something else that went on here, too, something I've had dreams about all my life: and now it's coming back to me.' He pauses.

'Go on,' Ruth says encouragingly.

'Well, like I said in my court statement, my dad wasn't able to go to fight – he did try, you know, but they rejected him on medical grounds. So he volunteered for the Civil Defence and the Home Guard. There wasn't very much of that going on in the smaller villages, not as much as there should have been. We relied more on Cambridge and the bigger towns like Ramsey.

In Lower Wattage it was my dad and two older men, Ken Baker and Ed Woodward – both dead a long time now – and my dad was in charge, being the youngest, I suppose. This is how I remember it – he didn't talk about it much after the war.'

We all nod. He takes a few more sips of water.

'But one thing I remember, or think I remember, is the sticky bombs.'

'The what?' Ruth asks after a prolonged silence.

'The sticky bombs. An officer in uniform from Cambridge brought them for my dad. He said he was taking them to the Home Guard in all the towns and villages, and he explained to my dad how they were supposed to use them.'

'Archie,' Ruth asks, 'what…are… sticky bombs, exactly?'

'They were, like, magnetic bombs – well more like hand grenades, really, except they were magnetic – but we always called them sticky bombs. The idea was: when the German tanks arrived, we were supposed to rush out into the street, pull the pin out, put the bomb on the tank, and run away again, so it would go off before they could remove it. How you were supposed to do that without getting yourself shot, no one ever explained; but that was the idea, apparently.'

There is silence for some time, as those present begin to digest the significance of this morsel of Home Guard history.

'Mr Barratt,' I say in due course, 'history records that the German tanks didn't make it quite as far as Lower Wattage, doesn't it? So after the war, did an officer come from Cambridge to collect the sticky bombs and take them away again?'

'No, sir. That's the point. My dad didn't feel he could keep them in the house or even out in the garden – you know, I was running around there all the time, and my cousins would come to see us, and our friends from school. It would have been too dangerous. So – and this is the part I'm a bit vague on – but it came back to me just now that, once the threat of an invasion had passed, he and Ken Baker buried them here on the Middle Plot, to keep them safe. And then the war ended, and I don't know whether he asked Cambridge to send someone to dig them up again, or whether he just forgot about them.'

'Oh, my God,' Gwendolyn says. She sits down abruptly on the bench next to Archie. She looks a bit pale.

'I don't remember anyone digging them up. Of course, I could have been at school when it happened. But I don't remember anyone saying anything about it.'

'This is complete nonsense…' Andrew Pearce protests.

But Anand already has his phone out. 'Mr Barratt, do you have any idea exactly where they may be buried, and roughly how many of them there are?'

He shakes his head.

'The memory came back while I was standing down there, so I think it might be down there somewhere. It wouldn't have been near where we were planting, so I would say, down that way, nearer to the street. And as to how many – I remember seeing them laid out on the table in our living room when the officer unloaded them from the box. There might have been ten, something like that.'

Anand has tapped a number into his phone. Judging by the speed with which his call is answered, he's called 999. Of course, I realise belatedly, he will have been through drills for all kinds of emergencies at court any number of times, including full-scale building evacuations. He's used to taking charge in this kind of situation, even if an outdoor location is rather unusual for a courtroom setting, and if anything, the evacuation is on a far smaller scale than he's used to.

'Police… yes, I'm in Lower Wattage… W-A-T-T-A-G-E, a street called The Ramblings… R-A… yes, that's right, and I've just been alerted to the possible presence of unexploded World

War Two ordnance… yes, that's exactly what I said… a bomb, yes… well, possibly more than one, actually, it could be as many as ten… my name is Anand Gupta… G-U-P-T-A… could you expedite this, please? Yes, I will hold the line…'

He turns to me. 'Judge, I'd like everybody to make their way off the Middle Plot in an orderly fashion and convene in the Black Bull.'

'There's no need for all that, surely,' Andrew Pearce protests. 'There can't be any danger. Even assuming that there ever were any sticky bombs, or whatever you call them, buried here – which, I must say, I rather doubt – they've been here for at least sixty years, haven't they, with children jumping up and down, playing football and cricket all over the place? If they were going to explode, they would have done it by now, for God's sake.'

'Ordnance can deteriorate over time, Mr Pearce,' Anand replies. 'I'd prefer not to take any chances. In any case, the police will probably insist on evacuating the area so that the bomb squad can take a look.'

'Anand is right,' I say with as much authority as I can muster. 'Let's exit top right, up by the vegetable patches. From what Mr Barratt has told us, there shouldn't be anything in that area.'

I lead the way at a measured pace, the Pearces following behind me with an ill grace – as if to indicate that in their view, we are all falling victim to some desperate confidence trick on the part of Archie Barratt – and with Molly, doing a passable imitation of a border collie, shepherding the others into line behind them. We make a wide trajectory taking us to the right of the Old Rectory, and then turn towards the street. As we reach the street, I inform our limo driver of the situation, and advise him to remove the car to a place of safety, preferably the car park of the Black Bull. He sets off immediately. I turn back towards Anand.

'No need to stand there, Anand,' I say. 'The police will find us. Come away.'

But he's talking on the phone, and as we reach the door of the Black Bull the sound of a single siren and the flashing of blue lights announce the arrival of the first police response in the form of the local bobby. I look at my watch: almost twelve already. It's a slightly ridiculous formality in the circumstances, but it's time to declare that the Court has decided to take an early lunch. Work is effectively over for the morning, anyway – the view has come to an abrupt end for now – and it doesn't take me long to see that the odds on any further case-related work being done today are getting longer by the minute. I make the announcement about lunch accordingly. The parties and their lawyers commandeer separate tables on opposite sides of the bar. Molly is explaining the situation to Dennis, who is alarmed at first, but when Molly explains that there is no threat to the Black Bull, recovers admirably and starts taking orders for coffee, soft drinks and sandwiches. I order coffee and a Cheddar and pickle sandwich; I have my eye on the bar, but it will have to wait until later.

I call Marjorie, who is in chambers receiving periodic reports on the progress of the repair work going on at the front entrance. All is quiet, she tells me. Apparently word of Chummy's miraculous recovery has spread, and the police haven't detected any enthusiasm among his mates – a number of whom are in any case in custody, facing serious public order and explosives charges – for a repetition of the events of yesterday. All the same, DI Derbyshire isn't ready to release Legless from her protection just yet – she's planning on keeping him in her clutches until the end of the week, just in case. But all in all, everything seems to be under control. Stella is hard at work revamping the list for the next few weeks, and Marjorie thinks she may be able to list a few urgent bail applications tomorrow, and perhaps some guilty pleas and sentences on Thursday and Friday, so that the week isn't a complete write-off. She asks me what I'm doing.

'Funny you should ask,' I reply. 'As a matter of fact, I'm in the Black Bull pub in Lower Wattage with the parties and their lawyers, hiding from some explosive devices.'

She laughs hysterically, and rings off.

* * *

Tuesday afternoon

Just after one o'clock, a uniformed police inspector arrives, accompanied by a sergeant and by Anand, for whom Molly has thoughtfully ordered a ginger ale and a vegetable wrap.

'Inspector Jeffrey Whittaker, from Cambridge, my Lord. I just wanted to give you an update on what's happening out there, and I must say I'm grateful to Mr Gupta here for his help.'

'My pleasure, Inspector,' Anand replies, taking a grateful gulp of his ginger ale.

'We've got officers from the bomb squad on the way from RAF Alconbury, sir, ETA one thirty. My lads have evacuated the houses opposite the Pearce and Barratt residences, just to make sure, and the occupants have been advised that they won't be allowed back until the Middle Plot has been thoroughly inspected.'

'How long is that likely to take?' I ask.

'It's impossible to say, sir, until the bomb squad boys know what they're dealing with. If you want my honest opinion, it could be a long afternoon. I would settle in for the long haul if I were you, make yourself comfortable.' He grins. 'Look on the bright side, sir. It could be worse: there are lot of less comfortable places you could be holed up in.'

I have to agree.

The leader of the bomb squad team, an amiable young lieutenant by the name of Jonathan Dawson, calls to pay his respects just after two o'clock. Everyone leaves the refuge of their separate tables to gather around – they all want to hear this.

'My team are running the metal detector over the entire area now, sir,' Lieutenant Dawson assures us. 'I say "metal detector", but obviously it's a bit more sophisticated than the version people use to search for old coins and the like. Actually, it's more like clearing a minefield.' This causes a couple of gasps and sharp intakes of breath among those assembled. 'Don't worry,' he adds quickly. 'We're taking every precaution. We're going to be very careful, but if there's anything there, we'll find it. '

'And then what?' I ask.

'If there's anything there, sir, we're going to dig the blighters up one at a time. We'll make an assessment of their condition. If they're stable, meaning they're not about to blow, we'll remove them back to base and detonate them remotely under safe conditions.'

'What if they are about to blow?'

'Well, sir… then we might have to detonate them *in situ*. That's why no one can return home just yet. I don't know how long it's all going to take, to be honest. We have a couple of very powerful arc lights on the way, so we can continue work after dark if necessary. We're not going to leave these things where they could cause harm a minute longer than we have to, believe you me; and at least we have one major advantage in this situation.'

'What might that be?' I ask.

He grins. 'Well, they're ours, sir, aren't they? Usually when we come across ordnance of this vintage, it's German, and before we can do anything else we have to identify the type and work out how it's made; and often the markings have faded and they're all in German anyway. But these will be ours, and we should have a blueprint on its way to my phone less than a minute after we've dug the first one up.'

A soldier opens the door and puts his head inside.

'Sorry to interrupt, sir,' he says, 'but you need to see this.'

'Do excuse me,' Lieutenant Dawson says. 'Duty calls. Further update as soon as I can.'

It's after three by the time we are given the further update. Lieutenant Dawson is in company with the soldier who put his head around the door earlier, and he's cradling, with obvious care, an almost spherical silver metallic object lying in his gloved hands on top of what looks like a filthy old towel. Once again, everyone gathers round. He spots Archie, who's standing to his left, next to Ruth.

'You would be Mr Barratt, would you, sir?'

'Yes. I would.'

He grins. 'Recognise this, by any chance, sir?'

Archie looks closely, and backs away rather quickly. 'Oh, my God. That's one of them. That's one of the sticky bombs.' This causes a general movement away from the door.

'It's all right,' the Lieutenant assures us. 'It's completely stable. The pins are in as tight as the day it left the production line. I just wanted to show you. Ladies and gentlemen, say hello to anti-tank hand grenade Number 74, more commonly known as the "sticky bomb", issued to the Home Guard for use against enemy tanks in the event of an invasion. There are actually two pins in place, one to release the sticky core from the outer casing, and one to activate the device. The core is a glass sphere filled with nitroglycerin – very nasty potentially.' He looks directly at Archie. 'But I'm glad your father never had to use one of these, sir. I know I wouldn't want to.'

'Oh? Why is that, then?' Archie asks.

'Well, for one thing, even if you could get near enough to the tank to plant it, it might not stick if the tank was dirty and muddy, as they usually are. The only reliable method of getting it to do real damage would be to climb up and throw it into the interior of the tank, in which case the explosion would almost certainly kill you as well as the crew. Also, it had a nasty habit of sticking to your clothing instead of the tank if you weren't careful what you were doing: and obviously, that wasn't good. Apparently the government advertised sticky bombs to the public with the slogan, "At least you can take one with you". Not the most inviting call to action, if you ask me, but I suppose those were different times.'

'My dad would have taken his chances,' Archie insists.

'I'm sure he would have, sir,' Lieutenant Dawson agrees at once. 'And that's not all we have to thank your father for. It's down to him that they've lain there all these years without blowing.'

'Oh?'

'He kept them in good nick for us by wrapping them up in these oilskins before he buried them. The oilskins help to keep the dirt and moisture out. It's thanks to him this one's not going to hurt anybody.'

'This one? So there are more, Lieutenant?' Anand asks tentatively.

The Lieutenant nods. 'We think there are twelve altogether. That's what the machine is indicating, and if so it's going to take us a while to dig them all out. But if they're all in the same good nick as this one, we will be able to bring them up safely. Anyway, I should get back, but I wanted to show you this. It seems that Mr Barratt's memory is completely accurate, and we're certainly glad that you remembered about these little blighters, sir.'

'I'm sure we all are,' I add, with a pointed look in the direction of Andrew Pearce, who nods towards Archie, though not as graciously as one might have hoped. They return to their respective tables.

Lunchtime turns into very late afternoon, with no further

updates. But as dusk begins to settle we can see the arc lights casting their bright light down on the Middle Plot, and from the movement of the dark figures around the excavator and the occasional shouted instructions we know that the delicate work is continuing. Oddly, despite the police cordon around quite a stretch of The Ramblings and the evacuation of a handful of residents, the population of Lower Wattage seems to be taking the day's excitement in its stride, and a good number of locals have joined us in the Black Bull to partake of their usual pints, as if there were nothing out of the ordinary going on. Just before six o'clock, bowing to the inevitable, I declare court to be adjourned for the day and advise everyone that they are now free to drink whatever they want. Leading by example, I order a pint of Abbot for myself, a vodka and coke for Molly, and another ginger ale for Anand, who, he intimates, doesn't do alcohol. The Pearce and Barratt camps make their own separate ways to the bar to follow suit.

By eight o'clock I'm on the phone, chatting happily away with Marjorie, who in contrast to yesterday evening is relaxing at home with her feet up and a gin and tonic close to hand. The atmosphere in the bar of the Black Bull has also become considerably more relaxed, and there has even been a little tentative cross-table contact between the parties in my case – until Lieutenant Dawson suddenly returns, looking rather more serious than hitherto. He has with him a soldier carrying a walkie-talkie.

'Right, everyone,' he says, raising his voice against the din in the bar, 'if I could have your attention, please: just to let you know, we've removed ten of the devices without any problem – they're very stable and not presenting any threat. However, the remaining two are buried very close together and one is showing signs of serious deterioration. The outside pin is highly unstable, and we don't think it would be safe to try to remove it. Unfortunately, this leaves us with no alternative but to detonate it *in situ*. When we do it will also set off the twelfth device, so there will be a rather big bang, and, I'm afraid, some damage to the frontages of the houses, especially those on that side of the street. I'm sorry, but there's nothing we can do. Stand by.'

'Are we in any danger here?' Dennis calls across the room from the bar.

'No, sir,' Lieutenant Dawson replies. 'But,' he adds as an afterthought, 'everyone stay back from the windows – just in case.'

'Oh, my God,' Dennis mutters to himself.

'Charlie, are you still there?' Marjorie is asking.

'Yes, sorry,' I reply. 'There's something going on here. Hang on a moment.'

'All personnel clear, and no civilian activity visible, sir,' the soldier is saying, holding the radio to his ear. 'The sergeant is awaiting your order for remote detonation, sir.'

'Proceed,' the Lieutenant replies authoritatively.

'Proceed. Roger that, sir. Proceed!' the soldier fairly bellows into the radio.

'Charlie, what on earth is going on down there? Are you –?'

There is the most almighty bang, and the sound of glass breaking.

'Oh, my God,' I hear Gwendolyn shriek.

'Charlie, Charlie, for God's sake. What's going on? Are you all right?'

'Yes, I'm fine, Marjorie,' I reply. 'They had to detonate a Number 74 anti-tank hand grenade, that's all. Nothing to worry about, all in a day's work; we're all at a safe distance. I think it's all clear, now.'

'Charlie…'

'Just one of those noises that give delight and hurt not,' I say. 'Look, I need to go and talk to the parties, make sure they're all right. I'll call you back later.'

* * *

Tuesday evening

Feeling fairly sure that events in Lower Wattage will by now have attracted the attention of the media, and that the Reverend Mrs Walden may well have learned of them, I make a pre-emptive call home. Fortunately, she's been in a Parochial Church Council meeting for two or three hours and hasn't seen the news yet, so I'm able to reassure her that, whatever alarming images she may see, I'm safe and sound and happily contemplating a third pint of Abbot without a care in the world – except for the nagging thought that fairly soon, despite the recent trauma it has suffered, I'm going to have to decide the fate of the much disputed Middle Plot, and for all today's excitement I'm still no wiser about which way I'm going with it.

The bomb squad and the police have left now and Lower Wattage has returned to some semblance of normality. Thoughtfully, the bomb squad have left behind the arc lights – the ground around the Post House and the Old Rectory is cracked and uneven, and there's broken glass everywhere, so it would be a real hazard in the dark. Molly and Anand are deep in conversation at the bar, and I'm just wondering about finding our driver and making my way back to the George for the night, when I see Robert and Ruth approaching. I wave them into chairs at my table.

'How are they all doing?' I ask.

'I think Archie's in a state of shock,' Ruth replies. 'He keeps asking what would have happened if he hadn't remembered about the sticky bombs. I think it's beginning to dawn on him what a lucky man he is. That device could have blown at any time, Lieutenant Dawson said.'

'He's led a charmed life,' I reply.

They look at each other. 'Are you in a hurry to get back to Huntingdon, Judge?' Ruth asks.

'I suppose not,' I reply. 'Were you thinking of another drink? I daresay it would do us all good. Allow me…'

'Well, no, actually, Judge,' Ruth continues. 'I mean, we could, but also we were thinking that we might be able to take advantage of the parties being in something of an altered state as a result of today's events.'

'An altered state? Oh, you mean, the shock of it all?'

'Exactly, Judge. Well, that and a couple of strong drinks apiece, certainly in Archie's case.'

I look at Robert. 'Are the Pearces also in an altered state?'

'They're certainly rather traumatised by it all, Judge, and I daresay the gin and tonics have something to do with it too at this point. She's quite weepy – and she's not someone who does weepy. I've certainly never seen her like this before.'

I nod and swirl the remains of my pint around in the bottom of the glass.

'Are you seriously suggesting,' I ask, 'that we should take advantage of the trauma and inebriation the parties are experiencing?' I can't think of anything less likely to happen in a criminal case at Bermondsey. I'd be more likely to remand the pair of them in custody if they showed up at court in that condition. But then again, I did declare court closed for the day.

They exchange looks. 'Indeed we are, Judge,' Robert replies.

'What – to promote a settlement of some kind?'

'Exactly, Judge.' He smiles. 'I know it's not something you're used to in the Crown Court, but in civil cases we can often do a bit of mediation while the trial is still going on, and there's no difficulty about the judge joining in, as long as the parties have no objection.'

'If you don't mind telling them that you haven't made your mind up which way you're going yet,' Ruth adds, 'so there's still everything to play for.'

'There is,' I reply honestly. 'Even leaving the facts on one side, I'm going to need your help with the law before I can decide anything, so I still have a long way to go.'

'Sounds good, Judge. Do you want to give it a go?'

'I've never actually done a mediation,' I admit. 'I have no experience of them at all. But I had no idea that it was the practice to do them after two or three pints, or gins and tonics.'

'It's not usual, Judge,' Ruth concedes. 'But they do happen in all kinds of circumstances. For a successful mediation you need everyone in the right frame of mind, and sometimes you find yourself in a situation they don't teach you about when you do your mediation training.'

'Such as doing it in a pub when everyone's had a couple of drinks,' Robert adds.

'It's just a matter of taking advantage of circumstances when they arise,' Ruth says. 'Are you up for it?'

'Do you really think it might work?'

'It might, Judge,' Robert replies. 'The key is to get the parties to tell each other what they're really upset about – which often has nothing to do with the things they're suing each other over – and set the stage for apologies. You'd be amazed how many cases settle once the parties are prepared to apologise to each other. And with their guard down – who knows? *In vino veritas*, as they say.'

I'm wondering what Marjorie would have to say about this, and hoping that I'm not making a complete fool of myself. I could, of course, easily call her and find out what she thinks. But I'm here and she isn't, and I have a gut feeling that these two barristers, who know their clients far better than I do, know what they're doing and aren't going to lead me down the garden path. And in any case, what's the worst that can happen – that they won't let me do a civil case again? I'm in uncharted waters, and perhaps part of it is the Abbot talking, but it seems worth taking a chance.

'All right, then. Why not?' I reply. 'Let's give it a try.'

'There's a long table by the wall at the far end of the bar,' Robert observes. 'Why don't I move everyone over there? Do you want to take the lead, Ruth?'

'I'd be glad to.'

Cooperation once again, I note. I make my way over to the long table, where Ruth places me at the head of the table, with Robert and herself on either side of me, the Pearces next to Robert and Archie next to her, with Anand, Molly, and the solicitors at the far end of the table.

'With the Judge's agreement, and yours,' Ruth begins quietly, 'we thought we might explore whether there is any ground for you to come together and talk about the case, away from the more formal atmosphere of the courtroom. Robert and I understand, obviously, that what's happened today has been very distressing for you. It's come as a shock to us all. But as a result, there may be a window for you to talk to each other and see if you can come to a better understanding of what it is you're really angry with each other about. The discussion will be completely off the record, so it won't be binding on anyone, it can't be referred to in court, and it won't affect the judge's view of the case.' She turns to me. 'In fact, Judge Walden, I believe you feel that you're not in a position to reach any conclusion about the case yet?'

'That's quite right,' I confirm.

'Archie,' Ruth continues, 'would you like to kick it off for us?'

I'm fascinated. I assume there's been some prior discussion

between them about the process of mediation, from which Ruth has emerged fairly confident that Archie would indeed like to kick it off – because otherwise this may turn into the shortest mediation on record, which wouldn't do anything positive for the future management of the case, and might well be a disaster for her side of it. My previous observation of Archie Barratt doesn't predispose me to think that a holistic practice like mediation would greatly appeal to him, but looking at him again, I note that the events of the day do seem to have had an effect, and an altered state isn't a bad way of putting it. He looks somewhere between shocked and chastened, or perhaps both. I'm still not entirely sure how spontaneous his recovered memory of the sticky bombs was – the cynic in me insists that having twelve lethal explosive devices buried so close to your home is not the kind of thing you're likely to forget, even if they were buried there more than sixty years ago. But the fact remains that he didn't make any effort to have the grenades disposed of during that time despite the obvious risk, and there's no doubt that, as the Reverend Mrs Walden would say, he's altered the chemistry of the case.

'Well,' he replies after some time. 'I suppose what's happened today has made me think – think how lucky I've been, and my boys have been, over all these years. And when I think about that... about what could have happened... well, it sort of puts everything else into perspective. So, I suppose what I want to say to you, Mrs Pearce – Gwendolyn, if I may...'

I wouldn't put money on that permission being granted... but to my amazement...

'Of course, Archie...'

'I suppose what I want to say, Gwendolyn, is that I'm sorry about ripping up all your trees and flowers and such like. It was a childish thing to do. But, you see, I got annoyed when you started mucking us about when you'd only been here about five minutes, trying to make Lower Wattage into some kind of show village – which it isn't and never has been – and I suppose I resented you as a newcomer, having had the Pitt family as my neighbours for so long. But anyway… I shouldn't have done it, and I want to apologise to you.'

Ruth is smiling at me. As Dorothy once put it: 'Toto, I've a feeling we're not in Kansas anymore.' This isn't a different state from the Crown Court, it's a different planet, and it's one on which I can't immediately get my bearings. I return the smile. There's nothing I can do but sit back and watch the experts work.

Gwendolyn gives a deep sigh. 'I'm the one who should be apologising, Archie,' she replies. 'We could have been killed today, too, and somehow all this arguing seems so trivial after that. It was insensitive of me to rush into the village and think I was somehow entitled to change your way of life, which you and your family have had for centuries. I'm so embarrassed. I want to apologise to you in turn, and so does Andrew – don't you, Andrew?'

Andrew nods, although he doesn't seem to be in quite such an altered state as his wife.

'Accepted, of course,' Archie replies graciously.

'It was all so silly, anyway,' Gwendolyn adds. 'I can't even get my own garden under control. Mr Pitt left it in such a state I don't even know where to start with it. It was stupid of me to think I could transform the whole village when I can't even transform my own garden.'

'Bill Evershed could help you with that,' Archie volunteers. 'He lives down on Market Street – the far end, by the new housing estate – and he does a bit of landscaping. He's got some good heavy equipment that will rip all that long grass and the weeds right out of the garden and churn up the ground, and once you've got rid of all that kind of stuff you can take your time and plan what you want to do with it. I'll call him tomorrow and ask him to drop by.'

'Thank you. That would be very kind.'

'And – first things first – his brother Joe is a builder. We should ask him to come and look at the damage first thing in the morning. Well, we can't leave it as it is, can we? He should at least be able to put some temporary boards up for us until we can get some new windows made, and he can clear away the worst of the mess so that we can at least get in and out of our front doors. Shall I see if he's available?'

'Yes please. That would be wonderful.'

'And there is one funny thing about all this, isn't there?' Archie says.

'What's that then?' Gwendolyn asks.

'Well, the Home Guard managed to do what Hitler and his lot couldn't do in five years of trying, didn't they? They finally blew up The Ramblings.'

Even Andrew sees the humour in that, and we all have a good laugh.

'Well, that all sounds very positive,' Ruth says. 'Thank you both. I feel you've both come a long way. Don't you, Robert?'

'Very much so,' Robert replies.

'Does anyone feel differently about the case, now that we've cleared the air to some extent?'

'I'm not sure what we're even arguing about,' Gwendolyn says, after a longish silence. 'It's not as if the Pitts ever made any use of the Middle Plot, is it? Archie, if you're willing, I think we should treat it as a joint project, and see what we can do with it. If the lawyers can work it out, so that you can come on to the land and work it, as long as we can talk about what we want to do with it – what would you think about that?'

'I'd be very happy with that, Gwendolyn,' Archie replies. 'I never really wanted to own the Plot all on my own. I didn't have any use for that, but I didn't know what else to do to get access to it. If we could work out some arrangement like that, I'm ready to drop the case and agree to it.'

He offers her his hand. She takes it. Ruth turns to me.

'Judge, if you could give us until after lunch tomorrow, that should be enough time for Robert and I to work on some wording and produce a draft agreement. We should at least be able to present you with a basic agreement, subject to liberty to apply if we need your help with the final version.'

'They will both need the morning to secure their property after the damage,' Robert adds. 'We can work on the agreement while they do that.'

'Of course,' I agree immediately. 'I'll be ready to start at two o'clock, but let me know if you need any more time.'

Andrew Pearce is taking orders for drinks. Robert, Ruth and I discreetly remove to a table closer to the bar, so that they don't have to worry about saying the right thing in front of us. Of course, there is some small chance that being left alone together will cause the agreement to unravel as quickly as it was made, but there's no sign of that at the moment. I get drinks in for the three of us.

'So, does this kind of thing often happen in civil cases?' I ask.

'You'd be surprised how effective it can be if you can just find the right space for the parties to get together away from court,' Ruth replies. 'Admittedly, this was a bit unusual by any standards, but – well, whatever works.'

'We hope today's experience won't put you off doing more civil cases, Judge,' Robert adds, 'and perhaps you'll come out this way to see us again.'

'Who knows? Perhaps I will,' I reply.

We toast each other silently.

On arriving back at the George, after some hesitation, I call

Marjorie. It's late now, and I'm not really expecting her to be awake; but she's on her own – Nigel is in Frankfurt for work – her memories of yesterday continue to linger, and so she's sitting up on the sofa with the lights dimmed, wide awake, with a mug of cocoa and a glass of something stronger, watching old films on TV. I regale her with the full story of the events of my day, and to my pleasure and relief she laughs uproariously.

'I know it's late at night,' I say, 'but may I ask you a technical question?'

'At your own risk,' she replies.

'Well, if a member of the Home Guard buries sticky bombs in his neighbour's plot during the war and then leaves them buried there for more than sixty years without saying anything, could that constitute evidence of adverse possession?'

'Absolutely. Why do you ask?'

I smile to myself. 'Oh, nothing really. It's just that I have a shrewd suspicion that the Barratt family are not quite the country bumpkins people like the Pearces take them for…' I pause for a moment or two. 'Tell me honestly, Marjorie, do you think I did the right thing?'

'What, you mean getting everyone around the table together when they were all as pissed as newts?'

'Yes. I mean, you don't think it could all go horribly wrong, do you?'

She is silent for some seconds.

'Well, Charlie, sitting the parties down in a pub and plying them with drink probably isn't in the best classical tradition of mediation. But apparently, it worked. I suppose the only potential for it to go wrong is if the parties wake up this morning with a hangover and start to get buyer's remorse. As you know, until the ink's dry on the settlement agreement, they're free to change their minds, and I'm not sure I'd want all this coming out in the Court of Appeal.'

'But counsel implied that things like this are all in a day's work for you civil types.'

'Yes,' she replies, 'and you had good counsel in front of you, who wouldn't have let it happen unless they were pretty sure of a good outcome. Besides, the sticky bomb trauma probably played just as much part in it as the drink. Sometimes, that kind of thing focuses people's minds in a way a mere trip to court can't. I wouldn't worry about it, if I were you. Well done! You've successfully concluded your first civil case.'

* * *

Wednesday afternoon

'My Lord,' Robert begins, 'I'm pleased to inform your Lordship that the parties have reached an agreement to settle this case, and we will not require your Lordship to give a judgment.'

I've had a nice, relaxed morning – certainly more so than the parties, who will have spent it assessing the devastation caused to their homes by the sticky bombs, and making the buildings secure until permanent repairs can be made. I enjoy a full English breakfast at the George, cooked for me personally by Darla, who's sad that I'm leaving and hopes that I will return soon – the prestige of having The Judge in Residence, one assumes – and recommends that I have a stroll around the Wednesday morning market in Market Square, which after perusing *The Times,* I do. It's no match for the legendary Bermondsey market, but it has a certain rustic charm, and strolling among the various stalls I realise that I'm actually unwinding from the cares of being the RJ of a London Crown Court and, like the barristers in my case, enjoying the slower pace of life away from the big city.

'In essence, my Lord, the claimants have withdrawn their action to assert title to the Middle Plot, and the defendant has withdrawn his claim to have acquired title to the Plot by adverse possession. Instead, the parties have signed a memorandum of understanding: the gist of which is that while the claimants will continue to have sole paper title to the Middle Plot, they will grant Mr Barratt, his heirs and assigns, a right to enter on to the land at reasonable times and to a reasonable extent for horticultural purposes. This memorandum will form the basis of a formal settlement agreement, which should be ready for signature by the end of the week.

'The reason for the slight delay is that the parties' solicitors want to consider whether to achieve that goal by means of an easement or licence, or in some other way. They are confident that they will find the most appropriate way, and copies of the documentation will be filed with the Court at that stage. The memorandum also contains an understanding between the parties, which will not form part of the formal settlement agreement, as both parties accept that it is essentially unenforceable. This understanding is that the parties will collaborate on the future use of the Middle Plot before engaging in any works there.

'Finally, my Lord, Mr and Mrs Pearce also agree not to enter Lower Wattage in the Cambridgeshire Best Kept Village Competition, or any similar competition, until such time as both parties are satisfied that doing so would command the support of the inhabitants of Lower Wattage as a whole.'

'That is correct, my Lord,' Ruth adds, 'and in the circumstances we invite your Lordship to make no order as to costs.'

'So ordered,' I say. It's a phrase I seem to remember civil judges using in films and on TV, and it's always sounded pleasingly definitive.

'The only other thing, my Lord,' Robert adds, 'is to express the gratitude of the parties, and indeed the gratitude of my learned friend and myself, to your Lordship for his willingness to adopt such an unorthodox approach to bringing the parties together. Without your Lordship's innovative approach to mediation it is very likely that we would still be contesting this case instead of settling it in such a constructive manner.'

I look up. 'I hardly think I can claim any credit for that, Mr Mason,' I protest. 'You and Miss Bannerman educated me about the possibilities available to a judge sitting without a jury in a civil case, so it wasn't really a case of innovation on my part.'

'Nonetheless, my Lord,' Ruth says, 'that's what we're going to tell Mr Justice Gulivant, as senior Presiding Judge. It's the best hope we have of making him send you back to see us again.'

Back in chambers, I thank Molly and Anand for their outstanding work during what on any view has been a remarkably challenging case, and promise that their contribution is something else Mr Justice Gulivant will be hearing about.

After Molly has left us to clear up in court, Anand and I share a pot of tea.

'Couldn't you find me something else to do for the next couple of days, Anand?' I ask. 'They won't have anything for me at Bermondsey until next week and I'm rather enjoying sitting at Huntingdon. It wouldn't be a problem for me to stay for a couple of days and help out.'

'I'm sorry, Judge,' he replies with a smile. 'I wish I could, but we just don't have that much work here. We've got nothing else scheduled until next week. Look, if you're not in a hurry, why don't you just take a couple of days for yourself, extend your stay at the George, rent a car, take in the sights? And I can recommend a couple of good restaurants, Indian and Italian, not too far away, if you like. I'm not entirely sure about the Italian, but I can claim to know a little about Indian.'

Once I'm alone I call the Reverend Mrs Walden.

'I know you're busy, Clara,' I say, 'but couldn't you take a couple of days off and come up here and breathe some fresh air with me? I'll have you back in good time for Sunday, I promise.'

'Oh, I don't know, Charlie. I've got so much to do…'

'I'm in need of pastoral care,' I whine. 'You are my vicar, you know, as well as my wife.'

She hesitates. 'Well, you have been through a lot this week,' she admits, 'so I suppose it may be my duty – spousal as well as pastoral – to assist in your recovery, and if a short foray into the country would help…'

'It might make all the difference,' I say.

'In that case, I will see you in time for dinner this evening. Get the noises, sounds and sweet airs ready for me, as long as they give delight and hurt not.'

'I think I'll forego any further noises, if you don't mind,' I reply, 'but I'll have the sounds and sweet airs ready in the George by six.'

SOMETHING BORROWED, SOMETHING BLUE

SOMETHING BORROWED, SOMETHING BLUE

Monday morning

'St Paul,' the Reverend Mrs Walden told her hushed congregation yesterday morning, 'showed us what he thought of marriage when he wrote to the Corinthians, didn't he? "It's better to marry than to burn," he advised them. Well, I'm sure he was right: but isn't that a bit like saying that it's better to eat cold porridge than to starve? It may be true, but it's not exactly a great advertisement for marriage, is it? I don't think it was marriage that concerned St Paul, as much as sex. When he said, "better to marry than to burn," he meant, of course, that it was better for a male follower of Jesus to find a woman to have sex with than to spend his whole life walking around too frustrated to think straight; and in his world a man couldn't have sex with a woman unless he was married to her. Obviously, he wasn't going to put it as directly as that, but neither was he about to offer the Corinthians the full range of choices we have available to us in our lives today.

'For St Paul, it was marriage or nothing and given that stark choice, St Paul himself apparently preferred the burning option. But is that how we should think of sex and marriage today? I don't think so; and I suspect most of you don't think so. Let's be honest about it – St Paul is great on many things, for example the supreme importance of love, but he isn't necessarily the most reliable authority when it comes to sex and marriage. He comes across as pretty uptight when it comes to anything involving sex, and he didn't think much of women, married or otherwise. So, where should Christians living in today's world, with its constant emphasis on sex, start when it comes to the subject of marriage? The church recognises marriage as a sacrament, but...'

Sitting dutifully in my pew in the parish church of St Aethelburgh and All Angels in the Diocese of Southwark, as is my wont on Sunday mornings, I am frequently in awe of the Reverend's willingness to depart from the script, so to speak. Today her subject is marriage, but I've listened to her on many other Sundays when she's raised some eyebrows on a variety of different subjects – her support for the medicinal and recreational use of cannabis and her exegesis of the biblical texts dealing with the relationship between Jesus and Mary Magdalene have caused the occasional stir in the past. But, as Abraham Lincoln, or John Lydgate, or somebody once said, 'You can't please all of the people all of the time'; and it's a lesson the Reverend Mrs Walden has taken to heart over the years. She is unapologetic about departing from the party line when she disagrees with it, and I applaud her for her willingness to dissent, as (thank goodness) do her bishop and most of the younger members of her congregation. As I say, it's not always about marriage. But at certain times of the year, when there are a good number of marriages pending at the church, the subject does tend to resurface in her sermons and just now she has something of a deluge of them. So for a week or two, marriage is going to get the full treatment.

The full treatment actually encompasses rather more than marriage in the strict sense of the term, and tends to range from the traditional Church of England wedding model – something old, something new, and all that kind of thing – to long-term cohabitation, experimental cohabitation, gay marriage, civil unions, and even to young people learning to enjoy sex responsibly with the benefit of education from both school and parents. The Reverend leaves her audience in no doubt that, in contrast to St Paul, she is in favour of Christians feeling free to express themselves sexually, whatever proponents of some other religions – not to mention the great majority of her own co-religionists – may believe. There are occasions when she holds out our own relationship as a good example of what marriage can be, and sometimes even condescends to a certain degree of detail to make her point. Mercifully, yesterday was not one of them. But she did conclude by telling her congregation that, after thirty plus years of marriage to me, her enthusiasm for marriage remained undimmed.

That made me feel good, of course, and it's a sentiment I share unreservedly. But perhaps we don't need to have quite the same degree of enthusiasm for marriage as Marcus Findlay-Smyth, whose case I am to try today: and as I arrive at court, latte and *Times* in hand, I do find myself wondering whether her open-mindedness about marriage would extend to the kind of history that awaits an unsuspecting jury this morning.

'Members of the jury, my name is Aubrey Brooks, and I appear to prosecute in this case. My learned friend Miss Cathy Writtle appears for the defendant, Marcus Findlay-Smyth, the gentleman in the dock.'

An ironic case for two unmarried counsel, I reflect, although both more than make up for their lack of the matrimonial experience in other ways. Aubrey moves in the best of circles, in which he has the reputation of being quite the ladies' man; while Cathy, who mixes in more mundane circles, is happily cohabiting with a charming South African anaesthetist whom I've met once or twice at legal dinners. They are just as different in court. Both are regular members of the Bermondsey Bar, and both are very good at what they do. Aubrey, known for his invariably elegant appearance featuring his trademark double-breasted jackets, is low-key and urbane, and polite to a fault; but quite capable of a sudden, deadly blow to the jugular when the opportunity presents itself. Cathy is equally capable of wreaking havoc on an opponent. She can sometimes be a bit frantic in court and occasionally gets a bit dishevelled as the day wears on; but she's a dogged, relentless pursuer of dishonest and evasive witnesses. She starts her assault on the prosecution case with the first witness and never lets up; and very often, something eventually gives way.

Our jury is the kind of fascinating mix of people we always seem to get at Bermondsey: it includes one man and one woman of Bangladeshi ancestry and two men originally from Eastern Europe, one of them, to judge from his dress – and the fact that he asked to take the oath on the Old Testament – Jewish. What this typically cross-cultural group is going to make of the evidence they're about to hear, and what they would have made of the Reverend Mrs Walden's sermon yesterday, is anyone's guess; but I'd love to be a fly on the wall of the jury room when they start their deliberations. Aubrey asks if they can have copies of the indictment, and as I glance over at them they are receiving their copies from Dawn, today resplendent in a bright pink dress under her black gown.

'Members of the jury,' Aubrey continues, 'this defendant, Marcus Findlay-Smyth, is a director of a small family-owned international investment bank. He earns a substantial income from his position with the bank, and in addition has some older family money of his own. In other words, he is a successful and wealthy man – the kind of man you would probably expect to have a wife and a family by the age of forty. And indeed, you will hear that in September 2012, when he was forty years of age, Mr Findlay-Smyth apparently married a woman called

Deborah Jane Martineau. The apparent marriage took place here in London, at Holy Trinity Church, Brompton. After their apparent marriage, Mr and Mrs Findlay-Smyth, as they were known to their friends and neighbours, lived together in a large flat on the top two floors of an elegant house in Park Walk. For those of you who don't know it, Park Walk is a prestigious residential street in an affluent district of the Royal Borough of Kensington and Chelsea. They lived there in some style; and about six months after the ceremony of marriage, Deborah Jane Martineau, who is some twenty years younger than Mr Findlay-Smyth, gave birth to their daughter, whom they named Charlotte.

'Now, you may have noticed, members of the jury, that I was careful to say that Mr Findlay-Smyth "apparently" married Deborah Jane Martineau. I put it in that way because, although the ceremony of marriage celebrated at Holy Trinity Brompton appeared to be perfectly regular – in other words, it appeared to comply with all the necessary legal formalities and the rules of the Church of England – it was in fact unlawful. It was unlawful because in June 1998, Mr Findlay-Smyth had married a woman called Monica Harhoff in Scotland, at a church in Edinburgh. That marriage, members of the jury, was lawful; and although, sadly, she has since died, Mrs Monica Findlay-Smyth was alive and well in September 2012 when her husband apparently married Deborah Jane Martineau.

'It is, of course, a requirement of a valid marriage that both parties are free to marry; and being free to marry means, among other things, not being lawfully married to anyone else. Members of the jury, it follows that Mr Findlay-Smyth was not free to marry Deborah Jane Martineau in September 2012, and the Crown say that in going through that apparently regular ceremony of marriage with her at Holy Trinity Brompton, he committed the offence of bigamy.

'If you would look at the indictment with me for a moment, you will see that it charges Mr Findlay-Smyth with a single count of bigamy, contrary to section 57 of the Offences against the Person Act 1861, which alleges that he, "on or about the 8th day of September 2012, married Deborah Jane Martineau during the life of his wife, Monica Harhoff Findlay-Smyth."'

The jury are looking confused, and you can't really blame them. Whoever drafted section 57 of the Offences against the Person Act 1861 overlooked the self-evident proposition that you can't 'marry' a person during the life of your wife. If you already have a wife, at best you can purport to marry another woman by going through a ceremony of marriage with her; your 'marriage' is unlawful and would be declared void by any court in the land. Why this obvious drafting error hasn't been corrected in the more than a century and a half since the act was passed is anyone's guess. I will explain it to the jury when I sum the case up to them, of course: but it doesn't reflect much credit on the law and it doesn't make the jury's job any easier to have such nonsense perpetuated in indictments. Marcus Findlay-Smyth, smartly dressed in a dark grey suit, white shirt, and a red and blue striped tie, doesn't look in any way confused. He is listening attentively but without any obvious show of anxiety, almost as if he were attending a board meeting at his bank.

'As I said a moment ago,' Aubrey continues, 'Mr Findlay-Smyth's wife Monica is deceased, and so he is technically a widower. Monica Findlay-Smyth died of natural causes in November 2016. As far as we know, Monica died without any knowledge of the ceremony of marriage celebrated at Holy Trinity Brompton in 2012 between her husband and Deborah Jane Martineau, and the two women never met.

'Indeed, both women appear to have believed, not only that they were married to the defendant, but also that they were living with him as husband and wife in perfectly normal circumstances. Deborah believed that their home was in Park Walk in Kensington and Chelsea, while Monica believed that their home was the flat in the New Town district of Edinburgh they had occupied ever since their marriage in 1998. Mr Findlay-Smyth's bank has an office in Edinburgh as well as in London; and the Crown say that he was in effect commuting between his two homes in London and Edinburgh. Cleverly, he spent enough time in turn with his wife and with Deborah to convince both women that he was simply dividing a busy work schedule equally between the two cities. Unfortunately, Monica Findlay-Smyth is no longer with us to tell you about her experience of this relationship, but the Crown will call her brother James to tell you what he observed, and Deborah Jane Martineau will give evidence about her history with the defendant.

'It may well be, members of the jury, that Mr Findlay-Smyth would have got away with this deception indefinitely, had it not been for the vigilance of a junior civil servant at Her Majesty's Revenue and Customs, who during a routine review of his tax affairs noticed some irregularities in tax returns filed by Mr Findlay-Smyth for the tax years 2015-2016 and 2016-2017, which covered the period during which Monica Findlay-Smyth died. This young civil servant, Alice Clegg, told her superiors of her findings, and they in turn passed their file to the Crown Prosecution Service.

'Members of the jury, you may well be wondering what explanation the defendant could give for his extraordinary behaviour; and you may be surprised to hear that he has put forward, not one, but two quite different explanations. When he was arrested and interviewed by the police, he did not deny any of the facts I've just told you about. On the contrary, he told the police that he was entitled to be married to two women at the same time because he "enjoyed being married"; and because polygamous marriage formed part of his religious belief and was, therefore, protected under European human rights law. You will hear evidence of the interview from the officer in the case, DI Bairstow, in due course, and the Crown say that you will find his explanation of his religious belief to be, shall we say, lacking in substance.

'But, members of the jury, we say that even if he genuinely held such a belief, it affords him no defence in law. I anticipate that when he directs you about the law later in the trial, His Honour will tell you that English law does not recognise polygamous marriages as valid if they are contracted in this country between British citizens; so even if Mr Findlay-Smyth sincerely believes that he is entitled to marry polygamously – and I'm afraid the prosecution doesn't accept the sincerity of that belief – but even if he does, it would afford him no defence to a charge of bigamy.

'Members of the jury, it seems that even the defendant himself doesn't have much confidence in his defence of religious belief. I say that because in his defence statement he puts forward a second and quite different defence: the defence of duress. He claims that he was forced to go through the ceremony of marriage with Deborah Jane Martineau because she was already pregnant with Charlotte at the time, and her father and brother threatened him with dire consequences if he didn't do the right thing by her. The Crown say, members of the jury, that this claim, too, is arrant nonsense.

'Members of the jury, the Crown bring this case and the Crown must prove the defendant's guilt so that you are sure of it, if you are to convict. If, having heard all the evidence, you are not sure of his guilt you must find him not guilty. But we say that the evidence will prove beyond any reasonable doubt that the defendant has committed the offence of bigamy, and that you will be sure that the only possible verdict is one of guilty.

With your Honour's leave I will call the evidence.'

I nod; but before Aubrey can announce his first witness, Carol stands quickly, turns to me, and hands me a note. Aubrey pauses to allow me to read it. It's short and to the point, surprising and rather worrying. The note tells me that Sir Jeremy Bagnall, of the Grey Smoothie High Command, is in my chambers and would like to see me immediately on a matter of some urgency. I can't imagine what could be so urgent on a Monday morning that it couldn't at least wait until lunchtime. But there have been times in the past when the Grey Smoothies and I have differed on the interpretation of 'urgent'; and I've been doing this long enough to know that they will get their way in the end: I don't really have a choice. Saying that I have to deal with an 'urgent administrative matter', I extend Marcus Findlay-Smyth's bail for the duration of the trial, and send everyone away for coffee.

Arriving back in my chambers, I find Sir Jeremy pacing up and down in front of the window, looking quite agitated. On seeing me, he walks over to me, we shake hands, and he takes a seat in front of my desk. I take my seat behind the desk, opposite. As Carol has accompanied me, I offer coffee, which he declines.

'And actually, Charles,' he adds, 'I would prefer it to be just the two of us, if you don't mind.'

'You don't want your meeting recorded, Sir Jeremy?' Carol asks.

'No, thank you.'

Carol raises her eyebrows: this is a distinct departure from Grey Smoothie protocol, which requires every conversation to be recorded if any official matter is to be discussed, whether urgent or not. But clearly the agenda is different this morning. In any case, Jeremy wouldn't rely on us to record the meeting for him: if he wanted to make a record he would have our cluster manager Meredith with him, pencil in hand, ready to take a comprehensive note of the proceedings. I nod to Carol to say it's all right, she can return to court, which she does. A number of seconds elapse.

'I'm sorry to drag you out of court like this,' he says, eventually.

'Not at all.'

Another lengthy pause.

'Charles, do you know how old Judge Drake – Hubert – is?'

I close my eyes. I've known ever since I came on board as RJ that I would be having this conversation with the Grey Smoothies sooner or later, and I've been dreading it. I'm not the only one. Everyone at court has been aware of the question of Hubert's age looming; it's been a recurring topic of conversation – in Hubert's absence, naturally – throughout the building. But as RJ, I've probably been more conscious of it than most, and I suddenly have a premonition that the day I have dreaded may have arrived. I pretend to make light of it. I smile.

'Ah. Well, Jeremy, that's one of the great mysteries of western civilisation,' I reply. 'He says, sixty-six.'

'Yes, I know. But for how long has he been saying sixty-six?'

I nod reluctantly. 'For a bit too long, I suppose.'

'Yes, that's what I was thinking.' He pauses. 'The ministry doesn't seem to have any formal record of his age. I think he's been on the bench long enough to date back to the days before the Judicial Appointments Commission. We didn't have application forms to become a judge in those days; it was all done by an exchange of letters, and in Hubert's case the letters don't seem to have much personal information about him. I even tried *Who's Who* but he hasn't got his age listed there, either. He must be the only one in the whole book who hasn't.'

He's still looking agitated. I lean forward.

'Jeremy, I must admit, I've never really pressed Hubert about his age. I suppose I should have, but I always thought that eventually there would be talk of retirement and we would find out then. But if you really need to know now, I suppose I could try asking and not taking "sixty-six" for an answer – or perhaps I could threaten to ask the secretary of the Garrick Club. That ought to do it.' For the first time Jeremy ventures the ghost of a smile. 'But I am curious to know why it's become urgent all of a sudden.'

He looks up at me. 'I've received a rather disturbing report,' he says.

'About Hubert? About his behaviour in court, you mean?'

'Yes.'

I shake my head. 'Oh, you know Hubert, Jeremy; he can be difficult, and he does march to the beat of a different drummer. Well – you remember the case of the solicitor with the pink hair, I'm sure. But he means well, and in the end he usually gets it right.'

'The report suggests that he may be losing the plot,' Jeremy replies.

I take a deep breath, exhaling audibly. Of course, the question of the plot underlies any discussion of a judge's age. In the old days, there was no retiring age for judges, and RJs hadn't been invented; so at the Bar, dealing with the occasional judge who was hanging on a bit too long after his 'best before' date was something you just learned to do. Sometimes, if you were a regular at the court, you had a quiet word with another judge you knew well enough; or sometimes you made sure that a judicious alert made its way to the Lord Chancellor's office via your head of chambers. But conditions that make you lose the plot are no respecters of age and nowadays it's something an RJ is expected to notice in any judge, regardless of age, and report as necessary. Despite his shyness when it comes to his age, I'm actually surprised to hear this about Hubert. He has always been eccentric – even by judicial standards – and he sometimes rubs counsel up the wrong way. I hear about that occasionally, but I've never had this kind of complaint about him.

'Losing the plot, how?' I ask. 'Losing his memory, seeming confused while on the bench, or what? What are we talking about?'

'Being seriously confused while on the bench.'

I don't respond immediately.

'When is this said to have happened?'

'Two weeks ago: a case called Karsten.'

'Jeremy, I have lunch with this man every working day, as do the other judges here. If something serious was going on, we...'

'The report is very specific, Charles. It suggests that Hubert was confused about the case he was dealing with. The case had been going on for three or four days, but he thought he was dealing with another case entirely.'

'Would you mind telling me the source?' I ask. 'We have a pretty small, close-knit bar here at Bermondsey, and I've always encouraged our regulars to talk to me if anything happens to alarm them. I'm very surprised I haven't heard about this already.'

'I don't know the exact source.'

I stare at him. 'What? I don't understand. How did you...?'

'It didn't come from the Bar,' Jeremy interrupts. 'That much I do know. Actually, it was an anonymous tip, in writing, sent directly to the Minister, which makes us speculate that it came from someone in an official position, fairly high up.'

'Not the court staff, surely?'

'Unlikely: they would speak to you first, wouldn't they?'

'I would hope so.'

'I'm sure they would. No, we think it's more likely to be a senior police officer, or someone with the CPS. But Charles, whatever the source, it's the content of the report that matters. If Hubert really is losing the plot, a dignified retirement with his pension fully intact may be the best way to go. If he's close to retirement, or, God forbid, already past retirement age, it will make it much easier.'

I allow some seconds to go by.

'Retirement? Is it really that serious?'

'That's my impression. But that's not my decision to make, as you know. That's for the Minister to decide.'

'But that's why you want to know his age?'

He pauses. 'It's not even about his age, really, Charles. I can probably get that from some other government department easily enough if I need to. But I'd feel much better if you would talk to him. He's bound to feel more comfortable with you than he would with me. Besides, I don't want word of this leaking out. I want to put the lid on any gossip before it starts.'

'If something happened in court, it may be a bit late for that,' I point out. 'But I will talk to him, of course, and see what I can find out. Hopefully, at least he will finally tell me how old he is.'

'It's in his own best interests,' Jeremy replies. 'You understand, Charles, I'm sure. I'm on Hubert's side, and I think I have the Minister's ear on this, but I need to be in a position to advise the Minister and answer any questions he has. I need to get a feel for what's going on.'

I nod. 'I'll do what I can,' I promise.

Deborah Jane Martineau is a young-looking woman with short blonde hair, visibly nervous, but nicely turned out in an elegant dark green dress. When Aubrey asks her name, she gives it as Deborah Jane Findlay-Smyth, which, of course, it isn't; but no one is going to embarrass her by drawing attention to the fact; and Aubrey is a master when it comes to diplomacy in this kind of situation.

'And is your maiden name Martineau?' he asks, without missing a beat.

'Yes, that's correct.'

'To make it easier, would it be all right if I call you Deborah?'

'Yes, that's fine.'

'Deborah, are you a citizen of the United Kingdom?'

'Yes, I am.'

'On the eighth of September 2012, did you go through a ceremony of marriage with the defendant, Marcus Findlay-Smyth, at Holy Trinity Brompton in the Royal Borough of Kensington and Chelsea?'

'I did marry Marcus, yes.'

'Had you ever been married before?'

'No, I had not.'

'How old were you at the time of your marriage ceremony?'

'I was twenty-two.'

'Whereas he was forty?'

'That's correct.'

'Before the ceremony took place, did you take any steps to ensure that there was no difficulty about the two of you getting married?'

'You mean, to make sure it was legal?'

'Yes.'

'I thought so at the time. We did all the usual things. We went to see the vicar at Holy Trinity, and produced proof of identity and so on, whatever he asked for. Apparently, that was all in order. He explained to us that the banns would be read in church, and that was about it, really.'

'Do you remember what proof of identity you showed the vicar?'

'We both produced our British passports.'

'Yes, thank you. Did the question ever arise between you and Mr Findlay-Smyth as to whether or not he was free to marry you?'

For the first time, a question causes some real distress. She removes a handkerchief from her handbag and wipes her eyes.

'I don't think we ever discussed it in those terms,' she replies. 'It was understood – or so I thought. He asked me to marry him. He didn't suggest that there was any problem. It's something that never occurred to me. I never dreamed…'

'No: of course. Did you ever hear Mr Findlay-Smyth say anything to the vicar to suggest that there might be a problem of that kind?'

'No: not a word.'

'Were you ever told that anyone had come forward to object to the marriage when the banns were read?'

'No.'

'And at the point in the marriage service when the priest asks anyone who has an objection to speak now or forever hold their peace, did anyone say anything?'

'No.'

'Did Mr Findlay-Smyth say anything at that point?'

'No. He did not.'

'And do you now produce a certified copy of the entry in the register of marriages relating to the ceremony, which describes Mr Findlay-Smyth and yourself as husband and wife?'

She looks away almost immediately after Dawn has shown it to her.

'Yes,' she answers, almost inaudibly.

'Exhibit one, please, your Honour,' Aubrey says.

Cathy Writtle leaps to her feet. 'No objection, your Honour.'

'Exhibit one,' I confirm.

She's using the handkerchief again, and Aubrey gives her a short respite by pretending to go through his notes.

'Deborah, how long had you known Mr Findlay-Smyth when he proposed marriage to you?'

'Not very long: less than a year.'

'Please tell the jury how you met.'

'I was living at home with my parents. My father is a… well, a businessman. He'd met Marcus at some conference or other and thought a private investment bank sounded interesting, prestigious, or whatever; and he invited him to the house for dinner one evening. Marcus obviously took a shine to me, and asked me out. Well, actually, first he asked my father for permission to ask me out. I assume that was for my benefit, to show me how sophisticated he was. He was always like that – so full of it.'

Cathy is already halfway to her feet. Aubrey raises a hand.

'I know it's difficult, Deborah, but please…'

'I'm sorry. Anyway, that's what he did. I was twenty-one, going on twenty-two: what did I know?'

'Were you working at that time?'

'No. I'd been to university for a year, a little more than a year actually, and I'd realised that it wasn't for me. I was thinking about what I wanted to do with my life when I first met Marcus. I eventually started working with a friend of mine who had started a day-care centre for men and women working in the City. Of course, Marcus was all over that, what a good idea it was, since he worked in the City himself. He even gave us one or two donations.'

'As a matter of interest, are you still involved in that work?'

She smiles for the first time.

'Yes. Eleanor made me a partner after a couple of years. We're doing really well now.'

'You knew that Mr Findlay-Smyth was a director of an investment bank, essentially a family business: is that right?'

'Yes. He wasn't shy about it. I used to hear about all the money he made. To be honest, I can't complain about him when it comes to money. He took me out to all sorts of fancy restaurants, the theatre, whatever I wanted, and when he proposed to me he bought us this lovely flat in Park Walk. It was something my parents could never have afforded. I suppose that shouldn't have mattered. But you know what you're like at that age.'

'Did you also come to understand that his family bank had an office in Edinburgh, in addition to the City office?'

'He told me they had offices all over the place: Edinburgh was one, but they also had one in Hong Kong, one in Singapore, one in Amsterdam, and, I think, one in Frankfurt; there may have been others, but those are the ones I remember.'

'Did he ever say anything to you about his work involving any of those other offices?'

She nods vigorously. 'He was gone a lot, for days or even weeks at a time. This was before we were married, but it got even worse after we were married. He said it was a small family company and all the directors had to take turns visiting the outlying offices to make sure they were working properly. But he would be away for weeks on end. I can't believe I fell for it.'

'Well,' Aubrey says quickly, 'I was going to ask you about that. Did Mr Findlay-Smyth ever suggest that you might like to accompany him on his trips to the outlying offices?'

'No. He always told me that it was just business, that it wasn't the done thing for wives to tag along. And the strange thing is, I don't remember ever questioning it, even when he didn't come home for the weekend from Edinburgh, when he could have just jumped on a train.' It's almost as if she's talking to herself for a moment, ignoring her surroundings. 'I never once asked myself, what's going on? I just accepted what he said. I feel like such a fool. But whenever he did eventually come home he treated me like a princess – restaurants, parties, the theatre, whatever I wanted.' She doesn't cry this time, but shakes her head sadly.

'Deborah, did you ever meet Monica?' Aubrey asks gently.

'No.'

'Tell the jury, please, when and how you discovered that

Mr Findlay-Smyth was already married when he wooed you, proposed to you, and went through that ceremony of marriage with you at Holy Trinity Brompton.'

'I found out about six months ago, when two police officers came round to the flat one evening, unannounced, and asked him to accompany them to the police station for questioning. Actually, I didn't really find out even then. They were very vague about what they wanted, and it was only after he'd been charged that I really found out that I wasn't ever married as far as the law was concerned. So there we were, suddenly cut adrift: me and my daughter.'

'Was one of those officers DI Bairstow, who is in court this morning?'

'Yes.'

'Deborah, this may be an obvious question: but if you had known, in September 2012, that Mr Findlay-Smyth was already married, would you have gone through a ceremony of marriage with him?'

'No. I would not.'

Aubrey consults his notes again. 'I think that's all I have… Oh, perhaps one last question. Did Mr Findlay-Smyth ever tell you, either before the marriage ceremony or at any later time, that he had a religious belief according to which polygamous marriage was acceptable?'

'No. He did not. He never told me he had a religious belief of any kind.'

'Thank you, Deborah. Please wait there. There will be some further questions for you.'

'We had a really nice reception,' she adds, again as if speaking to herself, 'at my uncle's golf club. It cost my dad a fortune. I wore a small blue patch on the inside of my dress; and I'd even borrowed my Mum's gold bracelet. Much good it did me.'

Cathy is on her feet in a flash.

'Deborah, how long after your marriage to Mr Findlay-Smyth was your daughter Charlotte born?'

She looks down. 'About six months.'

Aubrey stands. 'Your Honour, I don't know what the relevance of that is said to be.'

'If my learned friend had read my defence statement,' Cathy replies at once, with a touch of attitude, 'he would know exactly why it's relevant. But if he follows my next few questions all will become clear.'

'I've read my learned friend's defence statement,' Aubrey insists. 'I'm aware of the allegation of duress. But the Crown say that duress can provide no defence to a charge of bigamy.'

'That's not correct,' Cathy replies. 'But your Honour should hear the evidence before we address that question, so that we don't deal with it in a vacuum.'

I nod. 'All right, Miss Writtle. But let's get to the point as quickly as we can, shall we?'

'I always try, your Honour. But it will be easier if my learned friend reads my defence statement and lets me get on with it.'

'I have read the defence statement,' Aubrey replies, 'as I said before. And while I'm on my feet, I would be grateful if my learned friend would not refer to a "marriage" between this witness and the defendant, because there wasn't one.'

He sounds a bit stung by Cathy's insinuation that he hasn't read his brief. But he would be well advised to steer clear of getting into a slanging match with Cathy. It's not his style: as between these two there's only one likely winner in that kind of fight. Besides, thanks to the nameless draftsman of section 57, she's doing no more than repeating the language of the indictment. But I don't want this kind of squabbling going on in front of a vulnerable witness. I see Cathy's finger playing with the nuclear button, and decide to head it off.

'I think the jury understand that point, Mr Brooks,' I reply. 'Let's move on, shall we?'

Cathy shoots me a quick, chagrined grin that suggests I've spoiled her fun.

'Does it follow from your last answer, Deborah,' she asks, 'that you were about three months pregnant with Charlotte when you married Mr Findlay-Smyth?'

'Yes.'

'So, you had to get married: would that be fair?'

'I didn't *have* to. I *chose* to: and I thought he chose to. He asked me to marry him, knowing that I was pregnant.'

'Well, let me ask you about that,' Cathy continues. 'You say *you* didn't have to. But what about Mr Findlay-Smyth? Did *he* have to?'

'I don't understand what you mean,' the witness protests.

'Oh, I think you do, Deborah,' Cathy says. Aubrey is back on his feet in a flash.

'If my learned friend has a question, your Honour, perhaps she would ask it rather than making comments to the witness.'

I see Cathy about to argue back, but this time, Aubrey is right. I hold up a hand.

'Ask a question, Miss Writtle.'

'Yes, your Honour. Deborah, you described your father as a "businessman". What kind of business is he in?'

'Again, your Honour,' Aubrey protests, 'relevance?'

This time, Cathy opens a file, takes out a copy of her defence statement and slides it across the bench to Audrey. 'It's all in here,' she replies. The jury have a quick chuckle to themselves.

'Enough, Miss Writtle,' I say. 'Let's get to the point, shall we?'

'Yes, your Honour. Deborah, among other things, your father is in the business of loaning money to people, isn't he?'

'Yes, he is. What's wrong with that?'

'But unlike Mr Findlay-Smyth, he's not a banker, is he?'

'He doesn't work for a bank, no.'

'Would it be fair to describe him as a loan shark?'

'No. He lends money, but it's all above board.'

'In fact, he loans money to people such as gamblers and drug addicts who want to feed their habit: isn't that right?'

She hesitates. 'I've never been involved with my father's business.'

Cathy holds up a hand. 'I'm not suggesting for a moment that you have. But your brother Trevor has, hasn't he?'

'Trevor works with my dad sometimes, yes.'

'Yes. And was there an occasion when your father and Trevor were tried together at the Old Bailey for blackmail and causing grievous bodily harm? Were they both convicted and sentenced to four years imprisonment?'

Aubrey rises, uncertainly. 'Your Honour, these men are not here to defend themselves. It's hardly fair for my learned friend to attack their character.' But it's said without conviction. He has read Cathy's defence statement, of course, as have I, and she's entitled to the evidence.

'If they wish to defend themselves,' Cathy replies, 'I'm sure my learned friend will call them as witnesses. If so, I will have a few questions for them myself.'

'The question is quite proper,' I rule. 'Please answer, Deborah.'

'That was years ago,' Deborah protests.

'Actually, it was about five years before your wedding. But my point is this: the charges arose from their efforts to recover a loan from a man who didn't pay, didn't they? They used threats at first, and when that didn't work, they resorted to violence – serious violence, using baseball bats and rubber tubing – didn't they?' Deborah doesn't reply immediately. 'If you don't know, I can get it from DI Bairstow later.'

'I believe that was what was alleged.'

'Yes: and they were convicted, weren't they?'

'Yes.'

'Did you tell your father and Trevor that you had become pregnant by Mr Findlay-Smyth?'

'Yes.'

'And was that before the wedding?'

'Yes.'

'Mr Findlay-Smyth didn't want to marry you at that time, did he?'

'Of course he did.' She sounds rather indignant.

'Isn't it true that he agreed to marry you only when your father and Trevor explained to him exactly what would happen to him if he didn't?'

'What?'

'Is it within your knowledge that your father and Trevor threatened Mr Findlay-Smyth that if he didn't marry you, they would kill him or beat him within an inch of his life?'

Aubrey is back on his feet in no time.

'Your Honour, is my learned friend suggesting that this witness was present when such a threat was made?' he asks.

'No, your Honour,' Cathy concedes at once.

'In that case, your Honour, my learned friend is not entitled to ask her about it.'

'I asked her whether it was within her knowledge,' Cathy insists.

This is getting complicated. I decide to give witness and jury a coffee break, and send them out of court.

'Where is all this leading?' I ask when they have departed. 'Is someone going to call the father or the brother?'

'I may call them in rebuttal,' Aubrey suggests, 'if the defence actually produces some evidence of duress. I'm not going to call them as part of my case. My learned friend is free to call them as part of her case, if she wishes.'

'If he's thinking of calling them at all,' Cathy replies, 'my learned friend should have provided us with witness statements from both of them. It shouldn't be left to the defence to do that.'

'As my learned friend knows,' Aubrey insists, 'it's not that simple. If DI Bairstow has evidence that they may have committed an offence, he might feel that he has to interview them under caution, as suspects. In that case, they would be entitled not to answer any questions: and even if I call them, your Honour would have to caution them that they're not obliged to answer any questions that might incriminate them.'

'Your Honour,' Cathy persists, 'allegations are put to witnesses in court every day of the week. Just because they deny those allegations, that doesn't give an officer any basis for interviewing them under caution. We're entitled to witness statements.'

'Miss Writtle has a point, Mr Brooks,' I agree.

Aubrey shakes his head. 'Your Honour, if I could have some time with my learned friend, it may be that we can agree on something that will work for both sides.'

I look at the court clock. It's already twelve-thirty. I'm sure no one is going to mind an early lunch.

'I will adjourn now until two o'clock,' I agree. 'See what you can do.'

And so to lunch, an oasis of calm in a desert of chaos. But not immediately: first, I need to gather some information.

As always at this time of day, Stella is at her desk, feeding information into her computer in an effort to transform it into a paperless crystal ball that will tell her what cases she needs to list over the coming weeks. An untouched canteen egg and cress sandwich and a minute packet of cheddar and onion crisps sit forlornly at the side of the computer.

'Sorry to interrupt, Stella,' I say. 'I know it's your busy time.'

'Not at all, Judge,' she replies brightly. 'What can I do for you?'

'Do you by any chance remember a case called Karsten? It would have come in front of Judge Drake two weeks ago.'

She nods, briskly exits the file she was working in, and conjures up another instantly. She turns the screen towards me so that I can see for myself.

'It was a benefit fraud. Nothing unusual. He was convicted, and Judge Drake adjourned it for a pre-sentence report.' She looks at me. 'Why do you ask, Judge?'

I tighten my lips. 'Did you hear anything about Judge Drake in that case, under the radar?'

She nods. She knows immediately what I'm asking her. Two of the many things I like about Stella are: that she doesn't need to have everything spelled out for her; and that she's the absolute soul of discretion. Also, if there's anything going on under the radar, Stella will almost certainly pick up on it.

'No, Judge, nothing out of the ordinary, just the usual: he's to the right of Attila the Hun; his sentences are a bit steep; he gets impatient if you come up with points of law – you know the kind of thing.'

'Nothing more worrying than that?'

She smiles. 'No: and actually, Judge, the day I start worrying about Judge Drake will be the day I *don't* hear that kind of thing about him.'

I return the smile. 'Yes.'

'Is that why Sir Jeremy was here this morning?' she asks.

'Yes. He says they received some kind of report that Judge Drake was losing the plot in court. He didn't show me the report, needless to say. Actually, he told me that it was sent anonymously direct to the Minister. He thinks it may have been a police officer, or someone at the CPS.'

She raises her eyebrows. 'But Karsten was convicted, so they wouldn't have any reason to complain about the result, would they?' she suggests.

'That's true,' I agree. 'But I suppose if they were concerned... but why not raise it with me, through counsel? Who were counsel, by the way?'

She turns the screen back in her direction. 'Actually, Judge, the same counsel you have in front of you now, Aubrey Brooks prosecuting and Cathy Writtle defending. I remember now. They were in front of Judge Drake for two weeks. Karsten was actually the second of two related cases which Judge Drake had ordered to be listed for trial back to back. The first one was called Bourne. Both convicted.'

I think for some time. 'Surely Aubrey and Cathy would have let me know if there'd been anything untoward going on?' I ask eventually.

'I agree, Judge. But they couldn't have told you at the time,' Stella points out, tapping a key and turning the screen back towards me. 'You were away on leave that week. We had Recorder McCabe sitting in your court while you were away.'

'But they could have come to see me when I got back, couldn't they? I was only away for the one week.'

'They could,' Stella agrees. We are silent for a few seconds. 'Have you noticed anything yourself?'

I shake my head. 'Nothing to be concerned about.'

'Even so, Judge, you'll have to talk to him, won't you?'

'Yes,' I reply, standing to take my leave. 'I will. By the way, what did you think of Recorder McCabe?'

Stella folds her arms to make the shape of a cross in front of her.

'That bad? Really?'

'Impatient, bad-tempered, sarcastic, not clear in his summings-up. I could go on. That came from Carol and Dawn as well as counsel – Emily Phipson, Piers Drayford and Julian

Blanquette. I'm surprised it hasn't filtered back to you.'

'Apparently, if you go away for a week you fall out of the loop,' I suggest.

She looks again at her screen. 'Oh, and here's a coincidence. He's a member of Judge Drake's old chambers.'

I smile. 'What is it about those chambers?'

She giggles. 'I can't think, Judge.'

When I go into lunch, feeling rather tense, I am glad to see that Hubert is absent. That's something of a rarity, given his attachment to the dreaded dish of the day. Legless tells me he's in his chambers, working on a summing-up. It doesn't ring true somehow, but then I reflect, I may just have become a bit paranoid about Hubert as of this morning, and that's something I will have to live with until the situation is resolved one way or the other. I'm not ready to confront him just yet, and I am relieved that I don't have to make small talk with him this lunchtime.

* * *

Monday afternoon

As I hoped, Aubrey and Cathy have buried the hatchet for long enough to find a solution to the problem we discussed before lunch. Both father and brother will be visited by police officers and invited to make witness statements, after being cautioned that they have the right to remain silent. Whether or not they agree to make statements, the prosecution will produce them under subpoena for cross-examination by Cathy. All that isn't going to happen today, of course, so for now all we can do is to proceed with the evidence that is available.

'Before lunch, Deborah,' Cathy resumes, 'I was asking you whether you were aware of any threats made to Mr Findlay-Smyth to induce him to marry you. I ask again: is it within your knowledge that such threats were made?'

'Absolutely not,' Deborah replies. She sounds stronger this afternoon, as if she's been preparing herself mentally over lunch.

'How did your father react when you told him you were pregnant out of wedlock?'

She thinks for a moment. 'Well, obviously, he wasn't exactly overjoyed. He asked me how I could have allowed it to happen and all the rest of it, but once he'd got that off his chest he calmed down, and he was very supportive. He knew Marcus had agreed to marry me. He said we should arrange the wedding as soon as we could, and that's what we did.'

'What did Trevor have to say about it?'

'I don't think he cared one way or the other.'

'Really? He didn't think the family's honour had been violated?'

She snorts. 'No. The only honour involved was mine. It had nothing to do with Trevor. This isn't the Middle Ages.'

'You'd be surprised...' Cathy mutters, with a sly glance in the direction of the jury, but seeing both Aubrey and myself twitching, she quickly changes tack. 'So what you're saying is that your father and brother really didn't care that Marcus had got you pregnant out of wedlock?'

'My father and brother were happy to have a man as rich and socially connected as Marcus joining the family.'

'Happy enough to want to make very sure that he did join the family?'

'I don't know what you mean.'

'And you're not aware of any threat to kill or cause serious injury to Mr Findlay-Smyth if he refused to marry you?'

'Absolutely not.'

'Even though your father and your brother both have form for much the same thing?'

'Oh, really, your Honour...' Aubrey complains.

'Sorry, your Honour,' Cathy replies with a casual wave of the hand, before I can tell her to knock it off. 'I'll move on. Marcus told you repeatedly, didn't he, that he was in fear of your family, and that's why he was going to marry you?'

'No.'

'He told you that your father and Trevor had threatened him, and I'm going to use his exact language: that if he didn't marry you, the boys would be round, and he'd be lucky to get out alive?'

'No. That's ridiculous.'

'Is it? Did Mr Findlay-Smyth know about their convictions at the Old Bailey for blackmail and grievous bodily harm?'

She lowers her eyes for a moment. 'Yes. I told him about that.'

'Why? To make sure he understood what he was up against if he didn't marry you?'

'No. I just thought it was only fair that he should know something about the family he was marrying into.'

Cathy nods and takes a pause for breath. 'Did Marcus tell you that he has relatives living in the United States?'

'Yes. One of his brothers moved to America: Edgar. Marcus told me that Edgar didn't want to work for the family bank. He took his share of the inheritance and moved there. I never met him, but Marcus said he had a big ranch and he was doing well for himself.'

'In the State of Utah, is that right?'

'Yes, out in the country somewhere.'

'And did Mr Findlay-Smyth also tell you that Edgar was a Mormon by religion?'

She thinks for some time. 'Yes. He may have mentioned that.'

Cathy nods. 'Lastly, Deborah, I think I'm right in saying that Mr Findlay-Smyth has not lived with you since his arrest. He moved out, and you and Charlotte have been living on your own in the flat on Park Walk: is that correct?'

'Yes, it is.'

'Is it also correct that despite his arrest, and despite knowing that you would be giving evidence against him, Mr Findlay-Smyth has continued to support you and Charlotte financially, exactly as he did before his arrest?'

'Yes, that's correct,' she agrees.

'Thank you, Deborah,' Cathy concludes, sitting down.

'Your Honour, I will call James Harhoff,' Aubrey announces.

James Harhoff is a tall, thin man with a shock of hair in the process of turning from black to silver, and a slow, dignified walk. He's wearing a black suit that looks a little threadbare in places, and a red and green tartan tie that has also seen better days. He takes the oath with a pleasant, understated Highlands accent.

'Mr Harhoff, are you the brother of Monica Harhoff?'

'I am, sir.'

'Sadly, I believe your sister passed away in November 2016, is that right?'

'Aye, sadly she did.'

'And she died of natural causes?'

'She died of breast cancer.'

'Yes. Mr Harhoff, I won't keep you long. I don't have much to ask you. But on the twenty-seventh of June 1998, at about one o'clock in the afternoon, were you present at a church in Edinburgh known as the Canongate Kirk?'

'I was, sir.'

'Is that church in fact a kirk belonging to the Church of Scotland?'

'Aye, right enough. As the name suggests, it is situated in Canongate in the Old Town in Edinburgh.'

'Thank you. Mr Harhoff, what was your purpose in attending the kirk on that occasion?'

'I was there to witness and celebrate the marriage of my sister, Monica, to Marcus Findlay-Smyth.'

'Do you see Marcus Findlay-Smyth in court today?'

Without undue haste, he turns towards the dock. 'He's the man sitting next to the officer, sir.'

'Did your sister Monica and Mr Findlay-Smyth attend the kirk on that occasion?'

'Aye, they did.'

'And in your presence and hearing, did Mr Findlay-Smyth participate in the marriage ceremony, and did he exchange marriage vows with your sister Monica?'

'He did.'

'Were you one of the official witnesses?'

'I was, sir.'

'And do you produce to the court a certified copy of the certificate of the marriage celebrated on the twenty-seventh of June 1998 between your sister Monica and Mr Findlay-Smyth, bearing your signature as a witness?'

The witness produces the certificate from his inside jacket pocket and hands it to Dawn, who in turn rushes over to present it to Aubrey.

'Mr Harhoff, how do you come to be in possession of this certificate?'

'I'm the executor of my sister's estate, and so I'm in possession of all her personal papers. I found the certificate among them.'

'Your Honour, may this be Exhibit two? I do have a solicitor qualified in Scotland on standby if my learned friend requires formal proof of the certificate under Scots law...'

'That won't be necessary,' Cathy responds at once. 'I have no objection.'

'That will be Exhibit two, then,' I confirm.

'I'm much obliged, your Honour,' Aubrey says. 'Mr Harhoff, let me turn to another matter. Did your sister and Mr Findlay-Smyth live together as husband and wife after their marriage?'

'Aye, they did.'

'Where were they living?'

'They lived in what we call the New Town district of the city. Marcus had bought a flat in one of the older houses in George Street, not far from St Andrew Square.' He turns towards me, and for the first time there's a suggestion of a smile. 'Marcus was nae short of the odd shilling, ye ken, sir; and he was nae shy about splashing it around.'

The jury laugh, and I sense them warming to this quiet, modest man. In a few words and without being asked, he's giving us a picture of the lifestyle the defendant chose for himself in Edinburgh, and it bears an obvious resemblance to the one he established in London.

'Do you know why they lived in Edinburgh? Is your family from Edinburgh?'

'No, sir. The family hails from Inverness for more than three hundred years. I believe we once had some Danish ancestry, from which we take our name, but we're proud Highlanders. So no, Edinburgh's not a family home, but Marcus's bank has an office in Edinburgh, so it was the natural place for them to settle.'

'Where were you yourself living in 1998?'

'In Edinburgh also: I have the family home in Inverness, but I've also lived in Edinburgh for many a year now. I'm an academic at the university for my sins, in the faculty of History.'

'Yes, I see. Did you visit your sister's flat in George Street after the marriage?'

'Aye, usually once a week, or at least once every fortnight.'

'What did you observe about Mr Findlay-Smyth on the occasions when you visited the flat?'

The witness sniffs dismissively. 'The main thing I noticed about him was that he was nae there most of the time.'

Aubrey nods. 'When you say, "most of the time", can you be a little more specific?'

Harhoff looks up at me. 'I may have been a wee bit unfair tae the man when I said, "most of the time", sir, and I dinnae want to be unfair tae him. But he was away a good half of the year, from my own observation, and from what my sister told me, naturally.'

Cathy is thinking about rising to her feet, but Aubrey nods almost imperceptibly.

'I'm not allowed to ask you what your sister told you, Mr Harhoff.'

'I'm a historian, sir,' Harhoff replies. 'I know all about hearsay.' There is laughter, with the jury joining in. 'But from what I observed myself, it was a good part of the year.'

'And do you mean that he was absent continuously for a good part of the year, or that he was coming and going at various times during the year?'

'He would come and go. Half the time, Monica didn't know when he would turn up, or how long he would stay, and I'm not sure he knew himself.'

'Leaving aside anything your sister may have said, did Mr Findlay-Smyth himself give you any explanation for his absences?'

'He did, sir. He always said that he regretted being away, but he had to spend time at the London office, and also go abroad to the offices in Hong Kong and wherever else they had them.'

Aubrey pauses for a moment. 'To the best of your knowledge, did your sister ever know about Deborah Jane Martineau, or know that her husband had been through a ceremony of marriage with Deborah?

'Not that she ever said; and I'm sure she would have told me if she had known.' He smiles grimly. 'She would have told *him*, as well,' he adds. 'You can bet every penny you have on that.'

'From your own observation, how did your sister feel about being on her own for these prolonged periods?'

'She didnae like it, sir, I can tell you that; but she was never one to complain. She kept her feelings to herself, and whenever I asked her about him, she would make excuses for him, "Look at how hard he works" and such like. He was very generous with money, sir, I will give him that. She never wanted for anything, and if she ever asked him for money she would have it.' He pauses. 'So I will give him his due. The only thing I can never forgive him for is not coming more often when she was in her final illness.'

'Are you saying that he was away when she was dying from breast cancer?' Aubrey asks.

I can feel Cathy holding herself down in her seat. If she objected to this as irrelevant she would have a point, and Cathy finds it hard to resist any objection that has half a chance of success. But she's right to resist it now. There's no protecting the defendant from this consequence of his actions – at least, not without turning the jury against him for the very attempt.

'He kept the same schedule as he did when she was well,' Harhoff replies, 'and there's nothing hearsay about that: I was with her myself almost every day. She was diagnosed six months before she died: sadly, they didnae find it in time to save her. She was in hospital for surgery, she had chemotherapy, and then back to hospital the final time: and if he was with her for three weeks during that whole time I would be very surprised. He didnae come even when I rang the London office and left word that she wasn't expected to live though the week.'

Harhoff stops for some time, then turns towards the dock.

'And for that,' he adds, 'I will never forgive him. I had little affection for Marcus in any circumstances. But for not being with her when the end came I will never forgive him.'

A silence pervades the courtroom. When the jury and I eventually tear our eyes away from the witness box, we notice that Aubrey has quietly resumed his seat. I look at Cathy. Without standing, she shakes her head briefly. I thank James Harhoff for his evidence and wish him a good trip back to Scotland.

'Thank you, sir,' he replies. 'But if it's all the same to you, I will stay and observe the proceedings.'

I tell Mr Harhoff he is most welcome to stay, and he takes a seat unobtrusively in the public gallery. But there isn't going to be much in the way of proceedings for him to observe this afternoon. The two Martineau family enforcers, I'm told, have been contacted and will be brought to court to give evidence tomorrow morning, whether they want to or not. Understandably, Aubrey doesn't want to call DI Bairstow, the officer in the case, before the court has heard what they have to say. In the meanwhile all that can be accomplished is to provide the jury with some agreed facts, mostly times, dates and places; and to read to them the undisputed evidence of Alice Clegg, the bright young HMRC officer who triggered the investigation by spotting that something was amiss while ploughing through the defendant's tax returns. When this has been done, we adjourn for the day.

I have been greatly tempted to ask Aubrey and Cathy into chambers for tea this afternoon, to find out what they know about Hubert losing the plot. But out of caution, I prefer to be as prepared as I can before I throw that particular cat among the pigeons, and I decide, first, to acquaint myself with the related cases of Bourne and Karsten that Hubert was trying when the plot was supposedly lost. To my considerable satisfaction, I succeed in retrieving the files on my computer from the paperless court without any help.

But they turn out to be a bit of a disappointment: there's not much in the way of clues. Both were cases of benefit fraud, albeit somewhat more sophisticated than the usual case in which the claimant simply lies about his circumstances and waits to be found out. In both cases, there was a sporting attempt to cover the fraud up, similar enough in fact to suggest that Messrs Bourne and Karsten had colluded in cooking it up together over a taxpayer-funded pint or two in their local. They had originally been jointly indicted, but since there was nothing else to link them to what were otherwise completely separate offences, Hubert had ordered that they be tried separately – a decision I can't criticise at all. As Stella said, he had also ordered that they be tried back to back – probably not such a good idea, as jurors from the first and second trials were likely to be mingling together in the jury lounge during the mornings and at lunchtime: but he may have had good reasons for taking that risk, and in any case it hardly amounts to losing the plot. All things considered, I find myself none the wiser.

***

Monday evening

On the way home I remind myself of Marcus Findlay-Smyth's hint that in his religious universe, bigamy is not an offence. I've been more preoccupied today with what appears to be his current defence of duress, and I haven't really focused on the alternative scenario. But as I walk back to the vicarage, the spectre returns to my mind. In contrast to the Reverend Mrs Walden's world, in mine the spectre of religion never bodes well. It's an unwelcome complication, one that casts the long shadow of freedom of religion and the European Convention on Human Rights over a trial, and tends to obscure the more mundane aspects of the case. It also raises the spectre of being asked to rule on the subject of the defendant's human rights, and of an outing in the Court of Appeal for Cathy if I get it wrong. Moreover, unless Cathy has decided to ditch her client's religious defence in favour of the slightly more realistic story of duress – which would, to say the least, be untypical of her – the spectre seems poised to make an imminent appearance. I may have to deal with this tomorrow. I decide to consult an expert.

I find the expert in the kitchen cutting up vegetables for this evening's tagliatelle primavera. I open a bottle of Aldi's late harvest red table wine, and pour us both a glass. We clink glasses and toast each other.

'I'm interested in polygamy,' I begin.

She looks at me strangely and puts down her glass – though not the knife.

'What? After all these years, Charlie?' she asks plaintively. 'I can't believe it. After all this time I'm suddenly not enough for you? Who is she? Someone younger and prettier, I suppose…'

'Clara…'

'I suppose I'll learn to adjust. But where will we put her? I suppose she'll have to go in the big bedroom at the back, where we put the travelling missionaries.'

'Clara…'

'But I want you to know, I'm hurt…' At which point she seemingly can't continue. She suddenly gives way to laughter, which actually comes as something of a relief. I had been going somewhat hot and cold. As well as I know the Reverend Mrs Walden, when she's in a mischievous mood I can't always tell when she's joking and when she's being serious until she enlightens me. And at this precise moment she's holding a rather large knife.

'I'm sorry, Charlie, but you should see your face.'

'I'm sure I should,' I admit with a rueful grin.

'So, it's not personal? Well, that's a relief.'

'No, Clara, I assure you, I have no personal interest in polygamy.'

She resumes her vigorous destruction of the vegetables. 'So, tell me about it.'

'I'm trying a case of bigamy. Chummy married wife number one in Edinburgh in 1998, but not being satisfied with just the one wife, he – quote, married, unquote – wife number two in London in 2012. He then spent a number of years commuting between the two on a regular basis until wife one died in 2016.'

She looks up from the destruction. 'My goodness. That must have taken some effort, not to mention money,' she observes. 'And more than his fair share of good luck, too, if he got away with it for that length of time.'

'He had some cover,' I explain. 'He's a director of an investment bank which has offices in both London and Edinburgh.'

'Even so…'

'Yes, as you say, even so.'

'What on earth is his defence?' she asks. 'I thought the law was pretty cut and dried on this. We don't recognise polygamous marriage in England, do we? I know, during my training, we were always told we had to inquire about previous marriages before we could proceed to read the banns in church.'

I top up our glasses. 'Well, the current defence seems to be that it was a shotgun marriage. She was pregnant, and he says her father and brother threatened him with dreadful consequences if he didn't do the decent thing.'

'How wonderfully eighteenth-century,' she replies, laughing. 'And it didn't occur to him to disappear to Edinburgh or somewhere in the dead of night?'

'Apparently not. We haven't heard his story yet. We'll see what he says if he gives evidence. But father and brother do have a certain amount of form for hurting people, so there may be some basis for it. Cathy Writtle is suggesting that they're a couple of violent loan sharks. We're going to hear from them tomorrow, I'm told.' I take a long sip of wine. 'But that's not the story he gave the police.'

She smiles. 'I'm all ears.'

'He told the police that he liked being married, and that in any case polygamy was acceptable in his world, for religious reasons, details unclear. Is there any realistic basis for that, do you think?'

She is starting to fry the vegetables lightly in onion and garlic, and I'm suddenly starting to feel hungry.

'Well, there certainly could be. Polygamy features in Islam, obviously, and quite probably in early Jewish practice. There are some tribal cultures in Africa, too. But I suppose the most obvious example in the West would be the Mormons.'

I nod. 'Cathy asked a couple of questions today about the defendant's brother. He's a Mormon, living in Utah somewhere. But surely, they don't practise polygamy today, do they?'

She drains the pasta, adds the vegetables, gestures to me to take the garlic bread out of the oven, and we're ready to take our seats at the table.

'Officially, no,' she agrees. 'From my limited recollection of what I've read on the subject, polygamy got started during the great trek from New York State in search of a new home out west, which they eventually established in Utah. They'd suffered a lot of violence during their early days, resulting in a large number of deaths among the men and an imbalance between men and women. Brigham Young saw polygamy as an acceptable way to take care of the women who had been widowed, and their children. The religious overtones, about being fruitful and multiplying, may have come later.'

'But not today?'

'As I say, not officially. They had to agree to abandon the practice as the price of statehood for Utah: so, in Salt Lake City or Provo today, probably not. But in the rural areas, well – you hear all kinds of reports of groups living in compounds and keeping the old traditions alive. It wouldn't surprise me at all if polygamy is still thriving away from the prying eyes in the cities.'

'But what do you think about polygamy, Clara,' I ask after a pause, 'as a minister, I mean? You've always been pretty liberal about relationships from the pulpit, but I'm not sure I've ever heard you talk about polygamy.'

I pour the last of the wine for us, and she thinks for some time.

'I don't think I have,' she replies. 'I suppose it's one of those things that you don't hear about very much, so compared to the bigger issues, such as forced marriages, it doesn't register. But, now that I think about it, I think my reaction is more as a woman than a minister. What struck me about your case was that he kept the two women separate and apart. Did they ever know about each other?'

'No.'

'You see, that makes all the difference for me. He tells the police he likes being married and it's part of his religion, but actually he's living in two alternate worlds at the same time, worlds that never collide.'

'But he has to, doesn't he?' I suggest. 'Otherwise, he will be arrested and it all comes crashing down. Besides which, the second marriage isn't a real marriage. Legally, it's void.'

'Maybe so,' she replies. 'But that's not what marriage is supposed to be about, Charlie, is it? Even polygamous marriage: in all the religious traditions, younger wives are brought into the household and are part of an extended family. All the children grow up together and the more junior wives help the more senior wives, and the husband, as they get older. I'm not sure I like the idea: for one thing, how much choice do the women have in the matter? Probably not a lot in most cases. But, in theory, if everyone agrees freely, I wouldn't necessarily be against it.'

'But not if he's keeping them separately, at arm's length?'

'Well, that's not marriage, is it?' she replies. 'That's just a married man having an affair.'

* * *

Tuesday morning

The scandalous case of Marcus Findlay-Smyth having received more than adequate coverage on the TV news and in the columns of the *Standard*, I receive some less scholarly input on the defendant's conduct on my way to work.

'You just never know, do you, sir?' Jeanie asks, as she puts the finishing touches to my smoked salmon and cream cheese sandwich, an occasional break from my usual ham and cheese. 'You never know who's living next door to you. They may seem like a nice enough couple, but for all you know, the bloke could be leaving her the next morning to go and see one of his other wives somewhere else.'

'And how much money is that costing him?' Elsie joins in. 'Or costing us, I should say: because they're all on benefits, aren't they? It's us that's paying for it all, innit?'

'Not in this case,' I point out. 'At least he had the money to provide for both of them.'

'I'd kill mine if he was up to anything like that,' Jeanie adds. 'I'd be up in front of you for murder, sir.'

'Yes, but you wouldn't know, would you?' Elsie insists. 'That's how they get away with it. They're so clever, they never let one wife know about the other.'

'I'd know,' Jeanie replies. 'Mine's not clever enough to do that. He'd say something he shouldn't and give the game away, wouldn't he? You know, one day I'd say to him, "Where are you off to then, all dressed up?" and he'd say, "I won't be long. I just have to go and get married."'

This reduces both of them to laughter as I hand over my money and pick up my latte and sandwich.

'I'm sure neither of you has anything to worry about,' I say as soothingly as I can.

'I hope not,' Elsie says. 'But you never can tell, can you? I don't mean my old man. But my uncle Albert was a different story. I mean, he kept my aunt Gladys in Chigwell, but there were nights when he didn't come home. If you ask me, he could have had another wife in Epping Forest or somewhere, and we'd never have known.'

'You've got to hand it to him, guv,' George says, giving me *The Times* and my change.

'Do you?' I ask.

'Well, yeah. I mean, just think of the energy it would take to have two birds on the go at once and having to keep them both happy, without them knowing about each other. It takes all my time with just the one. And it's not like he just had a fling with the second one, is it? He actually married her. It makes me tired just thinking about it. No, I take my hat off to him, guv. All right, I mean, I know he shouldn't be doing it, which is why he's landed himself in court. But still, I reckon most blokes would have a secret admiration for him, guv, wouldn't they? They wouldn't say so, obviously, in case it got back to the old lady, but I bet you anything you like, they're thinking it.'

At Cathy's request, Aubrey calls the son, Trevor Martineau first. He invites me to remind the witness that he's not obliged to answer any question he thinks may incriminate him, which I duly do, and which Trevor acknowledges with a brief grunt and a nod of the head. It's an interesting feature of criminal trials that witnesses often give you a clue to the kind of conduct they're going to be accused of just by the way they look and behave. Trevor is no exception. He's a big lad and he's sporting several sinister tattoos on his neck and hands. He's wearing a suit and tie, but somehow they only serve to make him look even more threatening than if he'd come in a T-shirt and jeans. In his manner he comes across as truculent and uncooperative. Cathy couldn't have asked for anything better: a villain straight out of central casting. Aubrey is not going to ask him any questions, so she can wade right in.

'Mr Martineau, in November 2007, did you appear at the Old Bailey with your father, charged with blackmail and grievous bodily harm?'

He turns towards me.

'Is she allowed to ask that?'

'Yes, she is,' I reply. 'Please answer the question.'

He turns back towards Cathy.

'That was a misunderstanding.'

'Really?' Cathy says, with one eye on the jury. 'According to the record of the trial, a Mr Summerfield suffered a broken right tibia, three broken ribs, concussion, and numerous cuts and bruises consistent with having been assaulted with a weapon such as a baseball bat. Do you remember that?'

Trevor shrugs. 'Nothing to do with me.'

'Oh, but it was to do with you, Mr Martineau, wasn't it? The prosecution said that you were the leader of a group of men who attacked Mr Summerfield outside a public house in Hackney.'

'That's what they said, yeah,' Trevor acknowledges after some time. 'But it was all lies.'

'Well, the jury believed it, Mr Martineau, didn't they? They convicted you, and you were sentenced to four years inside.'

No reply. That's not going to throw Cathy.

'Did Mr Summerfield owe your father a thousand pounds he'd borrowed to cover his gambling debts?'

'You'd have to ask my old man.'

'Oh, I will. But you were present at a meeting between your father and Mr Summerfield, weren't you, about a week before he was assaulted?'

'Might have been. I don't remember.'

'At that meeting, your father said to Mr Summerfield, "If you don't pay up, the boys will be round, and you'll be lucky to get out alive." That's right, Mr Martineau, isn't it?'

Another shrug. 'Don't remember.'

'And your father was right, wasn't he? Mr Summerfield didn't pay up; the boys – led by you – did go round; and he was lucky to get out alive, wasn't he?'

'I wouldn't know.'

'But you were convicted of blackmail and causing grievous bodily harm with intent, weren't you?'

No reply.

'Let's turn to something else,' Cathy suggests happily. 'When did you first learn that your sister Deborah was pregnant by Marcus?'

He thinks for some time, evidenced by his lips tightening and a grimace on his face.

'A month or two before the wedding.'

'Did your father become aware of the pregnancy at the same time?'

'She told us at the same time, yeah.'

'How did you react to that news?'

'React to it?'

'Yes. How did you feel about it?'

'Well, we weren't exactly pleased, were we?'

'Why was that?'

For the first time, the witness shows some sign of being engaged with the subject.

'Why?' he replies animatedly. 'Why do you think? She's my sister, isn't she?'

'It was 2012, Mr Martineau. Your sister is an adult, isn't she? What she does is her business. What's it got to do with you?'

He stares at Cathy. 'You must be joking.'

'I assure you, I'm not,' Cathy replies calmly. 'Did you think her pregnancy was something you had to deal with in some way?'

'She's my sister.'

'So you said. Did you feel you had to protect her, make sure this man who had violated her did the right thing by her? Was that what it was about?'

The truculence finally subsides a bit. Apparently, it has finally occurred to Trevor that Cathy is leading him at a brisk pace down the garden path, and he doesn't like what he sees at the end of it.

'No. I mean, we weren't best pleased, obviously. But he was going to marry her, wasn't he? He wasn't short of money, and he was going to take care of her and the baby, and that's all that mattered.'

Cathy treats us to one of those dramatic pauses she does so well.

'Did the fact that Marcus agreed to marry Deborah have anything to do with a conversation you and your father had with him a day or two after she broke the news of the pregnancy to you?'

'Not that I remember. What conversation?'

'The one in which your father said – and apparently this is a phrase he's rather fond of, one that's worked well in the past, perhaps –"You'd better bloody-well do the right thing, mate; if you don't, the boys will be round, and you'll be lucky to get out alive." Do you remember your father saying that?'

'That's the same as what they said at the Old Bailey,' Trevor protests.

'Exactly my point, Mr Martineau,' Cathy says contentedly, resuming her seat.

'Your Honour,' she adds, after Trevor has left court, 'I ask that the record of Mr Martineau's conviction, and that of his father, at the Old Bailey be admitted as Exhibits three and four.'

'No objection, your Honour,' Aubrey says, sounding rather dejected. I have the impression that he's less than happy with the way things are going for the prosecution this morning.

The father, Oscar, is up next, and we have a virtual replay of Trevor's evidence: yes, he was upset; she's his daughter; but no, he never used threats against Marcus; he's not a violent man, and it was all a misunderstanding at the Old Bailey. By the time it ends, I'm abundantly convinced that the pair of them had a few words to say to Marcus, most probably in the vein Cathy has suggested, just to make sure he understood that he would be wise to honour his obligations; and I'm pretty sure that the jury will have reached the same conclusion. That's a long way from proving that the marriage took place under duress: but it's not a bad start.

No doubt convinced that the only way from here is up, Aubrey calls DI Bairstow. Much of his evidence is a low-key account of the investigation, beginning with Alice Clegg's chance discovery of an apparent irregularity in the defendant's matrimonial situation. But then he comes to the arrest. As Deborah said before him, the officers' appearance in Park Walk came as a bolt from the blue for both her and her non-husband. Mr Findlay-Smyth was taken from home to West End Central Police Station, where he was interviewed in the presence of his solicitor, a Miss Vickery, at which point the evidence increases in intensity quite considerably. The evidence of the interview is delivered in the usual manner, with Aubrey reading the questions and the inspector reading the answers given by the defendant. It includes the following passage.

DI Bairstow: So, Mr Findlay-Smyth, if I understand you correctly, you don't dispute that, when you went through your ceremony of marriage with Deborah, you knew you were already married to Monica. Is that right, or have I...?

Mr Findlay-Smyth: No, you're right. Of course I knew.

DI Bairstow: But... did you understand... do you understand that you can't legally be married to more than one woman at the same time?

Mr Findlay-Smyth: I'm aware of the law. Yes, of course.

DI Bairstow: So, when you tried to marry Deborah, you knew you were breaking the law?

Mr Findlay-Smyth: I don't see it that way.

DI Bairstow: Well, with respect, Mr Findlay-Smyth, it's not a question of how you see it. That's the law. What makes you think you're entitled to ignore the law?

Mr Findlay-Smyth: I enjoy being married.

DI Bairstow: What?

Mr Findlay-Smyth: I enjoy being married.

DI Bairstow: What do you mean, enjoy it?

Mr Findlay-Smyth: I mean what anyone would mean. I like the companionship, the home life, the comforts – the same things everyone likes. Don't you enjoy being married?

DI Bairstow: Since you ask, yes. But I'm happy enjoying marriage with one wife.

Mr Findlay-Smyth: Well, there you go. We're all different.

DI Bairstow: But why couldn't you enjoy being married to just one woman?

Mr Findlay-Smyth: I don't know. I just enjoy having more than one wife. They are different people, you know. And I do want to add that I wouldn't be married to more than one woman if I couldn't afford it. I supported them both to a very high standard – in Monica's case, until she died, obviously. I do want to make that clear. I would never marry a woman I couldn't support. In my book, that would be completely wrong. But fortunately, I've been blessed with enough money in my life. It's never been a problem.

DI Bairstow: I understand that, Mr Findlay-Smyth, and I will say, I've received no complaints about your financial support.

Mr Findlay-Smyth: Thank you.

DI Bairstow: But what you did is still against the law.

Mr Findlay-Smyth: Well actually, I think I'm entitled to do it.

DI Bairstow: Really? Well, let me ask you again? Why do you think you're entitled to ignore the law?

Mr Findlay-Smyth: I have the right to express my religious beliefs.

DI Bairstow: Come again?

Miss Vickery (solicitor): If I may… it may help if I explain.

DI Bairstow: Well, I wish someone would.

Miss Vickery: Mr Findlay-Smyth is asserting his right to family life and religious expression under articles 8 and 9 of the European Convention on Human Rights. Those articles give him the right to protect his family life and to express his religious beliefs through his actions.

DI Bairstow: Are you saying that there's now a human right to commit bigamy? Because, to be honest, that's a new one on me.

Miss Vickery: It's a new one on me too, Inspector. I will need to do some more work on it, but I think he may have an argument.

DI Bairstow: Well, I'm out of my depth, I'm afraid. I'll have to consult the CPS and get their advice. But in the meanwhile, unless Mr Findlay-Smyth has any other matters he wants to bring to my attention, I see no alternative but to charge him with bigamy. Is there anything else either of you would like to add? Would you like to tell me what religious belief you hold that permits you to commit bigamy?

Mr Findlay-Smyth: It's a form of Mormonism. I was introduced to it by a relative who lives in America, in Utah.

DI Bairstow: Mormonism?

Mr Findlay-Smyth: A form of Mormonism. Not all Mormons practice polygamy today. But it is a tradition, and there are those who carry it on.

DI Bairstow: They carry it on in this country, do they?

Mr Findlay-Smyth: Well, no: in America, mainly.

DI Bairstow: I see. Is there anything else either of you would like to add?

Miss Vickery: Nothing from me.

Mr Findlay-Smyth: No. Thank you.

Wisely, Cathy contents herself with a few innocuous questions about the investigation before DI Bairstow leaves the witness box to resume his seat behind Aubrey. Aubrey announces that he is ready to close the prosecution case. As expected, the spectre of religion and the European Convention has raised its menacing head, and I now have to deal with it. Cathy is about to ask me to stop the case. Suppressing nightmarish visions of constitutional law – and the Court of Appeal – I send the jury away until after lunch.

'Now then, Miss Writtle,' I begin once the jury are safely out of earshot, 'what's all this about family life and forms of Mormonism?'

'It's all about the European Convention on Human Rights, your Honour. Under article 9, Mr Findlay-Smyth is entitled to express his religious beliefs; and under article 8, he is entitled to the protection of his family life. If he chooses a kind of family life that happens to be different from most people's, that doesn't mean he loses the protection of the Convention.'

'So, if I declare myself to be a form of Mormon, I can marry as many wives as I like? Is that what you're saying?' I ask.

I see Aubrey grinning, and I see the look Cathy is giving me. This isn't an argument she'd have chosen to run with if her client and Miss Vickery hadn't tied her hands, and I sense that she wants to keep her powder dry for her real issue – duress at the hands of the Martineau family enforcers. The form of Mormonism argument is a diplomatic exercise for Mr Findlay-Smyth's benefit. Fair enough. Either way, I have to take it seriously – or at least appear to – because if the defendant is convicted, I wouldn't put it past Cathy to book herself a ticket for Strasbourg, and I don't want to come across as dismissing the Convention too summarily.

'Surely,' I continue, 'we don't allow polygamous marriage in this country, do we?'

'That depends on what your Honour means by "allowing" it,' Cathy replies. 'We don't *recognise* polygamous marriages contracted by British citizens. Such marriages are void here. But because they are void under our law, a British citizen who enters into polygamous marriage abroad, in accordance with local law, does not commit the offence of bigamy.'

'But Mr Findlay-Smyth didn't enter into such a marriage abroad, did he?' I counter. 'He entered into it in the Royal Borough of Kensington and Chelsea.'

'Yes, your Honour. But in this day and age, why should it matter where the marriage is celebrated?'

Aubrey suddenly intervenes. 'Because it has to be a country where polygamous marriages are legal,' he points out. 'England and Scotland don't fall into that group.'

'Yes,' Cathy responds at once, 'but that law dates from a statute passed in 1861 and a leading case decided in 1901. It's the "benighted foreigners" approach – based on how much more enlightened and civilised we are in England. Your honour, that kind of chauvinism might have played well in 1901, but in my submission it's not acceptable today.'

'Why is that chauvinism?' I ask. 'All the law does is to prefer the form of marriage recognised by English law.'

'The problem, your Honour, is that the law discriminates against people with a religious belief that permits polygamy. Since 1901 a lot has changed: we've had the European Convention. The Convention guarantees certain rights to British citizens – rights that didn't exist in 1901 – and those rights include: the right to believe in and follow the precepts of a religion of their choice, including any form of Mormonism; and the right to have their chosen form of family life protected by the state. The court today should read the Act of 1861 as if it allowed a British citizen whose religious belief permits it to enter into a polygamous marriage here, without committing the offence of bigamy.'

She sits down abruptly. She's said all she can, and said it

very well, in recognition of which I call on Aubrey to reply, *pro forma*, though I know what he's about to say, and I know that I'm going to agree with him.

'Your Honour, assuming that articles 8 and 9 have the effect my learned friend claims for them – which I don't concede for a moment – the Convention can't overrule an Act passed by our Parliament, even one passed as long ago as 1861. Your Honour has no power to strike a statute down simply because it appears to conflict with a Convention right. At the most, your Honour can certify that there may be a conflict. If Mr Findlay-Smyth is convicted and thinks his rights have been violated, he can go to the Court at Strasbourg. But even if he does, it won't affect his conviction.'

I look at Cathy. 'Unless you have something more to add, Miss Writtle, I'm afraid I'm going to have to agree with Mr Brooks', I say.

She's giving me a grin, indicating that she's done all she intends to do in the interests of diplomacy. 'As your Honour pleases. May I come to the next matter? I was concerned to hear my learned friend suggest that duress is not a defence to bigamy.'

I turn to Aubrey. 'Mr Brooks, I must say that I was rather surprised to hear that myself. Are you saying that the defendant has no defence, even if Miss Martineau's father and brother threatened him in order to force him to go through with it?'

'Bigamy consists of the act of going through a ceremony of marriage, your Honour,' he replies. 'It doesn't require proof of any kind of intent. Even if the defendant went through the ceremony reluctantly, he's still guilty of bigamy. It might affect the question of sentence, of course, but he remains guilty of bigamy.'

Cathy shoots to her feet. Her mood is much more buoyant now.

'That's simply not correct, your Honour. It's a defence to bigamy if you honestly and reasonably believe that you're free to marry – for example, if you believe that your spouse is dead, or that you've been divorced. If that's true, clearly the defendant's state of mind is relevant. If it may be the case that the defendant only went through with the ceremony because he was afraid he might be killed, or suffer serious harm, it would be outrageous to deprive him of the defence.'

I consider for some moments. Appropriately, given current circumstances, I find myself reminded of Hubert's most valuable contribution to jurisprudential wisdom: the wanker test. As expounded by its creator, the wanker test involves an exercise in imagination. When considering a doubtful question that may end up in the Court of Appeal, you imagine a group of your friends at your club sitting around before dinner, reading *The Times* over a drink; and that *The Times* has accurately reported both your decision and that of the Court of Appeal. Do your friends say, 'How could Hubert have made a decision like that? What a wanker.' Or do they say, 'How could the Court of Appeal have overruled Hubert like that? What a bunch of wankers.' The object of the exercise, Hubert explains, is to ascertain what's reasonable and what's unreasonable: if you go with what's reasonable, as opposed to what the law seems to require, then, even if you're overruled, the mantle of wanker will rest on the shoulders of the Court of Appeal, rather than on yours. This case seems to me to cry out for the wanker test. I could go either way: but if I go with Aubrey, I'm saying that the victim of a shotgun marriage is committing a crime, in addition to being forced into a life he doesn't want. What's reasonable in that situation seems pretty clear.

'I don't agree with you, Mr Brooks,' I say. 'I think Miss Writtle is right. Even if the statute doesn't say so in so many words, under general principles of law, his state of mind must be relevant. In my view, if the defendant wishes to raise the issue of duress before the jury, he is entitled to do so. But I'm not persuaded that the defendant has any right to commit bigamy as an exercise of religion, and for that reason I will leave the case to the jury.'

'I will call Mr Findlay-Smyth after lunch,' Cathy says.

And so to lunch, an oasis of calm in a desert of chaos.

'What are you going to give your chap if he goes down?' Hubert asks, looking up from his bangers and mash with gravy, today's rather greasy-looking dish of the day.

'I haven't thought about it,' I admit. 'I've been too busy thinking about whether we all have the right to indulge in polygamy – or polyandry in your case, I suppose, Marjorie – if we claim it's in accordance with our religious beliefs.'

'What conclusion have you reached about that?' Legless asks, smiling.

'I've concluded that while religious tolerance is to be encouraged, it doesn't go quite that far,' I reply. 'I don't know what view they take in Strasbourg, but it seems to me that restricting people to one spouse isn't a terribly serious violation of their human rights.'

'What's the maximum for bigamy?' Marjorie asks. Up to now she has been quiet, focusing on her egg mayonnaise sandwich.

'Seven years. But unless it's a case of a sham marriage, to facilitate immigration, or something like that…'

'Sounds about right,' she replies before I can point out the Court of Appeal's general preference for short or even non-custodial sentences. 'But he did support both women financially, so I might come down to five or six.'

There is an audible reaction around the table. It's usually Hubert whose starting point in sentencing matters is the Raj-era tariff. Marjorie is a judge who bends over backwards to avoid immediate prison sentences if she can. But we all have our blind spots, as I call them; crimes that offend us more than most and lead us into the higher echelons of the sentencing guidelines, if not actually outside them. Blind spots are one reason why talking over sentences with other judges over lunch is so important – because as the name implies, you don't always realise you have one until someone else points it out to you. Apparently, today, we've discovered Marjorie's.

'That's not like you, Marjorie,' Legless observes. 'I never knew you harboured such dark thoughts about bigamists.'

'It's beyond the pale,' Marjorie replies. 'Keeping two women who know nothing about each other; having children with one or both of them. It's a complete betrayal. Imagine what a woman in that position must feel when she finally finds out about him.'

'Is it so different from having an affair?' I ask, recalling the Reverend Mrs Walden's thoughts on the matter.

'Of course it is,' she insists. 'He's promised each of them that they will be the only one. And think about the children. How are they going to deal with it?'

Hubert looks up again from the dish of the day.

'I'd give him a suspended,' he volunteers. 'Eighteen months suspended for two years.'

Legless and I laugh out loud. The role reversal with Marjorie is complete. Marjorie, however, is not amused.

'Why on earth would you suspend it?' she asks indignantly. 'What kind of message does that send?'

'It sends the message that he's got to keep on supporting both of them, even after he's found out,' Hubert replies. 'As for where he lives, where the children live, whether they get to know each other, and so on – he's going to have to work all that out eventually, regardless of the sentence, isn't he? The important thing is not to leave them all destitute. If you send him inside he can't work, and they're all worse off. He's no threat to anyone once he's been convicted. Make him work and keep on paying: that would be my approach to it.'

I must admit to having, for once, some sympathy with Hubert's sentencing strategy. Marjorie is obviously unimpressed, and is attacking her sandwich with a silent fury, but it seems to me that Hubert makes a decent point.

'That was always the approach in the Regiment,' he adds, seemingly as an afterthought.

'The Regiment?' I ask.

'My great-grandfather's Regiment. He was an officer, my great-grandfather – full colonel by the time he retired – served in South Africa and India. He always said, the approach the Regiment took was, "Don't have more than you can afford". As long as a chap stuck to that rule, he wouldn't get in trouble. Of course, it gave the officers a certain advantage over the rank and file because they earned more, but that's what you'd expect in any Regiment.'

'Are you saying that the Regiment accepted that its soldiers might have more than one wife?' Legless asks.

'Oh, yes, of course,' Hubert replies. 'Many of the chaps already had one at home before they left, you see; and if you were sent out to Natal or Punjab for a few years, you were very likely to acquire at least one more. You couldn't just fly home on leave in those days, could you? And if the Regiment had court-martialled every officer or other rank who had an extra wife or two, they wouldn't have had time to deal with the important cases, much less run an empire. So the word went out that the Colonel didn't want to hear about women and children being left to fend for themselves, but subject to that, it was up to each chap to do the right thing. The rule was, "Don't have more than you can afford".'

'Very enlightened,' Marjorie comments, a touch venomously. 'I'm sure that's why people in the pink parts of the world get such a warm glow about the British when they think back to the days of empire. And what happened when a "chap's" tour of duty ended, and they shipped him off back to Blighty and his wife? What was the Colonel going to hear from the local wife, or wives, and their children then?'

'Quite a few chaps stayed on after they were discharged,' Hubert replies, apparently under the impression that he is answering Marjorie's point. 'Took up farming, or something like that.'

Sensing that Marjorie might well have a few further comments to add about the Colonel and the Regiment, I decide to change the subject before it gets out of hand. Quite apart from any question of keeping the peace, I've found myself scrutinising Hubert during lunch, to see whether I detect anything of concern. I'm going to have to broach it all with him before too long. I decide to begin the process gently.

'Hubert, do you remember, a couple of weeks ago, you had two benefit fraud cases called Bourne and Karsten?' I ask, as innocently as I can.

Marjorie glares at me. I was right. She did have more to say.

'Of course I remember, Charlie. A couple of real villains. They were fraudulent from the outset – they were claiming benefits they were never entitled to – and they got away with it for years. They had a scheme worked out to pull the wool over everyone's eyes, but of course they eventually over-played their hand and got caught. They always do, don't they, in the end, people like that? Nothing very remarkable about it, really. They were both convicted, and I'm waiting for pre-sentence reports. Why do you ask?'

'Oh, no reason. Somebody mentioned Karsten to me, that's all. Was there anything odd or unusual that happened during the trials?'

Hubert is looking at me strangely.

'Not that I remember,' he replies, and I have the distinct impression that he is defying me to inquire further. I blink first.

* * *

Tuesday afternoon

'Mr Findlay-Smyth, when did you first meet Deborah? How long before your marriage?'

'Slightly less than a year. Her father, Oscar, invited me to dinner at the house. We'd met at a tax seminar for small businesses I spoke at in the City.'

Findlay-Smyth seems confident enough in the witness box. Again today, he's immaculately turned out in a smart City suit and bright red tie. I can't quite see, of course, but I would lay a bet that his initials are somewhere on the sleeves of the hand-made shirt he's wearing – he strikes me as an initial kind of man.

'Was there some attraction between Deborah and yourself?'

'Yes: the first time we met there was a kind of chemistry. So I asked Oscar if I could take her out to the theatre, or to dinner, and he seemed to have no objection, so I asked her out, and it went from there.'

Cathy smiles. 'Mr Findlay-Smyth, Deborah was twenty-one. It may strike the jury as strange in this day and age that you would ask her father's permission to take her out. What do you say about that?'

He laughs. 'Yes, I suppose it was a bit old-fashioned of me. But I do like the old ways – it's how I was brought up – and Deborah seemed to find it all rather fun. Besides...'

'Besides...?'

'Well, I'm not sure quite how to put it: but even at that stage I had the impression that Oscar took his daughter's welfare very seriously, shall we say. I was a fair bit older than her, and I felt it was best to stay on his good side.'

'Did you in fact stay on his good side?'

'Not for very long, as it turned out.'

'Why was that?'

'The relationship soon became a sexual one – we would go to my flat in the City of course; we would never have risked it at her parents' place – and she became pregnant with Charlotte.'

Cathy pauses briefly. 'Mr Findlay-Smyth, throughout this time when you were going out with Deborah and having a sexual relationship with her, you were married to Monica, is that right?'

'Yes.'

'You had married Monica in 1998?'

'Yes.'

'Monica lived in Edinburgh, and you visited and stayed with her from time to time?'

'Yes, that's correct.'

'Did Deborah know anything about Monica?'

'No.'

'You never said anything to her about Monica?'

'No.'

'When you went away to visit Monica, what did you tell Deborah?'

'I told her I had to spend time in our Edinburgh office – which in fact, I was doing. But I was also staying with Monica for long periods.'

'Did you ever tell Monica about Deborah?'

'No.'

'When the two of you realised that Deborah was pregnant, did you discuss the matter?'

'Yes.'

I look at Cathy. She's giving nothing away, but I'm surprised at first that, having asked him about his commute between London and Edinburgh, she hasn't also asked Findlay-Smyth to justify his treatment of these two women. Perhaps she's saving it for later; but I'm not getting that impression. She must know that Aubrey is likely to ask him if she doesn't, and for a moment or two it doesn't make sense that she would allow Aubrey to put his own spin on it. But then it dawns on me that if she asks, Findlay-Smyth is not going to give her an answer she – or the jury – will like very much. Her client is clearly a man whose moral compass points in rather a different direction to most people's, and she's probably made the calculation that staying with the facts is a better shot than exposing the jury to a debate about the personal ethics of rich bankers. Cathy is a shrewd reader of cases, and the more I think about it, the more I think she may be right.

'And what, if anything, did you decide?'

'We didn't decide. Oscar and Trevor did.'

'You'll have to explain that to the jury, please, Mr Findlay-Smyth. Let me ask you this: did you decide on any course of action at all at that point?'

He takes a deep breath. 'We agreed that Deborah would have to tell her father. He would have found out sooner or later in any case, and we both thought it better that he should hear it sooner rather than later.'

'Were you present when she told him?'

'No. We agreed that it would be better coming from her first.'

Cathy allows a few seconds to pass by in silence.

'Mr Findlay-Smyth, I ask you to think very carefully about your answer to the question I'm about to put to you. It's very important. Before Deborah told her father that she was pregnant, did you ever offer to marry her?'

'No.'

'Was there any discussion about marriage between you at that stage?'

'No.'

'What happened after she'd told her father?'

'The next day I got a phone message instructing me to meet him at the house the following evening.'

'How did you react to that?'

'It didn't exactly come as a surprise. I'd been expecting him to say something.'

'Did you meet him at the house as he asked?'

'Yes, I did.'

Cathy nods. 'Just before I ask you about that, Mr Findlay-Smyth, had Deborah given you any information about her father and brother before this meeting took place?'

'Yes. I'd asked her about her father because of the sense I had of him of being a bit over-protective of her. She'd explained to me about the business he was in – loaning money to people at high rates of interest to cover things like gambling debts.'

'Did that come as a surprise to you?'

'It did. When we met at the tax seminar he came across as your average London middle-class entrepreneur; there was nothing obviously dodgy about him at all. He dressed nicely; he spoke well. There was nothing to suggest that he was involved with the underworld. He seemed completely above board.'

'Did Deborah give you any specific information about him and Trevor?'

'Yes. She told me about the time when Oscar and Trevor had been convicted at the Old Bailey because they went after a punter who hadn't paid up, and made a real mess of him.'

'Mr Findlay-Smyth, what happened when you kept your appointment with Oscar at the house?'

'He took me outside into the garden. They have quite a big garden at the back with a wooden shed, the kind of shed gardeners use to store their tools. Trevor was waiting for us there.'

'How did that make you feel?'

'I was nervous. I didn't think they'd do anything to harm me at the house. But I still felt a bit queasy about it all.'

'Tell the jury what happened.'

Findlay-Smyth takes a deep breath. 'Well, first Oscar paces up and down while he reads me a lecture about getting his daughter pregnant: who do I think I am? Do I think I can abuse his daughter just because I've got a bit of money stashed away? That kind of thing. While this is going on, Trevor's leaning against the door, saying nothing, but fingering a pair of secateurs they had hanging from a hook on the wall. Eventually, Oscar stops and asks me what I'm going to do about it.'

'How did you respond to that?'

'To be perfectly honest, I wasn't sure what he meant – whether he was asking me to marry her, or to provide money for the child, or even whether he wanted me to pay for an abortion. All he asked me was: what I was going to do about it. I had no idea what to say, and by now, Trevor had taken the secateurs down from the hook and he was opening and closing them, making a cutting motion. So in the end, I asked Oscar what he wanted me to do.'

'And what did he say?'

'He said what did I expletive-deleted think he wanted? He expletive-deleted wanted me to marry his expletive-deleted daughter, and make an honest expletive-deleted woman of her; and to do that within the very near expletive-deleted future.'

The jury have a little snigger among themselves.

'You're allowed to repeat someone's exact language in court, Mr Findlay-Smyth,' I intervene, to renewed chuckles in the jury box. 'Don't worry about swearing. We've heard it all before.'

'Thank you, your Honour,' the witness replies. But he doesn't elaborate, and Cathy doesn't ask him to.

'Did Oscar add anything specific to what he'd said?' she asks instead. 'Do you remember any particular words?'

'Yes. He said that if I didn't marry Deborah, the boys would be round, and I'd be lucky to get out alive.'

'Did those words sounds in any way familiar?'

'Yes. I recognised them as the same words he'd used to the punter in the case at the Old Bailey.'

'How did you know that? Is that something Deborah told you?'

'No. After she told me about the case, I asked my secretary to go to the library and copy some newspaper reports of the case.'

'Why did you do that?'

'I wanted to know a bit more about who I was dealing with.'

Cathy pauses. 'Mr Findlay-Smyth, as a result of what Oscar said – with Trevor practising with the secateurs while leaning against the shed door – what conclusion, if any, did you reach?'

'I concluded that I had no alternative but to marry Deborah.'

'When you say you had no alternative, what did you think would happen if you didn't marry her?'

'They would kill me, or at least beat me within an inch of my life.'

'Did you consider explaining to them that you were already married?'

'Somehow, that didn't seem like a very good idea in the circumstances.'

'No, I daresay not. Did you subsequently ask Deborah to marry you, and did she accept?'

'Yes.'

'Did you tell her what had happened between you, Oscar and Trevor?'

'Of course I did. I told her that there had been a rather unpleasant scene, and they'd threatened me with violence. I was perfectly honest with her about it.' He pauses. 'But at the same time, I did tell her that I wanted to marry her.'

'Why did you tell her that?'

'I enjoy being married. All right, I hadn't intended to marry Deborah originally, but I didn't dislike her at all. And as I had no choice in the matter, why not make the best of it? What was I going to tell her? "I'm only marrying you because your father and brother will kill me if I don't"? That's not exactly a great way to start married life, is it? No. It was better to let her think that I would have married her anyway, even without the threats.'

'Well, Mr Findlay-Smyth,' Aubrey begins once Cathy has resumed her seat, 'that's all very interesting. But are you seriously telling this jury that you had no alternative but to turn up at Holy Trinity Brompton on the eighth of September 2012 and marry Deborah Martineau?'

'That's correct.'

'No alternative at all?'

'None at all.'

'Well, let's think about that for a moment, shall we? What about telling Deborah – not her father – telling Deborah that you were already married? That would have done the trick, wouldn't it? There wouldn't have been any question of having to get married then, would there? She would have run a mile wouldn't she?'

'Oh, yes, great idea. Then I wouldn't have to tell her father, would I? She would do it for me. "Daddy, the man who got me pregnant is already married to someone else." Oh, yes, I'd really feel safe then.'

'But then you go to the police, don't you, and you tell them that these two men, who already have form for serious violence, have threatened you to make you enter into a bigamous marriage?'

'That would just have made it worse.'

'Worse? Worse than what? Worse than committing bigamy?'

'Worse, in the sense that they would have definitely come after me. The boys would have been round and I would have been lucky to get out alive.'

'Well, in that case, after you told the police, why not go on an extended visit to your Edinburgh office? You could even have stayed with your wife, couldn't you? There's a novel idea for you.'

'Your Honour…' Cathy mutters warningly.

'Or better yet,' Aubrey continues before I can admonish him, 'why not visit one of your offices abroad – Hong Kong, perhaps? The Martineau family's writ wouldn't run that far, would it? The boys aren't going to track you down to Hong Kong, are they?'

'I couldn't spend my whole life abroad,' Findlay-Smyth protests.

'We're not talking about your whole life, are we? All right, feelings were running high just after Deborah found out she was pregnant. But after some time, when things had calmed down a bit, you could have made other arrangements couldn't you?'

'Such as what?'

'Well, you're not short of a few bob, are you, Mr Findlay-Smyth? Everybody seems to give you credit for honouring your obligations financially, if not in other ways. So, once things calmed down, you could have instructed your solicitors to contact Deborah and offer to see her right financially, couldn't you? She's not going to let her father kill you as long as you're paying child support, is she?'

'I don't know.'

Aubrey nods. 'All right. In due course, you were arrested by DI Bairstow on suspicion of bigamy, weren't you?'

'Yes.'

'And you were interviewed under caution, in the presence of

your solicitor, Miss Vickery, at West End Central Police Station?'

'Yes.'

'You were present in court when that interview was read to the jury, weren't you?'

'Yes, I was.'

'Correct me if I'm wrong, Mr Findlay-Smyth: but to the best of my recollection, you didn't say a word to the police about having been threatened, did you?'

'No.'

'You understood, didn't you, that this was your chance to tell the police your side of the story?'

'I was too afraid.'

'You were cautioned that it might harm your defence if you failed to mention something you later relied on in court?'

'I was afraid.'

'Afraid of what, Mr Findlay-Smyth? Of two small-time loan sharks? You were in a police station, with your solicitor, talking to an experienced senior police officer. What was there to be afraid of?'

No reply.

'What you told the police was that you liked being married. Do you remember saying that?'

'Yes: and it's true.'

'But you were already married, Mr Findlay-Smyth, weren't you? If you like being married so much, why weren't you living with your wife in Edinburgh?'

'For the same reason he's not living with his wife in Amsterdam.'

The voice is female, and looking up I see that it belongs to a tall, thin woman seated in the second row of the public gallery, next to James Harhoff. She's wearing a casual brown shirt, khaki trousers, and brown boots, and is sporting a bright orange scarf around her neck, her hair cropped very short: mid-thirties, I guess. I'm taken aback, as, evidently are counsel and the jury.

'Please don't interrupt the proceedings,' I say reactively, without really focusing on what she's said. 'Otherwise I will have you removed from court. Who are you?'

This is known at the Bar as one question too many.

'I'm his wife,' she replies.

There is a stunned silence in court for some time. Recovering as best I can, I smile in the direction of the jury box.

'Members of the jury, why don't you take a short break?' I say. 'I'm sure you're ready for a cup of tea.'

They file out, obediently but slowly and reluctantly, twelve pairs of eyes riveted on the second row of the public gallery, as they make their way to where Dawn is holding the door open for them and trying to hurry them along.

'Would you mind telling me your name?' I ask, after they have gone.

'Elies van der Meer,' she replies.

'And did I hear correctly? You're claiming to be Mr Findlay-Smyth's wife?'

'I *am* his wife,' she insists. 'We met in 2014, when he came to work at his bank's office in Amsterdam. I was working for one of the bank's clients. I married him in Amsterdam in May 2017, after Monica's death.' Her English is faultless, with only the slightest hint of an accent. 'I am sorry that I interrupted the proceedings. But it seems that the court is not fully informed about the case.'

'It seems that you may be right,' I agree.

Both counsel look shell-shocked, Cathy especially. I suspect this is a detail of his life her client has omitted to confide to her.

'Mr Brooks,' I suggest, 'you probably want DI Bairstow to take a witness statement from Miss van der Meer, don't you?'

'Yes, I suppose I do, your Honour.'

'Yes. Very well. Then I will rise to allow that to be done, and once we have that statement, perhaps you and Miss Writtle might like to address me about where we go from here.'

'Your Honour,' Cathy says, getting to her feet rather slowly, 'I have no objection to a witness statement being taken from her, of course; but can I just point out that if what Miss van der Meer says is true, Mr Findlay-Smyth was legally free to marry her. He hasn't committed bigamy with her.'

'That's quite true,' Elies van der Meer replies before I get the chance, 'but he has with Veronica.'

'Veronica?' I ask. 'Who's Veronica?'

'Veronica Ho,' Elies replies. 'Hong Kong office. She's flying in today. She's planning to be at court tomorrow, I believe.'

'Oh, God,' I distinctly hear Cathy mutter to herself.

'Your Honour, I think we may need until tomorrow morning,' Aubrey ventures.

My last image on leaving court is of Marcus Findlay-Smyth, still standing in the witness box, staring fixedly ahead and looking distinctly white around the gills.

'Don't discuss your evidence with anyone overnight, Mr Findlay-Smyth,' I warn him.

'When I said tomorrow morning, Judge,' Aubrey says apologetically, 'what I should have said was, tomorrow afternoon.'

Counsel asked if they could come and see me in chambers about ten minutes after I left the bench. I've ordered up a nice cup of tea for us from Carol. I think we're all in need of one.

'It seems that Miss Ho won't be at court until at least mid-morning. If Miss van der Meer is right, Miss Ho represents a further act of bigamy, so Cathy and I will have to see what we can do to sort it all out. But we can't do that until we've seen what they have to say to DI Bairstow.'

'I didn't make it any easier for you,' I confess. 'I shouldn't have asked who she was, but it slipped out before I could bite my tongue.'

'I doubt it's made any difference, Judge,' Cathy says, generously. 'I don't see any way to keep it from the jury.'

'Neither do I,' Aubrey agrees. 'We'll just have to see what happens tomorrow.'

We all sip our tea in silence for a few seconds.

'Well, while I have you both here,' I say, 'there was something else I wanted to ask you about. Can we keep this off the record for now?'

They both nod. 'Of course, Judge,' Aubrey replies.

'I believe you both spent a couple of weeks in Judge Drake's court recently, doing two benefit fraud cases called Bourne and Karsten. Was there anything... I'm really not sure how to put this... was there anything about Judge Drake's conduct of those cases that caused you any concern?'

They look at each other for some time.

'The reason I'm asking,' I continue, 'is that someone has made an anonymous report to Sir Jeremy Bagnall, one of the senior civil servants responsible for Bermondsey, to the effect that Judge Drake may have lost the plot a bit. I understand that I'm asking a rather delicate question of you, but I'm not sure who else I can ask. Is there anything at all you can tell me?'

They continue to look at each other for some time.

'Well, Judge,' Aubrey replies, 'the first thing to say is that we didn't report anything. We'd have come to you if we'd had any concerns.'

'That's what I would have assumed.'

'Judge Drake handled the trials very well, I thought,' Aubrey continues. 'I can't disagree with any of his legal rulings.'

'That's because they were all in your favour, Aubrey,' Cathy adds laughing. We all join in, to break the tension a little. 'But I agree with Aubrey. He got the law right as far as I could see, and his summings-up were very clear – leaning towards the prosecution a bit, but that's normal for Judge Drake, and he never leans too far. I've advised my solicitors and clients that we don't have any viable grounds of appeal, if that helps.' She pauses. 'But there was that one episode, Aubrey, wasn't there – if that's the right word – I'm not sure it amounted to an episode exactly.'

Aubrey shakes his head. 'If you're thinking about the same thing I am, I would call it more of a moment of confusion.'

'What happened?' I ask.

'It was during the second case, Karsten,' Cathy replies. 'Mr Karsten gave evidence. Aubrey finished his cross-examination just before lunch – this would be on the Wednesday – and Judge Drake said he might have a few questions for him after lunch. But after lunch Judge Drake seemed to think that it was Mr Bourne in the witness box, instead of Mr Karsten. He asked him three or four questions he'd asked Mr Bourne the week before, and even called him "Mr Bourne" once or twice.'

'In fairness to Judge Drake,' Aubrey intervenes, 'as it happened, we were following almost the exact same timetable we had in Bourne. Do you remember, Cathy? Mr Bourne also gave evidence on the Wednesday, and had to come back into the witness box after lunch because Judge Drake had a few questions.'

Cathy nods. 'That's right. That was pure coincidence.'

'So, what happened?' I ask.

She shrugs. 'Nothing, really. It was obvious that Judge Drake had got himself mixed up for a few moments, but Aubrey stood up and reminded him that it was Mr Karsten in the witness box. Judge Drake apologised and had a bit of a laugh with the jury about it – "It comes to us all eventually, members of the jury", that kind of thing – and that was it. No big deal. We got on with the trial.'

'I thought he handled it very well,' Aubrey adds.

I think for some time.

'And neither of you thought it was serious enough to take any further?'

'Oh no, Judge,' Aubrey replies at once.

'If I'd thought that,' Cathy adds, 'I would definitely have come to see you – not to mention that I might well be taking both cases to the Court of Appeal. But no, it wasn't in that league at all, not even close.'

'Well, in that case,' I say, almost to myself, 'who would report it to Sir Jeremy, and why?'

'Did Sir Jeremy have any clues about it?' Aubrey asks.

'No, not really. He speculated that it might have been a police officer, or someone from the CPS.'

Aubrey shakes his head. 'Very unlikely' he replies. 'The officer in the case was very happy with the result, as were the CPS, as far as I know. If they'd had any worries, I would have been the first to know.'

Cathy puts down her cup. 'We're still off the record, Judge, are we?'

'Yes, Cathy, of course.'

She turns to Aubrey. 'I bet it was Andy McCabe.'

Aubrey nods. 'That's possible, Judge.'

'What? You mean, Recorder McCabe?'

'Yes, Judge.'

'He was sitting here the second of the two weeks,' I point out, 'while I was away on leave.'

'Yes, Judge,' Cathy replies, 'but he was continually coming to the robing room to see Aubrey or me.'

'What? But he was sitting as a recorder,' I say. 'He shouldn't have been anywhere near the robing room. It's totally improper. You sit yourself, Aubrey. You know that.'

'Yes, Judge, and I tried to tell him,' Aubrey replies. 'But he wasn't listening.'

'What did he want?'

'He wanted to bad-mouth Judge Drake, as usual.'

'As usual?'

'I assumed you'd know all that about that, Judge,' Aubrey replies.

'No: know about what?'

'Well, you know Andy is in Judge Drake's old chambers in Pump Court?'

'Yes, I know that, but…'

'Apparently, the two of them don't like each other very much.'

'That would be an understatement, Judge,' Cathy adds. 'This goes way back to when Andy applied to join chambers, years ago. Judge Drake didn't think Andy was barrister material, so to speak. He fought tooth and nail to stop Andy being taken on in chambers. But they took him on anyway. There's been friction between them ever since.'

'Did either of you tell Recorder McCabe about Judge Drake's moment of confusion?' I ask.

'Not me,' Aubrey replies at once.

'No, Judge, not at all,' Cathy says. 'I would think he got that from the court staff. Our usher told me he'd been pestering her to tell him all about whatever was going on in Judge Drake's court. So God only knows what impression he came away with. But he didn't get it from us.'

Before leaving court for the day, I make my way down to the list office, where Stella is putting the final touches to tomorrow's list.

'Stella,' I say, 'I assume Recorder McCabe was using one of our notebooks while he was sitting here?'

'Yes, Judge.'

'And we still have it, I assume?'

'Oh, yes, of course, Judge. We keep all your notebooks, for the permanent judges and for our recorders. They're always here if you should need them. If Recorder McCabe comes back to sit here again, we would find it for him.'

'Might I borrow it for a few moments?'

She raises her eyebrows slightly, but without hesitation walks over to a cabinet on the other side of her office, unlocks a door, and within a few seconds, locates the red hard-backed court notebook assigned to Mr Recorder Andrew McCabe.

'Don't let me interrupt you,' I say. I sit down in a chair in front of her desk, and, with Stella doing her best to ignore me but unable to resist glancing up at me from time to time, I begin to browse. It's the first and only time Andy McCabe has sat at Bermondsey, and he's been meticulous in noting the date of each entry. Mostly, as one would expect, the book contains his notes of the trial he did while he was with us, a four-day supplying class A drugs with two defendants. There are also a handful of bail applications Marjorie assigned to him. She was acting RJ during my absence, and would have been in charge of such things. But one page is of particular interest. Towards the end of the week, sandwiched between notes of two bail applications, in Recorder McCabe's admirably clear handwriting, there appears the following: 'Mixes up two cases. Losing plot?'

I show the page to Stella.

'Can we get this to Sir Jeremy in its original form?' I ask. 'Confidentially, of course.'

She examines it briefly.

'Yes,' she replies immediately. 'I should be able to scan the page and attach it to an email. If not, I'll copy it and fax it over to him.'

I nod. 'Good. Would you please also ask Sir Jeremy to check the handwriting against the handwriting on the report he received about Judge Drake, and to give me a call once he's done that?'

She smiles. 'It will be my pleasure, Judge.'

* * *

Wednesday afternoon

As expected, Aubrey and Cathy have asked to address me at two o'clock in the absence of the jury. Deborah Martineau and James Harhoff are sitting together in the public gallery, but there is no sign of any other wife, official or unofficial, of Marcus Findlay-Smyth. Just before lunch, I received copies of the witness statements taken by DI Bairstow from Elies van der Meer and Veronica Ho, which contain exactly what I'd expected them to contain: namely confirmation that, in the prescient words of Miss van der Meer, until now the court has not been fully informed about the case.

'Your Honour will have read the witness statements,' Aubrey is saying, 'and I've discussed the situation at some length with my learned friend. We are agreed that, if my learned friend asks your Honour to discharge the jury, and order a new trial in front of another jury at a later time, it's an application I can't resist.

'This is what we've got: Mr Findlay-Smyth went through a ceremony of marriage with Veronica Ho in Hong Kong in February 2018, after having validly married Elies van der Meer in Amsterdam in May 2017. In so doing, he committed a further offence of bigamy. I must now either seek a new indictment to charge him with that offence, or amend the present indictment to add it as an additional count. If I add it to the present indictment, I accept that it can't be right to proceed any further in front of this jury, certainly not without my learned friend's agreement. I understand, however, that Mr Findlay-Smyth would be prepared to plead guilty to the new count.'

'That's correct, your Honour,' Cathy replies immediately.

'And in those circumstances, one possible course, if my learned friend agrees, would be to say nothing to the jury about the new charge, to continue with the trial on the count involving Miss Martineau, and to allow Mr Findlay-Smyth to plead to the new count after the jury have returned a verdict as to Miss Martineau.'

I look at Aubrey. 'That's a very generous view, Mr Brooks. Many prosecutors would argue that the offence involving Miss Ho would be admissible evidence on the Martineau count, to rebut the defence of duress. You could apply to reopen your case to call her and Miss van der Meer.'

He nods. 'Technically, that must be right, your Honour. But I'm concerned with the question of fairness. I understand that my learned friend is anxious to continue with this jury, but we both agree that it would be unfair to Mr Findlay-Smyth to call Miss Ho and Miss van der Meer at this late stage of the trial. My learned friend has been taken completely by surprise: I accept that.'

I look in turn at Cathy.

'Your Honour,' she says, 'I'm very grateful to my learned friend. Having considered the matter, and having had a lengthy conference with my client, I do not apply for the jury to be discharged. We have no objection to the prosecution amending the indictment to include a second count of bigamy in respect of the ceremony with Miss Ho. Mr Findlay-Smyth will plead guilty to that count at the end of the trial, and the trial on the existing count involving Miss Martineau can continue. I submit that there is no need for the jury to be told about any of this, and I would further ask your Honour to direct them not to pay any attention to what I invite your Honour to call the "outburst" in court by Miss van der Meer yesterday.'

'Are you sure about that, Miss Writtle?' I ask. 'As Mr Brooks says, I wouldn't hesitate to discharge the jury if you were to ask me.'

'I'm quite sure, your Honour. Thank you.'

I have to admire Cathy's coolness under fire. I'm sure there was blood on the floor during her conference with Findlay-Smyth. In the hierarchy of abuses clients can commit against barristers, lying to and withholding vital information from them are the two cardinal sins. Findlay-Smyth's modesty about the true scale of his liking for marriage has pulled the rug clean out from under her feet, and knowing Cathy as I do, I have no doubt that she let him have it with both barrels when she got him to herself down in the cells. But after venting, she would have taken some time by herself and reflected on the mess her client has created for himself. At least nineteen out of any twenty given barristers would have run for cover. They wouldn't have hesitated to ask me to discharge the jury and order a retrial. That would have been the instinctive and natural path to take.

But Cathy has taken her time and thought this through. She knows Aubrey has Findlay-Smyth bang to rights for the offence involving Veronica Ho; and if she opts for a new trial, Aubrey will try him for both offences together, in which case Findlay-Smyth is going down like a lead balloon. The chances of a jury buying the defence of duress once they know about Elies van der Meer and Veronica Ho are somewhere between minimal and non-existent. But if she can deal with the Martineau count on its own, having inflicted some injury on the Martineau family enforcers in cross-examination, she still has some chance of limiting the damage to a single conviction. And, of course, there's always Strasbourg.

So we bring the jury back down, I tell them to ignore the "outburst" and we forge ahead. Aubrey resumes his cross-examination where he left off on being interrupted by Elies van der Meer, but he's not long about it. He treats us to an entertaining few minutes of exploration of Findlay-Smyth's form of Mormonism, demonstrating that the defendant is woefully uninformed about the theological background to polygamy in the Mormon Church, and indeed about any justification for polygamy other than his liking for marriage. He has the jury chuckling, and Cathy sinking ever deeper into her seat. Satisfied, he then wisely stops. We agree that we have time for closing speeches, but that I will sum up and send the jury out tomorrow morning.

Aubrey is short and to the point. Marcus Findlay-Smyth can't even get his story straight, he points out. Today, he asks the jury to believe that he committed bigamy out of fear of the Martineau family enforcers. But when arrested, he is interviewed in the safety of the police station, in the presence of his solicitor, and says not a word about duress: not even a hint. Instead, he tells the police that he likes being married, and suggests that he's expressing his religious beliefs. On the other hand, when he gives evidence before the jury, there's no mention of his religious beliefs until he's confronted about it in cross-examination.

Besides which, Aubrey adds, almost as an afterthought, his assertion of duress doesn't come close to the legal definition. Even if you believe every word he says, the idea that he was in fear of his life or of suffering really serious harm – which is the legal standard for duress – is laughable. All he had to do was to skip town, take himself off to Edinburgh, or Amsterdam, or Hong Kong, or wherever his abundant wealth could take him. As long as he supported the child financially, there was no real risk to him at all – it's obvious, isn't it, that money is what matters to the Martineau men? He could also have gone to the police, or simply told everyone involved – from a safe distance – that he was already married to Monica. The idea that he had no alternative but to appear at Holy Trinity Brompton, and participate in a ceremony he knew to be illegal, doesn't stand up to any serious scrutiny. There's only one possible conclusion the jury can draw from the evidence, Aubrey suggests: namely, that Marcus Findlay-Smyth is an unapologetic bigamist.

Cathy, of course, launches a frontal attack on Deborah Martineau's father and brother. She reminds the jury of their previous convictions at the Old Bailey. It's all very well for Aubrey to suggest that he could have made a run for it and hoped that his financial support of Charlotte would be enough: but is that the reality when you're dealing with organised crime? Is there ever really any place to hide? Would Marcus Findlay-Smyth have been condemning himself to spending the rest of his life on the run, looking over his shoulder every day of his life, wondering when the end would come? This wasn't just about money: these were men who were not about to allow their daughter and sister to be shamed. You can almost see Marlon Brando stroking his cat and murmuring instructions to Luca Brasi to avenge the family's honour.

The trouble is, it doesn't quite ring true. I'm going to have to direct the jury that Aubrey's right about the legal definition of duress. Legally, there has to be a certain immediacy about the threat. If Deborah's father were actually pointing a loaded shotgun at him in some rural barn, far from any source of salvation, and Findlay-Smyth had every reason to believe that he would pull the trigger unless he heard an enthusiastic 'I do', that would be one thing. But unarmed, in a church in central London with a vicar and any number of guests around him, Oscar Martineau doesn't pose quite such an immediate threat. Wisely, Cathy doesn't even attempt to explain Findlay-Smyth's failure to confide in the police about the threat hanging over his head, except as part of the overall picture of the terror that consumed him.

As I'm leaving for the day, I pass Hubert's chambers. The door is partially open, and I see that he's sitting at his desk, reading something in *The Times*. The time has come. I knock and venture inside.

'Come in, Charlie,' he says cheerfully. 'I was just thinking about heading off to the Garrick, but you look as though you could use a cup of tea.'

'That would be very welcome,' I reply. 'It's been an interesting day.'

Hubert self-caters when it comes to tea and coffee. He has his own kettle and a miniscule fridge for the milk.

'Still doing your bigamy case, are you?'

'Yes, but we've now discovered that Chummy has been unduly modest about his accomplishments in the field of bigamy.'

'Oh, yes?'

'Yes. Another case has turned up – one more genuine wife plus one more bigamous – and the way things are going, I wouldn't rule out further surprises before we're finished.'

'Extraordinary,' Hubert replies. 'And has Chummy been supporting all of them?'

'As far as I know. The Colonel would have been proud of him.'

'Extraordinary.'

When the tea is ready, we sit together on Hubert's sofa, a personal touch he insists on in chambers to supplement the standard government-issue chairs.

'Hubert,' I begin, 'there's something I want to ask you about. I don't want you to say anything immediately. Just listen, and then you can say something if you want to.'

'That all sounds very mysterious, Charlie.'

'No, not really. You remember those two benefit fraud cases I asked you about at lunch, Bourne and Karsten?'

Hubert takes a drink of his tea.

'Yes, of course I remember. I remember them very well. Why are you so interested in them?'

I take a deep breath. 'Well, you told me that nothing out of the ordinary had happened. But I've had a report that you were a bit confused for a short time during the second trial. I was told that you asked Karsten a few questions while under the impression that he was Bourne, the defendant from the previous week, and that Aubrey Brooks had to correct you.'

Hubert doesn't reply for some time.

'Did Aubrey tell you that?' he asks eventually.

'Only when I asked him. I have Aubrey and Cathy in front of me, and I happened to call them into chambers in connection with my case. The report didn't come from either of them.'

Hubert looks at me, puzzled. 'Well, who did it come from, then?'

'I'm not a hundred per cent sure yet,' I admit. 'It should become clear tomorrow. But the point is, Hubert, not where it came from, but whether it's accurate. Obviously you don't need to tell me anything you don't want to, but as RJ, I am supposed to keep an eye on things, and…'

I allow my voice to trail away.

'Am I in trouble with the Grey Smoothies?' he asks.

I think carefully about my reply. 'I'm almost sure the answer to that is no,' I say as reassuringly as I can. 'Neither Aubrey nor Cathy thought it was worth mentioning until I asked them, and neither had any complaint about your handling of the case – except, in Cathy's case, about your usual pro-prosecution summing-up, which she's not taking to the Court of Appeal, by the way.'

We share a quick laugh. He nods and stares into space for some time.

'It's something that happens from time to time, Charlie,' he says, 'not very often and never while I've been in court – at least before the Karsten case. I did get confused for a few minutes. But Aubrey helped me out very nicely and no harm came of it.'

'What happened, exactly, Hubert?' I ask.

'It was close to the anniversary of Joan's death,' he replies quietly, 'my wife, you know. Of course, she's been gone for several years now. But every so often, I see a woman who reminds me of her, and I seem to lose concentration for a short while. I suppose I still haven't recovered fully from her death, you see. Anyway, on the day in question, I came back into court after lunch, and there was this woman in the front row of the public gallery. I have no idea who she was, but she was wearing just the kind of jacket and scarf Joan used to wear. It threw me, Charlie. I should have gone back to chambers for a while to compose myself, I suppose, but for some reason I felt that I had to say something. The defendant was in the witness box, so I started to ask him some questions. But in my confusion, I had my notebook open at the wrong page. I was looking at my notes of the Bourne case from the previous week. That's all it was. As soon as Aubrey said something, I realised my mistake, said a few words to the jury, and we carried on.'

'And, apart from that...?'

'Apart from that, I'm as right as rain.' He smiles. 'Perhaps I should go and see your good lady wife, Charlie. I'm sure she could point me in the right direction, offer a few suggestions.'

'I'm sure Clara would be more than glad to talk with you,' I reply.

He nods. 'The thing is, Charlie – well, you know this as well as I do – marriage isn't just about the romance and so on, is it? It's not all about something old and something new. It's about friendship, isn't it, companionship, growing old together? That's what I miss. I liked being married.'

'And you did it very well, Hubert,' I reply.

***

Thursday afternoon

I sum up this morning, giving the jury what I hope is a balanced account of the law of duress, and reminding them that they must consider the defendant's case with the utmost seriousness, notwithstanding Aubrey's characterisation of it as laughable. I add that the defendant's religious belief, to the extent he has one, and the European Convention on Human Rights provide the defendant with no defence, and instruct the jury not to consider them. I send them out just after eleven.

Just after lunch, they send a note advising me that they have reached a verdict and are ready to return to court. We have a full house this afternoon: James Harhoff, Deborah Martineau, Elies van der Meer and Veronica Ho, all sitting together in an impressive show of solidarity – but mercifully, no one else claiming any relationship, marital or otherwise, to the defendant. Carol asks Findlay-Smyth, still immaculately dressed in his banker's suit, to stand. The foreman, a woman in her forties wearing not the friendliest of looks, also stands.

'Madam foreman,' Carol says, 'please answer my first question either yes or no. Has the jury reached a verdict on which they are all agreed?'

'Yes,' the foreman replies.

'On the sole count of this indictment, charging Marcus Findlay-Smyth with bigamy, do you find the defendant guilty or not guilty?'

'We find the defendant guilty,' the foreman replies emphatically.

'You find the defendant guilty, and is that the verdict of you all?'

'Yes, it is.'

I thank them for their service and invite them to remain in court for a few minutes longer. I know Aubrey is going to enjoy what's coming next, and besides, in the circumstances of this case I feel the jury are entitled to know that they have almost certainly arrived at the right verdict. Cathy is looking unperturbed, and not particularly surprised. I would guess she's personally not too unhappy with the outcome. Forgiveness for clients who lie to you doesn't come easily. She will do her best for him on sentence, but she's not going to lose any sleep over the conviction.

'As your Honour knows,' Aubrey says, taking his time, 'although the jury as yet do not: as a result of further inquiries a second count has been added to the indictment, alleging that in February 2018 Mr Findlay-Smyth committed a further act of bigamy by going through a ceremony of marriage in Hong Kong with a woman called Veronica Ho. That marriage was bigamous because, although Mr Findlay-Smyth's first wife, Monica, had died in 2016, as the jury heard, he had married a woman called Elies van der Meer in Amsterdam in 2017. That marriage, the Crown are happy to make clear, was perfectly legal, because Mr Findlay-Smyth was, at least as a matter of law, a single man at that time. Both Miss Ho and Miss van der Meer are in court today.

'Your Honour, I now ask that the new count relating to Veronica Ho be put to Mr Findlay-Smyth and that he be asked to plead to it.'

'No objection, your Honour,' Cathy murmurs.

Whereupon, to the visible astonishment of the jury, the count is duly put, and Marcus Findlay-Smyth duly pleads guilty to it.

I adjourn the case for three weeks for a pre-sentence report. It's one of those rare cases where I probably don't need one, but what I do need is time to think and I'm not going to pass sentence today. What I am going to do today is to take advice from those most qualified to give it, before the members of the Marcus Findlay-Smyth Wives Club disperse to their various corners of the banking world. One by one, Deborah, Elies and Veronica agree to step into the witness box and tell me what they know about this man, and what they think should happen to him. To my immense relief, none of them knows of any other wives, lawful or otherwise, so far unaccounted for. With any luck we may finally have the full tally.

To my surprise, I find that the Hubert Drake regimental approach to sentencing for bigamy is in the ascendancy – not one of them wants me to send Findlay-Smyth to prison. I'm sure this is largely a matter of self-interest. Although they have been grievously wronged, Findlay-Smyth's saving grace is his financial loyalty, and indeed generosity, which they would prefer to continue to enjoy while they rebuild their lives, and in Deborah's case, while she has a daughter to care for.

It's persuasive stuff, and in three weeks' time, it may well be the path I choose. But I'm not going to give Findlay-Smyth the comfort of believing that today. Instead, I tell him that he may well be facing a custodial sentence, and that I am allowing him bail pending sentence so that he can take steps to put his affairs in order. But at the same time, I do drop the hint that if, in three weeks' time, it is reported that he has taken steps to ensure that he can continue to fulfil his financial obligations to all these ladies over the long term, that is a matter that I will consider very favourably.

I've been expecting Sir Jeremy Bagnall to call, but in fact he goes one better and arrives in my chambers not long after I leave court, just in time for tea.

'This is extraordinary, Charles,' he says after dropping two cubes of sugar into his tea and giving it a very enthusiastic stir. 'There's no doubt about it. It's the same handwriting. See for yourself.'

He hands me the handwritten message sent to the Minister, together with the page from the notebook sent to him by Stella, so that I can play questioned document examiner for myself and make my own comparison. When I look at them, I see instantly that my suspicions are fully confirmed: we don't need an expert for this one.

I nod. 'So it is.'

'This was all this man McCabe's doing, then?'

I think about that for some time.

'The honest answer to that, Jeremy, is, "yes and no".'

He looks up at me. 'What do you mean by that?'

'Yes, in the sense that McCabe sent you, anonymously, a second-hand report of a case he wasn't involved in and knew nothing about. I've questioned two people who were actually involved – the two counsel who appeared in Bourne and Karsten – both of whom confirmed that they would have spoken to me if they'd thought it necessary, but that nothing happened that concerned them to that extent.'

'So, McCabe made it all up?'

I pause again. 'McCabe was guilty of a gross exaggeration, based on some tittle-tattle he got from a member of the court staff who should have known better. He passed on to you an account of the matter he hadn't checked, and which turns out to be very wide of the mark.'

Jeremy shakes his head. 'Totally irresponsible.'

'Yes.'

'Do we have any idea why he did it?'

'I gather there's been animosity between McCabe and Hubert for years. McCabe is in Hubert's old chambers. Years ago, Hubert tried to stop them taking McCabe on, and even though they did, it seems that McCabe isn't willing to let bygones be bygones.'

'It was purely vindictive, then? Is that what you're telling me?'

'Apparently.'

He sits back in his chair. 'Well, in that case…'

'There is more,' I add. 'I said the answer was "yes and no". Jeremy, I have talked to Hubert. He did experience a momentary confusion during the Karsten trial, which made him think for a minute or two that he was still in the Bourne case, which had concluded during the previous week.' I see Jeremy ready to jump in, so I continue quickly. 'Hubert gave me an explanation for what happened. It's a very personal matter and one that, in my opinion as RJ, does not affect his ability to carry out his judicial duties at all. If you insist, I will tell you the details, but I would very much prefer not to.'

He finishes his tea thoughtfully, and it is some time before he replies.

'What you're telling me, Charles, is that you, and the two experienced counsel present at the time, believe that there is no cause for undue concern about Hubert based on this one event.'

'Exactly,' I reply.

He nods decisively. 'Yes, very well, Charles. I'm satisfied with that, as long as you agree to keep me informed if there should be any change of circumstances.'

'Of course. Thank you, Jeremy.'

He smiles. 'Did he by any chance tell you how old he claims to be?"

'Oh, dear,' I reply. 'In all the excitement I completely forgot to ask. I will, of course…'

'Well… when there's a good moment to bring it up. I leave that to your discretion, of course.'

He gets to his feet.

'Well, thanks for the tea. I think I should ask Stephen Gulivant, as senior Presiding Judge, to see this man McCabe personally and give him a bloody good bollocking, don't you?'

'Yes, I do,' I agree immediately.

'Stephen can tell him that we will be watching him from now on, and if he wants to continue as a recorder, he's going to have to demonstrate better judgment in future. That ought to do it, I think.'

'I'm sure it will.'

'Is there anything else I should do?'

'I would be grateful,' I say, 'if you didn't send him to Bermondsey again. Quite apart from the animosity towards Hubert, to be honest, the court staff weren't unduly impressed with him.'

'Consider it done, Charles,' he replies, offering his hand. 'He can go and sit at Snaresbrook or somewhere, and we'll see how they like him up there.'

I take his hand. 'Much obliged, Jeremy.'

* * *

Thursday evening

I quietly ask the Reverend Mrs Walden whether, in the unlikely, but not impossible event of Hubert asking her advice, she would be happy to see him. As I expected, she agrees immediately. I open a bottle of Sainsbury's Founder's Reserve Chianti and, as she mixes the tomato salad to accompany our fettuccini with scallops, I regale her in what I hope is a light-hearted vein with the dénouement of the strange case of Marcus Findlay-Smyth. She listens in silence, although she raises her eyebrows more than once, particularly when Elies and Veronica enter the fray.

'So, what would St Paul have made of it all?' I ask. 'I imagine he would have disapproved, wouldn't he? Though if the whole idea is that it's better to marry than to burn, perhaps logically he should approve of a man increasing his odds of success in that department.'

She points a finger to indicate her wine glass, which emptied abruptly somewhere around the entrance of Elies and Veronica, and I refill it.

'The church had a teaching about only having one wife from quite early times,' she replies, 'though like everything else in the early church, there were probably any number of deviations from the standard practice.'

'You mean, like the Mormons?'

'Yes, I suppose so. But at least the Mormons had a rational basis for practising polygamy. A lot of the early pagan converts probably had polygamy in their cultural tradition, and didn't think much beyond that. Paul's take on it might have been not so much a moral one, but to make sure everyone understood that Christians were different from pagans, and they had to be seen to be different. Limiting yourself to one wife was part of that.'

We sit down to enjoy our pasta.

'So', she says with a smile, 'having listened to what you said about your case, a thought occurred to me.'

'Oh, yes?'

'Yes. If you're you still thinking about importing a younger, prettier model to join the harem, and putting her in the missionaries' room, you'd better make sure she has a good job. I'm not sure our finances stretch as far as Mr Findlay-Smyth's, and I'd hate you to be in a position where you can't afford us both.'

I put down my fork and take her hand.

'I like being married, Clara,' I reply. 'To you.'

NO EXIT PRESS

UNCOVERING THE BEST CRIME

'A very smart, independent publisher delivering the finest literary crime fiction' – ***Big Issue***

MEET NO EXIT PRESS, the independent publisher bringing you the best in crime and noir fiction. From classic detective novels, to page-turning spy thrillers and singular writing that just grabs the attention. Our books are carefully crafted by some of the world's finest writers and delivered to you by a small, but mighty, team.

In our 30 years of business, we have published award-winning fiction and non-fiction including the work of a Pulitzer Prize winner, the British Crime Book of the Year, numerous CWA Dagger Awards, a British million copy bestselling author, the winner of the Canadian Governor General's Award for Fiction and the Scotiabank Giller Prize, to name but a few. We are the home of many crime and noir legends from the USA whose work includes iconic film adaptations and TV sensations. We pride ourselves in uncovering the most exciting new or undiscovered talents. New and not so new – you know who you are!!

We are a proactive team committed to delivering the very best, both for our authors and our readers.

Want to join the conversation and find out more about what we do?

Catch us on social media or sign up to our newsletter for all the latest news from No Exit Press HQ.

f fb.me/noexitpress @noexitpress
noexit.co.uk/newsletter